THE LAST JUDGMENT

GIOTTO'S HAND

"Fine art, quirky characters and scenes set in Rome and an English country village add to the joys of *Giotto's Hand* ... A neat twist at the end is the cherry on this fudge sundae of a mystery."

—*Minneapolis Star Tribune*

"Pears has a whimsical take on the scruples of the art trade, on English food and plumbing and on Italian bureaucracy. It's a pleasure to get to the solution. A sweet, art world 'cozy.'"

—*The Mercury News*, San Jose, CA

"Art, crime, and Italy mix well ... Pears masterfully juggles his plot elements while providing delightful diversion in the contrasting manners of his English and Italian characters. Best of all is the moral ambiguity at the heart of the story. As in Michael Dibdin's Aurelio Zen series, good and evil are inextricably blended, like the ingredients in a good risotto."

—*Booklist*

DEATH AND RESTORATION

"Pears writes delightfully witty, elegant, well-informed crime novels."

—*The London Times*

"Pears' tremendous affection for Rome comes through strongly, making the city one of the most engaging characters."

—*The Sunday Times*

"The book dances with sunlight and colour, faded patinas and shifting standards, with humour and knowledge making easy companions."

—*Mail on Sunday*

MORE MYSTERIES FROM THE
BERKLEY PUBLISHING GROUP...

THE HERON CARVIC MISS SEETON MYSTERIES: Retired art teacher Miss Seeton steps in where Scotland Yard stumbles. "A most beguiling protagonist!"
—*The New York Times*

by Heron Carvic
MISS SEETON SINGS
MISS SEETON DRAWS THE LINE
WITCH MISS SEETON
PICTURE MISS SEETON
ODDS ON MISS SEETON

by Hampton Charles
ADVANTAGE MISS SEETON
MISS SEETON AT THE HELM
MISS SEETON, BY APPOINTMENT

by Hamilton Crane
HANDS UP, MISS SEETON
MISS SEETON CRACKS THE CASE
MISS SEETON PAINTS THE TOWN
MISS SEETON BY MOONLIGHT
MISS SEETON ROCKS THE CRADLE
MISS SEETON GOES TO BAT
MISS SEETON PLANTS SUSPICION
STARRING MISS SEETON
MISS SEETON UNDERCOVER
MISS SEETON RULES
SOLD TO MISS SEETON
SWEET MISS SEETON
BONJOUR, MISS SEETON

KATE SHUGAK MYSTERIES: A former D.A. solves crimes in the far Alaska north...

by Dana Stabenow
A COLD DAY FOR MURDER
DEAD IN THE WATER
A FATAL THAW
BREAKUP

A COLD-BLOODED BUSINESS
PLAY WITH FIRE
BLOOD WILL TELL
KILLING GROUNDS
HUNTER'S MOON

INSPECTOR BANKS MYSTERIES: Award-winning British detective fiction at its finest... "Robinson's novels are habit-forming!"
—*West Coast Review of Books*

by Peter Robinson
THE HANGING VALLEY
WEDNESDAY'S CHILD
INNOCENT GRAVES

PAST REASON HATED
FINAL ACCOUNT
GALLOWS VIEW

CASS JAMESON MYSTERIES: Lawyer Cass Jameson seeks justice in the criminal courts of New York City in this highly acclaimed series... "A witty, gritty heroine."
—*New York Post*

by Carolyn Wheat
FRESH KILLS
MEAN STREAK
TROUBLED WATERS

DEAD MAN'S THOUGHTS
WHEN NOBODY DIES
SWORN TO DEFEND
MURDER ON ROUTE 66

JACK McMORROW MYSTERIES: The highly acclaimed series set in a Maine mill town and starring a newspaperman with a knack for crime solving... "Gerry Boyle is the genuine article."
—*Robert B. Parker*

by Gerry Boyle
DEADLINE
LIFELINE
BORDERLINE

BLOODLINE
POTSHOT
COVER STORY

THE

RAPHAEL AFFAIR

Iain Pears

BERKLEY PRIME CRIME, NEW YORK

This is a work of fiction. Names, characters, places, and incidents are either the product of the author's imagination or are used fictitiously, and any resemblance to actual persons, living or dead, business establishments, events, or locales is entirely coincidental.

THE RAPHAEL AFFAIR

A Berkley Prime Crime Book / published by arrangement with the author.

PRINTING HISTORY
Harcourt Brace Jovanovich hardcover edition / 1990
Berkley Prime Crime mass-market edition / November 1998

The Penguin Putnam Inc. World Wide Web address is
http://www.penguinputnam.com

ISBN: 0-425-16613-9

Berkley Prime Crime Books are published
by The Berkley Publishing Group,
a division of Penguin Putnam Inc.,
375 Hudson Street, New York, NY 10014

The name BERKLEY PRIME CRIME and the BERKLEY PRIME CRIME
design are trademarks belonging to Penguin Putnam Inc.

PRINTED IN THE UNITED STATES OF AMERICA

15   14   13   12   11   10   9   8

To Ruth

Some of the buildings and paintings in this book exist, others do not, and all the characters are imaginary. There is no National Museum in the Borghese Gardens, but there is an Italian art squad in a building in central Rome. However, I have arbitrarily shifted its affiliation from the carabinieri to the polizia, to underline that my account bears no relation to the original.

THE

RAPHAEL AFFAIR

CHAPTER

1

Generale Taddeo Bottando walked up the staircase covered in stolen works of art slightly before the bell of San Ignazio struck seven in the morning, as usual. He had turned up in the piazza a good deal earlier but, as was his habit, had passed ten minutes in the bar opposite the office drinking two espresso coffees and eating a *panino* filled with fresh ham. The *habitués* of the bar had greeted him as befitted a regular breakfast customer: a friendly "buon giorno," nods of acknowledgement, but no attempt at any more conversation. Waking up, in Rome as in any other city, is a private matter that is best done in quiet solitude.

That pleasing early morning ritual over, he crossed the cobblestoned piazza and wheezed up the stairs, puffing and blowing heavily before he even finished the first flight. It was not that he was fat, so he reassured himself often. It was years since he'd last needed his military uniform let out. Portly, maybe. Distinguished-looking, he preferred. He should give up cigarettes and coffee and food and take up exercise instead. But what enjoyment would life have to offer then? Besides, he was nearing sixty, and it was too late now to start getting in trim. The effort would probably kill him anyway.

He stopped for a moment, partly to look at a new picture hanging on the wall, but more for a surreptitious opportunity to get his breath back. A little drawing by Gentileschi, by the look of it. Very handsome. Pity it would have to go back to the rightful owners when all the paperwork was done, the culprit charged, and the documentation sent over to the public prosecutor's office. Still, it was one of the compensations of being the chief of the Italian National Art Theft Squad. On the rare occasions when you did recover something, it was generally worthwhile.

"Pretty, isn't it?" a voice said behind him as he peered at the artist's work. Suppressing the last remnants of his breathlessness, he turned round. Flavia di Stefano was one of those wonderful women that Bottando believed only Italy could produce. Either they became wives-and-mothers or they worked. And if they worked, they had to strive so hard to stave off guilt feelings about not staying at home that they were twice as good as anyone else. For that reason eight of the ten researchers were women. This, he knew, had caused his department to win an unfortunate nickname in other parts of the service. But at least Bottando's Brothel, as his obviously jealous colleagues had dubbed his bureau, produced results. Unlike certain others he could mention.

He beamed a benevolent good morning at the girl. Or rather woman; he noted that he was now at an age when any woman under thirty counted as a girl. He liked her a great deal, even though she seemed totally unable to give him the deference to which his rank and age and wisdom entitled him. While some friends referred delicately to his certain roundness, Flavia called him, affectionately and without the least sense of shame, Old Tub. Apart from this, she was an almost perfect junior colleague.

Flavia, who also resolutely insisted on wearing sweaters and jeans to demonstrate that she fell into neither the policewoman nor serious businesswoman category, smiled back at his greeting. It was genuinely meant. In the last few years, the General had taught her an immense amount, mainly by leaving her alone to make mistakes, and covering for her afterwards. He was not one of those employers who see staff as a convenient herd of lambs to be sacrificed whenever something went wrong. Rather, he took immense pride in teaching his charges to do things properly and allowed them considerable, if always unofficial, independence. Flavia, more than most, had responded with enthusiasm and had become a full investigator in everything but name.

"The carabinieri near the Campo dei Fiori rang and want to bring someone around," she told him. "They arrested him last night breaking into a church on their patch and they say he has an odd story to tell. They seem to think it is more in our line of business."

She spoke in the harsh, nasal accent of the north-west. Bottando had hired her direct from the university at Turin, and she had abandoned a graduate degree to come to Rome. She always maintained that she would finish it eventually, and used this as her main reason for not joining the police fulltime. But she worked so hard in the department that it seemed very unlikely. She had the fair hair and light skin of many northern Italians. Even if she hadn't been simply but definitely beautiful, her hair would have made her stand out in Rome.

"Did they say what it's about?"

"No. Just something about a picture. They reckon he may be a bit crazy."

"What does he speak?"

"English and some Italian. I don't know how much."

"In that case you will have to talk to him. You know what my English is like. Let me know if he has anything interesting to say."

Flavia made a mock salute, two fingers of her left hand pressed briefly against the fringe of meticulously disarranged hair that edged half-way down her forehead. Both of them wandered into their respective offices, she to the small, cramped one she shared with three others, he to the more luxurious one, decorated almost entirely with more stolen objects, on the third floor.

Bottando settled down and went through the morning ritual of going through the mail left on his desk in a neat pile by his secretary. Normal nonsense. He shook his head sadly, sighed heavily, and tipped the entire pile into the bin.

Two days later, a bulky document awaited him on his desk. It was the fruit of Flavia's interrogations of the prisoner brought round by the carabinieri, and bore all the hallmarks of her conscientiousness. On top of it was a little note: "I think you'll like this one—F." In principle, the interview should have been conducted by a full policeman, but Flavia had swiftly switched into English and gained control of the proceedings. As Bottando flipped through the pages, he realised that the man clearly spoke Italian quite well. But the policeman on duty was fairly dull and probably would have missed almost everything of interest.

The document was a condensed transcript of the interview, the sort of thing that is sent along to the prosecutor's office if the police think a case can be made. Bottando got himself an espresso from the machine in the corridor—he was an addict of many years' standing who now could not even get to sleep at night without a last-minute caffeine fix—put his feet up and began to read.

For the first few pages there was little of any interest. The prisoner was English, aged twenty-eight and a graduate student. He was in Rome on holiday and had been arrested for vagrancy when found apparently trying to sleep in the church of Santa Barbara near the Campo dei Fiori. Nothing had been stolen and no damage reported by the parish priest.

All this took five pages, and Bottando was wondering why his department had been called in and why the carabinieri had bothered arresting him. Sleeping rough was hardly a major offence. Throughout the summer months, foreigners could be found snoring away on almost every bench and in every open space in the city. Sometimes they had no money, sometimes they were too drunk or too drugged to get back to their pensione, just as often there was not an empty hotel room for miles and they had no choice.

But as he flipped over the next page he became more interested. The prisoner, one Jonathan Argyll, informed the interrogators that he had gone to the church not to camp out, but to examine a Raphael over the altar. Moreover, he insisted on making a full statement because an enormous fraud had taken place.

Bottando paused. Raphael? The man clearly was off his head. He couldn't remember the church very well but was convinced that he knew the location of every Raphael in the country. If there was one in a tiny little church like Santa Barbara, he would know about it. He walked to the computer and switched it on. When the machine had hummed and whirred itself into readiness he went into the database that had been built up giving the locations of likely targets for thieves. He typed ''Roma,'' and, when it asked for more details, specified ''chiesi.'' He then typed in the name of the church. The machine instantly told him that Santa Barbara had only six objects that were potentially stealable. Three were bits of silver, one was a seventeenth-century vulgate Bible with an embossed leather binding, and two were pictures. But neither was a Raphael nor likely to be confused with one. Both, in fact, were very second-rate affairs that no thief worth his salt would waste his time stealing. The market for purloined, nine-foot by six-foot crucifixions by anonymous Roman painters was not exactly buoyant. Nor could he see much demand in the illicit international art trade for the altarpiece—a Landscape with the Repose on the Flight to Egypt by the magnificently mediocre eighteenth-century painter Carlo Mantini.

Going back to his desk, he read on for a few more lines, convinced that by ''interesting,'' Flavia merely meant that her document was yet another demonstration of the foolishness of mankind. She was very strong on this interpretation of human nature, especially as far as art collectors were concerned. Several times the department had abandoned the hunt for a minor work when they discovered that it had been bought—as a Michelangelo, Titian, Caravaggio or whatever—by a wealthy foreign collector with more money than sense. To get their revenge they wrote to the buyer informing him that he had been cheated, and passed on word to the local police. But, on the whole, they considered the humiliation the man would suffer was adequate punishment, and generally the work was too unimportant to go to all the trouble and expense of international arrest warrants and deportation orders.

So perhaps this fifty-page document simply catalogued the delusions of an unbalanced moron who had persuaded himself he could get rich quick? A few more glances rapidly persuaded him there was more to it than that. From being a question-and-answer session, the document settled into a sustained narrative, the result of a lengthy statement. Bottando read on, and became more puzzled:

". . . studying for a degree based on a dissertation about Mantini. During my research, I discovered a series of documents that proved beyond any doubt that Mantini earned money by working for art dealers in Rome in the 1720s and had taken part in a sizeable fraud. You mustn't think that Italy's restrictions on exports of works of art are new. Most old states had them even back in the sixteenth century. By the eighteenth century they were becoming onerous. The Papal States in particular were getting poorer, and lots of foreigners were coming here wanting to buy. So, various routes were worked out to bypass the regulations. The most usual was the most obvious: a series of judicious bribes. Pictures were also temporarily reattributed to some obscure painter, until an export licence was given. Occasionally, dealers would go so far as to cut the picture into fragments, ship it to London or Paris, then reassemble and repair it.

"The more important the painting, the more difficult it was to get it out of the country. I suppose that is also true now. And the most difficult of all were those by—or thought to be by—the great triumvirate of the Renaissance: Raphael, Michelangelo and Leonardo. Several times dealers or collectors bought works by one of these artists, asked the papacy for permission to export, and were turned down. In many cases the pictures are still here. So, when the di Parma family wanted to sell their most valuable possession, something illicit was clearly needed if they were to collect the money.

"The di Parmas had been a great family, one of the most powerful in central Italy. Like many others they had fallen on hard times, and when the Earl of Clomorton offered to buy their Raphael for an outrageous sum they agreed. To get it out of the country, they enlisted the aid of an English art dealer called Samuel Paris, and he turned to Mantini for extra assistance.

"The routine they came up with was beautifully simple. Mantini was to paint over the Raphael and the picture was to leave the country as one of his works. When it got to England the new painting would be cleaned off and the Raphael would take its place in the Earl's collection. Presumably Mantini used a coat of varnish to protect the painting underneath, and used only paint that could be removed easily.

"I don't know any of the details of how it was done technically, but I do know it was done. There is a letter in the Clomorton archives from Paris assuring the Earl that he had watched Mantini apply the paint and seen the Raphael disappear under its disguise. But Clomorton never hung his picture on his wall.

"At some stage something went wrong, either accidentally or deliberately. The picture must have been switched; the payment for the Raphael was handed over and a different picture was sent to England. Shortly after it arrived, the fraud was evidently discovered and the Earl died. The family doesn't seem to have mentioned the matter again.

"The point is, the Raphael *was* covered by Mantini—this was seen by Paris; it never got to England; and it disappeared from the di Parma collection. On the other hand, the family owned a Mantini in 1728 that they hadn't had four years earlier.

"Now, all of this suggests that the Raphael stayed in Rome under cover. If that was the case, I don't know why they never wiped the disguise off. But they didn't, the Mantini stayed in the collection and was evidently considered to be of such small importance that in the 1860s they donated it to Santa Barbara as an altarpiece.

"And there you are. The picture has rested unknown in that church for more than a century. I first saw it a year ago when I was working on my dissertation. Then I decided a Raphael may be underneath, came back to check, and it's gone. Someone has pinched the damn thing."

Even when seen through the stilted prose of an official document, the prisoner's sense of outrage was clear. Not only had he been jilted out of one of the most remarkable art discoveries of the decade, he had got himself arrested as a vagrant to boot. If, indeed, it *was* a remarkable discovery. Either way, if the painting had vanished, it was something to look into. Seeing an excuse for a stroll, he summoned Flavia, walked down the stairs, and set off for Santa Barbara.

One of the delights of his job, so Bottando thought to himself as they walked, was the chance of living in Rome. Although not born here, he considered himself very much a Roman and had spent most of the past thirty years in the city. Much of his dislike of his previous assignment in Milan had been prompted not by the job,

but because he had had to live in a city which he regarded as soulless and drab.

Then came his great opportunity. Bottando was summoned back to Rome to combat the growing number of
thefts of works of art throughout Italy. The creation of
his department was due to the theft of a dozen famous
works from one of the best—and theoretically best
guarded—museums in the country. The police, as usual,
hadn't known where to start. They had no contacts in
the art world, didn't know the likely instigators, hadn't
a clue what might have happened to the paintings.

In a country where the love of art is part of national
identity, the matter quickly bubbled up into a potential
scandal once it had been raised. The smaller political
parties in the ruling coalition began making speeches
about defending the national heritage from rapacious
foreigners as a way of irritating the larger group of
Christian Democrats. At one stage, it had even seemed
as though the socialists would pull out of the coalition,
and that love of art would bring down the government—
thus giving the country another unusual political first.

But it didn't happen. The polizia, spotting a way of
aggrandising itself at the expense of the rival carabinieri,
proposed a national task force to combat the problem,
and for once were backed up by their minister. And in
due course they had chosen Bottando to run it, the call
to duty rescuing him from the drudgery of fighting an
unequal and losing battle against white-collar criminals
and other semi-legitimate hoodlums in the financial waters of central Milan.

His return to Rome had been one of the great joys of
his career, and he had spent endless evenings walking
the streets, revisiting old and favourite sites like the
Imperial remains in the Forum, the quietly confident me-

dieval churches and the extravagant baroque monu-
ments. He was free to wander at his leisure, and blessed
the bachelor status which permitted it.

As he and Flavia walked now, he constantly looked
around him, and took his assistant on a slightly devious
route to their destination. The case they were on was not
so urgent that five minutes would make any difference.
It was one of those Roman spring mornings which turns
the city, for all its traffic jams, noise and untidiness, into
a place of magic. The ochre buildings stood out against
a clear blue sky, the smells of coffee and food drifted
out of bars and restaurants, there was a hum of preparation as the crisp and immaculate waiters set out tables
and chairs in small piazzas, talking incessantly as they
clipped the fresh white tablecloths in place and arranged
flowers in the miniature vases. A few tourists were in
evidence, looking tired as usual and dressed in the crumpled clothes and backpacks that were their invariable
uniform. But there were not many; the year was too
young, and the annual invasion was still several weeks
away. For the time being, Rome was for the Romans,
and it seemed like very heaven.

The way to their destination lay through the middle
of the Campo dei Fiori market. East of this ran the via
Giubbonari, a thin, straight lane lined with clothes and
shoe shops behind the ruins of Pompey's Theatre. It was
far too narrow for any sort of car, but nonetheless several
Fiats were wedged halfway down it, horns honking as
the pedestrians did their best to make their way past.
Just beyond these, in a small passageway on the left that
was lined with second-hand booksellers, was Santa Barbara.

It was a tiny church, unvisited even by Bottando. It
appeared virtually derelict, and was small enough to

look almost like a model. Unlike the great basilicas of the city, this was very much a parish church. Built probably in the seventeenth century, its design was entirely conventional, the sort of thing that even an attentive tourist would pass by without bothering to visit.

The first view of the inside confirmed that the tourist would probably have been correct in his decision. The ceiling was of plain greyish plasterwork, there were no chapels along the side and the decorations were commonplace. Nonetheless, it still gave Bottando that brief moment, as his body registered the coolness of the interior, his nose caught the faint smell of old incense, and his eyes slowly adjusted to the gloom, that always made him delight in visiting even the most modest of Rome's churches. Like nearly all small churches, there was something sad, neglected, but entirely welcoming about Santa Barbara. The one discordant note was that someone, evidently the priest, had decided to erect a modern altar, which stood out brashly in the old and worn building. Bottando heard Flavia sniff with disapproval.

''Modern priests trying to drum up fresh trade,'' she commented.

''Maybe,'' Bottando replied. ''I suppose in this area you have to do something. It would be a pity to wake up one day and find that your entire congregation had died of old age.''

''I suppose so. But I've never got on with hairy-chested clerical enthusiasm. The intense beady look in their eyes always makes me uncomfortable. Give me corpulent corruption any day.''

Bottando began to remark that he would never have thought she was interested in priests. He was trying to push his mind off the subject of his own little paunch, and the worry that this signified decadence in his assistant's mind, when the subject of their discussion came through a small door behind the old altar.

At first sight, he didn't fit the caricature of the tall, gaunt, jesuitical type that Flavia evidently had in mind. He didn't look at all like the sort who spend a few years doing good in the suburbs before rushing off to upset the Pope by running guns in South America. Short, pink and fleshy of face, he seemed more inclined to stay in Rome with a cosy sinecure in the Vatican. But, thought Bottando, you never can tell with priests. At least his greeting when Bottando introduced himself was courteous.

"I gather that you have lost a painting," the policeman began once the preliminary polite noises were over. "As I have been told it might have been stolen, I thought I had better make some enquiries."

The priest frowned, cupping his hands together in front of his stomach in a gesture of clerical thoughtfulness. "I can't imagine who told you that. There used to be an altar painting, true. But we sold it a month or so ago."

"Sold it? To whom? Isn't that church property? I thought these sales normally went through the Vatican. They generally tell us about them."

The priest looked uncomfortable. "Well, it's like this." He paused. "Do you have to make a report or something? I really don't want to get into a bureaucratic muddle over forms and things."

"It all depends. We've been told that a painting here was stolen. The niceties of Vatican routine are not our concern if it wasn't."

"It wasn't." He thought for a moment, then launched into an explanation. "I run a small programme for the addicts who live in the Campo area—food, shelter, some attempts to keep them off drugs, and awake.'' Bottando nodded and politely encouraged him to get on with it. He had come across dozens of these individual programmes in Milan, generally run by well-meaning priests. As a rule, they didn't even begin to scratch the surface of the problem, but the state provided no better alternative.

''We need a lot of supplies and, as you can see, it's a poor parish. We don't get any donations from visitors, not a penny from the diocese, nothing from the city. About a month ago a man appeared and wanted to buy the altarpiece. He offered enough money to keep the programme going for a year and I took it. The sale wasn't registered with the Vatican because it would have taken most of the money. I decided that my addicts needed it more.''

Bottando nodded again. It happened all the time and was understandable, even if it did make his job more difficult. ''How much did he pay?'' he asked.

''Ten million lire,'' the priest replied. ''I knew all about the painting. It's virtually worthless. I told him so, but he said it was for a collector who wanted a piece by Mantini and was prepared to pay over the odds for it.''

''Did he give you a receipt or anything like that?''

''Oh yes, it was all done properly. The deed of sale was even franked properly. If you will wait I'll get it.'' He hurried back to the sacristy and returned a few moments later with a large piece of white, lined paper with a stamp in the top-right corner. ''There,'' he said. ''Sold, One Reposo by Mantini from the Church of Santa Barbara, Rome, for ten million lire. Dated 15 February and signed by myself and Edward Byrnes, dealer. I see he gave no address. I'd not noticed that before. But he paid me in cash and gave me a donation for the programme as well, so I suppose that doesn't matter much.''

CHAPTER

2

At about eight that evening, Flavia di Stefano sighed, dumped the remainder of her work, finished and unfinished, in the "out" basket and walked briskly out of the office. It had been a busy day, and not a particularly satisfying one.

After the visit to Santa Barbara, the rest of her day had been taken up with routine enquiries about the Mantini, all of them frustrating for someone who loved finding corruption in high places. Everything about the transaction was entirely legal. The owner had wanted to sell, the buyer had taken the picture to England and had been scrupulous about informing everybody of his intentions. All the forms had been filled in properly, and every legal obstacle with the arts ministry, the treasury and the customs surmounted by the rulebook.

A model of a respectable art dealer in operation. Except that Sir Edward Byrnes, prince of London art dealers, might have been taking a Raphael out rather than some piece of junk. But an afternoon spent combing through the penal code had produced nothing which gave them a case. If Byrnes had painted over the Raphael and concealed the fact, a clear crime. If he had smuggled it out, ditto. If he had stolen it, no trouble. In all those cases they could probably have recovered the picture. But, as far as she could tell, there was nothing against taking out a Raphael covered with a Mantini, if you were not the one who'd put the Mantini over it in the first place. And Byrnes would say he didn't know there was anything special about the picture at all. He'd be lying through his teeth, of course, but nothing could be done about it.

It was annoying. Doubly annoying, in fact. Flavia took it for granted that all art dealers were crooked at some level. Their business, after all, consisted of buying things that they knew the sellers could get more for elsewhere. Byrnes, however, was an absolute model of propriety. Utterly fluent in Italian, he often donated works to Italian museums and lent other pieces for exhibitions. His services in other matters had been rewarded with honours in Italy and France, as well as with his knighthood. By reputation a distinguished and learned man, there was not a trace of his ever having even bent the rules, let alone broken them. It was infuriating and, to Flavia, merely demonstrated that he was too clever to get caught.

It was also annoying because the Italian woman, in this if not much else, was patriotic. For hundreds of years the rest of the world had picked over Italy and removed its greatest art treasures. Nowhere in Italy now was there a museum that compared with the National Galleries in London or Washington, or the Louvre in Paris. Many paintings only remained in Italy because they were stuck on to the walls, though she had even heard that one American millionaire in the twenties had offered to buy the church in Assisi so that the Giotto frescos decorating it could be shipped back to Arizona. For Italians to lose a Raphael was dreadful, even if they had not even known they had it.

Grumbling thus to herself, Flavia walked quickly along the streets, heading towards the Piazza Navona. She had agreed to meet her erstwhile prisoner for dinner, so she could go over some of the details of his story in an atmosphere that might make him more forthcoming. Not that she thought Argyll had been lying. But an interrogation by the police after a night in the cells often makes people forget little details.

The hurry was because she had almost forgotten. As she walked, she checked her handbag; the strap around her neck, Roman fashion, to guard against pickpockets. There was enough to pay for dinner for two. She had a feeling that her fellow-diner was short of funds, and taking men out to dinner always gave her an agreeable feeling. Her mother would never have gone out with a man on her own. Although she was a liberal sort of mother and countenanced such behaviour in her youngest, the idea of her daughter paying would still have shocked her greatly.

She had arranged to meet her guest at a nearby trattoria. It was not a particularly special one, but near to her apartment, and reliable. Like most Roman eating establishments, it served wonderful pasta, magnificent antipasti and dreadful main courses. Unlike Turin, which really knew what meat was, Romans seemed satisfied with any sort of boot leather. No matter: she was used to it now. But Roman food was still about the only thing that made her nostalgic for her home town.

Argyll was sitting at a table in the corner and waved cautiously at her as she entered. Ordinarily he would have been good-enough looking, in an English sort of way, not that that sort of thing normally appealed much to her. Tallish, fair-haired, conservatively and not very well-dressed by Italian standards. Most remarkable of all, perhaps, were his hands, which were long and delicate. He had wrung them together incessantly during the formal interview. They looked as though they would have been better employed playing the violin, or something. At least, he didn't now seem to be twitching and fiddling so much.

Being freed from temporary incarceration indeed seemed to have done him good, and Flavia remarked on the fact.

"For someone who has just mislaid a Raphael you seem remarkably cheerful," she said.

He beamed at her. "I suppose so. By rights I ought to be dreadfully depressed. On the other hand, of course, the whole business proves I'm right, even though it wasn't quite the type of public acclaim I'd had in mind. Besides which, being arrested by the police is quite interesting, in an odd sort of way."

"They didn't treat you badly, then?"

"Not at all. Charming people. They even let me go out for lunch, as long as I promised to be back in my cell in three hours. I can't see the boys in blue in London operating in quite such a free and easy fashion."

"I imagine that by then they'd decided you weren't a public menace. Didn't the whole business upset you at all, though?"

"Well, yes, it did," Argyll replied, tucking in to his plate of pasta. "It wasn't what I'd imagined at all. I rather saw myself uncovering the picture and making a grand announcement—after warning the parish priest—in some suitably scholarly magazine. Great sensation.

Career made, one happy parish priest and the whole world one Raphael the richer.''

He was speaking in Italian, which he spoke with some fluency. Not perfect by any means, and heavily accented, but more than acceptable. Flavia always believed in speaking Italian to foreigners if possible. Not many of them could, and those who tried could usually only manage phrases culled from guidebooks and street signs, but she felt she should make them practise. She herself had spent years learning English, and saw no reason why others shouldn't make a similar effort.

''But now we have one very unhappy parish priest, an even more unhappy Vatican, Byrnes with the picture, and your career very far from made,'' she pointed out. ''You're sure that there's something under it?''

''I wasn't at all sure, that's why I wasted so much money to come here and check. It took me months to get enough to buy the ticket. And I couldn't check it because it wasn't there any more. I was just standing around wondering what to do next. And before I could make up my mind, those flatfooted policemen of yours saw the door was open and collared me. But,'' he added, ''I'm sure there is now. Someone like Byrnes wouldn't pull off a stunt like this unless he knew it was worthwhile.''

''What I don't understand is why you didn't just write to the priest months ago, tell him your idea, and get permission to have the painting examined. Then he wouldn't have sold it until it had all been cleared up.''

''Oh, that's simple. I'm an idiot. And an apprentice academic as well, which is worse.'' Argyll looked gloomy, put his fork down, the idea clearly having made him lose his appetite. ''Art history, as you probably know, is a nasty, vicious profession. I reckoned that if

I said a word to anyone in Italy, some big shot in the Museo Nazionale would get there first and take the credit. That's happened before, and who could resist the temptation? It would've been the greatest find for years.''

"It still will be," added Flavia a little unnecessarily, dealing a further savage blow to his appetite.

"Thank you," he replied.

Flavia looked at him sympathetically. By all accounts all he'd wanted was a little bit of fame, a small boost to a career in a desperately overcrowded profession. And even that had been snatched from his grasp by Byrnes's desperate desire for even more money than he already had. "Can't you just write the article anyway? And why tell Byrnes in the first place? You haven't exactly been playing the master tactician through all this, but *that* seems the daftest course you could possibly have taken."

"I didn't tell him," Argyll said indignantly. "I may be dim, but I'm not that bad. I haven't told a soul. Well, except my supervisor. I had to tell him. But he's awfully discreet, hates art dealers and has been incommunicado in Tuscany ever since. Can't possibly have been Tramerton. Nice man really," he continued, going off at a conversational tangent. "I suppose I should send him a letter about all this. Going to jail to forward historical knowledge should impress even him.

"As for my article . . . Well, I will write one. But I'll have to do something a bit faster to stake my claim. It takes months to get a piece in a decent journal. By the time it came out, everybody would be sick of hearing about bloody Raphael. The moment Byrnes is sure he's got the right picture, the press will be called in. Sensational discovery, the works. His tame academics will write glowing articles about translucent masterpieces. And when the enthusiasm reaches its peak, the damn thing will move to Christie's.''

Argyll paused as the waiter brought the next course, which he looked at with distaste. ''And every museum, every loony millionaire in the world, will be there to bid,'' he went on. ''Something like the Getty would mortgage its grandmother to have it. Can you imagine what sort of price it will fetch? It will make a bunch of sunflowers by Van Gogh seem bargain basement.''

''Why so much? It's not as if Raphaels are thin on the ground. He churned out dozens of pictures.''

''I know, and they're all in museums or painted on the walls of the Vatican. There hasn't been a real one on the market for decades. Let alone a new one discovered. It's all supply and demand. Even if it doesn't turn out to be very good, it'll still fetch a fortune. Especially with a story like this attached to it.''

''Not a bad return on a ten million-lire investment.''

''That's what he paid?'' Argyll paused to consider the iniquities of the world. ''That makes it even worse. Even I could have raised that much. Well, almost, anyway.''

He had a well developed, if somewhat morbid, sense of humour, Flavia noted. He was also self-deprecating and appeared to be intelligent, despite apparently deliberate attempts to hide the fact. From being a simple business venture, the meal was turning into a moderately enjoyable occasion.

''Tell me,'' began her guest in an ostentatious attempt to change the subject, and demonstrate that he wasn't entirely obsessed with errant masterpieces, ''What's your job like? Plenty of work? Job satisfaction?''

She grimaced. ''Certainly plenty of work. It's like living under a permanent avalanche. Someone or other calculated that one work disappears every ten minutes. It's amazing there's anything left to steal.''

Argyll observed that, so far, Italy seemed to have plenty left.

''That's just the trouble. There seems to be an almost infinite amount kept in tumbledown country churches and half-abandoned houses. It keeps vanishing, and often as not the thefts aren't even reported.''

Argyll discovered to his delight that Flavia smoked, so fished out his own crumpled packet and lit up. ''Why not? What's the objection to reporting a theft?''

She counted the points off on her fingers as she spoke. ''One: basic distrust of the police. Two: conviction that we won't get it back anyway. Three: desire to stop the authorities knowing what else they have in case it gets taxed. Four: threats. What do you think? If I had to choose between a painting and my ears, I think I'd also choose to wave goodbye to the painting.''

It was not a bad evening. Argyll listened with every appearance of genuine interest in what she had to say, which made a nice change from the usual sort of meal where she was expected to listen with open-mouthed admiration as her date for the evening demonstrated his great qualities. He also had a fund of miscellaneous anecdotes and kept his end of the conversation going. There was only one minor incident after she had paid the bill in the restaurant when, with his hands between his knees, and rocking forward and backward slightly in an agonised fit of embarrassment, Argyll had squinted at the ceiling and said, ''I don't suppose . . .'' and then paused, and smiled foolishly.

By Italian standards it scarcely counted as an advance: one ardent suitor had only been stopped when Flavia smacked him in the face with a handy frying pan. But she had met enough Englishmen to realise what was intended, even if the technique was so reticent as to make the suggestion almost unnoticeable. Fortunately, dealing with the problem was easy: she had smiled back, and suggested an ice-cream. It seemed to be a more than suitable alternative, and the offer was accepted with evident relief.

They finished off the evening by taking a turn twice round the Piazza Montecitorio before heading for Giolitti's. Flavia was Italian and Argyll had spent enough time in the country to accept that a day without an ice-cream was a day wasted. And slowly eating it while walking the streets along with the rest of the population was a good way of restoring faith that the world was an essentially benevolent place, despite all the recent evidence to the contrary.

CHAPTER

3

Argyll swung in through a door in the via Condotti and mounted the stairs. He walked quickly past the janitor at the bottom, waving in a familiar sort of style. He should, properly, have shown the card which proved he was entitled to visit Rome's foreign press club. As he didn't have one, that was difficult. Janitors in Rome, anyway, don't often care too much about minor details.

He headed for the bar, an unattractive, tubular steel and artificial wood affair, sat down and ordered an aperitif. Then he looked around and spotted his quarry. Rudolf Beckett could be seen in the next room, alone at a table, eating a late lunch. A large glass of whisky rested in front of him. Argyll walked over and sat down.

"Jonathan. What brings you back to Rome?" Beckett thumped him on the shoulder with one hand, and shook his hand vigorously with the other. He had become one of Argyll's closest friends during his stay in Rome a year or so back. They had run into each other at a minor diplomatic party on the via Giulia. Both had felt out of place, so had naturally spent much of the evening drinking their host's alcohol and being rude about the guests. Afterwards they had gone on to a bar near by and drunk some more. It had cemented the friendship.

Not that they had anything in common. Argyll was a quiet and somewhat introverted Englishman, Beckett an aggressive workaholic with a permanent shake derived from too much drink, too little sleep, and all-consuming neuroses about the next story, the next cheque and whether anybody really liked him. As Argyll clearly did, he had never borne the brunt of one of the tumultuous outbursts of rage that made Beckett's colleagues a little wary of his company.

"Wild geese," he replied to the greeting. "I've just been let out of jail."

Beckett suppressed a smirk.

"No jokes, please," he continued, to head off the quip that the journalist was obviously on the verge of uttering. "I'm not resilient enough yet. I was wondering if you wanted a nice story."

"Is the Pope Catholic? Course I do. Depending on what it is. As long as you remember I can't pay anything for it."

"I don't want anything like that. To see it in print would be enough."

Argyll then retold the story of his discovery and the incursion of Sir Edward Byrnes, ending with his night in the cell. "My discovery. Pinched. Just like that. Could you write something so everyone knows what really happened? Otherwise Byrnes will get all the credit as well as all the money."

"Nice story," commented Beckett, finishing off another whisky and moving straight on to a large grappa. "But the lead is the Raphael, not your being diddled. However, an expert hack like myself will be able to do it. Great discovery, famous artist, etc., etc. Then a bit of stuff about you further down, undermining the whole thing and making Byrnes out to be a proper toad. Easy.

"You'll forgive me, though, but I must check up on the story first. A few phone calls, here and there, that sort of thing. OK? Feel better? You don't look as though you've been greatly enjoying the eternal city."

"I haven't. The only good thing that's happened so far has been having dinner with that policewoman last night . . ."

"That does sound bad."

"Not at all. She's very lovely. Remarkably lovely, in fact. As I've got to go back to London tomorrow, it doesn't really matter, though."

As Beckett explained in a letter a few weeks later, it wasn't really his fault, and he sent his original article to prove it. He had written the story as promised: revelation about a possible new Raphael, attributed to "museum sources"; a quotation of cautious optimism from Byrnes, a few comments from a couple of art historians, then some quite well-researched background about other remarkable discoveries in the past few years. From there on, Beckett had written about Argyll and had clearly and concisely got the message across. Young graduate student cheated by machinations of sly dealer. It didn't actually say that, of course, but the general implication was crystal clear. It was a good article.

Unfortunately, it was a bit too good. He had sent it off to the editor of his paper in New York and this man had been excited by it. So it had gone on the front page, left side, single column, instead of in the arts section as Beckett had expected. But it was a busy time of year. A summit meeting was in the offing, another bribery and

corruption scandal had broken out among local politicians, the administration was indulging in another spate
of Libya-bashing. The editor hadn't wanted to run the
story over on to an inside page. So he made it fit by
cutting it down a bit, and had sliced off the bottom seven
paragraphs. With these went all mention of Argyll.

In every other respect, the article worked wonders,
and stimulated enormous public interest. Over the next
few months, all of Argyll's predictions to Flavia about
the Raphael came true. The story of the eighteenth-
century fraud and its discovery captured the imagination.
Both the *New York Times Magazine* and the arts sup-
plement of the London *Observer* duly carried lengthy
accounts of the art-historical detective work which had
led to the pot of gold. They, also, neglected to mention
Argyll, but were otherwise solidly written. Byrnes's
sales campaign was well under way.

Argyll indulged his sense of mild masochism by collecting the articles. All sorts of critics and historians in-
vaded what he had previously considered to be his turf.
The diligent research of others produced dozens of little
fragments to complete his partial picture and show the
results of his haste. One article reproduced letters from
the Earl's brother-in-law indicating he had died of a
heart attack from shock at the fraud, and that the family
had covered up their loss for fear of embarrassment:
"Rest assured, dear sister, no fault attaches to you for
the attack. Such an event was entirely due to his own
injudicious choice and hasty character. But these matters
will remain between us alone; the disgrace to our family,
and the scorn of certain of our friends could not be tolerated . . ." That particularly outraged him. He had seen
the same letter, but had decided it was inconclusive.
Now everything else was clear, so was the letter.

What was worse was that all these little articles meant that even the modest piece he had planned for the *Burlington Magazine* was not possible; everything had already been published at least once. He avoided his friends and found a peculiar form of solace in going back to the *Life and Times of Carlo Mantini, 1675–1729*. At least he could finish that. It wouldn't be so good now that one of his central chapters had become about as original as the plot of Romeo and Juliet, but it would do.

He was also correct in assuming that Byrnes, one of nature's salesmen despite his mild manner, would turn the whole process of cleaning and restoration into a media event. The best restorers from the museums were called in to scrape away the paintwork of Mantini and remove the layer of protective varnish over the precious object underneath. Almost every week, bulletins on television would show the team of white-coated professionals—half scientific, half artistic—applying a variety of exotic solvents that could be relied upon to do their appointed task and no more. Then yet more programmes and articles in magazines monitored the second cleaning process, which would restore the painting to its original perfection.

Almost everybody knew by now that underneath the painting by Mantini there lay a portrait of Elisabetta di Laguna, the mistress of an earlier Marchese di Parma and, by repute, the most beautiful woman of her age. What someone like Raphael, who had made much less attractive women look like veritable Venuses, would have produced with such a sitter was anybody's guess. Critics from the *London Standard* to the *Baltimore Sun* speculated freely. Some even ventured to suggest that

Leonardo's *Mona Lisa* would be knocked off its perch
as the world's favourite painting.

While the picture was under wraps, the jockeying for
position got under way amongst the likely buyers. The
Louvre indicated its interest, if it could afford the price.
Two large New York banks and three pension funds in
Tokyo also let it be known they might attend the auction.
In an attempt to frighten off the opposition, the Getty
Museum in Malibu Beach hinted that it might unleash
all its vast buying-power to take possession. And all over
the world, lesser millionaires and billionaires assessed
their position, counted their money and attempted to
work out whether they could, in a few years, sell it for
a profit. Many decided they could.

When the picture was finally revealed to the public,
the event was stage-managed in exquisite detail. The un-
veiling took place in a large meeting-room at the Savoy
Hotel in the Strand, and hundreds of people were invited. The picture stood on a raised platform, covered
with a large white sheet. Before the great moment, a
presentation was made to the assembled press, television
cameras, dignitaries from the worlds of museum and art-
history faculties. The senior curator of the Louvre sat
alongside the local staffer from Associated Press and the
great Japanese collector Yagamoto; while the keeper of
western art from the Dresdener Staatsgalerie was sandwiched between his great rival from one of the richest
museums in the American Midwest and a sweaty individual from one of the London tabloids.

All of them had been served with champagne, cour-
tesy of Byrnes Galleries, and all listened with appropriate attention as Byrnes himself ran through the now
well-known story of how the painting was discovered;
long forgotten in the little church in central Rome, and

covered by another painting as a result of one of the greatest artistic fraud attempts of all time. Byrnes did a competent job of it, but was far from coming across as the archetype of the smooth art dealer. A small, timid-looking man with horn-rimmed spectacles and a bald head which ducked and bobbed nervously as he spoke, he was not at all like most people's image of an international aesthete.

Nor, to Flavia in the fifteenth row on the right, did he look like the Machiavellian beast of Jonathan Argyll's evidently fevered imagination. She was there largely out of curiosity; the presentation having come during one of her visits to London for informal discussions with the London art squad.

Flavia had gently asked her opposite number in London to organise an invitation. The squad was out in force to guard the picture, and Byrnes could hardly refuse them. So she sat and listened to him making his concluding remarks. Then he introduced Professor Julian Henderson, doyen of Renaissance studies, who gave a brief lecture. The picture, he told them, in an eminently polished delivery, was, without doubt, Raphael's masterpiece; the apogee of the Humanist ideal of feminine beauty.

The lecture hall was not one that the journalists in the audience were used to, but they listened politely, and the photographers got on with their business. Henderson concluded by comparing the picture to other portraits by Raphael, and suggesting that the evidence now indicated that Elisabetta had been the model for the portrait of Sappho in the mural of Parnassus in the Vatican. The new work that the discovery would engender was enough to keep historians of the Italian High Renaissance in business for years.

Amid minor laughter and light applause he sat down and Byrnes moved towards the picture.

Flavia was beginning to find the showbiz style of the meeting a little wearisome, and was glad that Byrnes avoided any excessive display in the final stages. Not that it was needed; the audience's sense of anticipation needed no further stimulation. With only a minor flourish, the cover was gently removed, and there was a quiet gasp as the onlookers, and the cameras, focused on what had become one of the most famous paintings in the world.

Because of the incessant coverage it had received in the last few months, almost everyone had some idea what the portrait looked like. Seeing it in the flesh was nonetheless exhilarating. It was a beautiful painting of a very beautiful woman. From her position, Flavia could not see very well, but it seemed to be a bust length with the head turned slightly to the right. Fair hair was gathered loosely at the back of the head so that the left ear was partly covered. The left hand reached up to touch a necklace, and the subject was dressed in a closefitting dress of a gorgeously rich red. The background was conventional, but excellently produced. The sitter—lean and with none of the fleshy appearance that made many of Raphael's Madonnas look just a little overweight—was in a room. In the left background was a window giving out to a wooded hill, on the right, wall hangings, a table and some ornaments. The organisation of the figure itself radiated an air of remarkable tranquillity, with just a hint of the sensuality that the painter so often brought out.

But she was most struck by the reaction from the audience. They were not admiring the delicacy of the brush strokes, the masterly application of shading or the subtleties of the composition, that was certain. They were ogling. Not a usual reaction for connoisseurs. She herself was caught up in the enthusiasm. The picture, both in its history and subject, was extraordinarily romantic. This most beautiful woman, nearly half a millenium old, had been lost for nearly three hundred years. It could hardly fail to capture the imagination. She even felt herself forgiving Byrnes.

The enthusiasm that greeted Elisabetta's entry onto the world scene after her long absence carried the painting right through to the auction, held in the main sale room of Christie's about a month later. That affair also lived up to expectations.

The auctioneers knew how to put on a show. Expensively printed catalogues with full-colour photographs, a satellite link to sale rooms in Switzerland, New York and Tokyo, live television coverage in eight countries; these were the most obvious signs that an event of great importance was taking place. The atmosphere in the room, casually lined with other works of lesser significance, was electrifying. Like all good salesmen, the auctioneers had style. The sale was officially dubbed only "sixteenth- and seventeenth-century old master oils and drawings," and Elisabetta was humbly placed as number twenty-eight on the list. The only difference was that, unlike many of the other lots, the Raphael had not been given an estimated sale price.

The audience had risen to the occasion also. London auctions range widely in style, background and purpose. At one end, there are the routine sales held in the shabby auction rooms in insalubrious neighbourhoods like Marylebone where the main clientele are unshaven dealers who congregate to chat, eat sandwiches, and pick up paintings for a couple of hundred pounds.

At the very top of the pile are the great houses in St. James, where uniformed doormen open the broad brass doors, the employees speak with the accents of the privileged, and the clientele look as if they could buy a few hundred thousand pounds-worth of oil painting and not even notice. Even here, however, dealers tend to predominate, but these are the princes of their trade, with galleries in Bond Street or Fifth Avenue or the Rue de Rivoli. They are the sort of people who have enough to live on for a year if they sell one painting every three months, who own firms—not companies and never shops—that were often founded a century or more before. Not that this made them any more honest and less likely to break the law if necessary, but they generally did so more cautiously, more intelligently, and with greater decorum.

Like their clients, they knew how to behave appropriately. In the audience of maybe three hundred people, all but a dozen of the men wore their dinner jackets. The women, outnumbered around four to one, were dressed to match, with most in long ball gowns or wearing furs—until the heat of the camera lights made them intolerable. The air vibrated with the smell of a hundred mingling perfumes.

The sense of anticipation built up slowly as the lots were brought to the rostrum and the bidding started. A Maratta was sold for three hundred thousand pounds— the price instantly clicked up on the display board in four countries translated into dollars, Swiss francs and yen—and no one paid any attention. An Imperiali fetching a record price excited no interest whatsoever. Lot twenty-seven, a particularly fine old Palma oil-sketch which deserved greater consideration, was knocked down at an absurdly low price and bought.

Then came lot twenty-eight. The auctioneer, a man in his sixties who had seen it all before, knew well that the best way to generate excitement and loosen wallets was an utterly deadpan presentation. The slightest sign of enthusiasm or an apparent wish to manipulate the audience with a show of salesmanship would produce entirely the wrong effect. Understatement is always a virtue in such situations. As he spoke, two young men in brown overalls brought the picture and hung it on the easel to the right of the rostrum. It stood there, bathed in light—as one poetic television reporter put it afterwards—as if it were back on an altar as an object of worship itself.

"Lot twenty-eight. Raphael. A portrait of Elisabetta di Laguna, about 1505. Oil on canvas, sixty-eight centimetres by a hundred and thirty-eight. I'm sure many of you know the background to this work, so we will start the bidding at twenty million pounds. What am I bid?"

To start the bidding at such a high price was audacious, but just the right touch of muted flamboyance needed. Only a few years ago to have *ended* the session on such a figure would have been a sensation. Only four pictures in the world had ever fetched more. Without any noise, and without any member of the audience appearing to move at all, the bidding flashed past thirty million, then thirty-five, then forty. At forty-two million, some dealers manning a rank of telephones along one side of the room spoke to their clients in dozens of different countries. At fifty-three million, some put down their phones and folded their arms, signifying that their clients had pulled out. At fifty-seven million it was clear that the bidding was down to two people, a burly man in the third row who insiders knew had acted in the past for the Getty Museum, and a small man who made his bids with a nervous gesture with his hand, chopping sideways briefly as though making a point in an animated conversation.

It was this second man who won. After he had offered sixty-three million pounds, the burly man with the purple cravat looked up, hesitated and then shook his head. There was silence for perhaps three seconds.

"Sold. For sixty-three million pounds. Yours, sir."

The room exploded in applause, the tension welling up suddenly then bursting into relief and euphoria. It was not only a record, but an enormous record. The only reservation in the minds of the professional part of the audience was who the buyer had been. The art world is a small universe and almost everyone in it knows everyone else and who they work for.

No one had the slightest idea who this man was, and he vanished through a side door before anybody could ask him.

CHAPTER

4

It took only a few days before the word seeped through the secret passages riddling the world of dealers, connoisseurs and collectors that the small unknown man who had outbid the Getty was a senior civil servant in the Italian treasury, sent to the sale with a blank cheque from the government and instructions to get the work at any cost. The news itself caused another mild stir. Like most other state museums, the Italian system was given an annual budget that was wholly inadequate. Like the curators of every museum in Europe, the director of the Museo Nazionale had had to stand by, consumed by a mixture of rage and envy, as work after precious work reached prices that his entire budget for the next twelve months could not have covered. But he was a man who regarded the saving of works for Italy as a moral duty, and had been lobbying everyone in authority for months to set aside more funds. He had won his point and, when Elisabetta came up for sale, had cajoled and fought for the government to honour its promises.

Clearly, some remarkable maneuvering had been go-

ing on in the labyrinthine and obscure network of in-
trigue known as the Italian government. In fact, it was
another example of politics at work. The interest that the
portrait had generated elsewhere in the world was nothing compared to that seen in Italy itself. The way that a
cunning English dealer had snatched Elisabetta from the
hands of State and Vatican, and had legally evaded all
the restrictions designed to stop such an event, made the
government appear foolish, the museum curators slow-
witted, and the art historians incompetent.

And several members of the government remembered
the furore that had preceded the founding of Bottando's
sezione only a few years before. So the authorities gave
way to the ferocious and persuasive lobbying, made
available the special grant they had promised, and sent
off their man. In some ways it was a daring thing to do:
the opposition Communist Party instantly did its best to
make capital out of the move by pointing to a dozen
better ways of spending that sort of money. Others wrote
polemical articles in the newspapers on the Italian budget deficit and how the country could not possibly afford
such indulgences.

But the government, and particularly the arts minister,
had calculated correctly. He posed as a champion of the
Italian heritage, willing to defend the patrimony at all
costs. If Italy had lost such a valuable painting, then it
must have it back. If this cost money, then so be it; that
amount would be paid to safeguard the nation's artistic
integrity. It turned out to be a popular move; opinion
polls showed that the electorate's patriotic nerve had
been touched. Besides, there is something peculiarly
gratifying in owning the most expensive picture in the
world, and to have outspent the Americans and Japanese
in a fair fight. Outside the country also, the Italian move

was applauded. Directors from national museums everywhere cited the purchase as an example for their own governments to follow; some newspapers even began pointing to the minister—a man of little administrative ability and small intelligence—as embodying the sort of dynamism and vision that could make an effective prime minister.

Which didn't endear him to the current incumbent, but as the government as a whole reaped some of the advantages of being considered effective, swift of foot and cultured—the last quality in some ways more important in Italy than the first two—nothing was said. But it was noted, and the minister was marked down for special attention in case he should show further signs of getting above himself.

The actual return of the painting was conducted like a state visit from a visiting sovereign. A month after the auction, once it had been put through a series of tests and examinations in London by specialists, it arrived in an air-force transport at Fiumicino airport and was carried in a procession—with attendant motorcycle outriders and armoured cars—to the National Museum. The armoured cars seemed a little excessive, but Bottando's department, in liaison with his comrades in the regular army, was taking no chances. The Brigate Rosse, the urban guerillas of the seventies, had lain dormant for several years, but you never knew.

In the Museo Nazionale itself, Elisabetta was set up like an icon. A room was emptied to take the portrait which would rest, behind the rope barrier keeping viewers ten feet away, in solitary splendour. Again, caution prevailed. Both police and curators remembered the sledgehammer attack on Michelangelo's *Pietà* in St. Peter's a few years before; too many pictures in recent years had been slashed with knives or peppered with pellets from shotguns by maniacs who claimed to be the archangel Gabriel, or resented the adulation of some long-dead artist while their own talents went unrecognised. And everyone agreed that the painting's fame made it a perfect target for some deranged attention-seeker.

Finally, the room was bathed in subdued lighting, with a single spotlight illuminating the work. The museum's interior designers freely admitted to their friends, if not to anybody else, that this was a bit melodramatic. Drawings, such as Leonardo's *Madonna* in the National Gallery in London, actually needed such protection from light to preserve them. Oil paintings were much more resilient and could do perfectly well in natural light. But the effect was splendid, creating an atmosphere of almost religious awe and causing visitors to speak in respectful, hushed tones which added greatly to the work's impact.

Visitors there were in abundance. In the first few months attendance at the museum doubled. A visit suddenly became almost compulsory not only for tourists—who had often left it out hitherto because of its inconvenient location out of the centre—but even for Romans themselves. Thousands of postcards were sold; Elisabetta di Laguna T-shirts were popular; a multi-national biscuit company paid the museum a fortune for the right to put her face on one of their products. Combined with the hugely increased entry fees, the museum directors calculated the state would have recovered most of the vast cost of the picture within four years if the painting's popularity continued at this rate.

• • •

For Bottando and his assistant, the return of the painting had triggered one of their busiest periods for years. Setting up security, keeping tabs on known national and international thieves, worrying lest anything should go wrong, chained them to their desks.

Bottando, looking at the work through the eyes of an old-time policeman whose budget was already not big enough, spent much of his time in a frenzy of anxiety. He knew perfectly well that, whatever the picture's artistic merits, it was a painted time bomb for his department. If anything should happen to it, the blame would move around the government with the speed of a ball in a pinball machine before coming to rest on his desk.

Much of his work, therefore, consisted of preparing his defences. Although not a cynical man, and no politician, he was no fool either. A lifetime's work under the aegis of the ministry of defence had taught him a great deal about survival techniques in a world that made fighting in the army seem genteel and civilised. So he spent many hours sweating over cautiously worded reports, drafted and redrafted memoranda and wasted a great deal of time taking a few, carefully selected, bureaucrats and politicians to dinner.

The result was not entirely to his liking, but better than nothing. He had lobbied for extra manpower, using Elisabetta as a way of making his case for a larger budget. In fact, the result was that the security staff of the Museo Nazionale was doubled. Although it was never stated directly, the effective conclusion was that his department was relieved of any responsibility for guarding the picture once it was hung.

This provided some protection. But Bottando realised, with a perception honed by years of watching for trouble, that there existed no official document proving his lack of responsibility, and that was worrying. Especially because in Cavaliere Marco Ottavio Mario di Bruno di Tommaso, the sublimely aristocratic director of the National Museum, he was dealing with a man who would have been a natural politician had he not gone into the museum business. A smoother operator, in fact, was not to be found in the Camera dei Deputati. Tommaso had had a painting snatched from under his very nose, had been forced to buy it back at an outrageous price, and had turned it into a triumph. Impressive, without a doubt.

He was reminded of the justice of this opinion as he stood talking to the director at a reception thrown to celebrate the picture's installation in the museum. A very select junket indeed. A sizeable chunk of the cabinet and their inevitable hangers-on; museum folk, the occasional academic, a few journalists just so the affair would reach the papers. Tommaso was, if anything, Bottando's superior in making sure glowing reports of his activities frequently adorned the pages of the newspapers.

"Taking a bit of a risk, aren't you? I mean, all these dubious types around your prized possession?" Bottando gestured contemptuously at the prime minister and an army chief peering at the work, cigarettes in hand.

Tommaso moaned softly in agreement. "I know. But it's difficult to ask the prime minister not to smoke. He gets withdrawal symptoms after ten minutes. We had to switch off all the fire alarms to make sure they weren't all drenched by the sprinklers. Can't say it makes me all that happy. But, there you are. What can you do? These people will insist on sharing the limelight." He shrugged.

The conversation dragged on for a few minutes more, and then Tommaso slid off to talk to others. He was always like that. Everybody got the regulation five minutes of urbane conversation. He was a perfect host; Bottando merely wished that he didn't make you feel it all the time. He was always pleasant, always remembered everyone's name, always recalled something about your last conversation with him to make you think he valued your company. Bottando hated him. The more so because he'd just sprung a very nasty surprise.

There was to be another liaison committee, he'd said. Were there not enough already, for heaven's sake? A joint meeting of the museum and the police, to discuss security matters in the museum: Bottando heading the police end and Antonio Ferraro, the head of sculpture, the museum side. It had been Ferraro's idea, apparently. Serve him right. Had Bottando heard about this in advance, he could have sabotaged the whole thing. But Tommaso had gone ahead, getting all the various approvals, before broaching the subject.

It was, of course, true that what this place did need was a long, hard look at its security procedures, which were neolithic. But a committee wasn't going to achieve much and, in fact, it wasn't intended to. Instead, Tommaso meant it to serve as a layer of protection between him and responsibility if anything should go wrong.

The only person Bottando felt sorry for was Ferraro, standing over on the other side of the room. Tall, broad, and powerful-looking. Dark hair, of the sort that clung to his scalp as though it had been heavily annointed with hair dressing. A voluble conversationalist, one of those who tends to interrupt you in mid-sentence so that he can continue his enthusiastic narrations. Mid-thirties, with a permanent look of mild sarcasm on his face. A clever, impatient man. No wonder he and Tommaso never got on well; neither was prepared to accept the other in anything but a subservient role. Maybe Bottando could have him replaced on the committee with someone a bit more amenable?

"You're scowling," said a voice by his side. "I deduce that you've just been talking to our beloved chief."

Bottando turned around, and smiled. Enrico Spello was unofficially the deputy director and someone he had a certain liking for. "Right as usual. How did you guess?"

Spello clasped his hands together to indicate the mysteries of human intuition. "Simple. I always look like that after a conversation with Tommaso as well."

"But he's your boss. You've a right to dislike him. He's always pleasant to me."

"Of course. He's always delightful to me, as well. Even when he's cutting my budget by twenty-five per cent."

"He's done that? When?"

"Oh, it's been going on for a year or more. No interest in the Etruscans any more. For archaeologists and antiquarians. What's needed is more brightness, stuff to bring in the crowds. As you know, he's a bit of a whizz kid, our Tommaso. My department gets sliced so he can afford some very expensive beige fabric on the walls of western art."

"Is yours the only department to be cut?" Bottando asked.

"Oh, no. But it's one of the worst. It has lost our friend over there a lot of popularity." He smiled whimsically. Bottando felt for the man. He was a real scholar, the sort of person who was dying out in the museum world. He lived, breathed and slept Etruscan antiquities. No one knew more about those mysterious people than Spello. His sort were now being replaced by administrators, by fund raisers and by entrepreneurs. Not at all like the short, stout and eccentrically dressed Spello.

"I didn't know he had any popularity to lose," Bottando commented.

"He didn't really. I don't know why he bothers. He's got so much money he doesn't have to."

Bottando raised an eyebrow. "Indeed? I never knew that."

Spello looked sideways at him. "And you call yourself a policeman? I thought you were meant to know everything. Vast family riches, so I'm told. Won't do him any good. One day he'll be found in his office with a knife in his back. Then you'll be spoiled for suspects."

"Where should I start?"

"Well," Spello began, considering the matter. "I trust you would do me the honour of making me top suspect. Then there's the people in Non-Italian Baroque, who've been shunted into a tiny little attic where no one can ever find them. Impressionism doesn't at all like his decision to merge them with Realism, and Glassware greatly resents the imperialistic designs of Silver. Quite a hornet's nest, in fact. Our little dining-room resounds daily to tales of his outrages, past and present."

"And which past ones do you have in mind at the moment?" Bottando prompted. He loved gossip, and realised Spello wanted to tell him some anecdote. Besides, he was irritated that he hadn't known of the Tommaso money.

"Ah. I was thinking of the Case of the Bum Correggio. This was back in the sixties, when our friend was keeper of pictures at Treviso. Nice museum, traditional starting place for One Who is Destined to Rise in the World. Being an ambitious and aggressive young man, Tommaso began to buy pictures from abroad, commandeering almost everyone else's budget to do so.

"He bought dozens of pictures and established his reputation as a thrusting up-and-comer. He likes buying pictures, you may have noticed. He alienated everyone else in the museum by doing so but, what the hell? He'd soon be moving on to better things.

"But he made a false step. He bought a Correggio for a considerable amount of money, and hung it in the gallery. Then the whispers started. An article appeared, saying that on stylistic grounds it might not be genuine. Then some pieces of provenance were dredged up suggesting it was merely a copy. He forces the dealer—none other than Edward Byrnes—to take it back. But the storm over his competence continues, nonetheless.

"This is where our friend's genius comes in. His friends in Rome whisper into ears. He bludgeons his director—a sweet and naïve man—into taking the fire. The director resigns, and Tommaso, enhancing his reputation, resigns out of loyalty. He goes out into the wilderness for a brief period but is soon back, climbing the ladder to the stars. And there he is, in his firmament.

"So you see," Spello added, looking around him at the now thinning room, "we may seem a happy family, but what a maelstrom of discontent is there. One mistake from our friend over there, and there'll be a queue, half a kilometre long, waiting to tear his throat out."

CHAPTER

5

Despite the concern that the presence of Elisabetta continued to create, the work of the department had to go on as much as possible. If the public was entranced by the picture, the art thieves paused only momentarily before getting back to their proper business.

In fact, the furore might have encouraged more activity; with contemplation on the value and transportability of a small piece of canvas tempting more people to try their luck on other, less illustrious objects. This was tiresome, but in some ways satisfying, as the department's success rate improved by picking up the amateurs. Removing an Italian statue or picture is often very simple, merely a question of breaking down an often frail door, loading the work into a car and driving off. Any second-rate crook can manage it. Getting rid of it afterwards, however, is a different matter. You can't just take a hot painting in to a sale room and sell it, and if you want to pass it on to a dealer you have to know the honest ones from the dishonest ones. Successfully stealing works of art is a highly skilled occupation which, unlike many others, continues to breed practitioners of great ability.

It was because of the quiet but persistent activity of a master craftsman that several months after the arrival of Elisabetta in state to Rome, and once much of the excitement had died away to little more than an expanded inflow of income to the Museo Nazionale's coffers, Flavia returned once more to London.

It was for yet another liaison meeting, a gathering of policemen from France, Italy, Greece and Britain, all brought together because of one man, thought to be French and suspected of running a thriving business in the theft of Greek icons.

Icons are relatively little known outside the art world, an obscure area that interests only the enthusiast. The pictures, generally on wooden panels and hung in Orthodox churches to assist the focusing of attention during prayer, are often difficult to appreciate. With simple backgrounds of gold, their stylised appearance is an acquired taste, especially as the absence of perspective makes them difficult for viewers brought up on the dynamism of the Renaissance. But once the taste is formed, they can become a passion, the stark elegance and uncluttered forms giving an aura of peacefulness and tranquillity which the more robust, active pieces produced in the West rarely approach.

More importantly, perhaps, they command high prices and the market for them is notably more crooked than for other types of art. Because one of the major sources is the Soviet Union, smuggling them is commonplace. Russian icons are also regularly brought out by *émigrés* who are forbidden to take out currency. They are smuggled to Vienna and on to Tel Aviv, then sent on to the market via New York and London. Buying them is cast almost as a blow for freedom, and few dealers or collectors worry themselves about their origin.

All these factors help create a market which Jean-Luc Morneau evidently found attractive—assuming that the deductions of the Sûreté were correct and that it was this Paris-based dealer who was behind the thefts. When the monastery on the island of Amorgos in the Cyclades contacted the local policeman, who in turn passed a message to Athens, which in due course made enquiries around Europe, Morneau's name kept on appearing, although no hard evidence could be produced to warrant any sort of action.

Whoever it was, the technique used was simple. A tourist appears on the doorstep of the monastery asking to see the church. Once inside, he takes photographs, and particularly snaps away at the icon above the altar. He then thanks the monk at the gate, makes a donation and departs.

He returns many months later, sporting a beard, moustache or dark glasses to make recognition unlikely. He is again left to wander as he pleases. He checks to see the church is empty, goes up to the altar and unzips the large camera case. He takes out the copy he has painted from the photographs, swaps it for the genuine one over the altar and puts this carefully into his bag. He leaves the island on the next boat—the visit is timed so that the boat leaves only an hour or so afterwards—heads for Crete or Rhodes where airport customs are scarce, and flies out of the country.

The copy left behind on Amorgos, and on about twenty other islands, as well as a few sites in the northeast of Italy, is detected as a fake the moment that experts examine it. But it is very competent and quite able to withstand the normal scrutiny it receives, half-hidden in the semi-twilight of the church, from both monks and the occasional sightseer. According to the best recollection of the monks, it had done so for more than a year. Other monasteries had been admiring their copies for even longer. ·

The finger pointed to Morneau firstly because he was a dealer in icons, secondly because he had been trained as a painter, and thirdly because he was not known for his honesty. But, there the evidence had dried up, and the meeting had been called so that efforts could be directed towards tracking down some of the paintings by discreet enquiries.

The Greek police also wanted help in the search for Morneau, who had vanished from sight. French checks had established that he had vacated his studio in the Place des Abbesses some time ago. Without knowing where he was, it was that much more difficult to establish where he had been. Certainly the evidence of the monasteries was of little help; one reported the visitor with the camera case as French, others as Swedish, German, American and Italian. They had all failed to identify him from photographs.

The meeting to discuss the matter was largely inconclusive, mainly because one young and none-too-serious Englishman had sighed and ventured that he wished he could have thought of a crime like that. The remark irritated the Greeks, who had responded by making remarks about crooked French dealers, which sent the Gallic contingent into a sulk. The encounter, indeed, was no great symbol of European cooperation.

It was also as an indirect result of this somewhat inconclusive meeting that Flavia met Jonathan Argyll once more. He had written to her several months before, asking to see her if she should come to England, and saying that he wouldn't mind returning the favour and taking her to dinner. She had not written back, partly because there had been no immediate plan to go to England, and partly because she hated writing letters; which, to her mind, made up a pretty good reason.

But evenings alone in big cities can be very dull, especially when the days are short, the weather is cold and the rain, as always in London, is coming down in a light, but persistent drizzle. It was impossible to walk around either to see sights or to window-shop. Going to restaurants on your own has little attraction, the cinemas weren't showing anything that interested her, the one play she wanted to see was booked solid and the thought of a lonely evening in a hotel room with an improving book made those little twinges of imminent depression noticeable.

So, having exhausted all other possibilities, she picked up the phone and gave him a ring. He was instantly delighted to hear her, and invited her to go and eat immediately. She accepted, and he suggested she come round to his flat. This she considered, assessed for possible trouble, and refused. Even Englishmen could act funny when in their own apartments and, while she had no doubts about her ability to deal with any awkward situation, it always ruined an evening.

"Oh go on. I'm not sure which restaurant to go to and it would be much easier if you came here first. It's not very far from the tube."

A sort of uncalculating friendliness in his request made her change her mind. She agreed to meet him at his flat at seven-thirty, was given directions, and put down the phone.

• • •

Getting to Notting Hill Gate from her hotel was easy. On the whole, Flavia's main objection to London was simply the size of the place and the inhuman way it was laid out. In Rome, she lived about fifteen minutes' walk away from the office, in a quiet and inexpensive part of town near Augustus's mausoleum that had an abundance of restaurants, innumerable shops and a boisterous population. But London was entirely different. Almost no one seemed to live anywhere near the centre and everyone spent hours every day on the tubes or trains either going to work or going home again. And the neighbourhoods they lived in were generally unutterably dull, with few shops and an atmosphere of respectability that made you think they were all tucked up in bed by nine-thirty with a glass of hot milk. The constant cavalcade of streetlife, of people wandering around for the sake of it, greeting their friends, having a drink, everything that made city life worthwhile, scarcely existed. London was not Flavia's idea of a good time.

Argyll's part of Notting Hill lay beyond the respectable bit that surrounded the tube station, in the less opulent regions beyond. The building was neither among the best nor the worst that the area had to offer. He lived on the top floor of a terraced house halfway along the street and, when she rang the doorbell, bellowed into a faulty, crackling ansaphone that she should keep walking up the stairs until she ran out.

His flat showed distinct signs of a very hurried and only partly successful attempt at flight. Mounds of notes lay in boxes; open suitcases, half filled with clothes and books, were on the floor; a pile of miscellaneous socks nestled up against the bottle of white wine that Argyll had evidently just been out to buy in her honour.

"Moving, are you?" she observed, noting that this

was not the sort of conclusion that required the brains of a Sherlock Holmes to reach.

"Yup," he replied, uncorking the bottle and peering into it to see how much cork was left floating in the wine. He frowned in disapproval at the debris, then looked up with a happy smile. "Farewell London, hello again Rome. For about a year, maybe more. Until I finish the damn thesis. I've done all the English end, so everything I need is in Italy. Which is pretty convenient, if you ask me."

"I thought you were impoverished."

"So I was. However, not at the moment. It's one of the unforeseen spin-offs of that Raphael."

"How so?"

"Well, you see, I was invited to a party, and there was Edward Byrnes. He sort of sidled up to me in a sheepish fashion and we got talking. The upshot of it was that he as near as dammit apologised for pinching the picture. Not, of course, that he admitted any double-dealing. Independent research leading in the same direction, and so on. Not his picture, anyway, you know. Entire coincidence, the whole thing. That's as may be. I don't believe it. He got wind of it through me, somehow. The important thing was, he offered a disguised form of compensation. His firm has a scholarship for art historians, and basically he said that if I applied for it, I'd probably be given it. So I did, and so I was."

"And you took it?"

Argyll paused for a moment. "Well, I thought, why the hell not? The picture's out of my reach for ever, Byrnes has a lot of money thanks to me. I could have stood on my dignity and refused to touch his filthy money, how dare you insult me, sir. But he'd still be as rich, and I'd still be as poor. By rights, I suppose, he should have offered me a couple of million. But he didn't, and it was this or nothing.''

''What did he mean, not his picture?''

''Just that, apparently. That's the story he's evidently putting around, probably because of jealousy in the trade. He was acting on commission. Someone else got him to buy it and so someone else now has the money, presumably.''

''Who?'' asked Flavia, intrigued.

''Didn't say. I didn't ask, to tell you the truth, because it's such obvious nonsense. Besides, I was too busy fantasising about going back to Italy.''

''You'd never make a very good policeman,'' she observed.

''I know. But I don't plan to. It struck me as such a silly story, I dismissed it instantly. I mean to say, can you see any self-respecting dealer having a Raphael on his hands and tamely letting it go?'' He paused for a moment while he fished for bits of cork with his finger, dredging them out a fragment at a time.

''Disgusting of me. Sorry about that,'' he said apologetically.

He poured, she sipped, he sat on the floor and they talked inconsequentially about her trip, his research, how he found his flat. They spoke in Italian and about Italy, and Argyll grew gently and fondly enthusiastic. He loved it in the way that only the repressed, monochromatic inhabitants of cold northern countries can fall for the colourful exuberance of the Mediterranean. But his was no goggle-eyed, blind devotion; he knew the country well, warts and all. The inefficiencies, rigidities, narrow-mindedness of Italy he understood and accepted. He also knew its art, and could talk with nostalgic delight of the long and weary trips he had made by bus and by foot to the more obscure delights that Italy likes to secrete in inaccessible places. It occurred to Flavia that he might get on well with Bottando. Then he changed the subject back and they talked about London, work and museums. He held up a finger as he poured her another glass of wine. "There was, by the way, another reason for taking Byrnes's money. It struck me as a sort of victory."

She looked at him, puzzled, "Some victory," she said.

"Wait and see," he replied, kneeling down by a large cardboard box and rummaging through dozens of bits of paper. "Now, where did I put it? That's the trouble when you pack. You always need the things at the bottom of the boxes. Ah. Here it is. I must show you. I think you'll find it funny."

Argyll explained that on his return to England, after the débâcle in the carabinieri cells, he had thrown himself back into the subject of Mantini with vigour. His motives were not any great love of art history, nor any particular devotion to resurrecting the reputation of his chosen painter—a man who by any stretch of the imagination was fairly second-rate. Rather, it had become a matter of pride that, having spent a few years on the subject, he was going to get something to show for it all, even if it was just a piece of paper and the right to be called Doctor Argyll.

He went on to say how he had made a resolute attempt to forget about Raphael and associated subjects. His painter had been fairly popular among English tourists in Rome in the early eighteenth-century, and many of them had commissioned some minor work from him as a memento of their stay; the eighteenth-century equivalent of buying a postcard of the Spanish Steps. Generally speaking, he turned out somewhat derivative landscapes in the style of Claude Lorrain or Gaspard Dughet which were held in high esteem at the time. As he was compiling a *catalogue raisonné* of the artist's work, he had written to almost every country-house owner in England to ask whether they had any. He had also gone to visit several houses, to look through their archives for any evidence of when the works were bought, how they were acquired and at what price.

On one of these ventures he had ended up in Backlin House in Gloucestershire, a vast, chilly pile still lived in by the original family even though they could clearly no longer afford it. Had they been sensible, he said, they would have given the place away to the National Trust and gone to live in the South of France, like the Clomortons had done after the war.

The muniments room, where the family papers were kept in dusty, mouldy obscurity, had made the rest of the house seem positively jolly. One look had almost persuaded him to go straight back home.

"A man from the Historic Manuscripts Commission came round in 1903 to catalogue the papers but died of influenza halfway through. I'm not surprised. If I hadn't taken the precaution of bringing a pair of mittens, a woolly hat and a hip flask I might well have gone under myself. The experienced researcher is prepared for all eventualities," he added loftily.

Because of the poor gentleman's untimely demise, the papers had never been sorted and a catalogue never published. And because of that, no one had been near them for years. So Argyll, when he finally made his way into the attic that contained four hundred years of miscellaneous memories, found a huge number of dust-covered rolls of documents, chests of estate vouchers, bundle upon bundle of legal materials, and a whole series of nineteenth-century cardboard boxes labelled "first earl," "second earl" and so on.

On the whole, the thousands of papers were arranged randomly, or if there were any order, he failed to grasp what it was. However, a few boxes bore the traces of the old archivist, and had evidently been arranged for examination before he died. These were given rough labels. One large box was titled "eighteenth-century letters."

"This was my great discovery," Argyll said. "One sheath was entirely of letters to the owner of the house, Sir Robert Delmé, from his sister Arabella."

"So?" asked Flavia, her manners beginning to fight a battle for dominance over her impatience.

"Arabella was a great lady, the sort that died out when the eighteenth century was through. She had four husbands in all, and outlived the lot. She was about to take on number five when she herself keeled over from excess cognac at the age of eighty-seven. The point is that husband number two was none other than our friend the Earl of Clomorton—that noted connoisseur of Raphael—and ten of the letters dated from this period."

Argyll explained that most of the letters were of little interest—London gossip, details of the doings of the Prince of Wales, as well as scabrous comments about the innumerable inadequacies of her husband. Although wealthy, the second Earl clearly did not rate highly with his wife, was parsimonious to a fault and seemed greatly lacking in judgement.

"He was exactly the sort of person the average Roman art dealer could see coming a mile off. It would have been a point of honour amongst them to foist rub-

bish onto him at vast expense. All he really cared about
deeply were his haemorrhoids, if Lady A is to be believed. He seems to have kept up a non-stop monologue
on the subject for years on end. Painful, no doubt, but
they ruin the atmosphere at breakfast.''

Two of the letters came from the period in which the
earl died, one immediately before, the second afterwards. ''Here,'' said Argyll, shuffling through a set of
papers in a manila folder, ''I copied them down. Have
a look.''

Flavia picked up the first sheet of paper and squinted
at it to decipher Argyll's rapid and untidy scrawl. *Dear-
est Brother*, it began, *As I've no doubt you are acquainted from the* Gazette, *my Lord has returned to
these shores from his travels. My! how he is changed!
No more the ruddy sportsman; the soft airs of Italy have
turned him into a true connoisseur of the arts! I cannot
tell you how much his new occupation causes me mirth.
He parades all day in his finest French lace, giving the
servants orders in what he considers fine Italian. They
do not understand him so do as they please, as usual.
Worst of all, his fascinations have unclenched his fist. It
appears he has been attempting to buy up all of Italy,
and plunge his family into ruin in the process. Some of
his baubles have already been brought to the house; I
intend to hang them only in the darkest corners, so visitors will not easily discern how my husband has been
impos'd upon by these foreign sellers. He promised me
pictures by the finest Italian hands; he has brought me
the merest daubs, the grossest of impositions. Only in
price do his prizes rank with the fairest productions of
the masters. The final blow is yet to fall, however; he
has been in London with Mr. Paris for the past three
weeks fussing over one final consignment of ruins by*

those wretches of Roman scene-painters who delighted in taking his money. My Lord tells me—in his most mysterious voice—these will delight and amaze me beyond comparison. I confess, I do not see how I could be more amazed. It seems that he spent more than seven hundred pounds for one of these, which surely will turn out to be worth not more than half-a-crown.

The letter then continued with local gossip and politics, complaints about servants and news about the death of some obscure relation's daughter. Then it got back to her husband, and the writer's venom began to be given free rein: *I have told you many times in the past, dear brother*, she continued, *about my Lord's amorous adventures. But less so of late after I threw that scene over the miserable hussy he was disgracing himself with before he left for his tour. I confess, when I told him then that I would cut his throat should he ever humiliate me thus again, the colour drained straight out of his cheeks! My dear brother, I was so convincing even I believed I would indeed do so. But the threat restored him to the way of fidelity. A scrub is ever thus, however. He seems still determined to humiliate our family name. My Lord arrives from London in two days' time. I leave you to think of the welcome he will receive from, your most affectionate sister, Arabella.*

"There," said Argyll, triumphantly. "What do you think of that, eh?"

Flavia shrugged. "So he was a dirty old sod. What should I think of it?"

"Weren't paying attention, were you? Look again. 'Wretched scene painter'—Mantini. 'Air of mystery,' that fits it well. 'Seven hundred pounds'—a vast price to pay for a picture then."

"So she's talking about the imminent arrival of Elis-abetta. What of it?"

"But look at what she says. She says it is a painting of ruins—no doubt in a classical landscape—that is coming."

"So?"

"The painting of Elisabetta was found under a Repose on the Flight to Egypt. Odd, eh?" He leaned back in triumph after delivering a statement he evidently consid-ered stunning.

"Well, frankly, no. It isn't," said an unimpressed Fla-via. "Maybe she was referring to the quality of the pic-ture, not its subject. Besides, we all know it was the wrong one."

Argyll had the look of someone who had been ex-pecting dutiful admiration rather than counter-arguments. "Oh. Didn't think of that," he said.

"But," he said with renewed enthusiasm, lighting an-other of Flavia's cigarettes and tossing the match into his empty wineglass. "Listen. The common link here is the dealer, Sam Paris. He watched Mantini at work in Rome, and he saw the picture unpacked in London. If a different one had arrived on the boat, he would have noticed. But he evidently didn't, as Clomorton was still under the impression that everything was going to plan."

Flavia nodded thoughtfully, but without conviction. "Well, I'll give you that much."

"And it seems that no one noticed anything wrong until the painting was cleaned. Therefore Mantini must have painted a picture of ruins over the Raphael. Still OK?"

Flavia pursed her lips. "Well, maybe. But maybe Paris was in it as well, and agreed to send off a different picture. He was an art dealer after all, and if I remember rightly he disappeared afterwards. To any self-respecting policeman that would count as suspicious behaviour. And there is an internationally acclaimed Raphael hanging in the Museo Nazionale, which doesn't do your argument any good at all. Although I must confess I'm still not sure what your argument *is*."

"I don't really have one, yet. I don't suppose it's important. But it will make a nice footnote. Wouldn't it be splendid if they'd got the wrong Raphael? The very thought has kept me in good humour for weeks."

The idea had fully restored Argyll's good spirits, and he walked along the wet, shiny pavements with a light step, skipping nimbly out of the way of the showers of water thrown up by buses and cars plunging through the deep puddles caused by blocked-up drains. He opened a vast black umbrella, the sort used by professional walkers in the rain, and stuck his elbow out.

Almost without thinking, Flavia rested her hand gently on the proferred arm. She couldn't remember that anyone had ever done such a quaint thing to her before. Furtive arms sliding round the waist before moving northwards, yes, in abundance; a cold and deliberate distance from her, which had been her last boyfriend's way of communicating displeasure, she was used to. But this had a quiet gentleness about it, giving her the opportunity delicately not to notice and shun the offer if she chose. Extraordinarily old-fashioned. But practical, and sweetly charming; it kept them close enough together so that both could keep dry under the awning of the huge umbrella.

"I thought we could go to a Thai restaurant," he said.

"Roman food is very good, but when I was there I found myself craving something with spice in."

Flavia made no reply, and barely even heard him as he kept up a steady flow of chatter on inconsequential subjects. At the restaurant, she nodded absentmindedly as he asked if she wanted anything to drink, and nodded again when he suggested trying some sake, which she had never heard of. Then she applied herself to reading the menu.

"Why do you think it would be nice if the picture was the wrong one? I think it would be dreadful—the department is paying for this, by the way," she said, once the waiter had taken the order, delivered a bottle in a vase of hot water, and vanished. It occurred to her that it was the first time she had asked him a question and been properly interested in the reply. His newfound buoyancy had transformed his character into something much more agreeable, although he showed signs of tipping over the edge into smugness. He was, certainly, not quite as dimwitted as he seemed.

"Certainly not. You paid last time. Besides, this is meant to be a sort of apology for boring you to death in Rome. And don't worry, this is on Sir Edward Byrnes. I got my first cheque yesterday. As for the Raphael, just think of the number of respected authorities who are at this very moment battling with each other to get out their books on the New Raphael first. Think how many have made a fortune writing adulatory articles in magazines and newspapers. Better still, think what wallies they'd look if it was revealed that they had been heaping admiring adjectives upon a dud. You married?"

"No, I'm not." She paused and downed the small glass of sake. It tasted of almost nothing, but was warm. She filled her glass again and drank that too. The heat made up somewhat for its evident lack of alcohol. "Have you told anyone about this?"

"Not a soul. I learnt my lesson last time."

"Listen. Restrain yourself and be sensible. I know the whole business upset you, but the Raphael can't be a dud. Every art historian in the world has written an article about it. Every single one of them agrees that it's genuine. I know they make mistakes; but they can't all be wrong. You can't set up an inconclusive fragment by a woman concentrating mainly on her husband's sexual peccadilloes against the agreed opinion of the most distinguished art connoisseurs alive."

"I don't see why not. As you say, people make mistakes, sometimes whoppers. A sizeable chunk of art history consists of unravelling other people's errors and substituting your own. All the art galleries in the world are full of things labelled 'after Velazquez' or 'circle of Titian' which were drooled over for years as fine works from the master's hand. Boyfriend?"

Flavia refilled her glass. "No. But how do you prove it?" she asked. "If everyone has committed themselves to calling it a Raphael, it would be difficult to persuade them to change their minds. It's all a matter of opinion. If enough people say it's genuine, then it is. Besides, I think you're playing games. You don't really think it's a dud at all, do you?"

"Not really," he said sadly, ladling out the rice and experimenting with his chopsticks. "Wishful thinking, I suppose. I was enjoying fantasising about finding some conclusive fragment. Think of the embarrassment. 'New light on Raphael's Elisabetta.' Short, pithy little article. Bang. Art historians doing the decent thing and jumping out of windows or locking themselves in rooms with loaded pistols. Turmoil in the museum. Red faces in the government. All that taxpayers' money down the drain. I can almost see the editorials now. Attachment? Cat?''

He evidently found his train of thought quite delightful. He spooned some more food, and poured some more sake.

''No. What's that got to do with it?''

''Nothing. It's just that I like cats.''

They ate in silence, which Flavia eventually broke. ''At least I had better tell the General when I get back,'' she said, sipping meditatively. Extraordinary. The whole bottle was empty already. ''Then he can do with it whatever he wants. Wastepaper bin most likely. But if anything does happen, then at least he won't be able to complain that he wasn't warned. I am single, unattached, and intend to stay that way. Men,'' she continued, wondering both why she was saying this and why her head was buzzing slightly, ''are frightened of me. I dislike them. Generally speaking,'' she added cautiously, squinting at him. ''So we are all happy. I feel sick.''

In fact, she was extremely drunk, and remembered thinking very clearly to herself, before such an effort became too difficult, that she would resent her host a great deal when she recovered for not having told her that sake was a good deal stronger than wine, and much more vicious in its effects. ''My last boyfriend used to tell me . . .'' she began mournfully, but forgot what it was halfway through. It hadn't been nice though. He'd been very angry when she'd finally walked out. Thought that was his job. Accused her of being unfaithful. Silly sod. No, that was Clomorton. Not her. It was too much effort. She was probably fast asleep even before Argyll arranged her on his sofa. Must have been asleep, in fact. At least, she hadn't protested when he dropped her on the stairs.

• • •

Flavia woke in a panic and with a wicked head. She was booked on an Alitalia flight for Rome—all Italian civil servants travel on the national airline as a way of circulating revenue from department to department—which was due to leave at eleven-thirty. Argyll was nowhere around, but a note on the table read, "Had to go out. If I'm not back when you wake, coffee in kitchen. Hope your head is OK. You're a great drunk."

She had no time for coffee, despite the fact that she would clearly die without it. She had no time to dress either, so it was just as well she had been deposited on the sofa fully clothed. She reckoned she had about two hours to get back to the hotel, pack, check out and make her way to Heathrow: department accountants always frown on additional costs caused by missing planes.

The head and the hurry put all thoughts of art out of her mind. Instead, she behaved more like a dogged automaton, the determination not to miss her flight constituting the only flicker of mental activity in an otherwise inoperative brain. She forgot all about Argyll, sake, Thai food and Raphael.

Flavia made the plane, ran down to the toilets the moment the seatbelt sign flickered off, and did her best to restore herself to human appearance. For the rest of the flight she persecuted the stewardesses unmercifully, demanding cup after cup of thick, strong coffee, aspirins and glasses of orange juice. She had to pay for the orange juice herself, accountants also frowning on self-indulgence, and it wasn't even much good. But it had some positive effects, and she was recovered enough by the time she arrived back home—grateful, above all, that it was Friday—to check through her accumulated mail before stepping into the bath.

A quiet and relaxing weekend allowed her to recover fully from the effects of oriental brewing. She occupied herself by being utterly domesticated in a way unusual for her—tidying the flat, doing some shopping, taking some clothes to the dry-cleaners. She forgot about work almost entirely until she made the brief walk to the office at eight-thirty the following Monday.

Paolo, the colleague whom she liked the most, greeted her. She asked what had been going on since she left.

"One case of jewellery, two and a half thousand eighteenth-century books, four paintings, thirty-eight prints. All gone. And the usual threats against that Raphael; somebody or other decided *we* should deal with them. We've had about a hundred sent over from the museum—part of the General's new committee work. Poor man, it's driving him to drink . . ."

They were settling down for a good and relaxing early morning conversation when Bottando stuck his head round the door. "Ah, there you are, my dear. Good trip? Splendid. Come up to my office and tell me about it in five minutes, would you?"

He vanished again. Paolo looked at the door. "He seems very edgy these days. I think he's still worrying about how to avoid landing in it if anything goes wrong with that damn painting. Don't know why. In the last few weeks he's surrounded this department with more defences and bureaucratic outworks than Fort Knox."

Flavia shrugged. "Maybe. Still, that reminds me of something I wanted to tell him. It might make him relax a bit."

She went up the stairs, walked through his door without knocking, as usual, and sat herself on his armchair. She summarised the meeting swiftly, then briefly ran over Argyll's tale about his researches.

"I thought I'd better tell you," she ended lamely. Bottando had his Silly-Little-Woman look on his face. He rarely used it, especially on her. "What do you think should be done about it?" she said.

"Nothing. File it and forget it. Better still, don't even file it. I'm much too old to go looking for trouble, and the very thought of telling the curator of the National Museum that he might have an old copy on his hands makes my pension start to shrink before my very eyes."

"But we should do something, surely? A quiet warning, a little suggestion?"

"My dear, if you didn't have me to protect you you'd be eaten alive. Now be sensible and think. The minister of defence is a Socialist, correct? And the arts minister is a Christian Democrat. And they don't like each other. Now, an old southern Socialist under this Socialist defence minister lets out the word that the arts minister has goofed in a big way. Do they say 'thank you for the warning, good of you to tell us?' Not likely. They suspect a conspiracy by the minority parties in the government to nobble their newly rising star and bring the DCI into disrepute. But they look anyway, discover the picture is genuine, and one ageing general, looking forward to his retirement, is wheeled out on to the scaffold to restore peace and harmony in the coalition. Preceded, I might add, by his very best assistant who is a notorious member of the Communist Party . . ."

"No I'm not. Membership's lapsed."

"Ex-member," her boss amended, "who is exactly the sort of person who would come up with a naïve plot to undermine the government."

"But what if it really isn't genuine?"

"If it isn't, they have a scandal on their hands. But we keep out of it, stand on the sidelines and watch. Our job is to protect that painting, not to run around causing trouble. And whatever evidence we produce will have to be very, very persuasive. You remember that Watteau that caused all the fuss a few years ago?''

Flavia nodded.

''Pronounced as genuine by everyone, and sold to the States for a fortune. And what happens? Someone writes an article saying it's a fake. Says that if you look in the background you can see the word 'Merde' written clear as day. I've seen it myself, he is quite right. The painting popped up from nowhere, it has no history, no one has ever mentioned it before. It's ninety-five per cent certain it's a phoney. But who admits it? Not the museum, which paid three million dollars, not the art dealer who might have to give the money back, and not the critics and historians, who have already said how wonderful it is. So there it stays, despite clear and conclusive evidence that it's a monstrous hoax.

''Now you come to our Raphael, which cost twenty-five times as much, and has a history that can be traced back to the artist's brush. If it was a phoney the head of the National Museum would have to resign, and his patron; the minister, would have to go too, because he appropriated this purchase as his idea.'' He walked over to the window and stared out of it onto the façade of San Ignazio opposite.

''And he would have to be replaced, and the Socialists, the Liberals, the Republicans and all of them would demand that they be given his ministry because he had made such a mess. And the Christian Democrats would refuse because even now they only have a majority of one in the cabinet. And the government would duly collapse once more.'' He waved an arm in the direction of the Chamber of Deputies, up next to the ice-cream store where Flavia had taken Argyll.

"Can you imagine how much every museum head, politician, academic and newspaper critic would be mobilised to assert that, without any doubt, the picture was genuine? The proof that it was not would have to be three hundred per cent certain, absolutely unassailable and without the slightest glimmering of doubt.

"And what you and this man Argyll have got isn't. Any academic worth his salt would make mincemeat of it.

"I don't mind taking some risks," he added, sitting down again and staring at her firmly. "But I am damned if I am going to commit suicide for a hunch concocted by a walking disaster like that man Argyll. They would eat him for breakfast—that is if they took any notice of him at all—disappointed and impoverished scholar, nursing a grudge, tries to get his revenge by starting a slanderous rumour. They'd wipe him out. They might even be right."

CHAPTER

6

"Dear me, what a day," sighed Bottando, reaching out and tapping the waiter on the arm as he passed. "Another?"

Spello shook his head. "No, thank you. I find alcohol a very poor consolation for an afternoon like this. A coffee, however, would be welcome."

The policeman ordered the drinks, and the two men, both in their fifties, sat in companionable discontent as they waited. It had been a hard afternoon. A meeting of Tommaso's infernal committee. A bit of nifty footwork on Bottando's part had cut sessions down, but they had to meet sometimes. And Tommaso had worked himself into a frenzy of anxiety over his picture, demanding ever tighter security. This afternoon had been typical: a suggestion had come from Antonio Ferraro—demand was a more accurate way of describing it—that the entire building be rewired. It needed it, certainly, but, as Spello pointed out while vetoing the scheme, there wasn't enough money.

At least the machinations of museum politics had pro-

duced one pleasant change. Bottando had suggested that
Ferraro might be too busy to head the museum's representation on the committee. Ferraro had agreed, evidently not liking the job, and Bottando had suggested
Spello instead. The policeman felt a bit mean about this,
but he was coming to sympathise with Tommaso's distaste for the sculpture expert. A very prickly character,
he was unable to control a meeting without being gra-
tuitously offensive, and had absolutely no sense that the
opinions of others might have any merit at all.

The only thing to be said for Ferraro was that he exited from the committee with good grace, leaving behind
only the megalomaniac, outrageously expensive, and utterly impracticable schemes he had already dreamt up;
Spello was much more in tune with Bottando's disdain
for committee work, and rushed through the business of
killing them all off as fast as was seemly.

"So you told Tommaso he'd done it again, did you?
I wish I'd been there. Preferably with a tape recorder for
the amusement of my colleagues afterwards." Spello
said gleefully.

"I did not tell him he'd done it again," Bottando
replied testily. "I merely mentioned, in passing and during a routine check over security precautions, that someone might begin casting doubt over the authenticity of
his picture."

"Was this entirely wise?" the Etruscan specialist enquired, unable to keep a broad grin off his face, despite
Bottando's evident discomfort.

"No, it wasn't. In fact I told my assistant to keep it
to herself. On the other hand, I don't know who Argyll
knows, or who else he might talk to. I thought it best
for the department—and for the museum—if Tommaso
knew it might be coming, that's all."

"And like all messengers bearing bad news, you got precious little thanks for the information?"

"Mount Vesuvius in full form was nothing in comparison," Bottando said, shaking his head as he remembered the director's face turning puce and the accompanying bellow of rage. "I thought for a moment he was going to hit me. Extraordinary performance. Such a little man, as well. Who would have thought he could have made such a noise? The only time I have ever felt the slightest liking for that man Ferraro was when he intervened and tried to change the subject. Quite courageous of him, especially as I'm sure he would rather not have been there at all."

"So our Tommaso was not receptive to the idea?" prompted Spello, who would clearly have loved to hear the entire story again, for the simple pleasure of it all.

"No. Although, to give him his due, he calmed down pretty quickly, and even apologised. And told me why he was so sensitive about the matter. Although his version of the dispute over the Correggio is different from yours. In his account, he was a scapegoat slaughtered by the machinations of the dealer and the weakness of his director."

Spello sniffed. "You expected him to take full responsibility for his mistakes?"

"No. Anyway, that was a long time ago and not especially important. More significant is the fact that he's convinced that he hasn't made a mistake this time. Even gave me a huge pile of scientific tests done on the Raphael after the sale to prove it was genuine."

"You read them?"

"Not me. I'll give them to Flavia. It'll be her punishment for bringing the matter up in the first place. But Tommaso seems very confident, and he should know what he's talking about. After all, the thing has got a better pedigree than most paintings. If it came through all the tests as well, there can't be much wrong with it.''

"Oh, what a pity," Spello said sadly. "You quite got my hopes up for a moment there. Still," he said, visibly brightening at the thought, "it makes a good story. Or will do," he added with a touch of malice.

"It will not. If I ever hear a word, a single breath, of this from anyone else and trace it back to you I will personally ram your finest Etruscan figurine up your nostril and glue it in place. I'm telling you for information purposes only, not so you can have a good laugh with your colleagues."

Spello looked mournful. "Oh. All right then," he said with evident reluctance. "I suppose I'll just have to hope it will turn out to be a fake. Which it will, if it is."

"Why's that?"

"Forgeries always reveal themselves eventually, that's the one great consolation about aesthetics. Or at least it's what connoisseurs convince themselves to justify the outrageously high prices of originals. What people find beautiful changes over time; you only have to look at the pale, flabby women painted by Rubens to realise that. They were reckoned to be the peak of sensuality in the seventeenth century, now they're overweight matrons; the modern age prefers the skinny Botticelli types. Even if someone paints a mock Raphael that is perfect in every detail, there will be some trace in it of the twentieth-century mind of its creator. That's the theory, anyway. As preferences change, a genuine Raphael will still look genuine, even if people see different things in it, but a modern copy will begin to show its modern origins more and more. Someone will notice.

Have you ever seen those banks of Victorian fakes that most museums put on display?''

Bottando nodded.

"And what do most of the nineteenth-century hoaxes look like? Like nineteenth-century paintings, that's what. They're obviously copies to us. But to people in the nineteenth century they were beautiful examples of early Renaissance, Mannerist, Baroque art, or whatever. Do you see what I mean?''

"You seem to know a great deal about this," Bottando said.

"I'm a museum curator. Surrounded by fakes all the time. You remember those pieces in my office?'' He was referring to a glass display-cabinet that Bottando had often admired. It was full of delicate, filigreed bronze figures, all Etruscan work of simple beauty and power. "Beautiful, no?'' the old curator continued. Bottando nodded in agreement. "Every one a bum. Probably made in the 1930s for sale to the US. Some ended up in the museum, which wanted to melt them down when they discovered what they'd bought. I recovered them and kept them.

"I think they're wonderful. I'm an expert, so-called, and I can't tell. Only laboratory analysis proved they weren't genuine.''

Bottando sniffed. "Laboratory analysis proved the Raphael was genuine,'' he noted.

"So, there's nothing to it. Tests are highly sophisticated these days. I must say, if I were you, I'd forget about it. Then everyone will go on enjoying the painting. Sow the tiniest seed of doubt and its popularity will wane, even if it is original. Why stir up trouble? Who has lost out anyway? As long as the museum thinks it's real, and the visitors agree, everyone's happy. And it'll take a great deal to convince our friend Tommaso, considering all the very good reasons he has to think otherwise.''

Bottando laughed, turned the conversation, and put the idea from his mind. But he was uncomfortable, and his thoughts kept on returning to the subject as he walked slowly home.

The next time Bottando saw Flavia he handed Tommaso's report to her. ''There,'' he said. ''That'll teach you. Some bedside reading for you. Photocopy it and send a copy to your mad friend in London as well, if you like. It might rein in his imagination a little.''

''I'll do better. I'll give it to him this evening. He arrived in Rome yesterday, I think,'' she replied.

It lay on her desk for several hours as she plied her way through a host of boring chores which she always liked to get out of the way in the morning, quickly and before she was wide enough awake to resent them. When they were all done and resting contentedly in the ''out'' tray, she settled back into her chair, opened the report, and tried to concentrate on the harsh, technical data that was presented. A good deal of it was in the form of tables, surrounded by chemical signs which meant nothing to her. Evidently they detailed a series of tests that had been carried out.

Fortunately, there was a written introduction and conclusion, couched in the cautious language that marks both the scientist, not wanting to go beyond the limits that the evidence permits, and the bureaucrat, not wishing to stick his neck out. But the summary was clear enough.

The report began by formally detailing the project. The team, the permanent employees of the Museo Nazionale, had been sent to London to examine a painting, "supposed to be by Raphael," and determine its authenticity. They had been given free use of the apparatus at the National Gallery in London, as well as assistance from employees at the Tate. The tests had lasted a week which, they said, was more than enough time to make all the experiments they thought necessary. They noted, cautiously, that their work was of limited utility. They did not intend to comment on the aesthetic merits or otherwise of the painting.

"Just as well," thought Flavia, remembering the dry technocrat who had ruled supreme for years at the museum. "Without a spectrometer they couldn't tell a Botticelli from a Chagall."

She flipped through the pages of experiments and began on the conclusion, on the safe assumption that whatever the main body of the text contained would be duplicated in simpler language at the end.

The examiners had begun by looking at the canvas. This, they said, consisted of threads of varying width with irregular weaving, consistent with the canvases used in the late fifteenth century. The stretch-marks indicated that the canvas had not been cut down or stretched on to a new frame, and the wooden frame itself, made of poplar, also appeared to be of an appropriate age. A carbon-fibre dating of the canvas and the paint—done by snipping a miniscule fragment off the side, grinding it down and dosing it with radioactivity—indicated that it was not less than three hundred and fifty years old.

"Before 1600, more or less. Pre-Mantini, in other words," she noted. So far the picture was holding up well.

The experts had then moved on to the paintwork itself,

noting that as the picture had been covered over for more than two hundred years and had been cleaned and restored before examination, there were particular difficulties. They also noted that they had been instructed to keep any paint removed for analysis to the absolute minimum, and come from as near to the edges as possible. However, the report continued that, despite these strictures, they were able to complete a fairly full examination of the different colours used and of the techniques employed in painting.

Again, the portrait came through. The craquelure, the hairline cracks that appear in old oil paintings as they age and grow brittle, were irregular; artificially induced cracks generally ran parallel as a forger rolled the picture up to give a false impression of age. The remains of dirt in the cracks—most had been cleaned out—were composed of different substances while forgeries generally contained some homogeneous material, such as ink, used to give the impression of dirt.

All the paints were of raw materials used in the sixteenth century and X-ray examination, conducted at different electricity levels to build up a three-dimensional picture down through the paint, suggested that it had been painted according to techniques used in other Raphael works.

The final summary was as definite as any scientist was likely to be. Under examination and bearing in mind the limitations mentioned, the painting was consistent with a work produced at the start of the sixteenth century by a painter using techniques also employed in several of Raphael's works. The lengthy footnote, with citations, detailed the virtual impossibility of reproducing such characteristics in a modern picture. Of course, judgement was reserved on whether it actually was by Raphael, but there was not a shred of evidence to suggest that it was not. The report was dated and signed by all five members of the investigating team.

Flavia put the folder down, rubbed her eyes and stretched herself. That, certainly, seemed to nobble Argyll's suspicions. She turned her attention to the mound of mail that had built up on her desk while she was reading, and started methodically but absent-mindedly to transfer most of the envelopes to the desk of the temporarily absent Paolo. Her work was, perhaps, thirty per cent enjoyable and seventy per cent dull and routine. Running around interviewing people, tracing pictures, keeping up contacts among dealers, auctioneers and collectors was the fun part. Reading reports, checking journals and filling out the innumerable forms that the polizia considered a vital aspect of good security work was very much less so. A nice, juicy scandal would have tipped the balance more towards the entertaining end. Pity.

CHAPTER

7

Any lingering regret on the subject of Elisabetta in Flavia's mind had only until 10:37 the following Thursday to germinate before being consigned to the distant past.

She knew that it was exactly 10:37, because that was the time stamp that the ancient telex machine in the office placed at the end of the message from the French police saying that the case of the icon-stealing tourist had reached a conclusion, albeit not a very satisfactory one. The message from Paris read that Jean-Luc Morneau, connoisseur, aesthete, painter, dealer and suspected criminal, had been found. Unfortunately, he was dead, and so was likely to be of little use in helping the police with their enquiries.

The French were quite proud of their discovery although, as Bottando observed, they appeared to have no idea where all the icons had gone. The fact that Morneau had clearly died of a heart attack, brought on, so the Parisians said discreetly, by excess exertion, lessened Bottando's interest. Especially as there was a witness to both the exertions and the demise, and the graphic details provided by the young woman involved were convincing enough to rule out foul play. Bottando was not greatly concerned in the matter, as he had long since given up hope that any of the missing Italian icons would ever be discovered. But, for the sake of thoroughness, he asked the French to keep his department informed about any new developments.

In due course, the French ran the dealer's old mistress to earth. In return for their agreeing to ignore the state of her income-tax payments, she told them that Morneau had rented a safe deposit box in a Swiss bank. A bit of gentle arm-twisting of opposite numbers in Zurich produced a grudging permission to look inside it, and Bottando was invited to come along to the grand opening.

Six weeks to the day after Morneau's body was discovered, therefore, Bottando and Flavia flew into Zurich airport, where they were met by an official police car and driven swiftly into the financial heart of the city. As usual, Bottando had wanted to stay in Rome and grumbled incessantly during the flight. If he disliked travelling, he disliked travelling to Switzerland even more. The cleanliness, order and efficiency of the place profoundly upset him and he also found the Swiss insufferable, not least because of his utter failure to persuade them to do anything to stop the steady flow of smuggled art works over the Italian/Swiss border.

The only thing that persuaded him to get on the plane, in fact, was the realisation that it was an ideal excuse for not going to yet another of Tommaso's parties in the museum. Its purpose was uncertain, but the man had said something about fund raising and was insisting that all members of the Security Committee, as it was now grandly termed, were present. Bottando took considerable pleasure in ringing up, presenting his apologies, and pleading pressing police business.

Tommaso had not been happy. He was angling for a large donation, he said, and really needed Bottando there to impress the potential benefactors. It was only when Bottando explained, with some exaggeration, that he needed to go to Switzerland and had high hopes of recovering some invaluable icons, that the man gave way.

He did it, at least, with some grace. If Bottando could recover any part of the Italian heritage, then that must take precedence, he said somewhat pompously. The General should not even consider coming to the party. They would manage without him, and Spello would be there to answer any questions about museum security.

So he'd gone, and had slowly begun to wonder whether the museum folk were worse than the Swiss police, or the other way around. Attempts at international conversation as the large black Mercedes whistled down the autobahn were accordingly muted, and the atmosphere did not thaw until Bottando spotted his long-time French equivalent in the bank lobby.

Jean Janet was universally liked. One of the rare French protestants, he hailed from the Alsace region in the east of the country, and had headed his department before Bottando's position had even been a twinkle in a bureaucrat's eye. In the early years he had been unfailingly helpful in getting the Roman sezione into working order, illicitly handing over vast files of material, introducing Bottando to influential and knowledgeable gossip-mongers in the art world, passing on advice on some of the more subtle aspects of police work in the art field. Bottando had, in turn, gone out of his way to be helpful whenever possible. Any request from Janet was treated as a high-priority matter, and the direct and easygoing exchange of material had proved beneficial to both sides.

Apart from that, Bottando genuinely liked the man's sense of humour, and Paris had become one of the few places outside Italy that he travelled to willingly. Janet's only real disadvantage, apart from powerful halitosis, was that he refused to speak anything but French, and this limited conversation. Especially as Bottando was an equally idle linguist—although he could become positively fluent after a good meal and a cognac.

He stumbled through his greeting, again acutely conscious of what he was sure were the contemptuous eyes of the bilingual Swiss policemen, and made up for it by wringing his friend's hand firmly and beaming at him.

"I am delighted to see you once more, my friend," said Janet. "What do you think of our little bit of detective work, eh? And even," he added, waving his hand at the still silent Swiss, "persuading these secretive folk to let us look in one of the vaults! Not bad for an old Frenchman."

As they were led down the stairs and through a series of gleaming steel gates towards the deposit boxes, Bottando congratulated his colleague on his swiftness and fortune. "Fortune, poof! Good police work. Research, interviews, careful questioning. Well, perhaps some luck. But only a little."

Bottando confessed that he didn't think there would be much in the box to interest him. "After all, our icons disappeared nine years ago. The chances of him having kept one as a souvenir are a bit slight—even if he did take them."

"I, also, do not expect a treasure trove. But who knows? It is a pity he died so inconsiderately. A brief conversation would have been very interesting."

Playing the Gallic extrovert with gusto, a role he habitually adopted when dealing with any sort of foreigner, Janet rubbed his hands together with theatrical anticipation as the heavily armed security guard took out a key and inserted it in the door of a large steel box, one of about a hundred in the room they had entered. Bottando noted that most of the owners were probably under the impression that theirs was the only key to their box, and that whatever they chose to keep in it was absolutely safe from either theft or, sometimes worse, examination. Another example of Swiss duplicity, he thought.

Morneau's box was about two feet square and three feet long, with a door of angled sheet steel two inches thick. As one of the Swiss policemen had told them on the way down, it was one of the most expensive types he could have rented, and cost ten thousand Swiss francs a year. That in itself, he added, suggested that there should be something interesting inside.

He was wrong. There were no stolen icons, no convenient address books containing the names of icon collectors, no sets of accounts detailing payments received, nothing at all that would get the investigation any further along. But there was a lot of money: some half million Swiss francs, at least fifty thousand dollars in small denomination notes, and the same amount again in Deutschmarks and sterling. All in all, about four hundred thousand dollars in loose currency. Apart from that, the only contents were a bundle of sketchbooks, well-thumbed and spattered with blobs of paint, bound up with a length of red tape. While the money was being taken out and counted, and sets of serial numbers taken down so that attempts could be made to trace their origin, Flavia sat down in a quiet corner—she had been largely ignored all morning and had barely spoken a word since they landed—and flicked through the sketch-books.

Some of them were clearly many years old, and were full of details of arms and legs, different types of faces and costume, the sort of thing that every art student at one of the more traditional painting academies is required to turn out. She remembered that, in the thirties, Morneau had been at the prestigious *Académie des Beaux Arts* in Paris and had made the beginnings of a promising career as a painter before turning to the more financially rewarding business of dealing. He had also taught in Lyons before going commercial. As she looked at the sketches with a critical eye, she could see why. He was very skilled, and the line drawings particularly were executed with ease and dexterity. But they were old-fashioned in the extreme, and almost entirely derivative. Dredging up the remnants of her education, she spotted drawings after Rembrandt, legs copied from Parmigianino, endless repetitions of fragments from the Sistine Chapel, all done with minute changes as the artist experimented to see what the painters had been doing.

Intermingled with the sketches were voluminous jottings. The notes were probably part of the dreary lectures in art history that were churned out until the riots of 1968 produced a revolution in methods. The new way didn't produce any better painters, but it was probably less boring. Recipes for paints, quotations from artists, extracts from books on techniques, all written in a fast, ill-formed hand that was often barely legible. The other books, many in better condition than the first, were of the same type. The newest were the three at the top of the pile and, once more, followed the same pattern.

Flavia decided that recognition of painterly style was merely a matter of keeping the eye practised. In the first volume she examined she had had to concentrate hard to tell even Rubens from Correggio. Now, after only a few minutes, the recognition was coming much faster and more easily.

She looked again, concentrating hard, and then glanced up to confirm that the five men were still busy talking to each other and were ignoring her very existence. She slipped three of the books in the black leather handbag that everyone in her office always made fun of for being so absurdly large and unladylike, bound the rest in the red cotton tape, and replaced them on the table with the bundles of money.

Forty-five minutes later, the two Italians and the Frenchman were sitting in a restaurant ordering food. Lunch had been Flavia's idea, and it had been taken up enthusiastically by her superiors, if for different reasons. There had been a polite disagreement about where to go. Janet had suggested an Italian trattoria, Bottando had returned the compliment by insisting that they go French. Because he was very much of the opinion that this was by far the best decision, Janet had let himself be persuaded, but made up for his chauvinism by ordering a bottle of Montepulciano, which he considered one of the few Italian wines that might deservedly have been produced in his home country.

He took an appreciative sip then asked, "Well, my friends, and what is it that I can do for you?"

Bottando looked surprised. "For us? What makes you think we want something?"

"I do apologise, but I'm sure one of you does. I am a thoughtful person, and observant. And I know you well. You are a polite man, and you were very rude in disposing of those Swiss so that you could eat alone in

my company. I am flattered, and I know your opinion
of our Swiss colleagues. But you could have asked me
earlier and made it less obvious. So, I think to myself,
you want to ask me something that has only just occurred to you. And the invitation came after that whispering in your ear from your assistant here.
Therefore . . .''

"Entirely incorrect. I just wanted to enjoy my lunch
rather than have to suffer through it. Although I must
admit I do want to hear what you know about Morneau.
He sounds a character.''

"He was. I recommend, by the way, the trout. It
comes with one of the few sauces they do here which
doesn't have too much flour. Otherwise, stick to the veal.
It is very good to see you again. But, I must insist that
you play fair. I will tell you about the life and secret
career of Monsieur Morneau—as much as we know—
if you tell me the latest goings-on and scandal in Rome.
I haven't seen you for some time. There must be a great
deal I've missed.''

He fussed over the bread, spearing it on his fork and
using it to sop up some garlic sauce from his plate, while
Bottando considered whether he should break the policy
of silence about the Raphael which he had so convinc-
ingly explained to Flavia several weeks back. It was
about the only decent anecdote of recent vintage, and he
knew Janet would appreciate it. On the other hand, he
doubted the man's ability to keep it to himself.

"Well, then,'' Janet began, lifting his head reluctantly
from his plate and wiping a dribble of gravy from his
chin. "As you probably noticed, Morneau was an ex-
ceedingly rich man for an art dealer. He had an extravagant lifestyle, a house in Provence, a spacious
apartment in Paris, and a gallery which, although suc-

cessful, certainly did not generate enough income to support his expenditure. No mortgages, no debts. All his residences, incidentally, had been completely swept of any incriminating papers by the time we got there to have a look around. A very tidy man.

"So where did this money come from? Not from legitimate activities, and not from peddling stolen icons either. We know of twenty-five he probably stole. Even if there are another twenty-five we don't know about, that gives you, say, six or seven million francs over a ten-year period. He spent much more than that. So what else was he up to?

"Then he disappears. This is a man who turns up at almost every gallery opening, hasn't missed a performance of the ballet for nearly fifteen years, and is an artistic socialite of the first order. He ducks out of sight for nearly a year, and then he turns up, in an embarrassing position and dead. So where has he been, eh? Tell me that."

He finished his little speech and smiled, as if expecting applause for the brilliance of his logic.

"I was hoping *you* would. You haven't actually told us anything at all. What was he doing?" Bottando asked.

Janet shrugged. "There I cannot help you. Deduction can take you only so far. Any further requires more information. Now tell me. What about Rome?"

Before he could begin, Flavia, who had been staring absently out of the window, made one of her first comments of the day. She didn't like being ignored, although she was occasionally prepared to put up with being treated as merely a decorative appendage by Bottando. He didn't do it very often and, besides, he was old and southern and could hardly be expected to be perfect. But it was time, she decided, to make her presence felt.

"Maybe we should test the Commissioner's powers of deduction a little further," she said, smiling winsomely at the Frenchman. She always did that when she suspected she might be being a little rude. But before she could proceed further along these lines, Bottando interrupted her.

"Quite," he said. "But how good a painter was he? What were those fake icons he turned out like? It struck me that we might approach some of the more reputable forgers in Naples and ask a few careful questions there. Now he's dead they would probably be more forthcoming than usual."

Janet considered the matter for a moment. "As for Morneau's qualities as a painter, he was very good indeed, but he was born too late. He disliked modernism in all its forms. Had he been born a century earlier he would have had a great success.

"His icons were very variable. The earliest ones were good, painted on old panels, covered in dirt, quite well-executed. But once the technicians knew what they were looking for, they could easily spot them—something about paint in wormholes, which you don't get in the real thing. The later ones were sloppy. It looks as though he realised that they didn't really have to be that good to be convincing, so stopped wasting so much effort.

"Technical problems aside, however, they are remarkable, even the bad ones. They have a great spiritual quality, almost as if he were painting for his own sake. I'm not really surprised the monks were taken in. Once they had been aged and covered with dirt, they looked wonderful, even better than the originals. You should see them. One always tends to assume that fakes are not as good as the real thing. I'm not so sure. Morneau understood the paintings. That's where most of these people fall down." He smiled at the two of them. "There. All along you suspected your old friend was a Philistine, eh?"

They had reached the coffee, and the conversation showed signs of wandering off into the byways and alleyways of anecdote. Flavia stirred herself for another attempt.

"Commissioner," she began. "The bank's log of when Morneau opened his box. When was the last visit?"

"I don't know. We haven't been able to get that out of the bank yet. However, according to his passport, he last visited Switzerland in May," he answered.

She smiled in quiet triumph. She must remember to point out to Bottando what an extraordinarily good employee she was. Even if she occasionally caused him a great deal of trouble and heartache. As she was about to do now. She reached into her handbag and took out one of the sketchbooks she'd purloined. Apologising insincerely for abducting evidence in such a cavalier fashion, she handed it across to the two men. "Have a look at that. Ring any bells?" she asked.

Janet glanced at it, looked noncommittally puzzled, and passed it to Bottando. He was equally blank. Then Flavia detected vague stirrings of unease, and a sudden realisation. "Ah," he said as he handed it back. Very quick on the uptake, really, she thought.

"I don't mean to be inquisitive . . ." Janet said.

Bottando looked flustered. "Indeed not," he said. "But this must be kept very quiet. The slightest hint could wreak havoc on the market."

Flavia was again impressed. She'd had the entire walk to the restaurant to work out the implications of the discovery; Bottando had had only a few seconds and he instantly saw the problems and pitfalls. Especially the impact on the art market if the slightest breath slipped out.

"Of course, of course," replied Janet. "But what is it, exactly, that I'm not meant to hint about?"

Flavia handed him back the notebook. "These sketches," she said casually, "would appear to bear a remarkably strong resemblance to the portrait of Elisabetta di Laguna in Rome. By Raphael. Or perhaps we'd better begin to say, *attributed* to Raphael."

Janet looked again, then nodded. "I suppose they do. But so what? Every artist in the western world has probably made sketches of it."

"Before last May? Before the painting had been uncovered and before anyone could possibly have known what it looked like?"

Janet leaned back in his seat, and a broad smile slowly spread across his face. "How splendid," he commented eventually. "How delightful," he said after further thought. "How very awkward for you," he added apologetically as an afterthought.

"When you've stopped enjoying yourself," Bottando said severely, "you'll begin to see why it's important you keep very quiet. No gossip back in the office. Not a word. Not even to your wife. Or anybody."

"Oh, quite. Quite. But please, I beg you. Clear this one up quickly. Every day without telling someone will be a day wasted. And, of course," he added, with some attempt to return to professionalism, "any help you need of me, just let me know.

"Oh dear," he said, his face cracking with pleasure once more, "I wish I could be there when you tell that awful man Tommaso."

"Everybody says that," said Bottando gloomily.

"But I'm the one who is going to have to face him. I may not survive the blast."

The meal ended shortly after that, Janet heading back for France in good humour and with a promise to send on the log when he'd got it out of the Swiss. Bottando's spirits were considerably lower. Before they boarded the plane that was to fly them home from Zurich to Rome at four o'clock that afternoon, he phoned the museum and asked to speak to the director. He was in a meeting, and a secretary, clearly briefed to deflect all unforeseen calls, declined to bring him to the phone, even though Bottando insisted that it was an important matter and police business.

Bottando gave up the struggle. He'd have to go to the party after all, and catch him there. The worst of both worlds, he thought morosely.

CHAPTER

8

Once he arrived at the museum in the Borghese gardens, Bottando handed in his coat and made his way along to the ground-floor gallery where the reception was taking place. It was a big affair, well under way by the time he got there, and the main sculpture gallery had been thrown open to accommodate the dozens of guests. He took a glass of champagne from a passing waiter, noting that, as usual, Tommaso was deploying what he always claimed were scarce museum funds in a lavish fashion.

"Not at all," replied a museum member who had zeroed in on the same tray of drinks and to whom Bottando made this somewhat cynical comment. "Tommaso calls it investment. He has a point, in fact. This bash is in honour of those gentlemen over there." He pointed towards a group of half a dozen men leaning on a large statue.

"Doesn't anyone mind them using a Canova as a drinks trolley?" enquired Bottando. He looked at the group closely. They had all just come in to the room with the director, and were standing around one of the giant statues in the middle of the gallery. All wore light-grey suits, blue shirts and striped ties. They were talking intensely, and Bottando suspected they were not dis-cussing the artistic beauties which lay all around them.

"Certainly not. You see, they're American business-men who are hoping to win a government defence con-tract." The man made an expansive gesture which was meant to give an impression of gigantic wealth and the machinations that go along with it. It was a broad sweep of the arm, not very well co-ordinated. Bottando decided he'd been drinking.

"And what better way of creating the right impression than making a large donation to the national museum," Bottando finished for him. The young man, in his thirties with an open countenance that was currently shaded by alcoholic distress, nodded firmly.

"Exactly. Their big white chief is currently locked in discussion with Tommaso in his office. To be followed, no doubt, by a large cheque which will cover the cost of the party and leave a considerable amount over to deal with the abominable electrical circuits in this run-down old dump. Clever, eh?"

Bottando turned towards him. "Do you know," he said, "I think that you're the first person in this place who's ever said a positive word about Tommaso."

The man's face clouded. "Giulio Manzoni, by the way," he offered, holding out a hand which Bottando briefly shook. "Deputy restorer. I admit he's not liked. But he's really not as bad as he seems. And this place needed an awful good shake to knock some of the dust out. Not that my relatively favourable opinion will do me much good, alas."

"Meaning?"

"You weren't here earlier? Evidently not. He's gone

and resigned. Said he's decided to take early retirement
and go to live in his house in Tuscany. A bit of a shock,
all things considered. As you no doubt know, everything
in this place is done through patronage. My job, for instance, came through the assistance of Enrico Spello and
I'm seen very much as his protégé.''

"That's good, isn't it?'' Bottando enquired, a little
taken aback by the news. "I mean, Spello is next in
line.''

The restorer shook his head matter of factly. "Not any
more, he isn't. Because Tommaso at the same time appointed Ferraro as his successor and official deputy.''

"Goodness,'' said Bottando mildly as he considered
the implications. "I thought he couldn't stand Ferraro.
What prompted this?''

"Perhaps he's sick of being disliked. Maybe he's human after all. Besides, he's gigantically rich, so why
crack your head working? He does dislike Ferraro, but
evidently he dislikes Spello more. You can never tell
with him; it's difficult to penetrate the façade. Besides,
the only way people will look on his passing with regret
is to make sure his successor is even more unpleasant
than he is. You see why I'm heading for my fifth drink
of the evening?''

Bottando nodded sagely. "I think so,'' he replied.

"You think so? Well, let me show you, so there's no
mistake.'' Manzoni leant forward and poked Bottando
in the chest. "Ferraro is a little rat, right? Spello will be
his main rival. So he wants to chop Spello down to size,
whittle away at his support. He can't attack Spello himself, as he's got tenure. So how will he get at him?
Through me, that's how.'' He now poked himself on the
chest to emphasise the point, then turned and gesticu-

lated at the new deputy director, coming through the tall oak doors on the far side of the room.

"Look at him. He has the air of triumph on his face, don't you think? A man who has just conquered all. An air of vulgar triumph."

"Are you sure the appointment will go through? After all, it's not Tommaso's personal gift." So far, Bottando was finding the conversation decidedly upsetting. He had, on the whole, relatively few dealings with the museum. Although he never felt entirely comfortable with Tommaso, the two had at least worked out a *modus vivendi* so that life did not become too onerous. He doubted that Ferraro would be quite so easy.

Manzoni nodded, his aggressive mood swiftly fading into one of lugubrious resignation. "A few months back the succession would have been close. Spello would have been the inside candidate; the reconciler, someone everybody could work with. Then, of course, Tommaso pulls off his *coup de théâtre* with that Raphael and everyone in government thinks he's the greatest thing since sliced salami. Whoever he supports will walk in now."

The restorer looked extremely upset, and stared at his again empty glass. Then, without a further word, he shambled off in the direction of the drinks trolley. Bottando breathed a sigh of relief; sympathetic though he felt, he had other things to worry about at the moment.

But Tommaso wasn't around; that he realised as he surveyed the room in search of him. In one corner he saw Spello, and could tell by the man's slightly stooped shoulders that he was feeling very disappointed, and probably angry as well. He sympathised, but wasn't in the mood to listen to another outburst of indignation, no matter how justifiable. In another corner he spotted Jonathan Argyll and Sir Edward Byrnes. He was momentarily surprised that either should be there, and that such an evidently amiable conversation could take place, but them remembered Flavia mentioning Argyll's fellowship. There is nothing like a little money to soothe the passions. They, at least, seemed in a good mood, but he felt disinclined to talk to anyone even remotely connected with that Raphael. So, he spent the next ten minutes being talked at by some connoisseur and critic, while mainly keeping his eyes open, waiting for Tommaso's reappearance.

Eventually the door swung open, revealing a cameo of Tommaso shaking hands with the senior American and evidently bidding him farewell. The gracious look on his face suggested he'd got his cheque. Bottando waited for the right moment to go up and ruin his evening. He didn't want another public explosion on his hands.

He was staring idly around him, uncertain about what to do, and the indecision lost him his chance to catch the director on his own and escape home early. Ferraro had also materialised at the doorway and had engaged the man in an earnest conversation. Even at a distance of many metres, Bottando could see the expression of benign good humour drain out of the director's face like water out of an unplugged bath. It would be an exaggeration to say that he turned green, but a sickly shade of off-white was well within the bounds of accuracy. Ferraro, in contrast, looked in control of himself but decidedly grim.

He was spared the trouble of having to go over and find out what was so evidently distressing to both men. Tommaso walked swiftly over to him, the air of effortless grace still present in his every step despite the look of concern on his face. Perhaps he hadn't got the money after all?

"General. I'm glad to see you," he said shortly, leaving out, for once, the elaborate courtesies he habitually employed. "Could you come with me, please. I've just had a piece of shocking news."

The director set off at a fast clip through the museum, along the entrance hall and up the stairs. Bottando puffed along to keep up. "What is the matter?" he asked, but got no reply. Tommaso looked as though he had just seen a ghost. Ferraro was unusually silent as well.

There was no need for complex explanations. As they opened the door and went into one of the smaller galleries on the second floor, it was immediately clear what the matter was.

"Mother of God," said Bottando quietly.

The frame of the Raphael was still there, badly charred in its upper parts, but nobody could ever have suspected that the few blackened threads and dark congealed liquid that hung loosely from it had been, until very recently, the most expensive and treasured painting in the world.

Four or five square inches of the bottom right-hand side, Bottando estimated, had been untouched by the fire, which had reduced the rest of the canvas to charred rubbish. The smell of burning oil, wood, and material, still hung in the air, and wisps of smoke rose from the few pieces of cloth that had not been entirely consumed. Above the picture, the wallpaper was badly charred, and had evidently come close to catching fire as well. Bottando found time to be thankful the museum had not decorated the room with padded silk, as they occasionally did. If they had, the whole building would have been ablaze by now.

None of the three said anything at all, but simply looked. Bottando saw very grave difficulties, Tomasso the ruin of his reputation, Ferraro the end of his ambitions. "No," said Tommaso, and that was all. For the first time, Bottando felt sorry for the man.

Memory of his occupation reasserted itself. "Who found it?" he asked quietly.

"I did," said Ferraro. "Just now. I came back down immediately to tell the director and found him by the door."

"What were you doing in here?"

"I was going up to my office to get a packet of cigarettes. And I saw smoke coming from under the door. I knew something was wrong the moment I smelt it."

"Why?"

"No fire alarm. It's very sensitive. We turned it off for the rooms where the party was being held, but it should have been on for every other room."

Bottando grunted and looked around. It required no great genius to see what had happened. He crouched down by an aerosol tin on the floor, not touching it. Engine starter. High-grade petrol you squirt into carburettors to start the car on cold days. Spray the picture, push a lit match against it, leave and shut the door behind you. The fuel lit up the dry but still inflammable paint on the canvas, and the whole thing was burnt away within minutes. He looked at the picture once more. Someone right-handed, he guessed. He seemed to have sprayed in an arc from bottom left to top right. Hence the relative lack of damage in the bottom right-hand corner. He lightly and cautiously touched the remains hanging in the frame. Still warm.

He sighed, and turned to Ferraro.

"Close this door and put a guard on it. Go downstairs,

tell them the party's over but no one is to leave. Don't
say what's happened. We've enough to do at the moment without worrying about the press. I will phone for
reinforcements. Perhaps we can use your office, director?''

Bottando spent another three hours there, dealing with
the more stratospheric consequences of the evening's
events. Phoning his colleagues in other departments, informing the arts minister, mustering his forces. He occupied the desk, while Tommaso fretted around,
summoning assistants and public relations officials to
draft a release to give to the press. Despite Bottando's
strictures, they had already sensed something had happened, and they would have to be told sooner or later.

It was some time before the policeman and the director had time to talk. Tommaso was sitting listlessly on
the ornate nineteenth-century sofa, staring at a Flemish
painting on the opposite wall as though he'd suddenly
discovered it was a personal enemy.

"Do you have any idea why the fire alarm didn't
work?" the policeman asked him.

"The usual reasons, I imagine," Tommaso replied
with a barely concealed groan. "The electrical system
in this place is a menace. Hasn't been changed since the
1940s. We're lucky the entire museum hasn't burnt
down. That's why I submitted the proposal to have the
place rewired to the security committee. It's a pity
Spello vetoed it."

"Hmm," replied Bottando noncommittally. He
picked up the double implication clearly. Spello had
made this attack possible by stopping the proposal. Secondly, it wouldn't take much manoeuvring to divert any

blame for the destruction from the director to the committee.

That would have to be dealt with later. He concentrated instead on the matter at hand. "How often does the thing shut down?"

"Constantly. Well, about once a week. The last time was in the evening a couple of days ago. Ferraro was still here, fortunately. He had to pull all the fuses out to stop the entire building from burning down. The guards had gone off to the bar, as usual. It really is like trying to run a madhouse in here, at times," he added with some considerable despair. Bottando sympathised. He could imagine.

"Anyway," the director continued, "that, indirectly, was the point of this party. I persuaded those Americans to hand over a donation that was going to rewire the entire building. Thus overcoming Spello's prejudices about modernisation." He laughed bitterly. "Shutting the stable after the horse has bolted, if you like. I imagine they'll cancel the cheque."

"Was this problem generally known?"

"Oh yes. The bell going off at random all the time is not the sort of thing you can keep secret. Oh. I see what you mean. This indicates it was done by someone inside the museum, you think?"

Bottando shrugged. "Not necessarily. But I think we should go and have a look at that fuse box. Could you show me where it is?"

A few minutes and several flights of stairs later, they were standing in the basement. "There you are," said Tommaso. He opened the gigantic, rusty box on the wall. Inside was line upon line of heavy ceramic fuses. He searched around, pulled one out, looked at it, and handed it to Bottando. "Thought so. Blown again," he commented.

Bottando held it up to the light and looked, a favourite theory evaporating as he did so. No one had removed the fuse, no one had cut any wires. It had just burnt through of its own accord. Only in Italy, he thought to himself, would things be done in such a ramshackle fashion. He found himself beginning to have more sympathy with Tommaso's reformist efforts. Tactful, he wasn't. But no one could say there wasn't a job to be done here.

In such a conciliatory spirit, once back in the director's office, the General tentatively began to raise the subject that had brought him to the party in the first place.

"There are one or two aspects of all this I thought it would be best to discuss with you alone. It might take some of the sting out of this appalling evening."

The director placed the tips of his fingers together, and peered at him enquiringly. He didn't appear to believe anything could do that.

"I don't think your loss today was as grievous as it seems," Bottando continued.

The director grimaced and shook his head. "I assure you, the painting is beyond repair. Or perhaps you don't find the loss of one of the greatest triumphs of Italian art grievous?"

A bit pompous, thought Bottando uncharitably. Still, he has had a bad day. "A triumph, certainly. But not of Italian art. I think it was a forgery."

Tommaso snorted. "Oh, General, not this obsession of yours again. I've already told you it's impossible. You know as well as I do the tests that picture went through. It passed them all with flying colours. And every scholar in the field pronounced it to be a Raphael.''

"Experts can be wrong. Every scholar in the world in the 1930s said the *Supper at Emmaus* was by Vermeer. They only discovered it was painted by Van Meegeren when he confessed to avoid being hanged for collaboration with the Nazis.

"The fake Vermeers were detected easily when they were examined scientifically," Tommaso objected. "And techniques have improved immeasurably since the 1940s."

"So, no doubt, have the forger's. But this is neither here nor there. The evidence we have is circumstantial, but worrying enough."

"And what, pray, is your evidence?"

Bottando reminded him about the letter found by Argyll in the country-house muniments room. The director interrupted. "But this is no less feeble now than before. You surely don't expect the entire academic community to change its mind on the basis of that?"

"Indeed not. As you say, on its own the letter amounts to very little. However, earlier today, my assistant found something a bit more convincing, hence my telephone call from Zurich to that infuriatingly obstructive secretary of yours."

He briefly told the director about the hunt for Morneau, the safe deposit box and their discovery.

That clearly rattled Tommaso. He walked across to a shelf of leather-bound books, swung it open and took out a bottle. He poured some golden liquid into two glasses and handed one to Bottando. He swilled it around and rubbed his face with his free hand. All his pomposity had evaporated again.

"If I understand you correctly, your argument hinges

only on those date stamps in that passport? Someone else could have put those drawings in the safe deposit *after* the painting was splashed over every magazine and newspaper in the country?''

Bottando dipped his head in acknowledgement. ''Yes. I told you it was circumstantial. But we now have two fragments pointing at the same thing.''

''I really don't believe this,'' the director said eventually. ''And if it was true, why would anyone bother to destroy the painting? I mean,'' he said defiantly, ''it's obvious why this happened, isn't it?''

Bottando gazed at him enquiringly.

''This was an attack on me, clearly. Only today I said I was retiring, and that Ferraro would succeed. Destroying the picture was a retaliation, to make me look a fool. It only makes sense if the picture was genuine. I know I'm not popular here.''

He paused. Bottando wondered whether he was expected to demur and reassure the director on that score. But he decided even Tommaso wasn't that vain, so he kept quiet.

''Everybody has always resented what I've tried to do, tried to stop every improvement I've introduced. Ferraro is the only one here who's given me any support at all. The only one who doesn't live somewhere back in the 1920s.''

''Hence the preference for him over Spello?''

''Yes. I like Spello, and I don't like Ferraro much. But the future of the museum is at stake, and I could see no room for personal preference.'' Again, just a shade of the old pomposity peeked through his suddenly energetic explanations.

''Spello is a good deputy, but the director has to fight with the ministries, squeeze money out of donors. I decided that only Ferraro could do it. He's not an easy man, I admit, but he's the best possible choice I had. And there are a lot of people who'd be prepared to stop me and him. At any cost.''

It was a legitimate interpretation, Bottando conceded. ''But,'' he objected, ''I find it difficult to see how anyone who'd worked in a museum all their life could ever bring themselves to such an act of vandalism.''

''Don't you believe it,'' Tommaso snorted. ''I said this was a madhouse and I meant it. But don't you get the point of what I'm saying?'' he continued intensely, staring at the policeman and leaning forward on his chair in an effort to convince him, ''If that picture was a fake, why destroy it? It would be much better to leave it and have the fraud discovered.''

Bottando smiled and shifted his conversational rudder a little to the right. ''If that painting was a fake, everyone was fooled by it, not just you. If Italy hadn't bought it, the Getty would have. Or someone else. The psychology of its appearance was just right, so no one thought to doubt it. All the evidence suggested there should be a picture under that Mantini. Byrnes produces it. It was like a fairy tale. Everyone wanted to believe it. Perhaps even the man who burnt it believed it was genuine.''

Tommaso smiled wanly. ''But it was us who paid out the money. The fact that others would have done so, given the chance, is a relatively small compensation, compared to the damage to my reputation.''

There was little else Bottando wanted to discuss, so he got up and made his way to the door. He was tired as well. ''Tell me,'' he said casually as he was leaving, ''why did you decide to quit? I confess I was very surprised.''

''So was everybody. I enjoyed seeing their faces when

the announcement went out. Too much of the ambitious careerist, they thought. But I've had enough of this job and I don't need the money. All administration and backbiting. It needs a younger man.'' Tommaso smiled curiously.

"Hence Ferraro?"

"Yes. He's very able, despite his unfortunate manner, and knows how to spot an opportunity. He ran the place for a few weeks a year ago. He made some good moves then. It was that which got him the job.

"As for me,'' he continued in a melancholy voice, "I plan to go off to my villa outside Pienza and live quietly with my library and my collection. Who knows? I may take up painting myself again. I haven't done any for years. It'll be a pleasant change—especially now. You must admit my timing is impeccable. Or someone else's is.''

He opened the door and shook Bottando's hand.

"I know we've never been easy colleagues, General,'' he said. "But I'd like you to know that I appreciate your efforts to find the man who did this. All I ask is that you suppress this rumour of a fake. If you come up with real proof, that's another matter. But I will not stand for my reputation being dragged through the mud because of a bizarre hunch.''

Bottando nodded. "That's reasonable. And we have our own reasons for keeping quiet. Don't worry. Good night, director.''

While Bottando was being grudgingly impressed by Tommaso's reaction to the evening's catastrophe, Flavia, on his orders, was wading her way through the drudge work that is inevitably associated with crime.

It was too late to do formal interviews of all eighty-seven people at the reception. She merely took their names and addresses, and asked them, politely but with authority, to remain within easy reach. She then passed the list on to immigration on the off-chance that someone would try to cross the border. It didn't seem likely. The only ones she missed were the group of Americans, who had already left by a late flight from the airport. However, they seemed the least likely suspects.

And suspects, she thought, they had enough of already; and some of them were clearly smart enough to realise where they stood. Argyll, for instance, who came in almost last.

"I'd rather hoped I would only ever see you socially in future. I never thought you'd be interrogating me again," he said wistfully.

"I'm not interrogating. Just getting your address," she replied in her stern manner.

He waved his hand. "A mere detail. You will be. After all, I must be your top suspect."

"You flatter yourself."

"Not really. Oh, all right. Maybe not number one. But in the top five, certainly. I can't say I like it much."

Flavia leaned back in her seat and put her feet on the desk. She was tired, and it was difficult to remain entirely hard and professional with someone you knew and liked. Besides, she wasn't in the police, so didn't have to. Sometimes that gave her an advantage.

"If you're so sure, perhaps you should give me your reasoning?"

He looked up at the ceiling for a moment to arrange his thoughts. "You think that picture was a fake, correct?" he began.

"What makes you think that?"

He shrugged. "Must be. Either that or you're looking for a maniac."

Flavia said nothing.

"If it was, of course," Argyll continued, "Byrnes received umpteen million for a dud. Which I, incidentally, first discovered. An accomplishment I am now beginning to regret. And I am now associated with Byrnes through his fellowship."

He paused, so she prompted, "So why fry the thing?"

"Because when it's discovered and proven to be a fake, Byrnes would have to take it back and refund the money. I'm sure something like that is in the sale contract. If it's destroyed, no one can ever prove anything. So Byrnes is home free. As am I, as his accomplice."

Flavia nodded slowly. "Very convincing," she commented. "But why were you the first person to suggest it was a fake?"

He paused over that one, and rubbed his chin. "Ah. I don't know. I'll have to think about that." He looked at her hopefully.

Flavia rubbed her eyes, ran her hands through her hair and yawned. "Ah, well. Enough for one night. Tell me the rest later. You'd be great as your own prosecutor. A pity the system doesn't allow for it. But you're right. You are a leading suspect." She stood up to let him out.

"And I can only think of one way for you to get off our list of potential Raphael roasters," she said as he went through the door.

"How's that?" he asked.

"Find us another one."

CHAPTER

9

At seven the next morning, Flavia walked into Bottando's office to see what was going on, and to arrange for the speedy interviewing of their suspects. As usual, she forgot to knock, and the General looked up at her angrily as she came in. Very unlike him.

"Tired and moody, are you?" she asked breezily.

He didn't reply, but handed over the last editions of the morning papers. Flavia glanced at them, and conceded inwardly that maybe he had a right to be moody. "Oh. Hadn't thought of that," she said apologetically.

"I had," he snapped. "But I didn't think it would be as bad as this."

She looked over them again. Until yesterday, Bottando's known fondness for food had always endeared him to the press. Now they laid into him with some violence, and in remarkable detail. In truth, he did look a little silly over the affair. Head of the art squad quaffing champagne and having a good time while mad arsonist destroys world's greatest masterpiece in the next room.

"You have to admit, it's got a funny side," she began, knowing it was the wrong thing to say.

"Flavia," said Bottando sternly.

"Yes, boss?"

"Shut up, dear."

"OK. Sorry."

He leaned back in his seat and sighed heavily. "It isn't funny at all," he said. "We don't have much time. Either we get someone soon, or the department will be massacred. We are caught," he observed acidly, "on the horns of a dilemma."

"Meaning that if you say it was a fake, Tommaso will tear you limb from limb, and if you don't, the press will?" Bottando nodded at her summary.

"Couldn't you just tell the minister, and get him to keep quiet?"

Bottando laughed. "A minister? Keep quiet? Contradiction in terms. I'd sooner take out a full-page advert in *il giornale*." He gestured vaguely at the most hostile of the newspapers. "No, I'm afraid we've no alternative. We'll just have to get results quickly. Besides, our case about Morneau is beginning to look a little feeble."

"Why's that?"

He handed over a sheet of paper. "Telegram from Janet. He screwed the log out of the Swiss."

Flavia looked at it with disappointment. Morneau's box had last been opened in August by someone else. They didn't know who. But it was well after the painting had been revealed to the public. "Damn it," she said. "Still, it doesn't mean that those sketches were put in then, though."

"No, but it weakens our case somewhat. That evidence is now very inconclusive. I'm sure it's also dawned on you that after last night we can't run any more tests on the picture to see if it really was genuine."

"You could always arrest someone. Last refuge of the incompetent, I know, but it would win us some time. Looks good for a few days, even if it's the wrong person."

"I was thinking about that. Maybe pulling in Argyll. Mad Englishman. Disappointed hopes. It would go down very well. The press think all Englishmen are lunatics."

Flavia looked worried: "Oh, no. Not Jonathan. That's not a very good idea."

Bottando regarded her dubiously. "Jonathan? Jonathan? What's this Jonathan bit?"

She disregarded the question. "If Byrnes didn't produce the real thing, that means that the genuine article is still out there. Somewhere, someone has a Raphael hanging on their wall, even if they don't know it."

"Argyll," she continued carefully, minding her words, "is probably our best chance of finding it. After all, if the thing exists, it's under a Mantini, and he's the only person who would know where to begin looking. If you lock him up he won't be able to help at all."

"True. But if the press finds out that we are relying on one of our prime suspects to help us in this, it'll make matters worse, not better."

She smiled at him. "That's easy enough. You don't need to have anything to do with him. I'll do that. I'm not in the force, so you can honestly say that the polizia has no contacts with this man. If anyone asks."

Bottando grunted. "All right. But he'll need watching carefully." He picked up a sheet of paper he'd been writing on earlier and gazed at it mournfully. "We have quite a lot of suspects to talk to today."

"Such as?"

"Anyone who might have known Morneau, which is,

in theory, almost anyone in the art world. People who didn't like Tommaso, again everyone in the art world. People who wanted to be very rich. Again, everyone in the art world. Universal motive, universal opportunity.''

''Except that whoever burnt the picture must have been at that party,'' she pointed out, sitting down and putting her feet on the low coffee table.

''That still leaves us with an embarrassing surfeit,'' he responded. ''Dear me, what a mess. And if we don't get results pretty fast we're going to be roasted ourselves.''

He looked round at her. ''I suppose we'd better get going. So get your feet off my desk, damn you, and start dogging Argyll's steps.''

''We need to prove the picture was a forgery, which is difficult now it's destroyed. The notebooks help, but they're not conclusive. So we have to find the original original, so to speak.''

Flavia was sitting in the kitchen of Argyll's new apartment. He'd explained when she knocked on the door that he'd taken up the offer by his old friend, Rudolf Beckett, of a spare room. He looked tired and told her that he had not, in the circumstances, slept very well. Flavia might have been more sympathetic had she not been so alarmed at the possibilities suggested by the fact that suspect number one was living in the same flat as a journalist.

Argyll, however, reassured her. His flatmate was at the moment in Sicily on an extended trip to write stories about the Mafia. Flavia wondered whether any reporter ever went to Sicily to do anything else. He would not be back for several days, at least, so she stopped worrying and got back to the subject of Argyll's chance to rehabilitate himself.

"If the evidence about the forgery is so weak, why are you convinced?"

Flavia held up her hand and counted off the points, one by one. "Firstly, I want to be, because I hate the idea of a genuine Raphael being charred. Secondly, because otherwise we're looking for a real nutcase, and I don't want to believe that either. Thirdly, because we've got to explore all the possibilities anyway. Fourthly, intuition. Fifthly, because I trust your judgement."

Argyll snorted. "Sixthly, you're also crazy. Certainly you're the only person who trusts my judgement. But I'm just a graduate student. I can't really see myself wandering around looking for picture forgers."

"Indeed not. But you know more about that damned man Mantini than anyone else. He's now very much the artistic flavour of the month. The end of our troubles probably lies somewhere in your file cards."

Argyll brushed his fingers through his hair, hummed a little, then twiddled his thumbs, all symptoms that Flavia now recognised as symptomatic of embarrassment on his part.

"Yes, lovely. Glad to oblige. But, I mean, I hardly like to raise the subject and all that, but, well . . ."

"Why should you bother when you could possibly find it yourself and make a fortune?"

"I wasn't going to put it quite like that . . ."

"But I got hold of your general line of thought, correct?"

"Suppose."

"Simple enough," she said sweetly. "Step more than a centimetre out of line and Bottando will arrest you as a prime suspect, and throw you to the wolves to get the

press off his back. I had a very hard time this morning,"
she added with some exaggeration, "dissuading him
from locking you up immediately. He found your reasoning about why he should very convincing. And, of
course, if you are innocent, you would earn the immense
gratitude of almost everyone from the prime minister
down to myself, if you helped."

Argyll reached for another slice of toast, buttered it,
and covered it with about a quarter inch of Beckett's
expensively imported marmalade. "Oh, all right, then,"
he said grudgingly. "You have a persuasive way with
you. But I must warn you that even my inestimable services don't guarantee success."

"There is your catalogue of Mantini's paintings."

"As yet incomplete. And that only deals with paintings that still exist. The number that must have been
destroyed, or forgotten about, is probably huge."

"Do your best. We can talk about it this evening
when you've thought about it. I must go off on my er-
rands."

"One thing you can do for me. Could you use your
contacts to ask around all the auction houses and dealers
in order to trace any pictures that might have been
bought by Morneau? And anyone else you might suspect?"

"Where?"

"All over Europe. Or at least the main centres."

"All over Europe for all our suspects? Is that all?"

He nodded. "I suppose it's a big task. But if you
could find that one of them bought a picture the same
size as that Raphael, it would help."

"I see. Anything else you want, by any chance?"

"Just tell me one thing. Do you think I had anything
to do with this?"

Flavia picked up her bag and slung it over her shoulder, brow furrowed for a moment as she weighed up the options of being truthful or of upsetting him with her lack of confidence in his honesty.

''Pass,'' she said eventually, and headed off before he could reply.

After Flavia had run down the stairs in search of a taxi, Argyll wandered about his new apartment, tidying up in a halfhearted manner, wondering how best to go about his new task. It was hard to concentrate on the matter with the omnipresent thought that the slightest slip-up could land him in jail for much of the rest of his life. If he helped find the picture he might damn himself. But if he didn't, he would surely do so. It was not what had been in his mind when he thought of the pleasures of living in Rome once again. One thing was clear, however. He wasn't going to be able to confine himself to looking through file cards. He'd have to be a bit more active than that. Flavia, he thought, was basically well-disposed towards him, and disinclined to believe him responsible for all this. Her boss appeared to be of a different frame of mind.

Not that this one was going to be easy. He had never counted, but he reckoned that he had records of about five hundred pictures by Mantini. He knew that around half of these had been painted before 1724, before the painter covered over the Raphael. All the rest were either after that date or uncertain. He went to the shoe boxes of white cards which contained the records of the past three years' work and started flicking through. After a few minutes he decided that it would be easier simply to take cards out; putting them back in the right order could be taken care of later. Desperate situations require reckless remedies. About an hour's work produced a depressing result: even after the pictures which had been bought by the owner and stayed in the family's hands thereafter had been taken out, the pile of possibles was still about two inches thick—at about fifty cards to the inch.

Then he remembered Lady Arabella's letter, and went through again, removing everything but ruins and things that might get called ruins; this more than halved the problem to around forty-five pictures. He settled down, clamped his Walkman over his ears, put on a tape, and began to make a list. Not because it was especially vital, but because he couldn't think what to do next, and listening to music and making out lists he always found very therapeutic.

The rest of the day passed in industrious boredom for all concerned. At the museum, Tommaso and his cohorts were doing their best to retrieve the situation, pumping out press releases. Bottando spent some of his time in similar pursuits, but eventually gave up what appeared to be a losing battle and turned his mind to more immediate tasks.

Clearly someone in the museum—and it had to be Tommaso—was working furiously to shift the blame onto the police, Spello, and the ill-fated security council. He cursed the day he'd ever heard of that infernal committee. Not that he really blamed Tommaso, he thought in a fleeting moment of charitable objectivity, the man was trying to survive a calamity which had not been his fault. Perfectly understandable; it was simply that he wished the director wasn't trying to do so by offering Bottando's head as a substitute for his own. Perhaps Bottando would have done the same thing, in similar circumstances. Perhaps. But he was sure he would have been more tactful about it, and not tried to torpedo someone who, at the moment, was doing his damnedest to track down the real culprit.

His rivals in the various police forces were also well into a campaign against him, and he realised that the only effective answer to them was an arrest or two. So he dictated a bland statement about pursuing all possible investigations and being confident of making an arrest soon—which they could do, he thought gloomily. It was just that they would have no idea whether they'd collared the right man.

Then he deployed his forces to interview the party-goers, and himself went over to the National Museum to brief the director, as well as to talk to the man's principal enemies. Not all of them. There weren't enough hours in the day.

The briefing was tense, with Tommaso feigning concerned affability and Bottando pretending he hadn't noticed anything, so it was with considerable relief that he turned to the miscellaneous witnesses and suspects, whom he suspected would be more agreeable company. He started with Manzoni, summoning him to Ferraro's office, which he'd taken over for the duration. The restorer came in, moving uneasily and looking like a wreck. Bottando wasn't certain whether it was from emotional distress about the picture or the after-effects of his drinking the night before. He didn't ask.

The questioning, on the whole, was routine. Where was he, who did he talk to, and so on. All accounted for up to the moment when he had wandered away from Bottando. "And then?"

"To be perfectly frank, I can't remember. I haven't the faintest idea who I talked to. I remember lecturing someone about the restoration of prints. I know that, because I thought to myself that, if I'd been sober, I'd realise I was being extraordinarily dull.''

Bottando considered this and then, with apparent indifference, started off on another tack. ''Tell me,'' he said, ''were you one of the people who did the tests on that picture? I looked through the report the other day. You signed it, didn't you?''

Manzoni nodded. ''I did. I was in charge of the operation. The actual tests were carried out by the English experts called in by Byrnes who were more familiar with the machinery.''

''I see. So Byrnes's people actually had their hands on the painting?'' The man nodded.

''And you were entirely satisfied?''

''Of course,'' he said a little primly. The question had evidently pricked at his pride. ''If I hadn't been I would have said so. They were men of the highest reputation. The picture passed every test with room to spare. I didn't have a shred of doubt.'' He stopped and bit his thumbnail thoughtfully, then looked up. ''At least I didn't until about thirty seconds ago.''

''What do you mean?'' asked Bottando uncomfortably, conscious of a certain lack of subtlety in his interviewing technique.

''Not all technicians are idiots, you know,'' the man continued, the slightly priggish air growing, rather than fading in strength as he spoke.

''Tommaso's reputation rested on that Raphael. But if there's something wrong with it, Tommaso's credit-rating falls and Spello will get the job. It was burnt either as a way of getting at him or for some other motive. You, for no apparent reason, are spending some time reading the technical reports when presumably you have more urgent things to worry about. Which leads me to suspect . . .''

"Which leads you to suspect nothing whatsoever. But you've got a good imagination.'' Bottando hurriedly got up to end the interview, feeling slightly alarmed at the way the conversation had run away from him. Hung over or not, that young man had forged connections far too fast. He didn't like it.

He accompanied the restorer to the door, showing him out into the small anteroom that was normally occupied by the secretary. His next candidate sat there, placidly waiting.

"I see you're going to have a busy day,'' Manzoni said by way of farewell, "but I'd like to talk to you again, if you don't mind. If you want I'll go through the report again and see if there were any holes.''

"Could there be any?''

"I'd rather read it again first, to make sure of my facts. And give it a bit of quiet thought. Besides, I don't want to disrupt your schedule. Maybe I could come round to your office after work to give you my impressions? About seven this evening?''

Bottando agreed, watched him go, then turned to ask Spello to come in. One down, eighty to go, he thought. Maybe Flavia can help out this afternoon. He watched the Etruscan specialist sit himself cautiously into the chair, and considered how best to start the questioning.

He needn't have bothered. Spello began on his own, with a forthright statement of fact. "You're talking to me because I'm one of your more promising arsonists,'' he stated. "Jilted out of my rightful job as the next director by Tommaso's machinations.''

"So, burned up inside, you took your revenge by burning up his prize picture?''

Spello smiled. "And thus, at a stroke, creating a scandal, wrecking Tommaso's power to recommend anyone and assuring myself of the job. Easily done, especially as you'd already told me it was a fake, so there was no harm done. No. I did nothing of the sort, but I admit it's a convincing hypothesis."

"Except, of course, that our main evidence of faking has been considerably weakened. The painting may well have been genuine."

The man blanched visibly at the statement. Why was that? Simple objective distress at the loss? Bottando felt intensely awkward. Spello seemed positively eager to explain why he should be arrested immediately.

"Were you ever alone yesterday evening? Could you have slipped off without anyone noticing?"

"Nothing simpler. I hate those gatherings. I have to turn up, but I find the heat, the conversation and the company oppressive. I normally sneak off and go and read a book or something to recover myself, then go back again. I was up here for about an hour yesterday evening. All on my own. No one saw me come, no one saw me go."

How distressingly honest. If he'd wanted to make life easy for the police, he should either have come up with a cast-iron alibi, or with one that could be undermined. Candidly admitting he had none at all made everything very much more difficult.

"When I told you about the possible forgery, you kept it to yourself," Bottando began, swinging on to a new line. He was not happy. So far his performance at these interviews, where he was meant to be so masterfully in charge, was not at all good. He had lost the upper hand with the restorer, and seemed to be repeating the process with Spello. Perhaps the pressure was beginning to tell on him. "If you'd really been after the directorship you would have started spreading rumours, surely?"

Spello shook his head. "Not necessarily," he said in a reasonable and distant tone. "Firstly, it could have been traced back to me. Secondly, without proof, Tommaso could brazen it out and put the rumours down to a smear campaign by the discontented—which it would have been. I'm still very doubtful. No matter what Manzoni thinks, I doubt he'll be able to punch a hole in those tests."

Bottando grunted, and tried again. "The fire alarm," he pointed out. "How did you do that?" He noticed that he'd stopped using the hypothetical language of conditional clauses. Spello noticed it as well, and for the first time the policeman saw a flicker of unease on the old man's face.

"*If* I did," he replied with emphasis, "I did what was actually done. Removed the perfectly good fuse, and replaced it with one that was burnt out. Thus, it would seem as though the fuse blew at random."

Bottando sat up in his seat. "How do you know that's what happened?" he asked.

"I talked to the electrician. He's an old fogey like me. Been here for years, like me. We've always got on well. He was a bit upset when he saw the fuse. Said he was sure he'd changed it over and put a new one in. Not at all like the well-used one found in the slot. I thought it was obvious; they'd been swapped. Chances were that no one would notice, or draw any conclusions if they did."

Bottando sat silently, thinking it over. Spello's account made perfectly good sense, and at least solved one problem of how it was done. It also tended to swing suspicion more firmly on Spello. Who realised it.

"So you see. Motive, opportunity and no alibi. Enough to arrest me on, if that's what you feel like doing."

"Yes," he agreed, then went on more formally. "For the time being, however, we're not arresting anyone. But I must warn you not to leave Rome for the next few days. Any attempt to do so will be treated as attempted flight. Do you understand?"

"Perfectly, General," came the equally stiff reply, which then turned into a conspiratorial smile. "But I can tell you that if you do arrest me, you'll be making a big mistake. It'll be all Tommaso needs to restore his reputation. Because of that committee, you'll go down with me."

10

It was seven-thirty in the evening. Bottando sat in his office, waiting for Manzoni to show up. He wanted to see the man, especially since Manzoni had rung up in the early afternoon to say that he had found something which might be of interest. But the restorer was late. Often the case with these sort of people, but Bottando, who still retained some vague elements of his earlier military training, was irritated nonetheless. Punctuality, he thought, was a very great virtue; not that so many of his countrymen agreed with him. He filled the time catching up on some work and trying to control his mounting ill-humour.

While he was muttering about lack of consideration and the indignity of full generals being made to wait by junior restorers, Flavia had arrived at Argyll's flat to see what progress he'd made during his day's work. There was no answer. Despite her express request that he be there, he'd gone out. Damn him. She thought for a moment that maybe the bell didn't work. It was an old, run-down block and that was a distinct possibility. So she went into a bar and telephoned. Still no answer.

She was furious, and starting thinking along the lines that were currently occupying her boss back in the office. She'd had a tiring day and was frustrated at having worked so hard for almost no result. And to be stood up by someone who was lucky not to be in jail already was outrageous.

The high point, or low point, of her day's business had been a visit to Sir Edward Byrnes. Unlike Bottando, she had not been faced with a virtual confession, and she'd found it difficult to ask all the questions she needed without bringing up their suspicions about the origins of the picture.

Byrnes had to believe that all they were after was the person with the wandering aerosol. There was no need to show all their cards, especially as, in her book, the successful and wealthy Englishman was far and away the most likely suspect.

She found him in his hotel: it was highly expensive and, typically, not one of the more obviously opulent affairs that are to be found around the via Veneto. Rather, Byrnes's combination of money and exquisite taste had landed him in a highly anonymous but very private and splendidly elegant palazzo off the Corso, where the few guests allowed in reposed as though they were at home with the servants.

In the delicate pink-and-white drawing room, deserted apart from the two of them, Byrnes sat Flavia down on a sofa, arranged himself opposite her in a tapestry-covered armchair, and summoned a waiter with a brief wave of his hand. He was at their side in a commendably respectful matter of seconds.

"A drink, Signorina?" he asked in flawless Italian. "Or are you going to say 'not while I'm on duty,' eh?"

He blinked in an amiably owlish fashion from behind thick pebble-like glasses as he spoke. There were two ways of interpreting that, Flavia decided. On the one hand, it might be a good-natured look that goes along with someone trying to make himself agreeable. On the other, it might be an expression of contentment from someone who knows he's got away with it.

"Not me, Sir Edward. I think that's only for the English police. Besides, I'm not in the police."

"Good. Very sensible." She wasn't sure what part of her reply he referred to. He ordered two glasses of champagne kir without asking her opinion on the matter. "Now, how can I help you?"

Not, thought Flavia, "What do you want?" He's keen to sound more accommodating than that. Doesn't mean he will be any more forthcoming, mind you.

Flavia smiled at him. He was ordinarily not someone who let anybody do the talking, let alone a woman. "Obviously it's about the Raphael, and the events of yesterday . . ."

"And you want to know whether I habitually go around with aerosols of gasoline in my pocket? Or if I saw anyone looking especially furtive?"

"Something like that. Routine questioning of everyone in the museum yesterday evening, you understand."

"Especially if they happened to be responsible for the picture being there in the first place," he observed, taking out a short stubby pipe and beginning to fill it from a leather pouch. The trouble with everybody in this business is that they're too quick on the uptake, she thought.

"I wish I could provide you with some helpful comment. I am, of course, deeply upset by the whole thing. I'd formed a great attachment to the picture, and was very proud of my role in it. I gather it's beyond repair?"

If Byrnes hadn't been responsible for burning the picture, he would, naturally, want to know how successful the attack had been. Flavia nodded, and he nodded back in acknowledgement. He was still filling the pipe, which was evidently a highly complex and technical operation. His head was bent over as he shovelled a remarkable amount of tobacco into the bowl, then tamped it into place with a little metal device apparently designed for just such a purpose. While he was doing this, with immense concentration, she couldn't see his face at all well. Eventually he looked up at her again, stuck the pipe in his mouth and continued, not having noticed the long break in the conversation.

''You get fond of them, when you're with them for a long time,'' he said absently. ''Especially this one. I watched over it very carefully, once I realised what it was. The high point of my career. And now this. It was an appalling thing to happen. From what I've read, it would have been difficult to prevent as well. You seem to be looking for a madman, and it's impossible to guard against random acts.'' He now began on the equally intricate business of turning the pipe bowl into a minor inferno. Smoke billowed out in profusion, and drifted in a thick smog across the room.

''I'm sure you understand that we have to establish everybody's whereabouts for the entire evening?'' Flavia said, tearing her eyes away from the pipe and getting back to business.

''Of course. That's simple. I arrived at the hotel at about six, checked in and walked straight to the museum. I talked to various people and was still there when the announcement about the, ah, incident was made at about eight.'' He reeled off a list of names. She jotted them down.

"And how long did you spend talking to each of these people? With Argyll, for instance," she said casually. He didn't appear to make any connection of significance.

"With him longer than most, I suppose. As he may have told you already, I'm financing his trip here, and I quite like talking to him."

She nodded. "May I ask why you gave him this money?"

"Mild guilt. Or rather sympathy. Or is it empathy? I heard afterwards that he, like the person who commissioned me, was on the trail of this picture, but that I got there faster. That often happens, of course, and I've been pipped at the post myself. Ordinarily I just see it as the luck of the game. Except that it was such a big prize and Argyll was clearly counting on it for his work, rather than for simple financial profit. So I thought that the least I could do would be to offer some form of recompense. He does, in fact, deserve it. His work is much better than he makes out. A little sloppy over details . . ."

That's true, thought Flavia to herself.

". . . but essentially well-researched and interesting. Not nearly as narrow as the subject suggests. So I'm not giving favours to the undeserving poor," he concluded.

"So you noticed nothing at this party and were never on your own?"

"Only when Argyll disappeared off to the toilet, or to get some drinks, or something like that. He was quite flustered all evening. I think he was excited at being back in Rome."

Well, maybe so. She switched the subject once more. "You talk about being commissioned?" she prompted.

"My little secret," he replied. "Most of my colleagues and rivals still believe I owned the picture. I let them think it because it drives them into such paroxyms of jealousy. All I did was act as an agent. I shipped it back, sent it to the restorers and organised the sale.''

"Why did you choose these particular people?''

"No reason. They were available, I'd worked with them before and knew them to be reliable. They were very excited. They were in the office from the moment the crate arrived: we could hardly keep them away from it.''

"Could you give me their names?''

"By all means. I'm sure they would be pleased to talk to you. One of them rang me this morning, very upset indeed. They became very proprietorial about it—always saying how lucky I was to own such a picture. I couldn't bear to disillusion them.''

"Who did it belong to then?'' Flavia leant forward in her chair in anticipation. He might lie. Almost certainly would. But even so it might provide something to go on. Even if it turned out to be a lie, his assertion would prove something.

Byrnes spread his hands over the desk. "I wish I knew. I was given instructions by letter from a lawyer in Luxembourg. It was a bit odd, I know, but such procedures are not entirely unknown. There is often a certain amount of disguise when some rich family wants to raise some cash discreetly. To buy and sell a picture anonymously is more unusual, but at the time I thought the picture was not especially valuable. So I could see no reason for not going ahead.''

"But you weren't tempted to keep the picture when you knew what it was?''

Byrnes smiled at her. "It occurred to me, of course. But by that time I'd signed a contract as the agent. Besides, it's not the way I operate. As you know, the art-dealing community is not noted for its impeccable integrity,''—here Flavia grinned—''but there is a sort of honour among thieves, and not pinching someone else's discovery is part of it. That's why I felt a little guilty about Argyll.

''But quite apart from the moral issue, I didn't know who was behind it all. For all I know, it might have been the Vatican itself. It always needs ready money these days, and this method might have been a way of circumventing the objections to the sale which would otherwise have developed. It never does to offend someone if you don't know who you are offending. Besides, the retainer alone was very generous.''

''You were never suspicious that something might be wrong?'' Flavia asked doubtfully.

''Of course. I haven't worked in the art business for quarter of a century without learning to trust no one. But I chose the people who tested it. They were in no doubt that it was genuine, nor was the Museo Nazionale. I could see nothing wrong. If I'd had the slightest doubt, I'd never have agreed to the museum's terms in the sale contract.''

''Which were?''

''Simply that if the painting's authenticity was called into question I'd be responsible for refunding the money as agent for the owner. Very tight and carefully drafted. They included it, I suppose, to satisfy the finance ministry that they were being careful with the taxpayer's money. Besides, Tommaso was involved and we've never got on, even though we keep up an appearance of friendliness.''

Flavia said nothing in reply to this, but sat quietly, waiting to see if he would continue on his own. In a fit of what was either calculating revelation, or confessional zeal, he did so.

"You see, I once sold Tommaso a Correggio. Doubts were cast on its authenticity, and Tommaso threatened me, saying that if I didn't take it back, I'd never sell another picture in Italy. There was nothing in the contract which said I had to. But I did, out of a sense of pride. Nonetheless, he still made life as difficult for me as possible for the next fifteen years. So it was quite a triumph to get him to take that Raphael, even if the terms were stiff. He hated doing it, but his desire for the picture was too great."

He shrugged as a way of showing his bewilderment with the ways of God and men. "Ah well. That's all past history now. The terms of that contract seem to be redundant. The painting's destroyed." He smiled gently at her. "So there's nothing for me to take back even if they wanted me to, is there?"

That, essentially, had been the interesting part of the day; the rest was spent listening to people explain how—and why—they hadn't seen anything interesting or significant at the party. Out of more than eighty people, some sixty-five, Flavia reckoned, could easily have slipped out of the room unnoticed, gone upstairs, set light to the picture and come back down again. Of that sixty five, around fifty knew about the alarm system. Of the remaining fifteen, nearly all could easily have found out.

More frustrating and personally irritating was the fact that she found herself quite liking Byrnes and being seduced—well, perhaps seduced was not the right word—by his charm. She'd gone in to see him determined to be distant, cold and efficient, but despite these laudable intentions, she found herself enjoying talking to him, and warming to his odd combination of vagueness and business acumen.

And the man had taken advantage of the fact. As she was leaving, he'd casually mentioned he was going back to London that evening, and would he be required for the investigation any more? Damn right, he would; but she could find no pretext upon which to detain him. He was evidently intent on going and they could not require him to stay without announcing that he was a suspect. But on what grounds if she couldn't mention the forgery? Equally, by politely asking permission to leave, he had countered any suggestion that he was hotfooting it to safety.

All she could do was lamely say that, of course, it was quite in order for him to go. He'd spent some time laying out his motives for destroying the picture—revenge, greed, the works—and all she could do at the end was wish him a safe trip home. He'd thanked her soberly, and wished her luck in the investigation. Was he laughing at her? Surely he was, but that poker face, moderated by thick glasses and clouds of smoke, had been impenetrable.

Then there had been the interminable interviews, often tramping over ground that—she found to her irritation—had already been worked over by Bottando, and, on top of that, her ears ringing and her head spinning, her useless visit to Argyll's apartment. At quarter to eight, tired, weary and wanting only to go home and have a bath and an early night, she dragged herself up the stairs of the office to write up a few reports. This made her feel virtuous, but did nothing else to cheer her up at all. She had a feeling that disaster was just around the corner.

She was wrong, as she often seemed to be these days: it was lumbering down the stairs, in the shape of a perspiring, out of breath and evidently troubled Bottando.

"Flavia. Good. Come with me," was all he said as he hurried past her. She turned round and followed him to his car in the square. Clearly it was serious; it took more than a small crisis to break the General out of his habitual slow amble. They both got in the back, Bottando gave the driver an address in Trastevere, and told him to hurry. He did so, complete with sirens, horn and screeching tyres for dramatic effect.

"What's happened now?" she asked as she regained her balance after a particularly vicious corner.

"I told you about Manzoni, the restorer?" She nodded. "He was meant to come and see me at seven. He didn't show up. The Trastevere police just rang: he didn't come because he was dead. It seems that someone has murdered him."

Flavia sat stunned. Things were going from bad to worse. "Are they sure it was murder?"

"Knife in the back," he replied simply.

"Oh dear," she said. Complications, nothing but complications. It wouldn't make Bottando look any better to have a witness murdered under his nose. It made solving the case more difficult, and now there was a murder mixed up in it all, there would be demarcation disputes with the murder squad and others, as they squabbled over who should be in charge. The investigation could disintegrate into one of those well-known Italian situations where everybody spends their time fighting their colleagues, and nothing whatsoever gets done. She'd seen it before. The General was evidently thinking along the same lines.

"Listen," he said as the car drew up at their destination. "Leave the talking to me here. Don't say anything more than you need to, all right?"

Following behind him at a distance suitable for a junior tagging along, therefore, she climbed the stairs and entered Manzoni's apartment. It was full of policemen, photographers, fingerprint men, neighbours and people just hanging around. The usual chaos. Bottando was spotted by the senior local detective, who came over and introduced himself.

"When we discovered he worked at the museum I decided it might have something to do with you, so I called," he explained after relating how the body had been discovered by a neighbour peering in through the open front door as she passed.

Bottando shrugged and walked over to the body, ignoring the invitation to talk. "Any idea when he was killed?"

"After five-thirty, when he was seen coming home, and before seven, when the body was discovered. So far we can't be more precise than that. Right-hand blow to the back and into the heart. Kitchen knife."

"No one saw any strangers hanging about, I suppose?"

The detective shook his head. "Any idea what it may be about?"

Bottando pursed his lips and shook his head slowly. "No," he lied. "My first inclination is to suggest coincidence, much as I dislike them. He certainly wasn't a hot tip for our arsonist. Nor was there any connection I know of between him and any of our suspects."

The detective looked disgruntled. He knew Bottando was being elusive, but in the very hierarchical police force, there is no way you can press a general without running the risk of getting yourself into trouble. He would have to find someone of equivalent rank to do that for him.

While the little interchange was going on, and while her boss wandered around the apartment looking vainly for hints, Flavia leant on the small round table in the sitting-room and pursued her own thoughts. They didn't lead anywhere, except to the depressing conclusion that while they had had two crimes and too many suspects this morning; now they had three crimes and too many suspects. Not her idea of progress.

She told Bottando this after they left the apartment. He dismissed the car, explaining that walking helped him think. Besides, it was one of the few things he found pleasant at the moment. She fell in step with him and talked. He marched morosely by her side, not saying a word in reply for several minutes.

"So what you're basically saying is that we're no further on at all? And in fact we're more confused than ever?" he said when her exposition was finished.

"Well, yes, I suppose I am. But we could try and narrow it down a little." Bottando grunted, but kept quiet. Flavia was wearing baggy trousers and a jacket, and now thrust her hands into the pockets to help her concentrate. They crossed the Tiber as the dusk was deepening into dark. A thin but chilly wind was coming up the river, making her shiver as they walked.

"OK then," she began after a few moments. "Either the picture was a forgery or it wasn't. If it wasn't, then we must look for a madman or someone in the museum. Correct?" It was a rhetorical question. Even had it not been it probably wouldn't have got a reply from her companion, who was staring moodily at the pavement.

"Main candidates, Manzoni, deceased, and Spello. Both disliking Tommaso, prompted into desperate action by the announcement of his retirement."

"Who killed Manzoni?"

"Spello," she said firmly. "Realised Manzoni had wrecked the painting. Overcome with rage that he'd destroyed such a beautiful object. Or realised Manzoni knew *he'd* burnt the picture, so killed him to shut him up."

"This is narrowing it down, is it?"

Flavia ploughed on, ignoring the interruption. "Other candidate: Argyll, overcome with remorse at his lost opportunity . . ."

She got no further in what she considered a masterly exposition of the options. "Flavia, dear, this is not cheering me up. Do you, in fact, have the slightest idea who might be responsible for this?"

"Well, um, no."

"I thought not. Now, why the timing?"

"What do you mean?"

"I mean, why was the picture burnt yesterday? After all, we'd just come across the evidence it was a fake and hadn't told anyone. And the evidence, it seems, wasn't as good as we thought. So why destroy it?"

This one stumped her, so he carried on on his own. "I think," he pointed out, mentally counting, "you have just listed about a dozen combinations of possibilities, without a shred of real evidence for any of them. Which goes to show that armchair detection is no good for anything. We need evidence of something. I reckon it's about time you stopped thinking and started looking."

"Where do you suggest?"

"Go to London. Manzoni seems to have come up with something, and we need to know what it was. If those tests have a hole, the only place you'll find out is there. Go and see those restorers. That might provide something. Could you get on a plane tomorrow?"

She nodded. "As long as someone can keep an eye

on Argyll while I'm away," she said. "Perhaps," she added, "I should nip off now and see if he's back in. You never know, he might open the door covered in blood."

"And might stick a knife in you for good measure."

"I can't see him doing something like that. But I can't see any of them doing anything like that. That's the trouble."

"Don't let your intuition run away with you. If it wasn't for the timing of all this, he'd be charged already. So watch yourself. Unless he comes up with a very good reason for what he's been up to, let me know and I'll pull him in.

"I feel uncomfortable about all this," he continued. "I'm missing something which should be obvious. Something a long time ago which isn't right. I woke up this morning and almost had it, but it slipped away. It's driving me quietly crazy. Having an impossible task is bad enough, but when you suspect it's because of your own failing memory it becomes insufferable."

They parted at the next corner, Bottando walking northwards, slowly, absent-mindedly and morosely; she with the brisk step of a person who cannot remain bothered and overburdened for too long.

Argyll was at home this time, let her in, and burbled happily about his day for the first few minutes, not letting Flavia get a word in edgeways. She sat quietly and waited for him to stop.

"There's nothing like the prospect of spending the rest of your life in jail to make you get a move on," he said. "I reckon if my supervisor had threatened to send me to Wormwood Scrubs for a year or two, I could have had my thesis finished ages ago."

He gestured over to a desk piled high with files, file-cards, used coffee cups and stacks of paper. "See that? I've been working like a demon all day."

"All day?" she asked quietly.

"Yup. Non-stop. Quite possessed I was. I've got it down to about twenty possibles. Assuming, that is, that it exists at all. But if I didn't assume that, I'd lose heart. With a bit of luck I'll be off your list of potential jail fodder within a week or so."

"All day?" she repeated. "What about when I came round at seven?"

He paused. "Oh. I'd forgotten all about that. That's what comes of concentrating. You were meant to come round, weren't you?"

She nodded. "And I did. At seven. And you weren't here."

"Yes I was. I'd just forgotten all about it. I had my Walkman on, so I suppose I didn't hear the bell."

"Was anyone else here? Can anyone give you an alibi?"

Argyll looked flustered. "An alibi? For heaven's sake! Of course not. I was here all on my own. I know it was careless of me. I'm sorry. But is it really such a big thing?"

"Yes," she said. And explained why. The colour drained from his cheeks as she spoke.

"So you think I slipped out, knifed him, came home and pretended I'd been here all the time, not hearing you because of the music?"

"Fits the facts, doesn't it?"

"Rather well," he agreed unhappily. "Except, of course, that it's not at all what I was doing. I was here."

He rummaged around in Beckett's drinks cupboard, pulled out a bottle of grappa and poured a healthy glass-

ful. "I don't suppose he'd object in the circumstances."
He took a heavy suck on the glass, coughed slightly,
then offered her a drink herself. She declined.

"I suppose," he restarted with some hesitation, ferociously scratching the top of his head in a way that
indicated profound misgivings inside, "I suppose that
what I was planning to do next will make things worse."

He stopped, and she gazed at him enquiringly. "I was
about to tell you," he went on, "that to finish the search
for this picture I would have to go to look at some things
in London. I was thinking of going tomorrow."

He looked at her hopefully. "Remarkable timing,"
she said sarcastically. "Especially considering that
Byrnes headed off for England this evening as well."

It was not the reassurance that Argyll had been looking for. Indeed, it made him even less comfortable. The
drink rested on the floor, completely forgotten.

"So it would look better if I stayed here?"

"It would look better. But practically speaking, I suppose, it might be better if you went. As long as I go
with you and you tell me exactly where you'll be at
every moment of the day. One more slip and I'll pull
you in. And I mean that. Depending on what turns up,
I might do it anyway. Agreed?"

He nodded. "I suppose so. I'm grateful for your trust
in me."

"Don't be sarcastic. And I don't trust you. Except, of
course, that I find it difficult to believe that anyone could
have forged a picture like that and act as dimwittedly as
you have. At the moment the only thing you've got going for you is stupidity. You're very lucky not to be in
a cell already."

So, sometimes you say the wrong thing. Flavia could,
at times, be a little harsh in her conversational gambits,

and the characteristic tended to show itself when she was tired or frustrated. This evening she was both of these, and worried as well. The combination eroded the natural kindness which generally masked her occasional tinge of verbal brutality.

Argyll, however, disregarded these extenuating circumstances and exploded.

"I think we ought to get one thing clear here," he began coldly. "I never said that picture was a Raphael, I simply came out to Rome to check. I went by the rulebook, not making claims I couldn't substantiate or prove. Whatever happened thereafter was nothing to do with me. So remember that. Secondly, it was me, not you, who first suggested it might be a fake. If it wasn't for my research, which you sneer at so much, you'd be running around wringing your hands at the loss of a masterpiece. Thirdly, you don't have any evidence against me at all. If you had, you'd have locked me up already. So don't imply you're doing me any favours.

"And finally, at the moment, you need my help more than I need yours. If you think you can find that picture on your own, go ahead. But you can't. I can, maybe. And I'm not going to help you if I'm going to be subjected to sneering little taunts from you all the time. Is that clear?"

On the whole, it was not a bad speech at all. Later on, lying in bed, thinking about it and making little improvements for the benefit of posterity, he was struck by his simple eloquence. Forceful, no-nonsense stuff, in fact. He was quite pleased with himself. Opportunities for righteous indignation come up only very infrequently, and he normally never thought of the appropriately devastating response until, on average, about forty-five minutes afterwards.

More satisfying still, it stopped the voluble Italian woman dead in her tracks. He was ordinarily very mild-mannered; his expressions of rage were most visibly expressed in a faint look of distress or a mumbled sentence of mild disapproval. Oratory was quite out of character and the suddenness of the speech, combined with the real feeling that apparently went into it, momentarily caught Flavia unawares. She stared at him in surprise, dismissed the temptation to fire back a full broadside, then apologised.

"I'm sorry. It's been a bad day. Truce? No more comments until you're cleared?"

He stumped around the room, closed the curtains, shut a cupboard door or two while he worked off his indignation, then nodded. "Or arrested, I suppose," he added. "OK. A deal. When do we leave?"

"There's a plane at seven-thirty. I shall pick you up here at six-thirty."

"That early? How horrible."

"Get used to it," she said as she got ready to leave. "In Italian prisons they wake you up at five . . . Sorry," she added quickly. "Shouldn't have said that."

CHAPTER

11

Not to be outworked by his assistant, Bottando was sitting down at his desk, the inevitable coffee before him, around the same time that Flavia and Argyll were boarding the plane for London. In the cold light of dawn, he was less than convinced that letting either of them go was a good idea.

But he'd allowed himself to be persuaded by her arguments. Which were, essentially, that as things stood they had no real evidence of anything at all; that if Argyll was guilty he had to be allowed to make some mistake, and if he was innocent he had to find that picture, or prove that it didn't exist and the one in the museum had been genuine. Besides which, as she somewhat tactlessly pointed out, they'd made so many mistakes so far in this business, one more would hardly make any great difference.

The comment accented the still ferocious assaults in the newspapers that lay before him. They had discovered about Manzoni, and were painting lurid pictures about what they had now dubbed the "museum of murder."

Tommaso had been no friendlier when he'd told him of the latest developments. He'd been clearly upset about the restorer's demise, no doubt concluding that, if this whole thing was a plot against him, then he might be next in line for a knife in the back.

Bottando had misjudged that man, it was clear. In the immediate aftermath of the party, the director had presented a humble, subdued, almost likeable side, though this was evidently an uncharacteristic reaction brought on by shock, because it wasn't lasting. Tommaso was now getting very nervous, tense and short-tempered; not that such a condition stopped the politician in him operating at full power. He was manoeuvring with all the grace of a synchronised swimmer, rapidly and successfully shifting all blame on to the committee, Spello, and Bottando's department. Already stories hinting something along those lines had appeared in one of the papers.

One thing was certain. Bottando felt himself getting too old for this sort of thing. Wearily, he counted up the forces and assessed his chances. On his side, he had the ministry of defence, who could be counted on to look after him. He thought. Against him, he had the newspapers, the arts ministry, the interior ministry, and Tommaso. The treasury represented a floating vote, whose mind would be made up by the chances of getting its money back.

If they ever got that far. According to the legal department in the arts ministry, the contract stated clearly that if the picture was a fake, the seller—that is Edward Byrnes—would have to refund. Any loss of a genuine picture would be borne by the state. If Byrnes was telling the truth, if he hadn't owned the picture and didn't have the money, he'd still have to refund. But, as the man had told Flavia, the picture was gone. So the only way of proving it was a fake was to find the original.

Essentially, it came down to the fact that the future of his department and of his career now depended on a foreign graduate student, who had already made one mistake and who might very well be an arsonist, forger, conspirator, murderer, and half-cracked as well. The thought did not bolster the General's confidence. He was starting to suspect that, at long last and after many campaigns, he was outnumbered, outflanked and outgeneralled.

And Bottando's sense that he was missing something still nagged away at him. He'd paced the streets, sat in armchairs, tossed and turned in bed. All to no avail. He *was* missing something and was no nearer to discovering what it was. The more he tried, the more the wisp of memory receded. Hence the vast piles of dossiers on his desk. The personnel files of everyone in the museum, combined with what they knew about Morneau, Byrnes, Argyll, and anyone else concerned.

He picked up Tommaso's file. Might as well start at the top, he thought as he opened it. Cavaliere Marco Ottavio Mario di Bruno di Tommaso. Born March 3, 1938. Father, Giorgio Tommaso, died 1948, aged forty-two. Mother, Elena Maria Marco, died 1959, age fifty-seven. He jotted idly on his notepad and sighed heavily.

Pages and pages of the stuff, a monument to the excessive zeal of an overstocked bureaucracy with nothing better to do. Education, careers, opinions, recommendations. All repeated hundreds of times in each dossier on everyone. And he was going to go through the lot of them, for the one piece of information that might jog his memory.

• • •

Bottando had polished off the Renaissance department when the plane touched down, and was progressing on to Early Medieval Painting by the time the taxi drew up outside the Victoria & Albert Museum to let Argyll out.

As agreed, he gave her a detailed itinerary; a couple of hours there, followed by a brief stop at the Courtauld in Portman Square, with an option on a visit to the British Museum later on. She told him to meet her at six, and concluded with dire warnings of the potential penalties should he miss the rendezvous again. He grinned nervously at her and made his way up the steps.

He had always hated the V & A, especially the library, which was his present destination. It was not just the fact that it was cold; nearly all libraries he had worked in were underheated. Nor was it particularly the clear evidence of a chronic lack of funds: the little donation boxes hopefully primed with five-pound notes to give visitors the right idea; the lack of proper lighting; the general air of woebegone neglect.

But in he went, walking through the museum along the echoing corridors, resisting the temptation to buy an overpriced bun in the café, up the stairs and into the library. For the next ten minutes he rummaged around in the catalogues, occasionally scribbling call numbers on bits of paper and handing them in at the desk. Then he gave in to temptation, took his newspaper and went down for a coffee. Long experience had taught him that no books would turn up for at least forty-five minutes.

Feeling oppressed and out of place, he took his coffee and soggy doughnut and sat in a far corner of the room, away from the other students and the small number of miscellaneous tourists. He concentrated on the paper and pretended, as best as he could, that he was somewhere else. His thoughts on the subject were interrupted by a clattering of plates as someone sat down at his table. The newcomer instantly fished out a packet of Rothman's from the pocket of his old, battered jacket—which had clearly once been the top half of a suit—and lit up.

"Thank heavens for that. First today. I've almost been chewing my fingers off up there."

"Hello, Phil. How are you?"

The newcomer shrugged. "As ever," he replied. He puffed furiously on his cigarette. He was one of Argyll's oldest associates. As Philip Mortimer-Jones, he was a child of privilege, public schools, and superlative contacts through his father, who was some big wheel in the National Trust. As plain Phil, he was short and stocky, abominably dressed, with dark greasy hair and a look on his face which made you suspect he was about to fall asleep, or that his eyes were caked with grime, or that he had just eaten some substance of which the police would disapprove: in all the five years he had known him, Argyll could never decide. Possibly all of the above. But for all his dormouse-like appearance Phil was a bright lad. He was also more finely tuned into the nuances of academic gossip than anyone else Argyll knew. He confirmed this with his next statement.

"Surprised to see you here. I thought you'd still be mourning over your great Italian disappointment."

Argyll groaned. If Phil knew then everybody would know. "Who told you about that?"

"Can't remember. Heard it somewhere."

How *did* he know, though? Argyll was certain he had told only one person, and that had been his ever-so-civil and discreet supervisor. It had been an awkward meeting, because his idleness had finally caught up with him. His university had become somewhat impatient and had threatened to wipe his name off the books. His super-visor, old Tramerton, had been asked for a recommendation one way or another, and he had asked Argyll for evidence that any sort of mental activity was still flickering.

He'd had to produce something convincing quickly. So in the space of four days he had gathered the only material to hand, accumulated an impressive-looking bibliography and posted off to Italy his tentative conclusion that underneath the Mantini rested a genuine, lost Raphael.

It seemed now, of course, that it was the wrong conclusion, but he refused to take responsibility for that. If the university authorities had not been so unreasonably demanding, the little paper would not have been written and Byrnes would not have got to the picture before him. Quite a pleasant chain of events, if you thought about it. Anyway, Tramerton had been convinced—of his efforts if not his scholarly merits—and had done the decent thing. The threat of execution was withdrawn and Argyll had thought no more about it.

Until now. Evidently either Tramerton had given the paper to someone or had told someone about it. Find who it was and the route to Byrnes would open up like magic. But who? His supervisor had been out of circulation in Italy, staying at a colleague's house west of Montepulciano, so a letter had said. How had Byrnes got at him there? He'd write and ask. Maybe that would produce something useful.

It would all have to wait for the time being; the aromatic confines of the library awaited him. He stopped his colleague just as he was getting into conversational second gear, astounded him with the announcement that he was desperately keen to get back to his desk, and dragged himself up the stairs again. A brief conversation, and not at all a satisfying one.

Working proved less easy than he'd anticipated. The excitement of the previous couple of days wrought havoc on his concentration. As did the pressure he was working under. As Flavia had pointed out to him, find that Raphael and all was well. The penalty for failure was not, however, merely a raised eyebrow from his supervisor this time. This is not, he told himself as he flipped through the books he'd ordered, what academic work is meant to be like. The marines would be less dangerous at the moment. It was all very well to say "find a Raphael." But if it was that easy, it would have been found years ago.

Of course, he'd made progress, but only of a negative sort. He knew better where the painting *wasn't*. That, however, was not going to bring him many congratulations. From the initial two hundred and something or other possibilities, it was now down to a few dozen. What was he meant to do? Visit every one with a sharp knife and give it a little scrape? Apart from the fact that the owners might protest, presumably someone else was also on the same course. If Byrnes had destroyed that picture so it wouldn't be revealed as a fake, he was smart enough to know he'd have to get rid of the real thing as well, which was the last possible proof of his initial fraud.

The idea made him think; he paid less attention to his books and stared up at the wire netting strung across the ceiling to stop falling bits of roof from the decaying building hitting the students below. The books didn't seem quite so important now. He could accumulate information for months, and still never find anything convincing. If he was going to get anywhere, he'd have to

work with what information he already had. He had to
find the picture to catch a culprit. But what if he did it
the other way round? Lateral thinking, it was called, and
once he started thinking along these lines, everything
began to seem quite simple. And after a few hours, he
even began to get a smell of where the picture might be.

Later that evening he met Flavia on schedule and in the
right place, and the two of them walked into a cutesy
little wine-bar in a street running parallel to Wardour
Street. It was called the Cockroach and Cucumber, or
somesuch, which prompted Argyll to make a few dis-
paraging comments. ''It'll probably be full of the elder
brothers of the students who work in the V & A,'' he
sniffed at Flavia, who missed the reference and smiled
politely. She'd had a tiresome day, talking to the other
restorers. Not that it had done her much good. They'd
all taken refuge in technicalities and refused to come out
of their shells. This was her last chance to make the trip
worthwhile. It made her determined, and sliced the edge
off her sense of humour.

   The clientele around the bar generated a rubicund air
of confident and artificial jollity that settled around Argyll like a suffocating smog. He felt unhappy already.
''Hardly the place for a quiet and confidential chat,'' he
bellowed into Flavia's left ear.

   ''What?'' she yelled back, then sighted the Tate restorer. ''Doesn't matter. Tell me later.'' She weaved her
way over to the bar. Anderson, her target, was standing
there, waving a five-pound note in a hopeful fashion.
Flavia rapped him on the shoulder firmly, just at the
moment his long vigil was rewarded, and the barmaid
was headed in his direction. He turned to greet the Italian, lost eye-contact with the other side of the bar, and

the woman drifted off to serve someone else.

"Goddamn," he exclaimed. "Missed her again. No matter. We can go next door where it's quieter. They have table service through there."

As they walked through, Flavia introduced Argyll. Anderson looked disappointed. "Oh. I thought you were coming alone." Argyll was instantly offended and found himself disliking the man intensely. They sat down at one of the few remaining tables and ordered a bottle of white wine of uncertain origin. "You see? It's a lot quieter in here. Nice place, eh?"

Argyll smiled and nodded. "Remarkable. Nice is not the word." He'd wanted to say that for years. Flavia smiled at him and trod heavily on his toe with her heel. They were not called stilettos for nothing. Tears came into his eyes from the pain.

She then went on to try and rescue the conversation, parroting out a largely erroneous explanation of her presence in England.

"And you want my help. Willingly. If, of course, you tell me why."

"Just routine enquiries, as I believe they say in this country."

"Nonsense. Nothing I could possibly say would be of the slightest use to you unless there was more to it than that. I knew nothing about the painting except that I was called in by Sir Edward Byrnes to clean and restore it. Apart from the occasional incursion by television cameras, I worked alone with the other restorers. Why send someone all the way from Rome just to ask about that?

"And of course, you turn up here bringing Mr. Argyll—" for some reason Argyll disliked that Mister bit, "—who Sir Edward once told me was miffed about the whole business. Why search for motives when you take the number one suspect along with you? Unless, of course, there is something else going on. Cheers.'' He raised his glass to salute his cleverness, and screwed his face up in an exaggerated demonstration of disgust.

''I never realised that I had achieved such fame,'' commented Argyll, uncertain whether Anderson's facial antics referred to the wine or him.

''Don't worry. You haven't. But Byrnes mentioned you once and I have a very good memory for minor details.''

Argyll decided to retire from the conversation as much as possible. Minor details, indeed. He leant back in his chair, nursed his glass of wine, and tried to look nonchalant. If it hadn't been for his afternoon's labours he would be in a bad mood. However, what he had to tell Flavia made him feel smug. It would be agreeable to be in control of events for once.

''Will you give me your word that this conversation will be confidential?'' Flavia asked.

''I can give you my word and you can decide how much it's worth,'' Anderson replied. Flavia thought some more. She not only wanted information, it would be nice to rattle this little bugger's confidence a little. Suggesting he might have been one of the prime victims of a hoax might sober him up a bit. Also, she didn't like that crack about Argyll: maybe he had been a little objectionable, but basically she agreed with him. This worried her. Becoming protective was always a bad sign.

''It was a fake,'' she announced bluntly.

The statement did the trick nicely. Anderson didn't exactly turn pale, but clearly felt like it. ''Oh shit,'' he said, very slowly and distinctly. ''Are you sure?''

Flavia shrugged and smiled prettily at him, but didn't reply.

"And can you tell me why you think that?"

She shook her head. "No. I'm afraid not. Just take it that we're right." It was a gross and unreasonable exaggeration, but Bottando had always instructed her that the one golden rule about police work was never ever seem uncertain of your facts. Besides, she reckoned that the more upset Anderson was, the more he'd talk. She switched into concerned and attentive mode.

"I think I ought to buy you something to eat here. I'm pretty hungry."

So was Argyll. And he appreciated that the little gesture was, perhaps, a good way of establishing a better rapport with Anderson. He was the sort of tactless person who not only can't resist a free meal, but who is also made hungry by bad news. For the next hour he munched his way steadily through a large plate of jumbo prawns, a sizeable slice of fish pie, two plates of vegetables, a dessert that was meant to be pecan pie but wasn't quite right somehow, two cups of coffee and an unfair share of a second bottle of wine. Flavia also matched him pretty much forkful for forkful. As on the first occasion when he had watched her prowess in this field, Argyll wondered how on earth someone of such a delightfully trim shape could possibly stuff that much food inside her.

To help Anderson in the right direction, Flavia began telling him about the scientific study of the picture. The scientist waved her aside. "I know all this. I was in charge."

"I thought Manzoni was?"

"Him?" Anderson said contemptuously. "He never came near it. Just read the report afterwards, said he was sure we'd done it all correctly, and signed the thing. Scarcely lifted a finger."

Flavia was quite unjustifiably irritated at the aspersions cast on her fellow-countryman by this large and cocky Englishman. His comments smacked too much of anti-Italian prejudice for her taste. Moreover, it meant one of her pet theories was weakened. If Manzoni hadn't directed the tests, he couldn't have fixed them either. Her focus came back to Anderson, who was pronouncing at great length, not noticing she hadn't been paying any attention.

". . . That's why I'd like to hear your evidence. I can't see any way that picture could be a fake. It looked right and tested right. The evidence would have to be absolutely overwhelming to make me change my mind," he concluded.

She evaded again. "Just tell me, how would someone fake a thing like that?"

"In principle it's easy. It's just doing it that's the trouble. From what I remember of the report, the forger would have had to get hold of a sixteenth- or late fifteenth-century canvas to start off with. One the right size as the final picture so there wouldn't be any new strain marks from the new shape of the stretcher. You clean off some, but not all, of the original paint. Then you start painting your own picture, using the same techniques and the same paint recipes as the original artist."

Flavia nodded. So far what he was saying fitted in exactly with the jottings in the Swiss sketch-books.

"Once you've painted it, then it has to be artificially dried and aged. An oil painting takes years to dry completely, sometimes half a century. There's no bigger giveaway than a Renaissance picture which is sticky. That, incidentally, is how Wacker, the Van Gogh forger, got caught in the 1930s.

"Drying can be done in several ways," he continued.

"The traditional method is to bake it—preferred temperatures vary from forger to forger—then roll it up in several directions to crack the surface, then dip it in a solution of ink to darken the cracks and make them look dirty. That, at least, was the Van Meegeren method, and he was one of the greatest. Couldn't paint for tuppence, but a great forger.

"Of course, there are ways of checking all that. The Elisabetta was analysed for the way it had dried, the direction and type of the cracking were examined, bits of paint were scraped off and tested in a dozen different ways, the dirt boiled up and analysed chemically. All perfect, as I say."

"So you've told us how to get caught. How about not getting caught?" Argyll suggested.

"There are some ways, I suppose," Anderson replied reluctantly. "As far as drying goes, you might try a low-voltage microwave oven, perhaps. That would produce a different method of drying out. Not foolproof, by any means, but it wouldn't produce the tell-tale signs one looks for to indicate normal baking. Cracking is also relatively simple if you are careful to preserve the original pattern on the host painting. Doing it is incredibly hard, but it is possible.

"In the case of the Raphael, you could dissolve the dirt from the original painting in some solution of alcohol and spread that over the surface. When it was tested it would be seen as being of a mixture of different substances, which is what it should be. The alcohol would also show up, but in this case might be confused with the substances we used to clean the thing.

"But it's paint itself which proves it. It's difficult to see how to get round that, and we tested it endlessly. Spectroscope, electron microscope, dozens of different routines. There can be no doubt. It was sixteenth-century, Italian, painted with Raphael's techniques. Genuinely old paint. Not just new paint mixed with old recipes. Old paint. Everything worked out perfectly. Which is why I don't really believe it was a fake.''

''I know how it was done,'' said Argyll quietly. They both looked at him. ''It's just occurred to me. Flavia, you told me the tests on the paint were done from a thin, long strip from the left-hand side of the picture?'' She nodded.

''So why couldn't the painter have left that bit from the original sixteenth-century picture? Paint over the central portion and match the background and portrait up. Then you could test to your heart's content, and the tests would have been positive every time.''

''Is that possible?'' Flavia asked Anderson.

He considered the matter. ''Technically, I suppose so. Of course it would be a bit difficult to hide the joins from X-rays, but that might be done if you add a small amount of metallic salt to blur the picture. If I remember, there *was* some blurring, but we were in a hurry, it was a new machine, so everyone assumed it was just a glitch. The real problem with that interpretation is how could any forger be sure the right bit of paintwork was tested?''

''That was no trouble at all. You were *told* to test that bit, weren't you? And who told you, eh?''

''The museum did.''

''You spoke to the museum yourself? They wrote to you?''

''No. Sir Edward told us. He said the museum didn't want any damage . . .''

''Aha.'' Argyll leaned back in his chair once more,

crossed his arms and nodded at Flavia. "There you are. Problem solved. Glad you brought me now?"

Argyll was in an excellent mood as he wandered round shops and libraries the next day, collecting the final bits and pieces he needed. In truth, the previous evening had been a triumph. Not only had he put that insufferable restorer in his place and come up with a nifty idea to prove Byrnes's guilt, he had compounded the achievement by giving Flavia his startling news as they walked back to the hotel she had chosen. He had, he told her, found the picture.

She was impressed. No doubt about it. Of course, she did insist on asking awkward questions like where was it? how had he tracked it down? and things like that. But he managed to sidestep those, saying mysteriously that she'd have to wait and see. That irritated her, but he stuck to his position. After all, he wasn't quite as sure as he'd implied.

So, whistling contently to himself, Argyll flitted in and out of art supply shops, accumulating equipment; and visited the literary-memoir, travel and history sections of the London Library, gathering an impressively filled plastic bag of possessions.

He looked at his watch. Eleven o'clock. Ten minutes to go, a brief visit to Byrnes as he'd arranged by telephone earlier that day, then back to Rome on the two o'clock flight. Perfect. He began to feel he was quite good at this sort of thing.

Inside the Byrnes Gallery he gave his name to the assistant, mentioned he had an appointment, and looked at the pictures while he waited. Five minutes later he was ushered into Byrnes's inner sanctum and shown to a seat. He declined the offer of a cup of coffee.

"Jonathan. I didn't know you were back in London quite so soon. How can I help you?" Byrnes smiled gently over the half-moon glasses he used for reading. Argyll disliked them; they always gave the wearer the opportunity to peer over them at you as if he was looking at some anatomical specimen. Very affected.

"Hardly at all," he said. "I was just passing so thought I'd drop in and say hello. Just to let you know I was around." He smiled inanely. He'd always been told he overdid the foolish look, but it came in decidedly useful now.

"And why are you around? I thought you would be hard at work in Rome by now. Or have you been roped into this Raphael business as well?"

Argyll shook his head with what he hoped was a look of despair. "Yes. Blasted thing. I curse the day I ever thought of it. The police of course suspect me, and you, and just about everyone else. So I'm here trying to work my way into their good books—by finding the real one." He said it lightly, then paused significantly, looking at the plaster ceiling as he did so.

Byrnes's left eyebrow shot up in a creditable look of astonishment. He did it well. Argyll was all admiration. "The real one? What are you talking about?"

"Did the police not tell you?" Argyll said in surprise. "The picture was a fake. A genuine Jean-Luc Morneau, may he rest in peace. It'll be a very great scandal when it all comes out. If it does, that is." They looked at each other with the glimmerings of mutual understanding.

"If?"

"No proof, you see. Except for the picture, which isn't there any more. Manzoni might have known something . . ."

"But someone knifed him, it appears." Byrnes continued. He was now leaning on his desk, having abandoned the air of easy relaxation that had greeted Argyll on his entry. "I see."

"So now," Argyll continued, getting to the point in a circuitous fashion which, on the whole, seemed justified by results, "it's all up to me. I've been asked—told might be a better word—to find the original. Prove the first one was a fake. The police think this will lead to the culprit and to Manzoni's murderer. Simple."

"If you can do it," Byrnes pointed out.

"I already have," he said smugly.

"Where is it?"

Argyll paused once again. That, of course, was the crucial question. He was not meant to tell anyone at all about this. If Flavia ever discovered, ever even suspected, that he'd mentioned so much as a word of it to Byrnes, she'd clap him in jail without a second thought. Even alluding to the painting as a fake was bad enough. On the other hand, Argyll had to think about saving his own neck. Reaching a careful understanding with Byrnes about what was going to happen next seemed the best way of doing it. He took a deep breath and stepped off the edge.

"Siena," he said. "But I've been told not to go into details."

"Of course, of course," Byrnes replied reassuringly. "Quite proper." There was no need to go into details, of course. He could see that by the thoughtful look in Byrnes's eyes. He'd said enough. The rest was up to Byrnes.

The conversation dragged on for a few more minutes, then, pleading urgent business, Argyll got up, made his farewells and left.

CHAPTER

12

Bottando groaned with impatience as the telephone rang once again. He'd had a dreadful morning. His secretary, hand-picked for her ability to persuade callers to go away, was sick. The very defensiveness he complained about in Tommaso's secretary, he treasured in his own.

In her absence, all the calls came straight through to his phone. Bottando had never realised there were so many; he'd managed to achieve virtually nothing all day. At first, he'd attempted just to let the thing ring and pretend to be out, but he couldn't stand the thought of missing something important. Some of the calls, at least, had justified his weak will. He had been busy, although his colleagues would have been a little surprised at his occupation. He was reading through his old cases, a carefully stuck-down folder of newspaper clippings reporting on his past triumphs. The past failures, of course, he left out. Lots of policemen have such things; it works wonders for promotion to be able, casually of course, to hand over accounts of how wonderful, how zealous and how effective you've been. Even if the opinions are only those of journalists, it looks good.

So he had the folder, which he occasionally took down and flicked through for nostalgic reasons. It also boosted his confidence when things were not going so well. Look, the folder told him, don't worry, see what you've achieved before. He was reading through an account of his great triumph in the Milan financial scandal. It reassured him he hadn't lost his touch.

The phone rang once more, and once more he lifted the receiver. ''*Pronto*Bottando,'' he said, all in one weary word.

''General, Ferraro here. I was wondering how the investigation was coming along.''

Bottando repressed a sigh as best he could. The man had become as much a menace as Tommaso. If one was nervous and irritable, the other was showing signs of having a breakdown. It was about the tenth call in two days. No form of vagueness, obstruction or even downright rudeness seemed to put either of them off. They had become obsessed with the Raphael, its authenticity, and demands that the culprit be found. Both of them had a lot at stake. At least this time he had something to report.

''Quite well,'' he said. ''My assistant has just rung to say that she is coming back to Rome this afternoon, bringing that man Argyll in tow. He seems to think he is making progress in the hunt for our missing artefact.''

''Excellent. And where is it?''

''That I can't tell you, I'm afraid. Argyll is a man with an overdeveloped sense of drama. Flavia says he is keeping it as a surprise.''

''Oh. Well, as long as he's right this time. His track record in these matters is not so good, after all,'' the voice on the other end of the line sounded disappointed.

"I appreciate your concern. We are also making some progress in other areas as well. But again, I can't tell you much, if you don't mind. Or rather, I'd prefer not to."

"That's quite all right. I understand. My concern is the Raphael. The criminal side of things is your business, I suppose. But please remember I want to be kept informed."

"How could I possibly forget? Don't worry. I'll come round to the museum later and brief you and the director fully."

It seemed worth trying as a way of deflecting further phone calls, anyway. Tiresome man. At least Tommaso was off the hook: he had an unbreakable alibi for Manzoni's murder. Dinner with the prime minister was fairly convincing. God only knew what they must have talked about. He shuddered at the thought. Ferraro had worked late in the museum and was seen leaving at nine o'clock, which seemed to take him out of the running, as well.

Bottando tried to get through some small routine tasks necessary to keep his superiors off his back, but abandoned the work after an hour. The phone was still going, and his head was starting to ring in sympathy. As was his stomach: he had not had any lunch yet, and it was already half three.

He went over to the bookshelf in his office, removed a thick volume, and walked out of the door. If he was going to read, he would do it in a restaurant, the book propped up on a roll of bread, with a plate of pasta in front of him. Where no more phone calls could disturb his peace for an hour.

●　●　●

They noticed him still sitting at his table in the Piazza del Collegio Romano, as they drove through in the taxi from the airport to the office. It was an eccentric route, but the driver insisted on the deviation, explaining that there was a demonstration at the end of the Corso and the more direct way was jammed solid with a screaming mass of protestors.

Flavia yelled to stop the taxi when she saw him, they paid, and joined him at his table. It was a restaurant he used often, one of the few that was willing to serve up food at such a late hour. In most, the diners had long since been hurried away, the tablecloths shaken off and the doors closed. For the tourists, who made up the majority of eaters at this time of year, there was little else to do for the next few hours but return to their hotels, sit on the edge of a fountain, or return to the foot-blistering work of hammering over the hard cobbles in search of more artistic delights.

Bottando fussed round them and insisted on summoning the waiter for some food. "You must be starving. Some good food will work wonders for you. I remember well what London restaurants are like." He made a good-natured face and beamed at Argyll, who was a little surprised at the amiable reception.

"Mr. Argyll, I'm pleased to meet you at long last. I gather you have made another great discovery. I hope you are right this time."

Argyll shrugged. "I think so. By a process of elimination I'm bound to get there eventually."

"It's the elimination bit that worries me. Must it be taken so literally?"

Argyll laughed a little awkwardly, and Bottando politely suspended the conversation while they ate. "What's that you've got there?" Flavia enquired.

"This? Oh, this is the bible." He read them the spine of his book, "*Who's Who in Art.* A positive treasure trove of useful information. Full of unsuspected details about our friends, colleagues and enemies."

He flicked through some pages. "Take, for example, my dear friend Spello. To look at him you'd never suspect he was once a senior advisor to the Vatican, back in the 1940s, would you? Such an unkempt man. And they're such snappy dressers at the Vatican. He must have been very young. I imagine he considered he had a great career ahead of him, rather than merely a secondary position buried in Etruscan statuary. Or that our beloved minister, a very lumpy dolt of military aspect and no apparent delicacy whatever, has a passion for bonsai gardening? Or that Tommaso's secret desire is to be a painter?"

"It says that?"

"Not exactly. But he told me he plans to retire and paint at his villa, and it says here that he once trained at an art school. In Lyons, no less. So, I conclude that he really wanted to be a painter. Evidence plus logical analysis. That's detection."

"And now I suppose you are going to say he was wonderful at it and made a particular study of Raphael?"

"No, Flavia, no. Would that it were so simple and easy. Alas, poor man, I think he was probably not good at all, and had the sense to look after the paintings of others rather than create his own. Besides, one of the few things we've established is that, if it was a fake, then Morneau was the faker. What we need now is proof of something. Which is a task you seem to have taken upon yourselves. So, tell me. Where is it?"

"Siena," Argyll replied simply. Bottando looked surprised. "Are you sure? How do you come to that conclusion?"

"Because it's the only conclusion to come to. It wasn't in the Clomorton collection, it wasn't in the di Parma collection, and it has disappeared. Therefore . . ."

"Therefore . . . ?" prompted Bottando.

Argyll looked superior. "I don't think I'll tell you. I might still be wrong. Anyway, you have the facts. You can work the rest out yourself. Evidence plus logical analysis, General. That's detection."

"Very funny. Still, as long as I know where you're going, and as long as you find the thing, I suppose the details can wait. Are you going up there?"

"Tomorrow morning. I don't think there's any need to rush up immediately. I think it's quite safe for the time being," Flavia answered, then broke off to order a coffee. It would play havoc with her stomach juices, but she reckoned she needed something to sip.

"*It* may be, but you may not. Some protection might be a good idea when you go," Bottando continued.

Flavia shook her head again. "No. If we go roaring up the autostrada in a fleet of armed police cars there'll be an enormous fuss. Initially it'll be much better to go up quietly and check the thing out. Then you can put as many armed guards around us as you like. The more the better, in fact. But if we go clomping about the place like that, someone will talk. And it'll be all over the newspapers tomorrow morning. Just make sure you keep it to yourself."

"Yes. You are possibly right. What time will you go?"

"First thing tomorrow morning. Before that I need to draw some money, make out an expenses slip to catch the deadline for the next paycheck, have a nice shower, and collect some clothes.''

"Tell me where to find you. Oh, by the way, you might want to look at this.'' He reached into his jacket and pulled out a sheet of paper.

"Telex from Janet. Poor man complains about having to do so much work for us, but don't let that concern you. I'm sure he got someone else to do it for him. He's been tracking down picture-buying. Score, Byrnes three, Morneau six, everybody else, nil.''

"May I?'' said Argyll, reaching over to take it. He unfolded it and read the communication carefully.

"That's it. That must be it.'' He pointed at a line of type after a few moments' perusal. '' 'Portrait of a lady, copy after Fra Bartolommeo.' Three thousand Belgian francs, to Jean-Luc Morneau. Seventy centimetres by a hundred and forty. Right size, more or less, and about the right age. Right style. That would have been perfect. Your colleague didn't send a photograph as well, did he?'' he asked hopefully.

Bottando rummaged around in his pockets once more. "Yes,'' he said, handing over another sheet of paper. "Not very good, I'm afraid. Just a photocopy from the sale catalogue. Pretty good service though, don't you think?''

Argyll was too busy looking at it to reply. He handed it over to Flavia, a satisfied look on his face. She looked disappointed. It was, in truth, unimpressive: very dirty, a three-quarter-length of a large middle-aged woman with a prospective double chin and a few other obvious attractions. Dressed in a dark, full-sleeved dress. Black hair, as far as he could tell through the dirt, and overloaded with vulgar jewellery: a tiara, a vast necklace and a thick, intricate ring.

"Not a great loss if it was used. The portrait of Elisabetta he put on top was much better," she commented.

"True. But look at the window and external scenery in the left background. Very similar to the fake Raphael, and exactly where the tests were taken. I think that's pretty conclusive, myself."

Bottando nodded approvingly. "You've got a good eye," he said. "I noticed the same thing myself, with a photograph of the Raphael to help."

"Which proves Morneau painted it, and that lets Spello off the hook," Flavia added with satisfaction.

"Alas, no. Morneau was also an advisor to the Vatican, back in the 1940s, and he must have known Spello then. That's one example of why these books are so useful."

He got up and brushed breadcrumbs from his lap. "Time to get back to the office. I have to work even if you two don't."

They parted, Flavia and Argyll heading east, while Bottando walked back to the office. He was worried. He hadn't mentioned it to Flavia, not only because Argyll was there, but also because he didn't want to concern her unnecessarily. But he knew he was about to take a huge risk with them. And it concerned him greatly.

Less burdened with cares than Bottando, Flavia and Argyll spent a delightful evening, once the business of washing themselves and their clothes, and other domestic matters had been taken care of. Flavia had put on the washing machine, opened her mail and fussed about the apartment while Argyll had read some of the books he had brought with him.

While he sat with his leg over the arm of her one comfortable seat, he read out extracts from the books he was looking through. This was a change from the plane flight home, when he had read intensely and said scarcely a word. Flavia had noticed that a guide book to the Palazzo Pubblico in Siena had been one of the volumes.

Argyll laughed. "Listen to this. It's a letter from Viscount Perceval about Lady Arabella. A great diarist and observer of eighteenth-century London, that man. She gets more and more remarkable every time I come across her. It wasn't only husband two who had wayward habits. Number one also couldn't keep his hands to himself either. She broke a cello over his head at a royal levee because of it. Then tried to beat him up with her fists. In public. Must have made everybody's evening."

Or later: "Another bit. Clomorton told the Duchess of Albemarle he was in love with a 'dark-haired beauty.' That was a mistake, poor sod. He must have known she was the worst tattletale in London. Perceval says she wrote to Lady Arabella directly. That must be what she was talking about in that letter I read you in London. Think of the reception the poor man would have got. Luckily for him he dropped dead first."

"What are you reading this for? Does it have anything to do with Siena?"

"No. I was just looking to see if there was any mention of Sam Paris, Raphael or whatever. A very arty man, Perceval, and a great observer of the London scene. Nothing happened without him noticing it and jotting it down in his diary. A Raphael on the market, or a scandal about one, would be in here somewhere. There isn't, which makes me more convinced I'm right."

"Are you going to tell me? Or am I to be treated like the General?"

He took her hand and kissed it absentmindedly, let-

ting go when he realised what he'd done. "Silly. Of
course not. After dinner you will hear all."

They had ended up digesting their evening meal by
walking blissfully around the city. Flavia pointed out to
Argyll her favourite buildings and spots; they had wandered around the old ghetto, looking affectionately at the
run-down buildings, Imperial fragments and tranquil,
beautiful piazzas that suddenly appear as you turn
unpromising-looking corners. Argyll gave an impromptu
disquisition on the beauties of the Farnese Palace. Flavia
wasn't entirely persuaded, but liked his sense of conviction. She had responded by dredging through the memories of her university days and identifying all the large
medallions on the Palazzo Spada a little down the road.

"I can do that too," Argyll said. "Come with me."
He grabbed her hand and led her to the other side of the
Piazza Farnese, down the via Giulia and then left down
a side street. He pointed to an emblem above one of the
large wooden gates that shut prying eyes from the courtyard beyond. "There. Two pelicans intertwined, surmounted by a crown and the symbol of a castle. Whose
is it?"

Flavia chewed her lip for a moment. "Don't know.
Whose?"

"That's the di Parma symbol. This was their Roman
palace."

She grinned. "So this is where it all started. I knew
the palace was around here somewhere, but I never got
around to looking. What's in there now?"

"Just apartments, I imagine. It looks very tatty. The
point is, however, that Mantini lived there, which ex-
plains why he was brought in for this job in the first
place." Argyll pointed to a door a few yards up on the
other side of the street.

"As for the picture," he went on, "The di Parmas didn't have it, nor the Clomortons, nor the dealer Sam Paris. Mantini was the only man involved who was left. Lots of motive as he was always hard up. Or maybe love of the painting was more important and he didn't want it to leave Italy and be bought by a clod like Clomorton. So he paints over the Raphael, makes a copy of the same picture which he gives to the dealer, and keeps the real thing himself.

"He couldn't uncover it either, because he lived almost next door to the di Parmas, who might have got upset. But there'd be no rush if he wanted the picture for itself, not the money it could bring. So it could sit there and wait until he retired back to his home town, or something.

"But he never made it to retirement. He has a seizure and dies in 1727, at the age of fifty-two. Perfect health, just drops dead one afternoon in the street. No time, you see, for deathbed confessions or secret instructions about his picture. His daughter inherits his small fortune and remaining pictures. She returns to her father's native *paese*, where she marries a silversmith."

"Siena."

"Quite right. And he, because silversmiths were highly thought of, gets on the town council and dies, wealthy and greatly respected, in 1782. And he leaves to the city a couple of pictures. One portrait of himself, naturally, and the other a memento of that great Sienese painter, his own father-in-law, the superlative Carlo Mantini."

"Very good. But how do you know it's the right one?"

"Because it must be. Process of elimination. It's a ruin, which fits in with the evidence available, and it's the only picture which could possibly have concealed the Raphael.''

This was the weak spot in an otherwise convincing argument, the area his supervisor would have pounced on, had he been there to listen. But he wasn't, and Flavia said nothing, so he hurried on. ''I did about a month's work in a day and a half. Quite a lot of shortcuts, I admit. But if no one else has it, and they appear not to, it's the only other possibility. I hope you're proud of me.''

Flavia patted him on the back. ''Well done. Now all we have to do is go there and see if you're right. Come on. Let's go home.''

CHAPTER

13

Flavia and Argyll set out for Siena at eight sharp the next morning, Argyll in the passenger seat, Flavia driving her old but well-maintained Alfa Spider like a banshee. In a brief moment of feminine submissiveness she had suggested that Argyll might drive. In a long-standing tradition of English cowardice, he had declined. Nothing, he declared as they forced their way onto the main northern artery, would ever get him to drive in Rome. Not after the last time.

It was a wise decision. Flavia drove with knowledge, skill and determination; Argyll would have driven with his eyes shut. The maniacal early morning traffic died away to something more human fairly quickly, and they made rapid progress north.

It's a long, five-hour voyage to Siena, even if you drive—as Flavia did—far too fast on the motorway. It's also a very beautiful trip. The autostrada, one of the best in the country and one of the longest in Europe, starts outside Reggio di Calabria at the very tip of the south-western peninsula. It curls through the parched hills of the south to Naples, then turns up through the poor countryside of Calabria and Latium to Rome. Then it heads for Florence and swings east, through a series of giant tunnels and dizzying climbs, over the Apennines to Bologna. Here it splits, one arm reaching out to Venice, the other travelling on to Milan.

Even on the relatively small segment between Rome and Siena, it takes the traveller within easy reach of some of the most wonderful places in the world: Orvieto, Montefiascone, Pienza and Montepulciano; the Umbrian hill-towns of Assisi, Perugia, Todi, Gubbio. The stepped hills of vines and lowland pastures of goats and sheep mix perfectly with the rivers, the steep drops, and the dozens of often largely ignored medieval fortress-towns, perched on top of their protective hills as if the Medicis still reigned supreme.

It was wonderful. Argyll had travelled around Italy for years, had seen nearly all the major sights several times over, but never tired of seeing them all again. For a brief interlude, he forgot his woes, enjoyed the scenery and tried to pay no attention to his companion's driving.

Five hours almost to the minute later, they swung off the motorway, paid the fee at the toll and headed down the hilly road through Rapolano to Siena, having spent their journey in a mood of cheerful contentment and buoyant optimism. Contentment on Argyll's part, optimism on Flavia's. Then Argyll said: ''How are we going to go about this little expedition? After all, we can hardly wander into the palazzo, take the picture off the wall and attack it with a knife. Curators don't like that. It upsets them.''

''Don't worry. I thought about it last night. We'll just go and make sure it's still there, then make an official visit tomorrow.''

They were a little delayed getting to their hotel. Siena is a town where the streets have changed not at all since the thirteenth century, and to cope with modern traffic flows, the authorities have instituted one of the most ferociously complex one-way systems ever devised. A single mistake anywhere, and you are flung off in entirely the wrong direction without the slightest chance of doing anything about it. They had driven—quite illegally as the area is closed to traffic—past the cathedral twice before Flavia reversed the wrong way down a narrow one-way street and found the road she wanted at the end.

She had chosen a comfortable, elegant and expensive hotel to serve as their temporary headquarters. It also served a remarkable lunch, which Argyll suspected might have weighed more heavily in its favour. They had a preliminary drink, and Argyll leaned back in his chair to gaze at the Tuscan hills out of the window. ''Wonderful,'' he said. ''The Italian police really do things in style.''

Flavia shrugged. ''The very last thing the General said to me was that we were to take care of ourselves.''

''I don't think this is quite what he had in mind.''

She spread her hands out wide in a very Italian gesture. ''Who can tell? Find this picture and no one will care. Besides, I've always wanted to stay in this place. And my expenses in London were derisory. This will make up for it a little. I've booked us in over the weekend. We can sort the picture out, then have a couple of days relaxing. Do you mind?''

''Am I complaining? This time last month I was sitting in a sandwich shop in London eating a cheese and pickle roll. This arrangement seems slightly preferable, whatever the dire consequences of failure.''

"Are you afraid of that?"

"Of failing or the consequences? Yes and no. I think you will have your proof by tomorrow, whatever happens. Do you carry a gun, by the way?"

Flavia frowned at the apparent *non sequitur*, trying to work out the mental leaps that took her companion from one subject to another. "No," she said, giving up the effort. "I'm not in the police, remember. Just a civilian. Why do you ask?"

He shook his head and smiled at her reassuringly. "No reason. Just wondering. This painting has been unlucky."

Getting back to a more comfortable topic, Flavia announced that they had more than enough time for lunch, and that, speaking personally, she needed some. Then they examined the local church, slowly and in a relaxing fashion, and walked, equally gently, into the centre. Striding up the hill was a little tiring, Argyll not having had much in the way of exercise for months, and his enjoyment of the stroll was spoiled by his trying to seem not too much out of breath. Flavia seemed not at all affected by the incline.

They reached the Campo at four, after a brief pause while Flavia did some shopping. How she could think of shopping at a time like this was beyond him, but he put it all down to cultural relativism. Some people do odd things to work off tension, and despite their relaxing start, he could tell that both of them were starting to feel just a little nervous.

The square they were heading for is a bizarre shape, like the outline of a cup, which runs downhill from the curved portion to a flat plane at the end. The straight side is almost entirely taken up by the palace; the centre of administration back in the days when Siena was a major city-state whose power, briefly, rivalled that of Florence itself.

The days of greatness had long since gone, however. A couple of unfortunate sixteenth-century decisions concerning the choice of enemies, a rapid war, and Siena settled into the role of minor provincial backwater. Since the seventeenth century, when some wise burgher had the bright idea of inventing the Palio—the annual horse race round the Campo—it had survived mainly on tourist income.

This year's contingent was beginning to flow in nicely. All the numerous cafés along the curved sides at the top of the Campo had laid out their chairs, tables and umbrellas, and waiters were flitting to and fro, delivering glasses of pastis, coffees, bottles of mineral water and the inevitable Coca-Colas. Little posses of tourists stood around gaping at the sight, or heading for the entrance to the palace.

There was not a lot of time to admire the view. Flavia led Argyll rapidly to the palazzo entrance, paid the two thousand five hundred lire entrance fee and wasted a few minutes complaining to the ticket seller about the disgraceful expense. This preliminary over, they crossed the courtyard and set about being sightseers. They had timed it quite well. Most Italian museums stop admitting new visitors at about twenty-five minutes before closing time; they had bought their tickets with five minutes to spare.

In the lower hall, where the great frescos by Sodoma are displayed, they split up, Flavia to examine the doors and windows, Argyll to locate the Mantini. An unpleasant shock awaited him when he arrived in the upper saloon. According to the picture in his guide book, 1975 edition, the picture should have been in a dark corner at the back, above a glass case of miscellaneous Renaissance silverware and just to the left of a vast nineteenth-century painting of Vittorio Emanuele, unifier of Italy, striking a heroic pose on a horse.

It wasn't. Instead, there was a group of early twentieth-century town councillors, done in the degenerate style of portraiture that proved that Italy was long since past its best in the picture department. Argyll's heart sank. After his enormous confidence that his plan would go off smoothly, he was now going to have to explain himself. This would be a little hard for Flavia to swallow. He could almost see the stern look of disapproval on her face, and her opinion of him dwindling into nothing as he told her.

He walked over to the guardian of the room, took out his guide book and jabbed his finger at the photograph. "You see this picture? Where is it? I've come all the way from England just to see it, and it's not there."

The guardian looked at him pityingly. "You came from England to see *that*? Listen: take my advice. Go downstairs to the *Mappamondo*. It's much better, one of the finest things in all Siena."

"I know that," Argyll retorted testily, feeling his aesthetic integrity was being impugned, "But I want to see this. Where has it gone to?"

The guard shrugged. "How should I know? I've only been working here a few weeks. I only know what's in here. Go next door and ask Enrico."

He did as he was told and found Enrico, a man of at least sixty, sitting lifelessly on a wooden chair by the door, staring without any sort of interest at the tourists coming and going. He did not look like a man who enjoyed his work overmuch. Argyll explained that Giulio had sent him, and did he know where this was?

Enrico looked at the picture. "Oh. That. Yes, that

went years ago. The curator reckoned it was cluttering up the room. They took it down when the room was restored. He didn't want anything before 1850 in there.''

Argyll was annoyed. ''They took this down and left that monstrosity of Vittorio Emanuele up? That's a disgrace.''

''That's different. It's after 1850. Besides, it's so big it won't go anywhere else.'' The guard shrugged again. The little fads of curators was evidently not a subject that enlivened him.

''Where's it now, then?''

The guard looked at the picture again and frowned. ''Tower room,'' he said. ''Don't know why everyone's so interested in that, all of a sudden. No one's shown the slightest concern about it for years. Listen, why don't you go downstairs and look at the *Mappamondo*. It's one of the finest . . .''

''Everyone? What do you mean? Someone else asked about it? When?'' Argyll interrupted the sales pitch in panic.

''About an hour ago. Man came in here and asked the same question as you did. Sent him up to the tower room, too.''

''Who was he?''

''You think I'm on first name terms with every visitor who comes here? How should I know?'' The guard turned to bellow at some Germans on the other side of the room, and moved away. They weren't doing anything wrong, but Italian museum guards don't seem to like Germans overmuch. Besides, it ended a conversation he clearly found tedious.

Jesus, why the hell didn't he tell me that in the first place, Argyll thought as he ran desperately up the two flights of twisting stone stairs to the tower room. It was a long way up, and the last room *en route* to the great Campanile that dominates both the Campo and all of Siena. He arrived breathless, in a small bare room, crowded with faded and dirty prints and a jumble of pictures. There was a small table of inlaid wood in the centre. It was evidently where the museum stored the pictures it thought no one wanted to see. Most people probably walked straight through on their way to the platform at the top, three hundred feet above the square below.

His anxieties faded a little. It was still there, at least. He had not been outmaneuvered yet. There, in one corner, surrounded by old maps of Siena in glass frames, was an undoubted, genuine piece of the *oeuvre* of Carlo Mantini. It was a landscape, which was a little awkward. Typical stuff: a stream in the middle background, and a few blobs of paint signifying peasants tending sheep or goats. Speaking personally, he wouldn't have called it a landscape with ruins. But, a small hill on the right had a ruined castle on it, which revived his flagging confidence a little. The sky was clear and, had it not been so dirty, would have been a light blue. All of Mantini's skies were light blue. He couldn't paint them any other way.

Argyll stared at it with adoration. There it was. What a beautiful piece. What a gem. What a masterwork. He squinted at it. Looked a little smaller than it should, but that might be the effect of the frame. A pity it would have to be a touch damaged, but he was sure Mantini wouldn't mind if he knew what it would do for his only biographer's career. And it was going to be famous, if all went well.

He was still staring when a deafening alarm went off. "Christ, please, not a fire," was his initial reaction. Then it occurred to him it must be the bell to warn visitors that the museum was closing. He ran down the stairs again, a much easier task, and went searching for Flavia. She was standing in the main council room.

"Where have you been? I've been standing here for hours."

"Nonsense. We only arrived twenty minutes ago. I was looking for the picture. They moved it upstairs. Listen, he's here. He followed us. The guard told me someone was asking about the picture. What do we do now?"

She looked very alarmed at his urgent tone. "Who's here?"

"Byrnes."

"The picture's not been touched?" He shook his head. "Good." She walked around in little circles and rubbed her chin thoughtfully. "We've no choice," she said decisively after a few moments. "We'll have to go ahead now. It's too risky to go outside and wait until tomorrow. Come on."

She headed off. "Where are you going?" he called after her.

"Just to the toilet. Don't worry."

Argyll's leg was long since dead of any sensation. He moved awkwardly, trying to get comfortable. "Was this the best you could think of?" he asked peevishly.

Flavia was sitting on his knee. "Keep quiet. I think it's perfect. They've inspected the place already. They won't come again. Now we just have to sit tight for another three hours or so."

"Three hours? We've been here for days already. It's all right for you. You've got my warm comfortable knee to sit on. I'm the one wedged into this damned lavatory seat. And you might have said, then I could've eaten more lunch. I'm starving.''

"Stop complaining. You were all secretive so why couldn't I be? Besides, I told you to eat up. Here, I bought this in the shop.''

She reached down by the side of the toilet bowl, picked up her handbag and fished out a bar of chocolate.

"Why are you so certain the alarms won't go off? We're going to be very unpopular if we're arrested. Wouldn't it have been easier to flash your ID card and ask to examine it?''

"And have everybody know within hours? You know as well as I do that people in the art world are incapable of keeping their mouths shut. Besides, if we wait, it might not be here tomorrow. Anyway, we won't be caught. The guards will only be round once more; I checked the rota in the entrance. And the alarms are only on the entrances and exits. Obviously they think that any robber will try and get away. We won't. We just examine the picture, wait until morning, go out with the first visitors, phone Bottando, and finish. There won't be anything missing, so no one will notice.''

"We've got to spend all night here?'' he hissed in horror. "In a women's toilet? Why not the men's, at least?''

"Yuck. What a dreadful idea. Dirty beasts, men.''

Argyll ate his chocolate morosely. "Couldn't we just forget the Mantini?'' he asked hopefully, trying to get his plan back on course. "After all, with Byrnes here, that's enough. I think we should just nip off to the hotel, call Bottando, have Byrnes arrested and come back in the morning.'' He finished the chocolate and remembered he'd omitted to offer her any.

"What makes you think it's Byrnes? The guard didn't describe him or anything like that."

"Well," said Argyll dubiously. "It must be, mustn't it? I mean, it stands to reason . . ."

"Not at all. All we know is that someone asked about that picture. Byrnes is the last person it could be. There's no way he could have found out where we are."

Argyll shifted uncomfortably on the toilet seat as she spoke. She took a hard look at him, an uneasy feeling coming over her.

"Jonathan? What have you done, damn you?"

"It's just that I thought, that, well . . . I told him, that's all."

Flavia didn't reply, but leant her forehead against the cool white tiles of the cubicle. "What did you do that for?" she asked faintly when she'd recovered herself.

"It seemed a good idea," he explained feebly. "You see, even if we found the picture, it wouldn't get us any further in finding who was responsible. So I thought, if I told Byrnes, he'd have to do something about it. He'd come trotting out to Siena, and the police could arrest him as he entered the city."

"And you didn't think it worth mentioning this before? Perhaps it just slipped your memory? One of those little details, of no significance, that you just forgot about? You great dolt."

"Of course I didn't forget," he protested, his voice rising in pitch as he realised that his masterstroke wasn't getting the appreciation it deserved.

"Don't squeak at me like that."

"Well, why not? I'm getting tired of this," he continued—might as well let off steam now—"Everything I've done so far you've taken as evidence of my guilt. You're rude, objectionable and too clever for your own good. Obviously I couldn't tell you what I planned. You would have locked me up. And if we're now in a mess, it's just as much your fault as mine. If you hadn't known best all the time, and maybe trusted me a little more, I would have been more forthcoming. Besides which . . .''

"Oh, no. Don't say that. I hate it when you say that. Besides what?''

Argyll positively squirmed, as much as any man can when sandwiched between a lavatory seat and a semi-official member of the Italian police. He shouldn't have said it. His burst of wounded indignation had been very impressively delivered, and now he'd gone and spoiled the effect.

"Besides which,'' he went on reluctantly, "I'm not entirely convinced I've got the right picture. I think I have,'' he hurried on before she could say anything, "but I did say I had to cut a few corners.''

"God preserve me,'' Flavia said quietly, to no one in particular. "We're up here, possibly on a fool's errand. Bottando is fast asleep in Rome and knows nothing about it. You appear to have successfully lured a murderer here without bothering to get any protection at all either for us or the picture. Well done. A fine achievement.''

"I'll protect you,'' Argyll said gallantly, hoping to make some form of amends.

"Gee. Thanks, mister. That makes me feel a lot better.'' She would have continued in this vein, but felt it hardly worth wasting her breath.

Argyll had lapsed into a sullen, morose silence and ate his way steadily through the contents of Flavia's handbag. She had stocked it with enough food to withstand a siege. He desperately craved a cigarette.

Flavia had also lost her conversational flair. Clearly little could be done to repair their once promising relationship until that picture had been looked at. Then, perhaps, all would be forgotten and forgiven. He still thought it was a good plan, and was a little hurt that she'd reacted so badly. Maybe she was jealous of him for thinking it up?

When she finally decided that it was safe and time to go, it took about ten minutes to restore life to his leg. When he stood up for the first time, it collapsed under him and he fell, knocking over a large bucket with a toilet brush in it. It rattled over the floor, and the noise echoed around the room. They watched as it rolled slowly to a halt in the corner. "Be quiet, for God's sake," Flavia yelled in fright.

"You're making as much noise as I am. At least I'm not shouting my head off," he hissed back.

"I don't want us to get caught now. It would be very embarrassing."

He smiled in a half-way attempt to be conciliatory. "I'm sorry. I'm not used to this sort of escapade. It's not included in the introductory course for art history graduates."

She glared at him, still not ready to forgive. "Just keep quiet, all right? Now, let's get going."

She poked her head into the corridor, then disappeared through the door, gesturing for him to follow. They walked down to the main saloon again, and tiptoed, quietly and cautiously, over to the door that led to the staircase. It opened. No alarms. That at least was one worrying part over.

Once on the top floor, she flicked on a small torch, another purchase from the shop. "Now tell me I don't think of everything," she murmured to him as they walked. She went lightly and without a sound. Argyll, wearing his usual heavy, metal-tipped brogues, clattered after, despite all attempts to keep quiet. Had she mentioned she was proposing amateur cat burglary, he would have dressed appropriately.

The room was as he had left it six hours earlier. Flavia went over, quietly closed the heavy wooden shutters over the windows, and flipped the metal fastener to keep them secure. Then she closed the door, and pushed down the light switch.

"There. I don't see why we shouldn't be able to see what we're doing for a bit. No one will be along here for at least an hour. How long will this take you?"

"Not long at all," he replied as they gently took the picture off the hook that kept it on the wall and blew off the thin coat of dust all over it. "I'll have to be careful, but no more than five minutes, I reckon."

He had taken a book on the restoration and cleaning of pictures out of the library and had read the subject up on the plane flight. In principle it was simple. You just needed some form of solvent and a cloth. Then you brushed away until the right amount of dirt or paint was removed.

He pulled the tools he had bought in the art supply shop in London out of his pocket. A very small but very sharp knife, a large bundle of cotton wool and a small aerosol. "Combination of acid and alcohol. The man in the shop said it's the best thing you can buy." He grinned at her. "I think of everything, you see." No response.

As is often the case, practice turned out to be more complex than principle suggested. Argyll wanted to be careful not to do too much damage to the painting; after all, he was no restorer and had only the vaguest idea of what he was doing. So he concentrated on a very small amount of canvas in the bottom-left corner. But this meant he could only spray a small squirt from the aerosol at any time, in case it spread out too far.

So he settled down to squirt and rub, squirt and rub, only removing a tiny amount of dirt, varnish and paint at a time. It was hard work that required a lot of concentration. Every time he swabbed the cotton wool over the canvas, he hoped to see the tell-tale signs that indicated a masterpiece underneath.

"How's it going? You've been at it for nearly twenty minutes now." She spoke quietly but urgently, leaning against a table a few feet away to give him light. She rubbed her arms. "It's freezing in here."

He rubbed for another five minutes, the pile of dirty cotton-wool balls getting ever bigger. Then, as he gently slid a new ball across the paintwork, he stopped, and stared intently, scarcely believing his eyes.

"What is it? Have you found it?" She spoke excitedly, leaning forward for a better view.

"Paint," he said. "Green paint underneath . . . Flavia, put that light back on. What are you doing?"

Flavia didn't hear the rest of the sentence. The room was plunged into darkness. If both of them hadn't been concentrating so hard on the picture, they might have noticed the movement of the door opening. But they didn't, and the first time Flavia realised something was wrong was when she was hit on the side of the head with a thick length of wood. She fell on the floor, silent, with blood flowing swiftly from a broad cut in her scalp.

Argyll looked up at the sound, saw her collapse, and saw a shadowy figure advancing towards him. "Oh my God . . ." he began, but had no time to finish the remark. He had never been kicked in the stomach before, certainly not that hard, and had never imagined that anything could hurt so much.

Badly winded, he doubled up in agony, clutching at his stomach as though that might lessen the torment. He was pushed away from the picture and fell heavily on the floor. He liked, later, to think that he was moaning softly. In truth, his groans were probably a good deal louder. He didn't notice; his stomach fully occupied his consciousness, but he did reach out and touch Flavia, afraid of what he might discover.

"Don't you dare die on me. Keep going or I'll kill you," he whispered in her ear. He felt for her pulse, and couldn't find it. But he'd never been able to find his own either. He reached for her head and brushed her hair lightly, and felt the soft breath coming from her mouth and nose. She was still alive. But she wouldn't be for long unless he got his act together here. Nor would he, for that matter. "Looks like neither of us thought of everything," he said to her sadly.

Try as he might, he couldn't move. The pain was too intense. All he could do was watch as the dark outline of the man who had given him such misery took a small, and evidently very sharp, knife and cut the painting, swiftly and without fuss, out of the back of the frame. At least, he assumed that was what was going on; all he could see was the occasional glint of metal. He didn't like the look of that knife, which was evidently a versatile instrument which could be put to many uses. He wheezed on the floor as the man rolled up the canvas, put it in a cardboard tube, and sealed it. Very methodical, in no rush at all.

That done, he picked up his knife again. "Oh, Lord," thought Argyll. "Here we go." He exploded from his sitting position and cannoned into the man's chest,

knocking him off balance by sheer fluke. It used up all
the reserves of energy and will-power he had. More, in
fact. Men with knives can bring out the best in you.

But it was immediately obvious that his best wasn't
enough. His antagonist slipped over, but Argyll simply
didn't have the resources to do what was plainly required; that is, leap decisively up and down on his head
with his heavy, metal-tipped shoes. Instead, he just stood
there, still half hunched over with pain as his opponent
rolled over, recovered his knife and began coming towards him again.

There was only one course left, and he took it. In the
gloom, he could dimly make out that the infernal creature was between him and the door leading to the staircase down. So Argyll dashed through the other one and
began to climb up. It was the best he could do to fulfil
his promise to Flavia to protect her, even though she'd
plainly been dismissive of his offer. With luck her assailant would follow him, giving Flavia a chance to regain consciousness and raise the alarm.

I *hope* he comes after me, anyway, he thought as he
wheezed and puffed his way up the stairs. But what if
he does something to Flavia first? Maybe I should have
stayed down there.

It was a noble thought, and the fact that it was plainly
impractical didn't make him feel less awful. He would
have been killed and Flavia would have followed soon
after. Which may yet be the case anyway, Argyll reflected.

He ran blindly up the stairs in the pitch dark, half-
tripping, missing steps, but going as fast as he could. It
got harder and harder. Earlier in the afternoon even the
climb up the hill had been enough to wind him; the way
he felt now, the man behind wasn't even going to have

to bother sticking in a knife. It was what came of sitting in libraries when he should have been out jogging away and lifting weights. If he survived this, Argyll promised himself, he'd buy a rowing machine. The next time some tall, dark forger tried to knife him in a Sienese tower in the middle of the night, he'd be prepared for it. Up the stairs like the wind, he'd go.

His thoughts were getting confused from the combination of fright, pain and cramps. At one stage he stopped climbing. Doing so scared him to death, but he simply couldn't go on. He listened over the whistling, rasping sound of his breath; the soft pad of footsteps was just audible. He evidently had a lead, and his pursuer didn't seem to be hurrying. But then, why should he?—Argyll thought with a flash of despair—it's not as if I can get away. Perhaps he's as out of condition as I am?

The thought of his pursuer keeling over with a heart attack halfway up the stairs cheered him momentarily, but dissipated as he realised it was hardly likely. Whoever it was, the man with the hefty kick was not Sir Edward Byrnes—an elderly gent who, whatever the circumstances, would hardly go around kicking people in the stomach. He could just about see Byrnes knifing someone, but this sort of crawling around with wooden clubs and boots and knives didn't really seem the man's style.

Argyll began climbing the stairs again. He was going slowly, but making progress. The apparent inevitability of death doesn't mean that you will do nothing to postpone it for as long as possible. He doggedly kept on going to the top. Had circumstances been different, he could have stared at the view from the parapet for a very long time: bent double over the wall, choking as he dragged air into his much abused and protesting lungs, he saw the whole of Siena laid out like something out of a fairytale. A crescent moon illuminated the Campo and the jumble of medieval buildings around it. It lit up the black and white marble stripes of the cathedral tower. Twinkling lights from dozens of windows showed where the town's inhabitants were still up and about, watching the television, drinking wine, talking with friends. A light, warm and refreshing breeze. Beautiful, safe and normal.

But Argyll was in no mood to ponder over either the scenery or his unfortunate situation. I could shout, scream bloody murder from the rooftops, he thought. But he didn't. No one would work out where it was coming from in time. And anyway, in the state he was in at the moment, he doubted that he could raise much more than a faint squeak.

He turned round at the creak of the door. The man was standing, quietly and still in the doorway, evidently evaluating how best to go about things. When Argyll had seen Flavia collapsing in a bloody heap, he had initially been furious, then desperation had sent him flying up the stairs. Now all these impulses had gone, and he was just frightened.

Knife me, push me over, or both, Argyll thought. Spoiled for choice. Probably push me over, he decided. More ambiguous.

An arm went round his neck, pushing him back so his head rested on the parapet wall. He saw the flash of the knife in the moonlight. He was choking. He grabbed the wrist below the knife, not that it made any evident difference. The planned resistance was useless; the unplanned response was much more effective: reflex action brought his knee up between the other's legs so fast and so sharply that the impact hurt it. To Argyll's faint astonishment, the grip relaxed as his attacker clutched at the offended area and let out a deep, and very satisfying yelp of pain.

But the respite was only brief. His assailant had kept hold of the knife and was still much too close. Argyll clenched his fist and hit him. He'd never hit anyone before, having led a quiet and largely withdrawn childhood in a world which disapproved of shows of temper among the young. He should have got into more fights when he was small. It was odd how small his fists felt, and how much his knuckles hurt when he punched the man in the general area of the chin. He made a few more desultory taps, then stopped. He could do no more and it didn't seem to be much use in the long run anyway. His assailant, at least, also seemed less than happy after his brief contact with Argyll's knee. They both paused, breathing heavily and looking at each other, eyes less than a foot apart. In the dim light, Argyll saw his face clearly for the first time, and was briefly shocked into inactivity.

Then the knife hand swung back for the last time, and Argyll reached into his pocket for his last weapon. A pity he hadn't thought of it before. He aimed the aerosol, and pressed the button.

There was a scream of agony, the knife clattered to the stone flagging. Argyll was appalled. He hadn't even considered what he'd been doing, just grabbed the one faint chance the moment it occurred to him. He backed away, and stood, dumbly, watching the torment he'd just caused.

One hand still trying to rub the acid out of his eyes, Argyll's assailant was scrabbling in the pocket of a heavy blue jacket.

Oh, Christ, not a gun as well, Argyll thought. This man's a walking bloody arsenal. It was no good even thinking of another round of fighting to try and disarm him. There was no strength left for that. With the certainty that only desperation can provide, Argyll ran forward once more and pushed with every drop of muscle-power and will-power he had left.

Without a scream, a cry, or any noise at all, Antonio Ferraro, deputy director of the Italian National Museum, disappeared over the edge and hurtled to the ground, three hundred feet below.

CHAPTER

14

Argyll sat there for twenty minutes, maybe more. He was too exhausted and in too much pain to move. The adrenalin washed out of his system, leaving a barely functioning wreck behind it. It was very quiet, now. His back resting against the parapet wall, he looked upwards, beyond the tall bell tower that rose from the middle of the Campanile, and stared at the stars. It wasn't really appropriate but he was far too washed out to do anything else. Flavia was, at the least, badly injured and might well be lying down there with her throat cut. He had, it seemed, just killed someone who would, knowing his current run of luck, turn out to be entirely innocent of any wrongdoing. All for that stupid, useless picture. The thought made him feel ill. It would have been better if he'd never heard of bloody Mantini.

Great. A good evening. Why can't you do something right for once? he asked himself bitterly. That's what comes of trying to be so clever. It'll take a lot of explaining this time. And the police will be all over the place soon.

They were evidently all over the place already. He heard sirens as cars drove into the Campo; shouted orders. Footsteps coming up the stairs. Oh well, he thought listlessly, here we go.

What happened next didn't really concern him much; he still ached and that seemed more important. He didn't even take his eyes off the sky when a couple of people came through the door and walked over to him.

A flashlight shone in his face, blinding him. He shut his eyes, and heard General Bottando say: "It's Argyll. He's still alive."

The rest of the night passed in a blur. Once Argyll realised he wasn't going to be instantly carted off to the local lockup, he had thrown a fit, refusing to let a doctor anywhere near him until he was told about Flavia. They said she was all right, but he refused to believe them.

Eventually, two policemen had to carry him down so he could see for himself. It was difficult, and with much cursing, they tried to help him down the steps without letting him fall. As far as Argyll was concerned, it was well worth it. Flavia was sitting against the wall, wrapped in a blanket, her head covered with a large bandage. A small spot of red was just visible around her left temple. She was conscious, complaining of a headache, and asking for some food. There was clearly not much wrong with her. Argyll was so pleased, so relieved and so exhausted, all he could do was pat her hand and look at her. Bottando stood over them with his arms crossed and looked disapproving.

"General, what about the picture, is it safe?" Flavia asked drowsily. She had been given a sleeping draught which was nearly taking effect.

He nodded. "Yup," he said. "Cut out of its frame

and damaged, but still basically in one piece. It'll be all right after a bit of work.''

This contented her, and she fell asleep. It was the moment for Argyll to say something, but he couldn't be bothered. It could all wait until tomorrow.

''Young man, she's fast asleep. If you would let go of her hand and stop staring like a lovesick cow, perhaps we could bandage up that arm of yours.''

Argyll hadn't even noticed, but he must have scraped his arm on the coarse, abrasive stone as he ran up the stairs. Now he did notice it and it hurt abominably. He stuck it out, and the doctor began washing and dressing it.

''What happened up there, anyway? How did he fall off?'' Bottando asked.

''I pushed him. But it really wasn't my fault.''

''Yes, yes, we know all that,'' Bottando said impatiently. ''But why did you push him?''

''He attacked Flavia and came after me. He was pulling a gun. It was the only thing I could think of.''

''I see. And he just stood there and let you give him a shove?'' Argyll didn't like the tone of that. Didn't seem entirely sympathetic.

''I doubt that he saw me coming.'' Argyll pulled the little aerosol tube out of his pocket. ''I sprayed this in his face while we were fighting. It's a cleaning solution for paintings.''

''Ah. That'll probably explain it. Needed to clean out his eyes a lot, I imagine. I sympathise with your caution, but he wasn't pulling a gun,'' Bottando looked at him with a weak smile. ''He didn't have one. I'm afraid you have pushed him off a three-hundred-foot tower because he was reaching for a handkerchief.''

• • •

The news upset him considerably, but not for long. He was also given a sleeping shot, and drifted off thinking how wonderful Flavia was. Which was generous, he thought, considering how badly she'd treated him. Like everyone else. A cruel and unjust world, when he was only trying to help.

Both of them slept deeply and soundly, even though much of the time was spent in the back of two police cars whistling back down the autostrada to Rome. They didn't even wake when they were lifted bodily from the cars and carried like sacks of turnips up the stairs to Flavia's flat.

Bottando supervised the operation, clucking over them with concern. As Flavia had only one bed, he wondered briefly where to deposit Argyll. But there was nothing for it: he conquered his prejudices and had the Englishman laid elegantly by her side, hoping she would understand it was an emergency measure and wouldn't protest too much the next day. That accomplished, he gave instructions to the policeman who was settling into Flavia's armchair that he was to remain until they woke, then bring them to the office as quickly as possible.

Flavia woke first, coming out of a drugged sleep so slowly she wasn't even aware of doing so. Argyll was curled up beside her, his hand holding on to her arm. She stroked his hair absentmindedly, wondering where she'd put the aspirin.

Then she remembered, began to resent his presence, stopped the display of affection and poked him violently on the arm. "What are you doing here?" she asked.

"Jesus. Be careful. That's tender." He woke up fast, shut his eyes again, then opened them and peered around. "This is your bed, isn't it?"

"Yes. I'll get some coffee. Then we can work out

why you're in it." Flavia crawled out of bed and headed out the door to the kitchen. She came back in immediately and grabbed her dressing gown. "There's a policeman out there," she observed. She nodded good morning to him on her second entrance and waved him into silence when he began to explain his presence. "Not yet. Can't take it."

She leaned heavily on the kitchen counter while she was waiting for the espresso pot to do its stuff. Her picture of the previous night's events was hazy, but enough to realise it had been a mixed achievement. Argyll had done his bit and found the picture, which went some way to repairing the damage caused by his rather bizarre behaviour in London. Then he had gone and spoiled it by pushing someone off the parapet. She should be grateful, she supposed, but still wished he hadn't.

When Argyll emerged from the bedroom, he was clearly in no more rosy a mood. His arm hurt, his stomach hurt, his lungs hurt, his legs hurt. He was also brooding over his performance. All that risk, that appalling danger, and for what? She could easily be lying in a little plastic bag with a label round her toe. So could he, for that matter. And not even a Raphael, fine painter though he was, was worth that. Too fast. Rush, rush, rush. That had always been his great trouble. Not enough attention to detail.

So they sat in companionable misery until the policeman, a veritable youth who had recently joined the force and who wasn't sure how to proceed in these circumstances, interrupted and, following orders, tried to escort them to the office. Flavia made short work of him, and he departed on his own, carrying a message that they'd be along in an hour.

They spent it having showers, eating breakfast, discussing the events of the night before and staring out of the window. If there had been any chance of Flavia persuading herself into a good humour, it evaporated slowly. Eventually she stood up, tipped the dirty dishes into the sink and turned to Argyll.

"Can't delay it any longer, I guess. We'd better go in and get it over with."

So they walked, as slowly as possible, to the office. "I'm not looking forward to this at all," Argyll commented on the way.

"What are you worried about? All he can do is shout at you. Me, he's going to fire." She had a point.

"But I'm the one who's lost his scholarship," he replied. He had a point too.

Bottando's greeting, though, was a pleasant surprise. "Come in, come in," he said after they had knocked tentatively on his door. "Good of you to come so early." It was a little after noon. Flavia couldn't decide if he was being sarcastic.

"I had a dreadful night last night. You shouldn't go about worrying me like that. Can you imagine how bad I would have felt if you'd got yourselves killed? Apart from the difficulties of explaining to the minister and getting a suitable replacement for you."

"Listen, General, I'm sorry . . ."

He waved her attempts aside. "Don't apologise. I feel bad enough already. These things happen. Of course, it's a pity about the business with the tower, Argyll. But I'm sure you didn't have much choice. Dreadful mess, he made. I'm a little surprised it wasn't you splattered all over the Campo, though. He was much bigger than you."

Argyll confessed that he was equally surprised.

"Ah, well. I don't suppose it will make any difference in the long run. How are you both? Feeling better yet?"

Flavia said they were. Bottando seemed in a remarkably jolly mood. But then he didn't know everything yet.

"Good," he continued, blithely unaware of the depressed state of his assistant. "I'm glad to hear it. In that case you can come along with me while I make my report to the director. I've given him a potted report, but he wants details. I fear he's not at all happy about Ferraro—the death rate in the museum is a little high, these days. Still, that's his problem."

As he led the way to his official police car and they all three squeezed in the back, Argyll was feeling uneasy.

"Are you sure you want me to come along? After all, I can't see Tommaso exactly welcoming me with open arms . . ."

"Probably not," Bottando replied. "No, indeed. You're responsible for nearly all his troubles, I suppose. If you hadn't leapt to the wrong conclusion to start off with, none of this would have happened. But don't worry. I'll protect you."

Driving up the Corso to the museum the conversation became muted, apart from Bottando muttering to himself: "Another Raphael, dio mio! A fine achievement . . ."

"Thank you . . ." began Argyll.

Bottando held up his hand. "Please don't. We can celebrate later. It's the grand picture we must concentrate on at the moment."

For the rest of the journey through the clogged streets of Rome he kept quiet, but Flavia could see in the reflection from the window that he would smile occasionally as he looked absently at the people in the streets.

"General, what about Ferraro?" she asked. "I mean, I don't understand how he did it."

Bottando patted her in a fatherly sort of way. "Too much running around, not enough thought, that's the trouble with you young things. I shall tell you when we see the director."

At the museum, the driver opened the rear door to let them out and saluted as they walked up the wide steps to the entrance. Then they strode quickly through the galleries, up some back stairs into the office leading to the director's studio.

"I'm afraid you can't see the director. He's busy."

Bottando searched out his most ferocious expression and put it on. "Nonsense, woman," he told the secretary. "Of course he wants to see me."

"But he's in a very important meeting . . ." she protested as he brushed past and opened the door.

Even someone like Argyll—who was not normally particularly perceptive over matters like the finer nuances of atmosphere—could tell that the mood in the room was not especially happy. Tense, in fact. Which was not surprising, really, as the only occupants, sitting in silence round an unlit coal fire, were the director, Enrico Spello and Sir Edward Byrnes. Clearly, their entry did not interrupt a lively conversation.

"Gentlemen. Good morning. I'm so glad you're all here enjoying yourselves." Bottando rubbed his hands together, his cheerfulness not even dented by the less than amicable air in the room. With exaggerated punctiliousness he introduced everyone, even though they had all met before. He sat down and beamed at the assembled group.

"Well, director, there are many details to go through. First, as you know, the museum now has a replacement

Raphael, and we can officially call the first one a fake.''

Tommaso nodded. ''That is a consolation. A shocking business all round. Ferraro of all people.'' He shook his head in a gesture which seemed more sorrowful than angry.

''Indeed. A distressing affair. As is the other transaction I have to perform.''

''Which is?'' Tommaso enquired.

Bottando fished around in his pocket and drew out a piece of paper, glancing around at the other five people in the room as he did so. ''It's just a little arrest warrant,'' he began in an apologetic tone of voice, clearly enjoying himself. He coughed to clear his throat so as not to stumble as he read out the legal phrasing. He always liked to get these little ceremonies right.

''Cavaliere Marco di Tommaso, I have here a warrant to arrest you on charges of conspiracy to defraud the state, conspiracy to commit forgery, conspiracy to pervert the course of justice, and non-declaration of income to the appropriate fiscal authorities.''

CHAPTER

15

They sat in Bottando's office, drinking coffee. Byrnes and Spello had occupied the only comfortable chairs, Flavia and Argyll perched on two tubular-metal affairs brought in for the occasion. Bottando sat at his desk, a look of radiant self-satisfaction about him, Byrnes and Spello had a neutral look on their faces, while Argyll and Flavia brought up the rear with an air of scarcely dissipated anxiety, slowly mingling with a degree of relief.

"Well, well. What a business. The look on the director's face when I read out that warrant was worth a small fortune. I never thought anybody could have spluttered so much," Bottando said with a happy smile on his face. "Couldn't have been better. I was particularly proud of getting him on his income tax. I shall greatly enjoy reading the papers tomorrow. One month before the budget submissions have to go in for next year. I think I'll take the opportunity to add on twenty per cent extra for wages and claim another five assistants. Probably get them now."

"I found it all rather alarming," commented Argyll. "I suppose you were bluffing. But what would you have done if he hadn't started confessing to everything? You would have been in a right mess then."

"Good heavens, young man, what do you take me for? Just because I'm a shade overweight and can't go running around Europe like a runaway train doesn't mean I'm completely senile, you know. Of course I wasn't bluffing: I would have been much more circumspect if you hadn't so brilliantly found that painting. Without that we wouldn't have been able to prove anything."

He smiled at the Englishman's look of blushing modesty.

"It was obvious that it was him. But you were so concerned to slam poor Sir Edward behind bars you ignored the evidence. While I, sitting quietly in my office with calm detachment, could see it all."

"Has anyone ever told you that you're really objectionable when you're smug?" Argyll asked.

"I know. But it's not often I have such a good day. Please forgive me."

"You were about to say why it was obvious."

"Yes. Firstly there was the problem of who knew about the picture in advance of Argyll's intemperate outburst here after his arrest. And you said you had informed only your supervisor, and that anyway he had been away on sabbatical in Tuscany. Right? And he wrote you a letter telling you he had been reading your paper and had written recommending that you be kept on at your university. He was staying with a friend east of Montepulciano. Interesting, eh?"

Flavia and Argyll leaned back in their chairs, folded their arms simultaneously, and looked exasperated.

"Well. And you remember I told you—I told Flavia anyway—that Tommaso had surprised me by saying he was going to retire next year to Tuscany. A villa outside Pienza, in fact. Ever been there? No? You really should. Very pretty town. A little jewel, in fact. It's very easy to get to: go to Montepulciano and keep on going a few miles east and you're there.

"And it seemed unlikely," Bottando continued, staring at the ceiling, "that two such eminent artistic types should be within spitting distance of each other without meeting. A brief phone call confirmed it. Your supervisor had been staying with Tommaso while he read the paper.

"So that's piece number one. Tommaso had the chance, at least, of knowing about that picture long enough in advance to get a forgery made. I couldn't find any way that Sir Edward might have known. Tommaso investigates, and discovers you're wrong. But he also goes through the evidence and realises that, although there is nothing under there, there should be. You said the same yourself. If someone uncovered the painting and found what looked like a Raphael, they would be predisposed to believe it was genuine.

"But he's no fool. You can't produce any old rubbish and expect to have it accepted. He needed an expert. And who does he think of? Why, good old Professor Morneau, the man who taught him all about painting when he was an art student in Lyons. He found the right man: Morneau was really good. He bought that old painting and used the others for practice. Then he cleaned off the central portion and painted a Raphael, along the lines you've described. Put the fake Mantini on top, dirtied and aged it, switched the pictures when no one was looking. Exit Morneau.

"Of course, I was just a little suspicious of Tommaso anyway, but I couldn't see my way past the fact that Byrnes was the most likely beneficiary, and that the director had a cast-iron alibi on every occasion. Flavia's view that Byrnes had probably been his own employer seemed most likely.

"Things really started crystallising when Byrnes rang me up, a little hot under the collar after Argyll had effectively told him that we knew the picture was a fraud, and that he was going to have to refund all the money." He paused and turned to the Englishman, "Why did you do that, by the way?"

Flavia looked at Argyll disapprovingly, and he looked sheepish again. "As I told Flavia, it seemed a good idea at the time. The idea was that Sir Edward would rush out to Siena, try to destroy the picture, and would get himself arrested. I suppose I owe you an apology," he said to Byrnes, who acknowledged it graciously.

"Very good idea," said Bottando with approval, surprising both Flavia and Argyll almost equally. "Wrong man, of course, but sound in principle. As you know, it was the same sort of plan as the one I adopted.

"In fact," he continued, resuming his monologue, "it was just as well you did go and see him. It was he who pointed out to me that Tommaso had been Morneau's pupil. Until that point, the only person I could see burning the picture and killing Manzoni was Argyll, which implicated Byrnes as I didn't think Argyll was able to think of the fake."

"Thank you very much," said Argyll.

"No offence. I was merely referring to your lack of experience. But you could kill someone; I couldn't see any of these slightly overweight—my apologies, gentlemen—aesthetes taking on Manzoni in a fight. So I reached a stalemate.''

Bottando twisted off the cap of a bottle of fizzy mineral water and poured a glass for himself, then offered it round to his audience. ''So. Byrnes is commissioned, buys the picture and takes it home, and the fraud is all set. Tommaso had also prepared his end by getting the minister to agree in advance that, should such an opportunity arise, they should leap in and save the Italian heritage.

''The museum buys the picture and Tommaso has the opportunity of directing his tests to the area he knew would pass. He calls Byrnes and gives directions that only the left-hand side of the picture is to be examined. Unfortunately, his secretary overheard the conversation, and told me about it yesterday morning when I was waiting outside his office to see him. It's the penalty for not seeing visitors promptly.

''Then Flavia goes to England and Argyll mentions his bit of evidence. I tell the director what Argyll suspects, and he explodes. But he doesn't do anything. It was only when I tried to get out of going to that party by telling Ferraro I was off to Switzerland in search of some icons, that the picture got wrecked. At this point matters get taken out of Tommaso's hands.

''That was another curiosity that fitted into place when you began to see Tommaso as a possible instigator. All of a sudden he names Ferraro as his successor and says he's going to retire. Odd, that, to do such a favour for someone you clearly and obviously disliked. I suspect that Ferraro found out what was going on when he ran the museum during Tommaso's and Spello's absence. The director said this was when Ferraro effectively clinched the job. I thought it was because he'd done so well, but it was more likely that it was because he'd then got his hold on Tommaso.

"Ferraro goes along and says he knows that I am about to prove the picture was a fake. He names his terms for dealing with the situation and not telling the police. Tommaso has no choice. He agrees and Ferraro, a very much more ruthless person, goes into action.

"Ferraro was in a difficult position. If the forgery survived and was unmasked, Tommaso's reputation and his own chances of becoming director would be damaged. But if it was destroyed and no one proved it was a fake, then Tommaso would again be damaged by the failure to protect a masterpiece.

"Unless of course, the blame could be shifted. Clearly a man who thought ahead. Hence, the rapid appearance of stories in the newspapers about the lapses of the security committee. It pushed Spello into the limelight as a suspect and made me a potential scapegoat. Once I stopped seeing it as a piece of bureaucratic politics and began to look at it as an aspect of the case, then the mist began to clear a bit.

"There were two final weak spots in their defence. Firstly, someone would see how the forgery was done. Manzoni works it out. He tells Ferraro, hoping to secure his position in the museum. Ferraro slips out of the office, murders him, and slips back to work afterwards, leaving late in the evening and making sure the doorman sees him go. The final detail was destroying the original picture, and this, fortunately, is where he slipped up.

"Now we all know what happened, of course, it is easy to see where we went wrong. We had the tendency to assume that the burning of the picture and the knifing of Manzoni were all done by the same person as was behind the fraud. And as Tommaso had a perfect alibi for the murder and for the burning, I couldn't see how he could be responsible.''

Flavia objected here. ''But Ferraro also had an alibi for when the picture was burnt. You told me so yourself.''

''True. Tommaso provided the alibi and the Americans provided an alibi for Tommaso. What we didn't have was an American alibi for Ferraro. Until yesterday, when I rang them again and they said he'd left the director's office halfway through their meeting about the donation. I should have thought of that, as well, because I saw him at the party ten minutes before Tommaso reappeared.''

He paused for a few moments to pick up his monologue where he'd left it. ''But that was only two days ago. I'm a bit slow. After Byrnes had called and everything began to fall into place, I had a dreadful day. I knew, but had no proof. So I had to take an anguished decision. You were going to Siena. Now, did I tell Ferraro? If I didn't, we'd have proof of the fake, but not of the instigator or the murderer.

''But if I did, Ferraro would inevitably turn up there, and try and destroy all the evidence once and for all. As that could well include you two as well as the picture, I was decidedly nervous.

''Very anguishing indeed. But Sir Edward persuaded me that if we saturated Siena with enough plainclothesmen we could protect you. So, essentially, I adopted the same plan as Argyll, only with a different target. I came up by helicopter to supervise, set up my headquarters in a hotel—not nearly as good as the luxurious effort you two chose, but I'm only a humble policeman—and off we went.

''And we could have protected you, if you hadn't

pulled that silly stunt of hiding in the toilets. Novel, but ridiculous. We were convinced you'd come out of the museum and we'd lost you. General panic. We scattered our forces and scoured the streets. And all the restaurants, of course. Nothing. I was convinced you were lying with your throats cut in some dark alley. The worry nearly set off my ulcer again.

"We found you, but only when Ferraro dropped off the tower. He landed a few feet away from a policeman we had watching the Campo for suspicious behaviour—he thought this qualified, and called me.

"No one had noticed him knock on the back door where the night porter hangs out, cosh the poor man and go in. That was because we were so busy wondering where you were. So that's the tale. Ferraro happily out of the way for ever, Tommaso under lock and key."

"What happens now?" asked Argyll. "What's he been charged with?"

"Oh, it doesn't work like that at all. Preventative incarceration first. That's to stop him hot-footing it to Argentina like all the other mobsters. He'll be locked up for, oh, about eighteen months while the prosecutor assembles the case. Then he'll be given a fair trial and found guilty. Lord only knows why it takes that long. It'll be a lovely trial."

Argyll stuck his hand up, tentatively, like a schoolboy wanting to go to the toilet, but had no chance to speak. Flavia got there first.

"I still don't really see why he bothered. After all, he was well off, had a wonderful job, highly envied and admired. Why throw a stunt like this?"

"Ah, well, that was what put me on to him in the first place. For the last six months or so everyone has been telling me how rich the man was. But it occurred to me, when I actually thought about it, that I'd never heard of this legendary wealth before. And I didn't think Tommaso was the sort of person to keep a fact like that to himself.

"So I spent some time looking through the dossiers and my old cases. A very useful exercise. And discovered that, as is often the case, he was christened with his mother's maiden name: Marco. The family was involved in a financial scandal I helped crack in my youth; it went bankrupt as a result. The young Tommaso was plunged suddenly from great wealth into abject poverty, which may have created a sense of greed and desire for revenge. He had no money at all. Not, at least, until he got his hands on the proceeds of this operation. Only then did tales of his wealth begin to circulate."

Byrnes stirred himself in his armchair by the fireplace, and spoke for the first time. "There is also my role in the affair," he began. "I imagine he would have gone ahead anyway, but luring me into the net made the triumph complete. He knew I would be the prime suspect.

"I told you of the Correggio affair. I took the painting back, which I gather made me more suspect. But I took it back when I needn't have because I was convinced it was genuine. I did research, proved it, and eventually sold it for more than Tommaso had paid. He resigned from Treviso for no reason at all aside from the criticism and doubts of a few connoisseurs.

"That rankled, and I can't say I blame him. He also resented me because I'd proved him wrong twice. When this opportunity came up, he took it. This time, he wanted to ridicule all those colleagues who had scorned him. The longer the fraud went on, the more articles and books would be written, and the more scholars would commit themselves. And eventually, possibly in his will so he wouldn't have to give any money back, he would reveal all and make a laughingstock of them.

"But this new evidence turns up, largely because Argyll sowed his first seeds of doubt, Morneau dies unexpectedly, and Ferraro takes the matter out of his hands. The whole thing stopped being an ingenious and well-conceived joke and turned nasty. A great pity. In some ways I rather wish he had got away with it. On the other hand, we do at least now have a real Raphael."

Argyll shook his head. "Ah, well, now then. I'm afraid not. I've been trying to tell you ever since we got here. I think I goofed again . . ."

There was a pause, followed by a quiet groan from the others in the room as it dawned on them what he had said. Only Flavia, who'd been waiting for this all afternoon, looked relieved that he'd finally got around to it.

"Again?" Bottando raised his eyebrows. "A second time? Another mistake? But Flavia said you'd found it. You told her there was a painting underneath."

Argyll smiled a little shamefacedly. " 'Painting,' not 'a painting.' There was. Green. Light-green paint. That's what I told her. But I was just about to explain when she was bopped on the head that it was a bad sign, not a good one. All painters use a dead colour to prepare the canvas in some way. Generally it's a sort of off-white. But Mantini used light green. That's what I was trying to say. It was a genuine Mantini from top to bottom. There was nothing underneath at all. I got the wrong picture."

There was a brief moment while everyone in the room looked at him sadly. Argyll felt like an insect.

"This really is very careless of you," Bottando said heavily. "I went in to Tommaso because I thought we had clear and absolute proof at last that the first painting was a fake. Think what would have happened if he had sat there and denied it all. We couldn't have touched him. You have now misidentified two Raphaels in the space of a year. Probably a record.''

"I know," Argyll said sadly. "And I'm dreadfully sorry about it. All I can say is that it should have been the right one, they both should, in fact. I really can't understand it. I must have missed something. Third time lucky, d'you think?''

"No. Absolutely not. Forget it. Even if you found the right one no one would believe you any more. You just concentrate on Mantini, that can't cause any turmoil. And do be a bit more reticent about this sort of thing in future.''

In the months afterwards, Argyll followed the General's advice and made steady progress in the task of restoring Carlo Mantini to his proper place in the artistic pantheon. His sudden and extraordinary dedication was not entirely due to a sense of scholarship, however. Byrnes had forgiven Argyll for entertaining the idea that he was a murderer, but he was quietly putting on the pressure for something to show for the fellowship. He also made a vague offer of a job in his Rome gallery once the dissertation was finished.

With the possibility of permanent residence in Italy to motivate him, Argyll slaved away at the Hertziana, the German art library at the top of the Spanish steps. Surrounded by the books he needed, and with a major incentive to work, he had little excuse not to. Flavia also bullied him mercilessly, while always reminding him that it was for his own good. By and large he agreed, and it caused no rupture in the close and companionable friendship that was slowly growing up between them, despite their differences in character.

His work was not especially exciting, but it was none too demanding either. He would put in a few hours in the morning, have a leisurely lunch at the Press Club, then return home to sit, hammering away at his typewriter. It all came out slowly and painfully, and he spent many an hour staring at the wall, searching for inspiration or, failing that, at least the will-power to get on with it. He fixed a photograph of the fake Raphael opposite where he sat: no matter what its origins, he still thought it a wonderful picture. Next to it he pinned the old copy Morneau had used as a base. Beauty and the beast. It reminded him of the whole business. Looking back, it all seemed like quite a good time.

Slowly, he made progress, but got bogged down in the central chapter—which dealt with the fraud—as he tried to find something new to say. And he'd agreed to give a paper at an art history conference in January— that would slow things down as well, especially as he could think of nothing to talk about. It would also require a trip to England at the worst possible time of year, but there was no way he could get out of it now.

Thus Argyll thought as he lay on the bed staring at the wall, cigarette in hand, taking a breather. Typing gives you a sore back. He looked at his two pictures again. The copy was indeed an awful thing. Who would ever wear such ostentatious and crude jewellery, even in the sixteenth century? Such a bizarre design, as well. A ring made of dead birds, indeed.

He walked around the room and thought, clarifying matters as an idea for his paper began to crystallise in his mind. It was going to need a lot of work, but that was fairly easy once you knew the general outline.

He was tempted to abandon his typewriter for the rest of the afternoon, amble off into the fading autumn light to see Flavia and tell her the outline. But he abandoned the notion. Flavia was a patient girl, but not that much of a saint. She would merely criticise him for not getting on with the thesis. Besides, she worked hard, and he didn't want to interrupt her.

So he kept quiet and worked discreetly on the side, accumulating the odd spots of information here and there. It was hard, but came in little drips until he had enough to throw a bit of his recently adopted caution aside. In late November, he went to London, where he saw Byrnes about his forthcoming job. His benefactor was most accomodating. A nice man, when you got to know him. Sense of humour, too. He also dug out Phil, and twisted his arm until he agreed to invite him to lunch with his father at the National Trust. Out of this meeting came an invitation to go north for a long weekend in the freezing cold of a Yorkshire October. Then he came back to Rome.

Flavia was amazed by his behaviour. He had begun working on his dissertation but was clearly not consumed by it. Now, to write a mere twenty-minute paper for the conference, he was working like a demon. Long hours, late into the night, writing, rewriting, and footnoting. He also refused to let her see what he'd written, despite her offers to check it through. She could hear it at the conference, he told her, if she wanted to come.

CHAPTER

16

Argyll was very nervous, not having given many papers before, and certainly not in front of such a large audience. "There must be about two hundred people here, even though some are leaving for tea. A couple of paragraphs of this and they'll sit down again," he thought as he walked to the podium.

He took out his paper and looked around, waiting for the hum of chattering art historians to die away. This might be fun. Certainly, the previous offering had not been much competition. This lot were about to get the shock of their lives. He spied his flatmate Rudolf Beckett, sitting morosely in one of the back seats, and gave him a little wave. The poor man had been persuaded to come along, and was clearly regretting the atypical gesture of friendship.

"In the past few months," Argyll began, "there has been a great deal of discussion, in journals and in more popular papers [polite laughter] about the purchase of a supposed Raphael by the forger Jean-Luc Morneau. As you all know, the former director of the Museo Nazion-

ale in Rome will shortly stand trial for complicity in the
affiar. I shall not, therefore, deal with this aspect of the
business for fear of contravening Italian restrictions and
in case anything I say prejudices Dottore Tommaso's
chance of a fair trial.

"Rather, today, I would like to go back to the original
proposition which started the whole sequence of events
off. That is the evidence that a painting by Raphael of
Elisabetta di Laguna, once owned by the di Parma family, was indeed painted over by Carlo Mantini to get it
through Papal customs and to England. Because of the
publicity surrounding the exposure of the forgery, the
question of the original has rather been lost sight of,
even though it undoubtedly existed. I intend to demonstrate that evidence exists to prove conclusively the last
destination of the picture."

There was a little stir in the audience. No more chattering from dissidents at the back now. The tea-trolley
brigade was settling down nicely into their seats. It was
true that Argyll had sacrificed something of scholarly
rigour for the sake of maximum impact, but it could
hardly fail. Compared with papers on "Manet's Con-
ception of Human Progress," or "Theorising the Male
Gaze," this was rock and roll.

"It has always been assumed that the painting disappeared either because it never left Italy, or because the
dealer Samuel Paris absconded with it at some stage."
Well, *he* had assumed that, anyway. But there was no
harm in generalising a bit.

"The main evidence for this was that the Earl of Clomorton died of a heart attack the moment the Mantini
arrived in England. A notoriously stingy man, it was
assumed that realising he had been robbed of more than
seven hundred pounds was too much for him.

"A letter from his wife, however, brings this interpretation into question." He read through the letter he had shown to Flavia in his flat. "This clearly states that Clomorton was expected in Yorkshire and had been in London with Samuel Paris for three weeks 'fussing over the consignment.' He died a week after this letter was written.

"A second letter from her brother appears to reassure his widow that unkind gossip about the fraud will never come out." He read out the document from the newspaper cutting he had taken. Not scholarly, but he had checked that it was an accurate transcription of the original. "Again, this reading is problematic. I find it unlikely that anyone, in possession of a Raphael, would wait for three weeks before looking at it. Paris was on hand, and he was a cleaner as well as a dealer. Surely it is more likely that he would have set to work the moment the picture was unloaded from the boat? And if that is the case, whatever lay under the Mantini would have been discovered within a matter of hours.

"So what did the Earl die of? It is scarcely conceivable that a man, however mean, would die of shock at being robbed a whole three weeks after the shock was administered. Moreover, Clomorton was buried in Yorkshire. He died in January, the month when English roads were at their most impassable. And he died on the date when his wife was expecting him to arrive home. If his death was caused by a shock received in the restorer's studio, would his family really have bothered to cart his body nearly three hundred miles at that time of year?

"So let us return to Lady Arabella." Here, he gave the extracts from Viscount Perceval's diary he had read to Flavia. "Perhaps this should be seen in a new light," he continued. "When Perceval referred to the 'dark-haired beauty' Clomorton said he was going to bring to Yorkshire, he was not referring to some mistress he had picked up. The phrase, after all, could refer to a painting of Elisabetta di Laguna. However, it was unfortunate that he made his little jest to the Duchess of Albemarle, who misinterpreted it and immediately wrote a warning to his wife. She naturally feared her husband was back at his old tricks and was outraged by yet another affront to her honour. She was, after all, a woman with a terrible temper. She had publicly assaulted her first husband and cheerfully confessed to threatening the second.

"So we have a possible solution. The Earl arrives home, complete with his latest consignment of pictures and excited at the prospect of showing them off. He does not get the welcome he expects. There is a blazing row, Lady A's temper gets the better of her and she lashes out. But this time she goes too far, and she kills him. This is what her brother referred to in his letters. Not keeping the fraud secret, but keeping the murder secret. It was put out that the Earl had died of a heart attack, and he was quietly and rapidly buried in the family vaults. I was present when the tomb, now the responsibility of the National Trust, was opened a few weeks ago. The Earl's skull was cracked, a symptom rarely associated with heart failure."

Another rumble from the audience, like a mass attack of indigestion. Argyll paused to let it subside, and winked at Flavia in the front row. He straightened his face to deliver the knockout.

"So what next? Lady Arabella has already delivered her opinion about her husband's pictures, and what she wanted to do with them. Copies and impositions that should be hidden away. This is exactly what happens, and they have stayed there, for the most part, ever since.

Those that weren't sold before the family vacated the premises in the 1940s are still in their original positions, in lesser bedrooms, down dark corridors or in the cellars.''

He paused for maximum effect. He'd been practising for days. ''According to surviving inventories, Raphael's picture of Elisabetta di Laguna—bought by the Earl, painted over by Mantini, uncovered and delivered in good faith by Samuel Paris—hung just outside the staff entrance to the kitchens, its true worth entirely unrecognised. It rested there, being splattered with gravy from passing trolleys, caked with smoke and covered with spilt coffee, for more than two hundred years. Its condition by the time it was sold at Christie's in 1947 was dreadful.''

Argyll had once heard a psychiatrist analyse the speeches of successful politicians. The man had explained that many of them, to create an air of excitement, persuade the audience to clap; then shout the next few lines of the speech over the applause, thus creating an impression of spellbinding oratory. He had wanted to try this for years. His statement about the gravy caused a respectable stir, so he raised his voice and ploughed on.

''From here on tracing the picture is a routine matter of provenance work.''

They calmed down a bit, so he paused, took a sip from his glass of water, and let them wait. Of all his discoveries of the past year—and he was the first to admit that some had proven embarrassingly below par—he was the most proud of this one. It called for observation, intuition and imagination, the sort of things he normally wasn't very good at. This proved he could do it when he tried.

''At the 1947 sale, the picture was bought by one

Robert MacWilliam, a Scottish doctor. He died in 1972 and it was sold at Parson's in Edinburgh, for two hundred and twenty-five guineas, to none other than Sir Edward Byrnes.''

A hushed silence at this, as they wondered what horrendous revelation came next. ''When I informed him of this, Sir Edward was greatly gratified. At any one stage I was afraid he might die of laughter. When he recovered and thought back, he informed me that he had never suspected that the picture was of any value at all. Indeed, he had not even bothered to have it cleaned. Someone came into his gallery one day, offered a price that gave him a small profit, and he accepted. After some searching, he found the record. The picture had been bought by a small private collector on the Continent. It remained in this collection until he also died a few years back.

''Now we come to the final stage, and I must apologise to you for delaying so long. The Raphael affair has been embarrassing all round. Technicians, in particular, are still upset by the fact that they didn't notice the fraud perpetrated on them. Raphael painted in a particular way, and they feel they should have noticed something wrong. I expect there can be few in this audience who do not know the process by which Jean-Luc Morneau created his fake. To do it required immense skill and sympathy for the painter he was imitating. He used Raphael's techniques, Raphael's recipes for paint mixtures, Raphael's style.

''I hate to have to tell you, but he also used a Raphael. The sale records show that the portrait of Elisabetta di Laguna was sold, as 'portrait of a lady, copy after Fra Bartolommeo' for three thousand Belgian francs, to Jean-Luc Morneau. There is one photograph of it.''

The picture Argyll had first seen in a Roman restaurant appeared on the screen. "The critical proof is the left hand," Argyll continued, indicating the area with a little pointer. "You see there is a ring." An even more blurred enlargement flashed up. "It is designed as two entwined pelicans. That, of course, is the symbol of the di Parma family. Elisabetta was the Marchese's mistress, and it was quite in order that she should wear the ring to show to whom she belonged. The liaison, after all, was hardly kept a secret.

"It needs only a brief comparison of the forgery and the original"—two slides flashed up on the screen—"to see the similarities in the backgrounds of the two paintings. That was why the tests failed to reveal that the picture was a fake. The bits examined were very much genuine.

"Morneau needed an authentic Italian canvas of the right period, and some passable paintwork to create the illusion of a real Raphael. It seems that he had better raw material than he could ever have realised. He scored through the accumulated dirt of two centuries, probably with some dilute acid, to prepare the surface for his work. I don't imagine that he ever paid much attention to the original painting that lay underneath the grime. To us, after all, it hardly appears to be the representation of a great beauty. Tastes change. Nearly all of Raphael's work, except this window and parts of the interior against which the figure is framed, was simply erased so that he could paint his fake Raphael on top. As you know, what remained was destroyed, along with Morneau's work, during the attack in the museum."

The result was better than he had hoped. He had expected tumultuous applause, roars of approval, programme notes thrown into the air. He got none of that, but the reaction was still more satisfying. Faced with the stunned amazement of the audience, he folded up his paper and stuffed it into his pocket. Then he clattered noisily down the steps from the podium, his metal-tipped shoes echoing across the silent hall. Flavia was waiting for him, beaming with delight.

"Slow but sure. What a clever thing you are, after all," she said. And kissed him, gently, on the nose.

PROFILE OF A TWISTED KILLER

"I want you to take pictures of the crowd. Do it in sections and take multiple shots from varying angles."

"You think he's watching us," Brady said as the detective left the stage.

"It fits the profile."

"Lord help us, Jack. We've got a real sick puppy on our hands."

"A classic sadistic sexual psychopath," Matthews said. "It takes a long time for someone to reach this degree of psychosis; this level of violence. He's on the extreme edge of depravity. And he's too organized; his fantasies too strong."

"Meaning what?"

"These aren't his first victims. He's done this before. And he's going to do it again. Soon."

COLD COLD HEART

James Elliott

A Dell Book

Published by
Dell Publishing
a division of
Bantam Doubleday Dell Publishing Group, Inc.
1540 Broadway
New York, New York 10036

ISBN 0-440-21863-2

Reprinted by arrangement with Delacorte Press

Printed in the United States of America

Published simultaneously in Canada

July 1995

10 9 8 7 6 5 4 3 2

OPM

COLD COLD
HEART

1

IT WAS HER favorite time of day, when the first rays of morning sun slipped slowly over the horizon and the grounds of the university were still and silent. She was near the end of her five-mile course through the heart of the campus and was still running effortlessly. She moved swiftly, with long, graceful strides, along the edge of a sprawling expanse of fading lawn, beneath towering maple trees ablaze with color, and past graceful white columns supporting the porticoes of imposing redbrick buildings.

As she reached McCormick Road, she checked her watch and slowed her pace to begin her cool-down walk. She breathed deeply of the crisp October air heavy with the scent of autumn as her eyes moved warily over the surrounding area. She zipped open her waist-pack to remove a small bottle of Evian water and her hand brushed past the can of Mace that she, and most of the other coeds, now took to carrying wherever they went.

The promise of a tranquil college life had been broken by a pervasive fear that gripped the University of Virginia's academic community. Four coeds had mysteriously disappeared in the past month, all under cover of darkness: the first was last seen leaving the Newcomb Hall student center, the second following an evening piano recital in Old Cabell Hall, and the third and fourth upon crossing the grounds after late nights at Alderman Library. One each week. None had been heard from since. And none of the missing students was troubled or given to erratic behavior. No demands for ransom surfaced. No contact of any kind from whoever was responsible. Nothing. Only silence. Followed by the worst kind of fear: not knowing.

After the disappearance of the second coed an escort service was arranged for female students and faculty. A telephone call brought one or two male students to accompany the caller to her dorm or parking lot after dark, waiting until she was safely inside or had driven away. The university police had tripled the number of officers who walked the grounds from dusk until dawn. But still two more abductions had occurred—both of the young women, forgoing the escort service, had refused to let fear dictate their lives and had paid dearly for their obstinate independence.

The young runner's breathing and pulse rate returned to normal as she skipped down the steps to the walkway in front of Garrett Hall. She then turned to descend another series of steps to the small outdoor amphitheater, where she sat on the top tier of the semicircle of stone bleachers to drink the last of her water and complete her morning ritual of watching the sun rise over the grounds.

The amphitheater was used periodically throughout the year by guest speakers, theater groups, and student organizations, but evening performances had been suspended indefinitely after the disappearance of the third coed. The walls flanking the stage below were still strung with banners advertising fraternity and sorority functions. The runner strained to read them, but she was nearsighted and could barely make them out without her glasses.

She noticed something in the center of the stage, and squinted at the blurred, indistinct form. She rose slowly and began to descend the stairs to the lower tier, where the morning sun had not yet reached. Her gaze was fixed on the deep shadows ahead, on what appeared to be an unclothed female mannequin sprawled on the stage in a suggestive pose. She shook her head in disgust at what she assumed was another tasteless and sexist fraternity prank.

Something made her move still closer, and as she crossed the grassy area in front of the stage the form came into sharp focus. An icy chill coursed through her veins and a wild panic suddenly gripped her and froze her in place. She tried to scream, but such was the horror of the image before her that no sound emerged. She stood in sheer terror, her body rigid, frantically gulping in huge breaths. A terrible sound finally erupted, again and again, in bloodcurdling screams that shattered the early morning silence and carried across the grounds to echo off the stately buildings.

2

AT SIX-FORTY-THREE A.M., in room 110 of the Cavalier Inn just off the University of Virginia grounds, FBI Special Agent Jack Matthews was jolted from a much-needed sleep by the telephone on the nightstand next to his bed. Before the first ring ended, he sat bolt upright, grabbed the receiver, and swung his legs over the side.

The caller was Neal Brady, the Charlottesville chief of police. His voice was tense and strained.

"We've got a body, Jack. And it's bad."

"How bad?"

"It doesn't get much worse. McIntire Amphitheater on the grounds. You know where it is?"

"Yeah. I'm on my way."

Assigned to the FBI's Richmond office, Matthews had been working out of the much smaller Charlottesville office since a joint task force of federal, state, county, city, and university police had been formed after the disappearance of the second student. Although there is no federal jurisdiction in murder cases, unless they occur during the commission of a federal crime, when the second missing coed turned out to be the twenty-year-old daughter of an FBI assistant director at the Bureau's Washington headquarters, the FBI had claimed jurisdiction under the guise of a suspected kidnapping.

Under the circumstances it was inevitable that the FBI would deal themselves in, and Chief Brady, who understood how things worked in the real world, harbored no resentment of the Bureau taking over command of the task force. Despite the turf battles inherent in any joint operation, he was, in fact, grateful for all the help he could get with what had quickly become a high-profile case receiving national media attention.

With the pressure from Washington, and the director himself taking a personal interest, Matthews had been working eighteen-hour days since coming to Charlottesville. He hadn't seen his wife and two-year-old daughter in two weeks, and he strongly suspected that Brady's phone call meant that he could kiss the promised family weekend in Williamsburg good-bye.

Matthews pulled on the same shirt and suit he had worn the previous day. He slipped his holstered gun through his belt, and ran his hands through his hair as he rushed from the hotel room to be jolted fully awake by the crisp morning air. He knotted his tie as he dashed across the parking lot to his car, his mind imagining the worst possible scenarios.

▽

FIVE MINUTES LATER Matthews swung into the small parking lot behind the amphitheater to find two

ambulances and a tangle of state, county, city, and
university patrol cars parked at odd angles across the
blacktop. Radios squawked from three of the cars left
standing with their doors open, and two of the cars
still had their light bars on, sending out swirling red
and blue flashes. To Matthews's dismay a mobile
news van from the local television station was already
there, and as he pulled his car into an open slot, a
newspaper photographer skidded a motorcycle to a
panic stop behind him, jumped off the bike, and
dashed around the building, cameras dangling from
his neck.

Matthews never ceased to be amazed at how
quickly the news media responded to any situation
that held the promise of a gory lead story: If it bleeds,
it leads. He had little doubt how they had gotten to
the scene so quickly this time; the local cops had
probably talked openly over their radios and the
newshounds, eagerly awaiting any break in the story
of the missing students, had picked them up on
their scanners.

Matthews rounded the corner to the lower level
of the amphitheater to see one of Chief Brady's men,
his hand held over the lens of a shoulder-mounted
television camera, ushering an intrusive and indignant
reporter and her cameraman from the area that was
now being cordoned off with bright yellow crime-
scene tape. The newspaper photographer suffered the
same fate. A burly state trooper in a sharply creased
blue-and-gray uniform blocked his path and ordered
him back to the parking lot.

A dozen or so uniformed cops and sheriff's deputies milled about the grassy area below the stage,
contaminating and destroying possible evidence that

was clearly within the dump-site scene. *It might have been worse*, Matthews thought; *at least some local official isn't posing for the cameras with his foot on the victim's chest.*

Matthews shouldered his way through the cops, noticing that a small crowd of onlookers had already gathered on the walk in front of Garrett Hall above the amphitheater. An occasional gasp and exclamation of shock drifted down to the lower level. Anticipating a mob scene once word spread throughout the campus, Matthews pulled one of the university policemen aside.

"Get some help and tape off the entire amphitheater. And the rear parking lot," he added, upon realizing that it was the most likely place the killer would have parked to unload the body.

The fact that the area had been inadvertently trampled over by himself, the reporters, and at least twenty cops who had rushed to the scene left little hope of finding significant trace evidence that could be positively attributed to the killer. He comforted himself with the thought that footprint casts would have been virtually useless anyway; hundreds of students walked across the grassy area every day.

The investigation had been hampered all along because no one knew the locations of the actual crime scenes—no one knew precisely where the victims had been abducted. As is the case with many serial killings, the abduction and murder sites might never be found. The dump site for a body seldom revealed the same quantity or quality of evidence that the actual crime scene did, since in moving the body, the killer had far more time to plan what he was doing and was in complete control of the situation. But for the moment the dump site was all Matthews had, and he could at least try to preserve whatever remained as yet undisturbed.

"I don't want any more vehicles in the parking lot," he said as the cop turned to go, "and those already there aren't to leave until the Crime Scene Unit is finished with the area. Keep everyone outside the tape, and I mean everyone except the CSU."

With that Matthews climbed the steps to the stage to join Chief Brady and two of his detectives. A chalk outline had already been drawn around the body, and the hands had been bagged to preserve any microscopic bits of flesh or hair beneath her fingernails. One of the detectives had just finished taking photographs of the victim and the immediate area of the stage, while the other was completing a sketch, after having taken measurements and directed a forensic technician to collect and bag any and all objects: fibers, hairs, scrapings, and particles on or around the body. They now stood over the medical examiner as he began his preliminary examination of the young woman sprawled before them. A quick glance verified that Brady had not exaggerated. It did not get much worse.

The once pretty student was grotesquely mutilated. Her head and limbs had been cut off, then crudely sutured back in place with thin wire. The same had been done to her hands and feet. Her breasts had been severed and similarly reattached, and the nipples from each breast had been sliced off and placed on her forehead above each eye.

The condition of the body caused Matthews to speculate on how the killer had transported it to the dump site: the limbs were so loosely attached that the body could have been folded like a rag doll and contained in a large garbage bag. All of the young women had been of the same type: approximately five feet four inches tall, slender with good figures and long, dark hair, averaging about one hundred and ten pounds. Carrying them would have been no problem for a man of average strength.

"What have you got?" Matthews said to the forensic technician who was placing evidence bags in a leather case.

"A few particles of what appear to be red clay mud," the technician said. "Strands of hair, probably the victim's. And this." He handed Matthews one of the clear plastic evidence bags. "I found it on the victim's chest, slipped partway into one of the gaps between the sutures. In my opinion the killer put it there to be found."

Matthews looked at the postage-stamp-sized object in the evidence bag. "A paint chip?"

"Probably. Your lab boys can puzzle it out later."

Matthews stood quietly for a few moments. Schooled at the FBI Academy by the Investigative Support Unit and Behavioral Science Services Unit, he was a trained psychological profiler, skilled at identifying serial crimes and tracking down the killers, and as such was involved in all of the investigations of suspected serial killings covered by the Richmond office. Most local police seldom, if ever, encounter grisly murders, but Matthews had seen mutilated bodies before. He had learned to maintain his composure and a semblance of detachment. But every killing claimed a small part of his soul, and he knew it. He found that complete professional detachment was impossible. The best he could hope for was compassion without emotional involvement.

He pulled on a pair of surgical gloves offered to him by one of the city detectives, then knelt on one knee across from the medical examiner.

"Jack Matthews, FBI," he said.

"Dave Maurer, medical examiner, University of Virginia hospital," Maurer replied without looking up from his work.

Matthews gently touched the cloudy white rim around the edge of one of the nipples affixed to the forehead of the victim. It was stiff and glossy.

"Epoxy glue?" he said to the medical examiner.

"Looks like it."

Matthews's eyes moved slowly over the body. "No bullet holes, stab wounds, or obvious fractures caused by blows?"

"None."

The inside of both thighs had circular sections of flesh missing; two on each leg, just below the crotch. The neatly cut-out sections were approximately three inches in diameter and one eighth of an inch deep. The medical examiner noticed Matthews studying them.

"I'm not sure of their significance," he said. "I've never seen anything like them before."

"They were probably bite marks," Matthews said. "Cut out to prevent us from getting a dental impression."

Maurer simply nodded and continued his examination.

Matthews then noticed the ligature marks above the wire used to sew the head to the neck.

"She's been strangled with a thin cord or rope."

Again the medical examiner made no response. His lips were pursed tightly together in a grim expression. Matthews suspected this was the doctor's first mutilation murder.

The victim's legs were spread improbably wide, and her arms were extended straight out from her shoulders. Other ligature marks, where handcuffs or some form of restraints had been used, were visible on the ankles and wrists. Matthews frowned as his eyes again moved over the body.

"Something's out of kilter here," he said, then realized what it was. "She has two left hands."

"That's not the half of it, Agent Matthews," Maurer said, a slight crack in his voice as he spoke. "She has two right arms, two left legs, two right feet. The breasts don't match, and I'm almost certain the nipples don't go with either of the breasts. What we have is one complete body made up of three or four different women."

"My God!" It was a young city cop who was guarding the steps leading to the stage.

"Indeed, Officer," Maurer said, looking up at the cop. "And we can only hope that He was there to comfort them in their hour of need."

Matthews's own thoughts and emotions were impossible to read as he said a silent prayer that the victims had not been alive when they were mutilated. But he strongly suspected the lab tests would prove otherwise. He would try to spare the families the gruesome details, but it was inevitable that some of it, if not all, would leak out.

Another troubling thought flashed through his mind as he knelt before the victim: Did any part of this body belong to the assistant director's daughter?

Not the head, he knew. From the photographs circulated among the task force and shown in the newspapers and on television, he recognized the face before him as that of the third missing coed, an Echols Scholar and member of the women's soccer team, if he remembered correctly. Sometime within the next twelve hours her parents, along with three other frightened and worried families, would learn the horrible fate of their loved ones. He did not envy those who would make the calls or the personal visits.

He reminded himself to focus on the scene, and he shut out the intrusive, disturbing thoughts. He stared at the trunk of the body where an incision had been made from the chest to the pubic bone, then sutured closed with the same wire used to reattach the limbs and head. The sutures were at least three inches apart. Matthews watched as the medical examiner gently probed inside the gaps between the sutures just below the sternum.

"Any organs missing?"

"The heart," Maurer said. "There may be others, but I won't know until I do the formal autopsy."

"I mean missing as in not there; not replaced by one that doesn't go with the body?"

"There's no heart. Period."

Matthews's attention was drawn to the glistening translucent gray-blue sheen covering the surface of the victim's skin. He gently traced his index finger along the length of one of the arms.

"The skin is cold and damp. Frozen?"

"If you want an educated guess," Maurer said, "this body was in a freezer until approximately an hour and a half ago. I can be more precise when the lab work is completed."

Matthews rose and stood next to Chief Brady. Both men clearly understood the significance of what the medical examiner had just said.

"What time was the body discovered?" Matthews asked.

Brady looked at his watch. "Thirty-five minutes ago. And one of the university cops made a sweep through this area about ten minutes before that. Says he would have seen the body if it had been here. The sun wasn't up yet and he played his flashlight over the shadows on the stage as he cut across the grass."

"That means the body's been here no more than forty-five minutes. So wherever this monster did his work is less than an hour away."

"Agent Matthews," Maurer said. He was using a pair of forceps to remove a folded piece of paper he noticed protruding from the vaginal cavity of the victim. He held it up for Matthews to take.

Matthews carefully held the small notepaper by the corners and unfolded it.

Four words were written in ink in neat block letters:

THE DAY WE MET

Brady looked at the note before Matthews slipped it into an evidence bag offered by the forensic technician.

Brady shook his head as he stared at the body. "He cuts out the bite marks, then leaves us a note and a paint chip. A cry for help? Please stop me before I kill again?"

"More like catch-me-if-you-can," Matthews said,

his eyes fixed in concentration somewhere in the middle distance. "He's playing with us, on his terms, selecting the evidence he wants us to have."

Matthews's own words made him act quickly. He turned to the detective with the camera standing opposite Brady. He pointed to the growing crowd now covering the entire perimeter outside of the crime-scene tape along McCormick Road and in front of Garrett Hall, spreading in a semicircle to Cocke Hall.

"I want you to take pictures of the crowd. Do it in sections and take multiple shots from varying angles."

"You think he's watching us," Brady said as the detective left the stage.

"It fits the profile."

"Lord help us, Jack. We've got a real sick puppy on our hands."

"A classic sadistic sexual psychopath," Matthews said. "It takes a long time for someone to reach this degree of psychosis; this level of violence. He's on the extreme edge of depravity. And he's too organized; his fantasies too strong."

"Meaning what?"

"These aren't his first victims. He's done this before. And he's going to do it again. Soon."

▽

ON THE SIDEWALK at the south end of McCormick Road, overlooking the amphitheater, a tall, slender man with broad shoulders and sandy blond hair, who looked to be in his early forties, stood quietly among the crowd of students behind the crime-scene tape.

He had a strong Slavic face with prominent cheek-bones, and large, expressive eyes. He wore a dark brown tweed jacket and tan slacks, and blended well with the faculty members who had gathered at the scene.

Transfixed by the activity below, no one paid any attention to him as he edged forward for an unobstructed view of the distant stage. A small smile creased the corners of his mouth as he saw the detective with the camera cross the grassy area and climb the steps leading up from the amphitheater. He watched for only a moment, then backed out of the crowd and walked slowly away.

3

ONE HUNDRED MILES north of Charlottesville, just off the Dulles Access Highway in Reston, Virginia, on the outer rim of the nation's capital, the reflective windows of a modern ten-story office building glistened in the midmorning sun. The first nine floors of the dark blue building housed an assortment of consulting and research firms, law offices, and the Washington representatives of various corporations doing business with the federal government.

The building index in the lobby lists the entire tenth floor as the offices of Global Demographics, Incorporated. The main elevators, however, go only to the ninth floor. To reach the top floor there is another elevator, located around the corner. It can be accessed only by inserting a coded card into a slot. Upon exiting onto the small lobby on the tenth floor, a visitor is confronted by an armed plainclothes security guard who asks for identification. Once properly identified the visitor then punches in the correct numbers in sequence on a cipher-locked door and enters the inner sanctum of the CIA's National Resettlement Operations Center.

NROC, pronounced "en-rock" when spoken by those who know of it, is a highly classified section of the much larger Operations Directorate, the Agency's clandestine services. NROC's sole purpose is to monitor the lives of the four hundred and thirty-six defectors, all intelligence officers from the former Soviet Union, Eastern Europe, Cuba, and China, who defected to the United States during the Cold War and immediately following the collapse of the Soviet Union.

Once brought to the United States the defectors are sequestered in safe houses in the Washington area and debriefed. The debriefings can last as long as one year, the average being eight months. The defectors are then resettled into new lives, with new identities, usually in the area of their choice within the continental limits of the United States. Most of the defectors in the program adjust well and settle into their new occupations and communities quickly, requiring little, if any, supervision other than a cursory semiannual report. The more recent arrivals, and those from the darker side of intelligence operations, receive the closest scrutiny.

The overwhelming majority of the defectors under the control of NROC are from the former Soviet Union. Consequently their value as intelligence sources and analysts has been greatly diminished by the huge turnover of personnel during the restructuring of the new Russian internal and external intelligence services. The CIA, however, is obligated to support all of the defectors for the rest of their lives at an average annual tax-free income of sixty thousand dollars with cost-of-living increases, regardless of what they may manage to earn at their new occupations.

Some of the defectors are less than satisfied with their lives in the United States, for reasons ranging from homesickness for their native lands to finding it difficult to adjust to a less adventuresome life-style. A few were simply bad apples to begin with and are a constant source of trouble for the case officers assigned to them.

It was one of the Russian defectors who was believed to have adjusted well, John Malik, who was responsible for the high-level meeting taking place in the NROC chief's conference room that morning. Present were one of the CIA's most powerful men, William Childs, deputy director for operations (DDO), Lou Gregus, head of the Operations Directorate's Special Operations section, Tom Walters, the case officer in charge of Malik's debriefing when he was brought to the United States, and John Quinlan, the head of NROC.

The DDO, a stocky, hard-looking man with the countenance of a dignified bulldog, did not suffer fools gladly. The frantic call he had received from the NROC chief that morning, informing him of what he immediately perceived as a potentially disastrous situation, had done nothing to improve his disposition.

"All right, lay it out for me," the DDO said, leveling an angry stare at Quinlan.

The NROC chief began to speak in a low monotone, consulting the notes he had brought with him.

"Four weeks ago a Crane Paper Company truck was hijacked. Crane manufactures the official currency paper for the Bureau of Engraving and Printing. The truck contained enough paper to print eight hundred million dollars if the denominations were fifty- and one-hundred-dollar bills. If expertly engraved plates were used in the printing process, the money would be virtually undetectable from the real thing."

"What does this have to do with the purpose of this meeting?" the DDO asked impatiently. Quinlan was known to go into far-ranging and unrelated discourses if not kept on track.

"The prime suspects for the hijacking were members of the Russian mafia operating out of Brighton Beach in Brooklyn, New York," the NROC chief continued. "The Secret Service had a serious crisis on their hands and they came to us for help. They needed the names of any recent Russian émigrés we might be aware of with ties to the Russian mafia inside Russia, and who also had a background in counterfeiting. Their usual sources couldn't give them anything, which led them to suspect that those involved were new arrivals. We came up with three former KGB officers who we know entered this country illegally about six months ago. They vanished into the Brighton Beach community shortly after they arrived. We gave the Secret Service their names and photographs, but said nothing about Malik."

"Malik was involved with them?"

"Our records show that Malik could have known two of them. They served in some of the same sections throughout their careers. And he may have been the one they were counting on to provide the engraved plates to produce the bills. Our files show that at one time he was suspected of being involved in KGB counterfeiting operations against this country and West Germany. He never admitted to that during his debriefing, and we're not certain if it's true.

"A few days later the Secret Service got lucky; a New York City detective got a tip from an informant. They raided a warehouse on the Brooklyn docks and found the pallets of currency paper—at least most of it. Enough paper to print thirty million dollars is still missing. They never caught the hijackers."

"I don't give a damn about the Secret Service's problems, John. Get on with it!"

"Yes, sir," the NROC chief said evenly. "But bear with me, the background is essential. We conducted our own investigation to determine if Malik had any knowledge of the hijacking or if he had the engraved plates hidden somewhere. We sent his case officer to Charlottesville to interview him. He couldn't find him."

"Couldn't find him? You mean he left town? Disappeared?"

"We believe so. He owns a small shop near the university, specializing in used textbooks and other student supplies. There was a sign on the door stating that it was temporarily closed. We were able to determine that he hasn't been there in the past two weeks. His home a few blocks away was also deserted. None of the furnishings was missing, but most of his clothes were. We accessed his bank accounts by computer and found they had been recently closed; he had withdrawn over one hundred and twenty thousand dollars over the past four months."

"His escrow money?"

"Yes, sir. After he bought the shop and the house it was what was left of the six hundred thousand dollars we had placed in trust for him over the period of six years he was operating as an agent-in-place. It reverted to his control when he defected four years ago."

The DDO's eyes narrowed. "You still have people down there looking for him?"

"We have a surveillance team watching both the shop and the house."

"I want them pulled out of there right now!" the DDO said.

The NROC chief immediately got up from the conference table and went to the telephone on the credenza near the door. He pressed three numbers on an in-house line and spoke softly into the receiver, then returned to the table.

The DDO turned his attention to Tom Walters, the case officer who had been in charge of Malik's debriefing four years earlier.

"Are you certain he's responsible for the murders of those college kids?" The news reports he had seen flashed through his mind. CNN and all of the regional television stations had been cutting into their regularly scheduled programs all morning with bulletins about the discovery of the body.

"The evidence is circumstantial, sir," Walters said, nervously clearing his throat. "But strongly so."

"Let's hear it."

"Approximately one year after Malik was debriefed and resettled, Boris Novikov, another of our agents-in-place, was brought out, just before the aborted coup in Moscow in August of 1991. The case officers who conducted his debriefing were cross-checking intelligence information Malik and others had given us, as we always do, looking for inconsistencies. When Malik's real name, Nikolai Lubanov, was mentioned, Novikov said he had known him for at least ten years, and said that he had been the subject of a long-running investigation."

"A murder investigation?"

"Yes, sir. Over a period of two years a series of eight murders had taken place in Moscow and Kiev, and according to Novikov, Malik was the prime suspect."

"Assassinations or murders?" the DDO asked.

"Murders. All of the victims were young women, small in stature, slender, with long, dark hair; the same as the missing coeds. And there were mutilations, though not as elaborate as the body they found in Charlottesville this morning."

"You had this information three years ago?" the DDO said. "And you still cut him loose?"

"Novikov's debriefers considered the information nothing more than hearsay," Walters said. "But they still made inquiries, and found no one who could support the allegations. We *were* able to determine that Malik was never arrested, accused, or even questioned about any of the crimes."

"He was a KGB colonel, for Christ's sake," the DDO said. "He had powerful friends. In those days if the local investigators were getting anywhere near him they would have found themselves transferred to Siberia."

"You have to remember that Novikov was a relatively low-level defector," Walters said. "He could have been lying to raise his status with us, or there may have been bad blood between him and Malik and he was lying to settle an old score. That's what his debriefers concluded."

"And you never gave it another thought."

"Unfortunately I never knew about it until yesterday," Walters said sheepishly. "When Novikov's debriefers passed the report on, someone in my office filed it with the transcripts from Malik's earlier debriefing, not with his active NROC file. I came across it when I was going over all of the information we had on Malik to see if there was anything there to suggest where he might have gone when he disappeared."

"Did you come up with any possibilities?"

"No, sir. If he is responsible for the murders of the students, he's still somewhere in the Charlottesville area. At least he was this morning."

The DDO sat silently for a few moments, looking out the window at the traffic streaming along the Dulles Access Highway. His thoughts were interrupted by John Quinlan, the NROC chief.

"At this point I can't see where we have any choice but to turn all of our information over to the FBI."

"The hell we will!" the DDO said. "We've got enemies in Congress who'd like nothing better than to see this agency brought down. There are people on the Hill right now who are seriously considering cutting our budget in half and turning all of our counterintelligence operations over to the FBI. They'd go into a feeding frenzy if they found out we turned a serial killer loose on the American people. And I don't even want to think about the media circus."

"But if he kills again?" Quinlan said.

"We've got to find some way to stop him before he does," the DDO said. "But we're keeping this in-house."

"Sir," Quinlan said, "I'm sure I don't have to remind you that our charter prohibits us from running operations inside this country. And the FBI is far better equipped to find him than we are."

With the strict compartmentalization of information in the CIA, and the policy of "need to know," the DDO was aware that the NROC chief knew nothing of Malik's operations as a KGB officer. He decided that now was the time to brief him, if he intended to win his full support for what had to be done.

"Let me give you some background on our friend Malik," the DDO said, leveling a no-nonsense gaze at Quinlan.

"He's as good as they come. Long before we recruited him he spent ten years in New York City as an illegal, operating under deep cover. And we never knew it. The KGB groomed him to operate in this country from the time he was thirteen. He understands our culture better than we do, and he speaks colloquial English without so much as a hint of an accent. And for good measure he's got a master's degree in political science and was working on his doctorate at the University of Virginia."

The DDO hesitated, carefully selecting what additional information he would reveal to Quinlan and the others. He then continued.

"During his ten years in New York, Malik ran a network of agents inside the United Nations right under the noses of the FBI's counterintelligence people. He carried out twelve assassinations and ten kidnappings during his career, that he told us about; God only knows how many there really were. Bottom line? I want Malik worse than anyone; this happened on my watch. But the FBI couldn't begin to cope with him on the best day they ever had."

The DDO again fell silent. His eyes fixed on Lou Gregus, the head of his Special Operations section. Gregus was his favorite troubleshooter and had handled numerous knotty situations in the past. Quietly and quickly. Doing whatever it took to get the job done. An instinctive, lateral thinker, his approach to solving problems was often innovative and daring. Precisely why the DDO had summoned him to the meeting.

Gregus, with a swimmer's physique and still boyishly handsome at forty-two, sat at the far end of the table. His hands rested in his lap, and his chair was pushed back, his long legs stretched out and crossed at the ankles in a relaxed pose. He had listened carefully to the discussions, and upon noticing that the DDO's attention was now directed toward him, he brushed a shock of graying blond hair from his forehead and raised himself to a more erect position in his chair.

"Lou?" the DDO said. "Any suggestions?"

"Yes. Our own low-profile hunt for Malik."

"How low-profile?"

"One man, supported by a twenty-four-hour operations center. We can set it up in one of our safe houses, away from headquarters. I won't need any more than two or three of my own people. We can tap into our sources, keep track of what the FBI and the locals are doing, and feed it to our man in the field."

"Who do you have in mind for the fieldwork?"

"Mike Culley."

The name had a galvanizing effect on the others. The DDO and Gregus were the only ones who knew him personally, but Quinlan and Walters were more than familiar with the name, as was everyone else in the CIA.

Culley had been sentenced to four years in prison for lying to Congress and contempt of Congress, in the course of protecting his CIA superiors, the DDO in particular, during Senate hearings into the BCCI banking scandal. Culley had been laundering money through BCCI to support "black operations" and illegal CIA proprietary companies. He was the only direct link to the operations, and was given assurances that the Agency would protect him if he kept silent about their activities.

But it had been Culley's misfortune to draw Oliver Hendricks, a hard-nosed judge from a wealthy, socially prominent family. The judge had little but contempt for the current administration, and despite numerous entreaties through the old-boy network, Hendricks had adamantly refused to give a slap-on-the-wrist sentence. He was intent on making an example of Culley, whose confrontational style and in-your-face attitude during his trial had done nothing to help matters.

The investigation and the trial had been pure politics. Enemies of the administration and those who hated the CIA had criminalized policy difference for their political benefit, just as they had done with Iran-Contra. The DDO still grated over Culley's fate, and had privately vowed to right the wrong. But the director of the CIA had told him in no uncertain terms that the matter was over. Any further intervention on the Agency's part could only cause them more problems if the press learned of it. The matter was to be forgotten.

"He's still in prison, Lou," the DDO said after a long silence. "With at least two more years left on his sentence."

"Permission to speak openly," Gregus said. "About the Judge Hendricks matter."

The DDO looked sternly at the others. "Nothing leaves this room. Understood?"

Quinlan and Walters nodded emphatically.

"Go ahead, Lou."

Gregus leaned forward, placing his elbows on the table. "When you told me the matter of the judge was closed, I still completed the investigation you requested after Culley's sentencing. I filed it away, just in case. Culley was a friend of mine. The information is still operable."

"Shame on you, Lou," the DDO said, without a trace of a reprimand in his tone. "And what are His Honor's peccadillos?"

"He likes boys. Very young boys," Gregus said. "He had a Brazilian housekeeper living at his estate in Middleburg. She has a five-year-old son. Two years ago she abruptly quit working for him and went back to Brazil, two hundred thousand dollars richer. There were other incidents, all very neatly covered up with a lot of money. I feel certain that Hendricks can be persuaded to vacate Culley's sentence and effect his immediate release from prison."

"A goddamn pedophile," the DDO said. But it

was perfect. The judge would have to be out of his mind to refuse them or report their approach. "Do it."

"Why don't we just use someone else," Quinlan said, "and avoid all these complications? Surely there are any number of special-operations people available."

"Because Culley's street smart. He's worked the field, alone, for years," the DDO said. "And more to the point, he was Malik's control for the six years we ran him as an agent-in-place in Moscow. He was the one who organized his escape from Russia, and he was the one who personally brought him out. He knows him better than anyone."

"What makes you think Culley will agree to help us?" It was Quinlan again, nervous about getting in too deep.

"I don't know that he will," Gregus said. "We were friends. We went through Agency training together, and I worked with him off and on. I can approach him in confidence. And I know him well enough to guarantee you this: If he agrees to help, he won't go back on his word."

"How can you be so sure he won't simply go to the FBI and tell them everything?" Quinlan said. "He certainly owes us no allegiance after what happened to him."

"For the same reason he ended up in prison," Gregus said. "Loyalty and a strong personal sense of honor."

"He's lost a lot, Lou," the DDO said, recalling the details of what Culley went through. "His wife committed suicide two weeks after he went to prison. His home and cars were seized for auction, and I think his daughter even had to drop out of college after his lawyers took whatever savings he had."

The DDO paused, then, as if in a personal apology to those present, said, "We had strict orders not to do anything for him. As far as the director was concerned, Culley was a nonperson."

Gregus nodded in recognition of the DDO's point. "As I said, I don't know if I can convince him to help. It might just boil down to how much he wants to get out of prison versus how much he hates us for destroying his life. But if he tells me he'll do it," Gregus said firmly, "he'll do it."

"Does he have to be told why we want to bring Malik in?" Quinlan said, again looking to cover bases.

"He's going to want to know why the full-court press," the DDO said. "If for no other reason, to assess what he's up against."

"The Secret Service may have provided us with the perfect cover," Gregus said. "All I'll need to tell Culley is we want Malik because of his involvement in the counterfeiting case. It's not a complete lie."

Gregus got an attaboy grin from the DDO.

"Good thinking, Lou. That will also cover our asses in the unlikely event the FBI finds out what we're up to."

The DDO raised an admonishing finger, intended for Quinlan and Walters. "One more time, fellows. Nothing leaves this room."

With that he turned to Gregus. "Get on it, Lou. Anything you need, talk to me directly. And you report only to me."

ENCLOSED BY A thirty-foot-high wall bristling with guard towers, the Lewisburg federal penitentiary rises like an Italian Renaissance fortress amid the gently rolling farmland of central Pennsylvania. Built in 1932 to confine one thousand inmates, the ominous brick compound now holds in excess of fifteen hundred of the most dangerous men in the federal prison system.

In the laundry, on the basement level of the main building that houses the cellblocks, Mike Culley brought a steam press down on a shirtsleeve, raised it, then rearranged the shirt and brought it down again. Most of the twenty-two inmates who worked in the laundry were talking to each other across the long, narrow room, shouting above the noise of the huge washers and dryers and presses. Some chanted rap songs, others whistled off-key; a few sorrier ones carried on animated two-way conversations with themselves.

Culley did his best to block out the constant human din that had permeated his every waking moment since he arrived at the prison fourteen months ago. But it was impossible to avoid, even at mealtimes; the mess hall had the acoustics of an elevator shaft and was packed with hundreds of prisoners at a time. There were no pleasures to be found in prison life, but the constant noise, the loud and senseless chatter and boisterous role playing and posturing, grated on him more than anything else.

Culley turned to get another shirt from the cart and saw the guard in charge of the laundry approaching, keys jangling from his belt.

"You got a visitor, Culley."

Culley gave the guard a questioning look, then continued with his work, slipping the shirt over the bottom section of the press and reaching for the handle.

"I didn't put anyone on my visitors' list," he said. "So I don't get visitors. And I don't want any."

"I don't know anything about that," the guard said. "Warden called down, says inmate 52176, Michael T. Culley, that's you, is to report to the visitors' room. There's an officer on his way to take you up. So let's go."

Culley stopped working and stared long and hard at the guard. He felt a sudden tightness in his chest. An unspoken plea screamed inside his head. *Please, don't let it be Jenny! Please, not Jenny!* He had told his caseworker that under no circumstances did he want to see his daughter. She was all he had left. His baby. His little girl. And he did not want her to see him like this. On the day he was taken away, he had asked her never to come to the prison to see him. She had promised that she wouldn't. And no letters; they would have been too hard to bear. Reluctantly, she had promised that too. When his wife committed suicide, she had left instructions that there was to be no funeral, no services of any kind. She wanted to be cremated, and Jenny had carried out her wishes, scattering her ashes over the pond on their small farm in Clifton, Virginia. Culley had broken his own rule and written Jenny a long letter upon her mother's death, comforting her as best he could, but he had again asked her not to respond in kind.

"Come on, Culley. Let's not make this difficult."

Culley brought the press down hard and held it in place much longer than necessary. When he raised it a large scorch mark streaked the back of the shirt.

"That's real smart," the guard said. "I'm gonna write you up for that. So you can count on moppin' the halls every night for a week."

Culley said nothing. If he refused to go to the visiting room the guard would call the goon squad. He would be wrestled to the floor, shackled, and hauled off to a strip cell. Solitary confinement for two weeks, maybe a month if he fought them. And if it was Jenny who had come to see him it had to be something urgent. They'd tell her he had refused. That he had been put in the hole. And he'd hurt her again. Better his own pain and embarrassment than causing her any more suffering. But, please, not Jenny.

▽

Lou Gregus sat in a bright blue molded-plastic chair at a cafeteria-style table in the visiting room at the front of the main building. He had purposely chosen a table in a quiet corner, removed from the dozen or so inmates scattered about the room. Gregus studied the khaki-clad prisoners with curiosity. Some talked with tearful wives, holding children in their laps, others held hands with girlfriends, rubbing knees under the table. Two were deeply involved in intense, whispered conversations with men in well-tailored suits with expensive briefcases open before them. Gregus assumed they were lawyers. Two guards stood nearby: one in front of the door through which the prisoners entered the room, the other beside the visitors' entrance.

Gregus's attention was drawn to the far end of the room when the door leading to the interior of the prison opened. He saw Mike Culley enter, looking apprehensive as he scanned the room. His eyes locked on to Gregus, and as though a mask had fallen from his face, his expression changed to one of contempt.

Gregus stood as Culley moved slowly toward him, then extended his hand as he reached the table.

"Good to see you, Mike."

Culley ignored the outstretched hand, pulled out an orange plastic chair, and sat down without a word.

"Well, I guess under the circumstances I don't have any right to expect a warm welcome."

Culley remained still and silent. He looked much the same as when Gregus had last seen him over a year ago. Maybe a few pounds heavier from the starchy prison diet, but still with a trim, athletic build with broad, sloping shoulders that suggested upper-body strength. They were the same age, but Culley, like Gregus, looked younger than his forty-two years. So far prison hadn't changed that. But something was different, and Gregus saw it when he looked into his old friend's eyes: the mischievous twinkle of the Irish rogue was gone. It was a flat, cold stare that greeted him.

"The DDO sends his regards," Gregus said. "He hopes things are going well for you." It was an inane thing to say, and he regretted it the moment he said it.

"What do you want, Lou?"

"Something's come up. Maybe an opportunity to set this mess right." Gregus again regretted his choice of words. With all that had happened to Culley, there was nothing that could ever make it right again.

Culley remained silent. The cold, hard stare unchanged.

"We need your help, Mike. If you agree I can . . ." Gregus paused, looked away for a moment, then leaned across the table. "Shit, Mike! I'm sorry. I know nothing can ever make this right. I'm sorry about your being in this rotten place. I'm sorry about Janet. I'm sorry—"

Culley's hand shot up from his side and clamped on to Gregus's throat. The pressure on his windpipe was tremendous, cutting off his airflow.

"Mike!" Gregus rasped.

Both guards in the room began moving toward the table. One raised a small portable radio to his mouth. Gregus saw them coming and held up a hand to ward them off. The guards stopped in their tracks, but stood ready to intervene. Gregus grabbed Culley's wrist with both hands and struggled to break his hold.

"Let go, Mike!" The words were barely audible. Little more than a squeak.

Culley stopped squeezing and relaxed his grip, then removed his hand altogether. The look in his eyes was one of pure hatred. The guards backed off and returned to their posts.

"Don't you ever mention her name again!" Culley's words were measured and emphatic. Filled with venom.

"Okay. Okay. All I was trying to say is, I'm sorry for everything that's happened to you. There was nothing I could do. Nothing any of us who cared could do. They shut us out, Mike. It was hands off or we were all out on our asses."

"What do you want, Lou?"

"As I said. We need your help." Gregus rubbed his throat. His voice slowly regained its full strength. "You remember Nikolai Lubanov? You ran him in Moscow and brought him out."

Culley nodded that he did.

"Well, he's resettled. His new name is John Malik. We got word that he's been a bad boy. Got himself involved in a counterfeiting operation. The DDO wants you to help bring him in. The Secret Service is bound to get on to him and we want him tucked away before they do. It's a damage-control operation. Same old story. Clean up our own mess. The Agency doesn't need the embarrassment."

"So? Pick him up. What do you need from me?"

"He's disappeared and we can't find him. And we can't mount a full-scale search without drawing attention to ourselves, not to mention violating the charter. You know him better than anyone. If you'll work the field, I'll set up a twenty-four-hour operations center to feed you everything we can get. Keep it all low-profile."

"Work the field? Am I missing something here, or are you forgetting where I am?"

Gregus smiled. "If you agree to help us, I can have you out of here tomorrow. It's already in the works."

Culley looked out across the room for a long moment, then back to Gregus.

"I'm not interested."

"Come on, Mike. How much time is left on your sentence?"

"With time off for good behavior? About two more years."

"You'd rather spend another two years in here than help us?"

"I'd rather do a lot of things than help you."

"Look, I don't expect you to forgive any of us for leaving you twisting in the wind. But you've got to believe we tried to help. We goddamn tried. At least let us get you out of here now."

"I said I'm not interested."

"Why?"

"Because you're lying through your teeth," Culley said. "You come in here with this bullshit story and expect me to buy in to it. You forget who you're talking to? I cleaned up a lot of messes for the DDO. What is it? He got in too deep somewhere and now the ex-con is perfect for the operation? Deniable and expendable."

"It's not like that, Mike. I swear. What I've told you is the truth," Gregus said. It was a lie by omission at best, but his guilt was partly attenuated by the fact that the counterfeiting story was true.

"I brought this on myself," Culley said, making a sweeping gesture around the room. "I believed in the wrong people. I've come to terms with that. I'll pay for it for the rest of my life, but I can deal with that too. So get the hell out of here and stay out of my life."

"Be reasonable, Mike."

Culley shook his head and chuckled softly. "Reasonable, huh? Tell me this: If it's so easy to get me out, where were you fourteen months ago?"

"It took some time to get what we needed." Gregus flashed a Cheshire-cat grin. "I had a little talk with your judge in his chambers a few hours ago. Let's just say he's reached a more sensible accommodation with reality. He's going to vacate your sentence."

"Is that right? What did you dig up on him?"

"Forget him, Mike. He's a piece of shit. Now, come on, are you in?"

After a long pause Culley said, "Get me a Pepsi."

He sat staring at the guards and the other inmates in the room as Gregus went to the machine and brought back the cold soda, Culley's first in fourteen months.

"What haven't you told me?" he said when Gregus sat down.

"I've told you everything."

"Everything there is, or everything the DDO decided I need to know?"

"Hey, Mike. Help us. Get out of here. Get on with your life."

Culley fell silent. The past fourteen months had been the worst experience of his life. He felt like a caged animal, hating every minute of his confinement. Hating himself for having destroyed his family and everything he had worked for. And there was Jenny to think of. In here there was nothing he could do for her. He remained silent for what seemed to Gregus an interminable amount of time.

"Spell it out," he finally said.

"As I said, I can have you out of here before noon tomorrow," Gregus began. "I'll have a car outside in the visitors' lot for you. Keys in the glove compartment, along with the phone number for the twenty-four-hour ops center. You'll also find a bio on Malik since his resettlement; his place of residence and business, any other personal information we have on him about his life-style, trips he's taken, social contacts, the details of the counterfeiting case, the works. And you'll find a briefcase locked in the trunk with twenty-five thousand in cash. Operating capital, all in small bills. Use it any way you want; you're not accountable for it."

"How long has Malik been missing?"

"His case officer went to interview him two days ago. Couldn't find him. He may have left before that, but we believe he's still in the Charlottesville, Virginia, area; that's where he was resettled."

"Why do you think he's still there?"

"A strong hunch," Gregus said cautiously. "NROC controls his passport, so he hasn't left the country."

"Who are you kidding? He could have gotten a phony passport from some of his Russian mafia buddies. He was in tight with those guys in Moscow and they're coming into New York like rats off a sinking ship."

"It takes time to get phony documents, Mike. Besides, you're just strengthening my case; that's why we need you to find him."

"I'm not going after Malik with just my wits,"

Culley said. "I want a piece, nine millimeter, and a shoulder holster."

"It'll be in the briefcase with the money," Gregus said. He met and held Culley's gaze with an apologetic look. "This is a one-op contract, Mike. No matter how much some of us would like it, there's no way you can come back to the Agency."

"There's no way I'd even think about coming back," Culley said. "I'm not doing this for myself."

"Then it's agreed?"

Culley nodded his commitment. "What about my house? My lawyer's been trying to keep them from taking it until I could get out of here and get on my feet. He ran out of ideas the same time I ran out of money. I haven't heard from the sleazy son of a bitch for a couple of months."

Gregus lowered his eyes. "Sorry. I checked before I came here. The IRS has it locked up. They're going to auction it in a few days."

"The contents . . . my car, motorcycle?"

"They seized everything."

Culley nodded in resignation. "If I find out you're lying to me, Lou, about anything, the deal's off."

"Understood."

"Tomorrow morning, huh?"

"Tomorrow morning," Gregus said, and extended his hand across the table.

Culley hesitated, then shook it.

Gregus looked over at a huge, tough-looking inmate who had just entered the room. His shirtsleeves were rolled up and every square inch of his forearms was covered with jail-house tattoos. Small swastikas adorned both sides of his neck.

"This is a scary place, you know?"

"I'll tell you what's really scary," Culley said. "Sooner or later, most of these guys are going to get out of here."

"Comforting thought," Gregus said, and got up to leave. He paused and turned back to Culley. "I took the liberty of looking in on Jenny every now and then."

Culley tensed and his eyes hardened.

"Don't worry, she never knew," Gregus said. "She got back in school last semester. Bright kid. Qualified for a scholarship. She's working three part-time jobs, but she's making it."

Gregus glimpsed the look of love and pride that passed over his old friend's face before it vanished.

"Check in with me at least twice a day for updates. If I'm not at the ops center they have orders to patch you through to me wherever and whenever. Good luck, Mike."

"Yeah," Culley said, and remained at the table sipping his soda long after Gregus had left, until the guard came and escorted him back inside.

5

SHORTLY AFTER SEVEN P.M., the CIA Learjet lifted off the runway of the Penn Valley airport and banked steeply onto a southeast heading toward Andrews Air Force Base. A few minutes into the climb-out the secure-voice cellular telephone in Gregus's briefcase chirped.

"Did he agree?" It was William Childs, the deputy director for operations.

"Yes," Gregus said.

"Good. Let's get this wrapped up fast, Lou."

"The paperwork is in progress. He'll be out tomorrow morning."

The DDO detected a hesitant note in Gregus's voice. "Something bothering you?"

"Yes, sir. I'd like to put him under surveillance. At least for the first few days."

"Put Culley under surveillance? Why?"

"A gut feeling," Gregus said. "Something in his attitude. In his eyes. I don't know; there was a distance. And he blew up at one point. He never had a hair-trigger temper before. It wasn't the same Mike Culley."

"Of course it wasn't. He's been in a cage for over a year, and we're partly responsible for it," the DDO said. "Did you expect him to waltz in singing 'Don't Worry, Be Happy' and give you a hug?"

"No, sir. But just the same I'd like to keep an eye on him until I'm sure he's got his equilibrium back."

"It's your call, but keep it loose. He doesn't have a lot of confidence in us to begin with, and if he spots a tail it's not going to improve his attitude any."

"Yes, sir. I'll put a transmitter on the car I'm having sent up here for him. We can follow him at a distance. It's only a three-hour drive from Langley. I can have a team in position in plenty of time."

"Keep me posted," the DDO said, and hung up.

Gregus tapped out the number for the safe house in Alexandria, where the twenty-four-hour operations center had already been set up. The call was answered immediately by the man he had selected to run the computers and the communications system.

"What's the latest from Charlottesville?" Gregus said.

"The FBI found a note on the body; they're keeping the contents to themselves. They also found a dark green metallic paint chip they think the killer left on purpose. The Feeb in charge of the task force, Jack Matthews, was pissed that someone leaked the paint chip to the press. They don't know what they have yet, but I think I do."

"And what's that?"

"I checked Malik's NROC file. He drives a Jeep Cherokee. Dark green metallic. Doesn't make much sense he'd give them something that could eventually lead them right to him, does it?"

"Don't apply conventional logic to a psycho who chops up women."

"Right. Anyway, the press is running wild with the story since the body was found this morning. It's all over the networks' evening news. Some insensitive moron has named him the Mix and Match killer, because of the way the body parts were—"

"I get the picture," Gregus said.

"I've set up monitors to keep tabs on any breaking stuff on CNN and the local television stations."

"Anything else I should know?"

"Yeah. Might be something, might not. CNN interviewed a crime reporter from *The Washington Post*," the assistant said, checking his notes. "Julie Houser. She's been doing a series of stories on the missing college kids since the first one disappeared. I think we should check her out."

"Why?"

"She's the one who got wind of the paint chip when nobody but the cops knew about it. She must have some good sources. It might be worthwhile finding out what else she knows. Give us some idea if the Feebs are getting close to Malik."

"Under no circumstances are you to break into the *Post*'s computers," Gregus said emphatically. "If they got wise to it we'd have an even bigger mess on our hands."

"No problem," the assistant said. "If she's like most reporters, whatever she's working on is probably backed up on a home computer. We can approach it from that angle."

"Put Simmons on it," Gregus said, and looked at

his watch. "I'll be landing at Andrews in about thirty minutes. That'll put me at the safe house no later than eight-fifteen."

Gregus returned the telephone to his briefcase and reclined his seat. He tried to grab a short nap, but his conversation with Culley kept replaying in his mind. Culley *was* bitter and angry. But the DDO was right. Who the hell wouldn't be under the same circumstances?

Gregus had read the Agency's report on the suicide of Culley's wife, and as he closed his eyes and listened to the muted roar of the jet engines, the details came back to him. It happened two weeks after Culley was incarcerated. On a Saturday evening, after seeing her daughter off at the Amtrak station for the trip to New York City to begin her freshman year in college, Janet Culley went home and killed herself.

She first wrote brief letters to her husband and her daughter, asking their forgiveness. She then went to the garage, closed the overhead door, ran a flexible hose from the exhaust pipe to the front passenger window of her car, sealed it in place with duct tape, got behind the steering wheel, and turned on the engine. She died listening to a homemade tape of her husband playing the guitar and singing to her at their twentieth-anniversary party only three months earlier. The small farmhouse into which they had sunk every spare cent, and had lovingly restored, in Clifton, Virginia, was well off the road, with no close neighbors. It was not until the following afternoon, when a friend stopped by, that Janet Culley was found dead from carbon monoxide poisoning.

Gregus shook off the depressing thoughts and looked out the window into the night sky. Below, off to his left, a solid string of sparkling lights spread south along the Baltimore-Washington corridor. He stared at them, deep in thought, as the sleek jet streaked homeward. Culley was their best chance of finding Malik quickly, and he hoped he had not made a mistake in choosing him for the job. The game was now afoot, as the DDO was fond of saying, and they would find out soon enough.

6

UPON ENTERING PRISON Mike Culley had quickly established himself as a loner. Once word spread throughout the inmate population about who and what he was and why he was there, he was granted a certain respect and status. Anyone who defied authority and refused to rat out his friends ranked high in the prison social structure.

After he rebuffed an offer by a white-supremacist group to become their East Coast *Oberführer* of counterintelligence, Culley was left alone. He knew few of the inmates by their names; Crazy Jack Hurley and Spaceship Smith were two of the exceptions. They had latched on to him for their own peculiar reasons, running around the track with him in the exercise yard, spotting for him while he lifted weights, and joining him, uninvited, in the mess hall or the recreation room in the evenings. They were good for comic relief, if nothing else, so Culley tolerated their intrusive presence.

Spaceship Smith claimed to have been abducted from his prison cell by aliens—eight times over the past six years. And he was tired of it. He hoped that Culley, with his CIA contacts, could arrange for the Agency to take him somewhere to study him. There was much he could tell them, he assured Culley, who assured him that the Agency probably would not be interested until after he'd completed the two-hundred-and-fifteen-year sentence he was serving for drug trafficking and triple murder.

Crazy Jack Hurley had killed two FBI agents who were coming to arrest him for a small-town bank robbery that had netted him less than eight hundred dollars. He would never get out of prison, but was intent on improving himself despite that minor setback in his long and lackluster criminal career. He had told Culley that he enjoyed talking with him because he liked to associate with people who knew more than he did. Five minutes after meeting him Culley suspected that that included most, if not all, of the world's population.

Culley had just gone through the food line in the mess hall and was looking for a table when he saw Crazy Jack motioning for him to join him. One last time, Culley thought.

Crazy Jack ate like a jackal on the Serengeti. His cheeks were puffed with food, his eyes shifted from side to side, and his arms surrounded his tray as if he expected someone to snatch it from him at any moment.

"Gimme the salt."

Culley passed the salt. *Thank you* and *please* were never heard in prison. Any sign of civility was perceived as weakness.

"Word is you're gonna be back on the street

tomorrow, Mike. Some spook was here to see you, right?"

Crazy Jack was wired into the prison grapevine through inmate friends who worked in the administration offices. There was nothing that went on inside that he did not know about within minutes after it happened.

"Looks like it," Culley said.

"Good for you," he said, then smacked him on the back. "I'll miss ya, buddy. I learned a lot from ya."

"I learned a lot from you too."

"Yeah?"

"Yeah," Culley said, and hoped he would not be asked to delineate exactly what it was he had learned.

"Listen," Crazy Jack said. "You might wanna avoid Spaceship. He heard about the spook comin' to see you too. He thinks this might be his big chance to get outta here; let people stick electrodes in his head and shit."

"I'll keep an eye out for him," Culley said.

"You do that. And good luck to ya, Mike. I gotta run. Got a poker game set up. Asshole already owes me ten cartons. I don't know why the fuck I even bother playin' with him no more. No competition. Can't learn nothin', ya know?"

"I know," Culley said.

Crazy Jack got up to leave, then bent down and put his head close to Culley's ear. "Look. You're outta here tomorrow, right?" he said in a conspiratorial whisper. "I ain't goin' nowhere, so who am I gonna tell? I gotta know. Did the CIA kill Kennedy?"

Culley simply looked at him and winked. Why ruin his day?

"I knew it! I fuckin' knew it!" With that, Crazy Jack wove his way through the tables and out into the main corridor, grinning in triumph.

Culley's eyes moved slowly over the three hundred or so inmates packed into the mess hall: black guys who thought they were Muslims, white guys who thought they were Nazis, an assortment of malignant sociopaths and snitches who huddled together watching each other's backs. All segregated into little pockets of hatred and conspiracy, organizing their prison scams and planning what they were going to do if and when they got out. He had spent more than a year in the company of cheats, liars, thieves, murderers, and rapists who couldn't be trusted any farther than you could spit them. But they never pretended to be anything other than what they were, which was more than he could say for the people he had worked with and believed in for twenty years.

Prison life had been regimented, structured, and predictable, every decision made for him. Culley had mentally prepared himself to spend the next two years in the same mindless limbo. The sudden prospect of regaining his freedom was unnerving. He picked at his food, eating little, then rose to leave, noticing Spaceship Smith entering the mess hall just as he left, his eyes eagerly scanning the tables.

Culley went directly back to his cell, skipping his evening run in the exercise yard. He lay on his bunk and stared at the ceiling until the seven o'clock count was over, and remained in his cell when the doors were opened for the recreation-room period. The conflict of emotions made him edgy. Get on with his life, Gregus had said. What life? There would be no pension, no offers from private security firms. He was an ex-con with a future full of menial jobs and sidelong glances.

His career as an intelligence officer, the only profession he had ever cared about, was over. He had been as good as any of them and better than most. Tested and not found wanting in life-and-death situations, as few of them had been. In the dark, snow-swept alleys of Moscow. In the grimy back streets of Prague and East Berlin. He had cleaned up their messes and run their black operations. He had been loyal and dedicated. Awarded an Intelligence Medal, the highest award the Agency gave. And in the end they had considered him expendable and betrayed him.

He got up off the bed and stood at the small barred window overlooking the narrow strip of grass between the cellblock and the facing hospital and isolation wing. He forced himself to think of other things, and his thoughts turned to Malik and the six years he had run the arrogant son of a bitch. He had never liked or trusted him. He had warned the Moscow station chief on numerous occasions that some of Malik's information was suspect, and that he was running black-market operations with the Russian mafia on the side, using the dollars and Swiss francs he demanded and got from the Agency. He long suspected that Malik was selling the same information he got for the CIA to the British and the West Germans, but he could never prove it. It did not surprise him that he had reverted to type. What the hell had they expected?

Despite Gregus's assurances Culley was certain

he had not been told everything. The counterfeiting story rang hollow. He had played the game far too long not to hear it. But then, that had always been the way they operated. And what difference did it make? He would keep his bargain and track Malik down. And that was the last he would have to do with them.

The bitterness and anger and hatred that had nearly destroyed him were still there. It came in the night. In the small hours before dawn when the mind feeds on itself. It rose like a bile from the depths of his soul. Choking him with rage. He had taught himself to hide it; to keep it under control. Any violent outbursts would have meant his "good days" would be taken away, adding time to an already unbearable sentence. On two occasions it had almost overtaken him despite his best efforts, but he had managed to repress it.

It came to him again that night. As he lay awake in the predawn hours. "It's over. It's over," he repeated softly. And the rage finally subsided. They had hurt him. Wounded him deeply. But they had not broken him. In a few hours he would walk out the front gate a free man. He would somehow put it all behind him, and find some foundation on which to rebuild a semblance of a life for himself and Jenny.

7

PETER DAVIDSON, *The Washington Post*'s city
editor, looked out through the half-glass partition
separating his office from the newsroom bullpen to
see Julie Houser headed for his door. He waved her
in as she was about to knock.

"I want to go down to Charlottesville," she said
as she closed the door behind her.

"Something breaking?"

"Not yet, but I have a feeling it's about to. The
killer was making some kind of statement when he
dumped the first body, and my instincts tell me he's
going to do the same with the other three. I'd like to
be there when it happens."

"Have you found out what was in the note he
left?"

"I'm working on it, but it's going to go a lot
faster if I'm down there where I can feel my way
around, talk to the local cops face-to-face. It'll also
give me a chance to get some background. Local
color on how all this is affecting the university and
the students."

Davidson nodded his consent. "I want to hear from you. Every day."

"My portable computer's got a modem," Houser said. "I'll just send my stuff in over the phone."

She paused as she opened the door to leave. "Oh, something else. I think my apartment was broken into last night."

"You *think* it was broken into?"

"I'm almost certain."

"Was anything stolen?"

"No. But unless I'm getting senile, someone was roaming through my computer files," Houser said. "My word-processing program has a feature that time- and date-stamps a file in the directory every time it's called up. When I got home last night around eleven, I decided to do a little work before turning in. When I finished, I checked the directory for another file and noticed that the one I'd been working on with all of my research on the missing college students was stamped with the right time."

"So?"

"I made a mental note when we went off daylight saving time to put the computer clock back an hour. I hadn't gotten around to doing it yet."

"Maybe you did and forgot."

"Maybe. But I don't think so. I think whoever was there checked the directory before he called up the file, noted the previous time and date stamps, adjusted the computer's clock and calendar before he went through the file, then reset it to the right time and date when he was through. Only, he hadn't noticed the computer's clock was still on daylight saving time when he first turned it on."

"Were your sources' names in the file?"

"No way. They're written in my own personal code in a little address book that stays with me at all times."

"Were there any signs of a break-in?"

"None. Whoever did it was good. No marks on the door or the locks. Nothing out of place."

"Who?"

"A 'black bag' job of that caliber? The FBI comes to mind. They weren't too pleased about my finding out about the paint chip. Maybe they wanted to see what else I know and who my sources are."

"I don't know," Davidson said. "The FBI's had its share of bad press lately. I can't imagine they'd chance searching your place without a court order, and they had no grounds to get one. I'd lean more toward you changed the time on the computer clock and forgot about it."

"Well, that isn't all of it. I don't want you to think I'm getting paranoid or anything, but I'm also pretty sure I had a tail on my way to work this morning."

Davidson raised a skeptical eyebrow.

"Don't give me that look. You're forgetting, I'm an ex-cop," Houser said. "I spotted a dark blue Mercury sedan with two men in it when I drove away from my apartment. They held off about three or four cars behind me. I made a few lane changes, increased my speed, then slowed down. They stayed right with me. They didn't break off until a few blocks from work. It could have been a coincidence. The FBI or the Secret Service working some case. But I learned a long time ago that when you chalk something up to coincidence, it usually isn't."

"If it happens again, get the license-plate number."

"Gee, boss, I'd've never thought of that," Houser said with a smile and a wink, then threw him a choppy salute and left.

Davidson watched as she went to her desk, grabbed her shoulder bag, and headed for the elevators. She had come to him for a job just two years ago, from New York City. Her credentials were not that impressive, two years at NYU with some journalism courses, and at thirty-one, with no track record in the business, she was a little old to be just starting out. But his gut told him to give her a chance. And his gut turned out to be right.

She was a natural, with great instincts for where the real story was. She knew how to interpret what she saw and how to follow a lead. She was hardworking, never missed a deadline, and the quality of her writing was far superior to that of most of her peers. And, as every male in the building immediately took notice, she was real easy to look at, with a swimsuit-model figure and a face to match.

He had assigned her as a court reporter for the first year, until he learned something she had left off her résumé. She had been a New York City cop for ten years. When he asked her why she hadn't mentioned it, she had simply replied, "That was then, this is now." At the time he was in dire need of another crime reporter and offered her the job. She refused, considering it a step down. He pressed, assuring her that in her case it wasn't. She reluctantly accepted.

A few months later, while having drinks with an old friend, a deputy chief in the Washington police department, Davidson got the full story. When Houser began covering crime, the local cops, wondering how she knew so much about how they operated, had checked her out.

Houser was twenty-one when she graduated from the police academy and immediately volunteered for an undercover narcotics assignment. It was high-risk police work, but a fast track to detective. Eighteen months later, after two commendations, and a combat cross awarded for her involvement in a shoot-out during a buy-bust operation, she got her detective's gold shield and was assigned to the homicide squad at the Seventeenth Precinct in midtown Manhattan.

Eight years later, while responding to a 1013, officer-in-trouble call, she took a bullet for her partner and was awarded the Medal of Honor, the department's highest award, earning her the respect of every cop in the department. Three months after that she retired from the force, for reasons she declined to discuss the one, and only, time Davidson had broached the subject.

The local cops, after word spread of her record in New York, trusted her and considered her one of their own. They granted her unheard-of access that other reporters could only dream of. She never violated a confidence, or attributed information to anyone who asked to remain anonymous, but she was more than capable of playing hardball if she felt she was being lied to or used.

Her story about the discovery of the body on the university grounds yesterday had gotten the front page that morning, and was filled with facts and background that none of the other papers had bothered to dig up, or were unable to get. Davidson had learned to give her a loose rein, and it had always paid off with top-notch stories. He thought about what she had said about the break-in at her apartment, and someone following her that morning. She wasn't given to exaggeration, and he had never known her to have an overactive imagination. He decided not to worry about it. If he had to choose which of his reporters was best able to handle themselves in a difficult situation, it would be Julie Houser.

▽

AT FOUR-FIFTEEN the rush-hour traffic on I-66 out of Washington was just beginning. Houser estimated no more than a ninety-minute drive to Charlottesville once she hit 29 South. She was singing along and drumming her fingers on the steering wheel to a Tommy James and the Shondells song as she glanced in her rearview mirror, downshifted, and swung into the inside lane to pass a truck.

And there it was again. Four cars back. The same dark blue sedan she had spotted that morning. She stayed in the passing lane looking back at the car, seeing two men in it, and that it had no front license plate. She saw them pull out just as she cut back into the right lane after passing the truck. Either they were damn poor at their job, or . . . No, that wasn't it. No one could be that incompetent. They wanted her to know they were there. It was an attempt to intimidate her. To scare her off.

Houser smiled to herself, then reached over and turned up the volume of the golden oldies station she was listening to.

"You want to play, boys? Okay. Let's play."

The 1967 Porsche 911S Targa was a real sleeper. The guard-red paint had long since faded, the vinyl on the removable section of the roof looked like it had been attacked by piranhas, and the chrome and rocker panels were pitted with rust. From the outside the car looked as though it was due for the junkyard at any moment. But ten months ago, after buying the relic for a song, she spent four thousand dollars to have the engine rebuilt, balanced, and blueprinted, and another three thousand on new brakes, transmission, and gearbox. The powerful six-cylinder sports car, the last of the Porsches to be equipped with three two-barrel carburetors, performed every bit as well as the day it rolled out of the Stuttgart factory, and that was exceptionally well.

Houser again downshifted to third gear, floored the accelerator, and quickly reached one hundred miles an hour. She looked back to see the dark blue sedan passing the truck, looking for her. She took one of the exits for Manassas at seventy miles an hour, braked hard, then swung onto a two-lane road heading south. She was around three sharp turns and into a long straightaway before she caught a distant glimpse of the dark blue sedan swinging wide out of the last turn.

Five minutes later, after turning off onto a narrow, winding state route, and then another, they were nowhere in sight. Houser slowed to the legal speed limit and lowered the volume of the radio. She took her miniature tape recorder out of her shoulder bag and spoke into it, noting the date, time, and circumstances of the incident.

A NIGHT BREEZE carried a promise of the winter to come through the old forest. It rattled the dying leaves of a stand of dogwoods and swayed the tall grass at the edge of the woods before continuing its errant journey over the surface of the lake, shimmering the glow of light from the cabin on the opposite shore. The profound silence of the place was broken only by the chirping of crickets and the soft strains of a country ballad that drifted out through windows open to the crisp evening air.

The rustic two-story log cabin sat in the middle of a six-hundred-acre private game preserve of dense woodland in the heart of Virginia's rural Fluvanna County. The cabin had served as a hunting and fishing camp for the Lawrence family of Richmond for over ninety years. It had been deserted for nearly two decades, ever since one of the present owner's sons found his wife there, in bed with his younger brother, and shot and killed them both. The senior Lawrence had arranged for repairs and maintenance over the years, but he had never set foot inside the preserve again. Stories of how the dead couple's ghosts haunted the cabin and roamed the woods at night were still told throughout the area.

Lawrence, having fallen on hard times and in need of money, had advertised the property in the Charlottesville and Richmond papers for more than a year without results. He was eager to rent the cabin until he could find a buyer for the entire six hundred acres. John Malik was his salvation. He said he was an adjunct professor at the University of Virginia looking for a weekend retreat. He had paid him cash in advance for one year.

The cabin had indoor plumbing and electricity, and a locked farm gate blocked access to the two miles of rough dirt track that led into the property from a lightly traveled state route. The isolation was complete. Malik had neither seen nor heard another living soul anywhere near the cabin in the month since he rented it. He spent most of his time there, first planning and preparing, and then satisfying the driving compulsions that, after lying dormant for the past three years, now dominated his every waking moment.

He could not believe his good fortune when he first saw the place. A forty-five-minute drive from his home and shop in Charlottesville, it was perfect for what he had in mind. And its former use as a hunting camp provided an unexpected bonus.

At the back of the cabin, in a separate twenty-foot-square room, a double-door refrigerator-freezer and two chest freezers, each with thirty cubic feet of storage space, took up most of one wall. A seven-foot-by-four-foot butcher's block, where deer had once been carved into roasts and steaks, dominated the center of the room. Above the butcher's block, hanging from an overhead rack, was the assortment of knives, saws, and cleavers necessary for carving and dressing the animals. A meat grinder, used for making venison sausage, stood on a table on the opposite wall, along with two large stainless-steel sinks.

The smooth concrete floor sloped gently to a drain in the center, allowing the room to be hosed down. Four meat hooks were attached to a metal bar that ran the width of one end of the room, where the deer had been hung while being gutted. Just outside the back door a gas-fired incinerator turned the waste products to ashes and bone shards. The room could not have suited Malik's purposes better had he designed and built it himself. Indeed, it had even sparked his creativity beyond what he had originally envisioned. He needed to add only a few personal items: a video camera mounted on a tripod at one end of the room, a roll of thin metal wire, a few large fishhooks with the barbs filed off, and four metal rings, to which he had fixed leather thongs as tie-down straps and which he had then nailed to the four corners of the butcher's block.

Most of the front of the cabin was taken up by a huge great room with a towering fireplace of natural stone. A half-wall at one end of the room separated an eat-in kitchen with a rough-hewn oak dining table and benches. Upstairs, four bedrooms, each with two double-deck bunk beds, opened onto a balcony that overlooked the great room. A porch, with a swing and a few old-fashioned rocking chairs, ran the length of the front of the cabin, completing the well-thought-out camp.

The chill night air, heavy with the scent of autumn, drifted in through the open windows as Malik tossed another log into the roaring blaze in the fireplace. The country ballad he had been listening to ended and he inserted another disc into his portable CD player. He skipped the first two tracks to select a raucous up-tempo tune, then turned up the volume. His head and shoulders moved to the rhythm of the music as he donned a cowboy hat at a rakish angle and began to line-dance by himself, stomping and twirling around the room. He held a small remote control in his hand as he danced, and pressed the repeat button to hear the song again and again.

When the song ended for the third time, Malik was perspiring and out of breath. He flopped on the overstuffed sofa and tossed his hat onto a chair opposite. His eyes went to the three oversized nylon duffel bags he had placed by the door, then to the bold headlines of the newspapers scattered about the coffee table. A smile spread slowly across his face.

"Mix and Match killer," he said aloud. Not bad. He picked up one of the papers and studied the front-page photograph of FBI Special Agent Jack Matthews, a dozen microphones stuck in his face. *You ain't seen nothin' yet, Special Agent Matthews. Tomorrow will be spectacular. Performance art at its best.*

His thoughts went back three days, to one of his little bitches, which was how he thought of them, and addressed them when he spoke to them. Was she the third or the fourth one he had grabbed? The fourth, yes. With her tight little ass and full, firm breasts. The first three had fulfilled some of his fantasies. Acknowledging his complete control and dominance. Whining and begging. One had even regressed to the point of crying in a childlike voice for her mommy and daddy. But not the fourth. The arrogant little bitch had spit on him. Spit on him! Defiant to the end; an end that he had carefully prolonged as an object lesson to the one he had kept alive, who was then totally submissive to his every whim. It was so much better with one of them watching. The sheer terror in her eyes, knowing she was next. Each scream from the one he was working on echoed and amplified by the other. It was an innovation, and heightened his pleasure immensely.

But he couldn't chance that luxury again. Keeping one alive until he collected another was too dangerous. The last one had almost escaped. He had underestimated the dosage. The drug had worn off too soon. Had he not forgotten something at the cabin, and returned twenty minutes after he left, she would have been free of the ropes and gone.

He hummed along to another tune as he smoked a cigarette and let his thoughts drift back over the years. To a small town, thirty kilometers north of Moscow, where it had all started simply enough. He was eleven years old, and the watching had thrilled him. He would finish his schoolwork as quickly as possible, then wait until his mother left for her night shift job at the tractor factory, locking him in his room, or so she believed. The timing was critical. The shank of the evening. Before the curtains were drawn or the shades pulled. Winter months were his favorite time with their early darkness.

He would roam the narrow alleys behind the crude one-story houses in his neighborhood until he found a lighted window through which he could observe those inside. In the beginning the simplest things aroused him. An old woman who sat alone each night at the kitchen table, eating her meager meals of black bread and thin, watery potato soup by candlelight, and crying. Watching a family at their evening meal, he would imagine what they were talking or laughing about. Making up conversations to fit their facial expressions and gestures. At times he could vicariously feel the warmth of a mother's embrace, or the security of covers being tucked under his chin before the bedroom light went out. He fantasized about what it would be like to have a father, even one who spanked him as the man in the house at the end of his street did to his children. But his mother did enough of that. She was quick to use the old leather strap whenever he disobeyed.

It wasn't long before he established a route. Making certain he reached favored homes at precise times. And he soon discovered other things. Things that excited him in new ways, made him short of breath and mesmerized him to the point of courting frostbite from staying out too long in the frigid Russian winters. The nightly ritual of a woman brushing out her long, luxurious hair as she sat before a dressing table in a loose-fitting nightgown, her breasts partially visible through the open front. The teenage girl and her father, who bathed together and fondled each other. And the huge, muscular man who beat his wife while they had sex, shoving her to her knees and forcing himself into her mouth. Sometimes that was all he did, holding her mouth shut so she had to swallow when he was finished. But other times he would enter her from the rear and bite her on the back as he satisfied himself. Any resistance was met with powerful slaps that sent her reeling across the room, or vicious body blows that doubled her over and made her retch. Later, when the man was asleep and snoring loudly, Malik would watch the battered woman get out of bed and stand at the window, staring out into the darkness long into the night.

By the time he was fourteen the watching alone no longer satisfied him. He began to feel a strong stirring deep within. One hot summer night, in a thick stand of evergreens on the banks of the river that flowed along the outskirts of the town, he saw the young girl who bathed with her father. She was alone, and he approached her and began to fondle her in the same way he had seen her father do. She slapped him. He slapped her back, hard, and she began to cry. He began to undress her and she offered no resistance, doing whatever he asked. He did not know what made him choke her to death, or what had driven him for the next three days to return to where he had concealed her body to sit beside her. And he was surprised to find that little was said about the girl's disappearance, and even less when her skeletal remains were found six months later by a man walking with his dog. In the worker's paradise of the Union of Soviet Socialist Republics, such crimes never happened, and consequently were never reported in the government-controlled press. Local police forces did not communicate with each other, and only those who lived in the same town as the victims heard of the murders, and spoke of them only in whispers.

When he was fifteen, he received a used bicycle for his birthday, and his horizons expanded. He would ride to nearby towns and villages at night selecting, then stalking, his next victim. He raped and killed two more young girls before his excellent grades at school drew the attention of a local KGB official and he was sent off to a private academy. It was three years before he raped and murdered again, two local women in the vicinity of his KGB school. By his twentieth birthday his fantasies had grown to include mutilation and torture and he constantly worked to improve his techniques, to prolong his pleasure and his victim's torment. He changed to selecting only prostitutes, knowing that their deaths would not be seriously investigated and would be attributed to the often dangerous lives they lived. But he soon tired of them. They were too hard and streetwise and often fought him to the end, refusing to be dominated.

By the time he was a fully trained KGB case officer, such were his skills in surveillance and countersurveillance that stalking and abducting his victims unnoticed and concealing any evidence that might incriminate him had become second nature. It was then that he began to choose only women of a type that excited him. He could recall, in detail, each and every victim. Dresden, Leipzig, Berlin, New York City, Moscow, Kiev, Leningrad, and now Charlottesville. Thirty-six since leaving his hometown. He could still see their faces, remember precisely what he had done to each of them, and where he had left their bodies.

As he sat on the sofa, his reverie fading, he thought of playing some of his videotapes. But there was work to be done in preparation for tomorrow. He looked at his watch. It was two A.M. Time to reconnoiter the dump site and go over his route one last time. Then, this time tomorrow night . . . "Show time, my little bitches," he said aloud. "Show time!"

9

A LOUD BEEP tone rose in pitch and intensity, filling the interior of the black four-door sedan. The man in the front passenger seat, acting as the tracker, looked down at the direction-finding receiver mounted under the dash. The bar graph on the signal-strength meter was moving steadily toward the top of the register.

The signal was coming from a magnetically mounted transmitter attached to the car they had been following since it left Lewisburg, Pennsylvania, forty-five minutes ago. Approximately the size of a deck of cards, the transmitter had a range of five miles under optimum conditions, allowing them to stay well behind the target vehicle. The increased frequency of the beep meant they were closing fast. A few moments later the beep became a steady tone and the motion sensor on the LCD display indicated the vehicle they were tracking had stopped.

"Turn down the volume on that damn thing, will you?" the driver said as the beeper sounded at an earsplitting level.

"He's stopped somewhere up ahead," the tracker said, rotating the volume control knob. "About a mile or so, on the right."

The driver's eyes returned to the road, looking for a place to pull over. A split second later his fist thumped the steering wheel as they drove past a gas station.

"A mile, my ass! There he is."

Mike Culley could be seen standing at the rear of the gray Ford Taurus he had found waiting for him in the prison parking lot at seven o'clock that morning. He was pumping gas and drinking a can of Pepsi.

"How can he need gas? He's only gone about fifty miles."

"I used three quarters of a tank on the drive up from Alexandria."

"I told you to fill the damn thing before you left it at the prison," the driver said.

"Nothing was open in that Podunk town at one in the morning. What the hell did you want me to do, siphon off some of ours?"

"Jesus, I hope he didn't spot us."

"I doubt it. Pull in someplace up ahead. We'll just wait until he drives by."

Ten minutes later Culley drove past the surveillance vehicle. He had not missed the quick head swings of the two men inside the black four-door sedan when it passed the gas station, nor did he miss seeing it parked facing the highway in the lot of a McDonald's a half mile down the road. He had known Gregus would put him under surveillance, at least initially. It's what he would have done.

Back on the highway, with the receiver emitting a low beep at five-second intervals, the surveillance team settled in two miles behind Culley. South of Harrisburg the compass display, which gave bearing and direction of travel on the target vehicle, indicated that Culley had gotten on the Pennsylvania Turnpike and was driving east toward Philadelphia.

"He's definitely not headed for Charlottesville," the driver said. "At least not directly."

"Maybe I ought to call it in."

"No. We'll let it play out for a while."

Ninety minutes later Culley left the turnpike, bypassed Philadelphia on the expressway, and drove south on I-95 toward Wilmington, Baltimore, and Washington.

The tracker took the secure-voice cellular phone from its cradle on the center console and dialed the number for the twenty-four-hour operations center at the safe house in Alexandria.

"He should have taken Eighty-one south out of Harrisburg if he was going to Charlottesville," the tracker told Lou Gregus. "It's the shortest route. Instead he took the turnpike east."

"Where are you now?"

"Delaware. Approximately fifteen miles south of Wilmington. Southbound on I-Ninety-five."

"Just stay with him and give him plenty of room," Gregus said. "I think I know where he's going. His home is in Clifton, Virginia, thirty minutes west of the Beltway off Route Sixty-six. If it looks like he's going anywhere else, let me know." One last look? Gregus thought. A sentimental journey? He hoped that was it.

▽

Twenty minutes later Culley pulled into a rest stop just across the Maryland border. It was the fourth stop he had made in the past hour. This time it looked promising; the parking lot was full. He went inside the restaurant and ravenously ate his first real breakfast in fourteen months. He ordered four eggs, scrambled, home fries, nearly a half pound of bacon, pancakes drenched in syrup, and three cups of coffee that actually tasted like coffee. He felt like a slug when he finally left the counter. But a contented slug.

Back outside he scanned the parking lot, making certain the black four-door sedan was nowhere in sight. He then began carefully going over his car. He looked under the dash, raised the hood and checked the engine compartment, then knelt on both sides and examined the undercarriage. It took him less than ten minutes to find the transmitter attached to a metal bracket behind the rear bumper. He removed it, put it in his pocket, and walked around until he found a likely prospect.

The large motor home was parked in the far corner of the lot. It had New Hampshire license plates and a rear bumper sticker that read: WE'RE SPENDING OUR KIDS' INHERITANCE.

Culley sat at a picnic table beneath a shade tree and waited until he saw an elderly couple exit the restaurant and approach the motor home. He walked by and smiled at them as they were unlocking the front door.

"Nice rig."

"Thank you," the old man said.

"Airstream, right?"

"Sure is."

"Beautiful," Culley said.

"You have a motor home?"

"No. But maybe someday."

"They're wonderful," the man's wife said.

"Where you headed?" Culley asked.

"North Carolina," the woman answered. "Nags Head. Then down to Florida for the winter."

"Sounds like the good life."

"We enjoy it," the woman said with a pleasant smile.

Culley stepped back and pretended to admire the sleek aluminum motor home. "Absolutely beautiful. Leaf or coil springs?"

"Coil springs, I think," the man said.

"Mind if I have a look?"

"Help yourself."

Culley knelt at the rear of the motor home and, unnoticed, slipped the transmitter from his pocket and palmed it. It took no more than a second to place the device on the undercarriage where the magnet held it firmly in place.

"Yep," Culley said, getting up. "Coil springs."

"Thought so," the old man said. "Rides real good."

"Well, have a safe trip," Culley said, and waved as he walked back to his car.

▽

THE DRIVER OF the surveillance vehicle had been caught on the busy interstate with nowhere to pull off without going into the same rest area as Culley—a chance he was not willing to take after the earlier mistake at the gas station. He had taken his only option and simply stopped at the side of the road, a mile from the rest area, then put on his flashers as he waited until Culley was moving again.

"He's rolling," the tracker said.

They waited until the monitor indicated their target was two miles ahead of them, then pulled out into the stream of traffic.

"He's not driving as fast," the tracker said. "Holding about fifty."

"Well, I hope the hell he stays on the road for a while this time. This is getting monotonous. The man's either got a hole in his gas tank or some real bad kidneys."

10

IKE CULLEY DROVE slowly along the narrow ribbon of blacktop that snaked its way through the Virginia countryside. He had made the drive a thousand times and its beauty never faded for him. It was at its most beautiful now, the brilliant fall colors of the dogwoods and hickories and maples accenting the fading greens of the pastures and hedgerows of the small farms and mini-estates throughout the area.

His home in Clifton had been more than just a place to live for Culley. It had been a state of mind, far removed from his professional world. A special spot, both physical and transcendental, an extraordinary clarifier where things that were obscure to the arrogant and self-involved were revealed to the humble. It was his refuge, where he returned to Janet and Jenny for the love, and peace of mind, and contentment he found nowhere else. There he could be refreshed and healed and made strong, and could calmly think things through to a solution.

He felt a tightening in his chest as he turned into the long tree-lined drive that led to the two-story

frame farmhouse. He stopped halfway there, overcome by a rush of memories as his eyes moved across
the familiar landscape. The rope hammock he had
long ago strung between a white oak and a sugar
maple still curved invitingly. The small barn with its
hayloft and split door where Jenny had kept her
pony, and then her horse, was shut tight. A few rails
were loose in the paddock they had all built together.
The old oak at the edge of the pond, with its long, fat
limb that swung out over the water like a bowsprit,
brought a bittersweet smile. On warm summer days
Jenny would lie stretched out on the very end of the
sturdy limb, watching the fish and ducks, and making
faces at herself in the calm surface. He could see part
of Janet's vegetable garden off to the right behind the
house. It was overgrown with weeds now. The empty
dog run brought a lump to his throat.

With all that had happened, Culley had all but
forgotten about Bubba, or had unconsciously forced
himself not to think of him. The black Labrador had
been Jenny's Christmas puppy fourteen years ago.
After Janet's death, with Jenny unable to keep the
dog at school in the city, Culley's lawyer had taken
him to the ASPCA, assuring him that he would
personally see to it that the dog was adopted. Two
weeks later the lawyer's secretary had thoughtlessly
sent Culley a letter in prison informing him that
Bubba, considered unadoptable due to age and in-
firmities, had been put to death. At the age of thirteen, arthritic and half blind from cataracts, the old
dog had known nothing but love and companionship
and warm firesides all of his life. That he had ended
his days in a cage, sleeping on a cold bed-board,
frightened and confused and lonely, with no one to

comfort him during his last moments, was the final, inescapable truth of the shambles that had been made of Culley's life.

Culley found his hands around the steering wheel in a death grip. He made himself think of happier times, and continued down the driveway. He parked in the circle in front of the house and sat in the car for the longest time, staring at the boarded-up windows and the shutters he had intended to paint before his American dream, if it ever was a reality, became his private nightmare. The paint on the shutters was flaking now. He got out of the car and walked tentatively up the steps to the porch, where he read the notice tacked to the front door.

The bold lettering warned trespassers that the property had been seized on behalf of the Internal Revenue Service, the state and county tax departments, and the law firm of Goodman, Roberts, and Kincaid. An auction of the home, its contents, the outbuildings, and the ten acres of land was to be held on October 18. Tomorrow.

Culley stood motionless, staring at the notice. A terrible sorrow slowly turned to anger. This time he could not control it. He did not even try. He tore the notice down and ripped it to shreds. He went to the car and took the jack handle from the trunk to pry off the plywood panel nailed across the living room window. The board came off easily, but the window would not yield. He smashed one of the small panes, unlocked the latch, then raised the window to climb inside.

He moved slowly through the house, room by room, feeling like an intruder in a past life. Nothing seemed to have been disturbed. Everything was as he remembered it. With one exception: On every piece of furniture, every painting on the walls—some of them Jenny's grade-school artwork—every framed personal photograph on the shelves and tabletops, every book, every knickknack, even Jenny's childhood stuffed animal collection in her bedroom, and her trophies and ribbons from her high school swimming team, was a numbered inventory sticker.

Everything Janet had selected with great care and love, everything that made the house a home and delineated a family's life together, was to be sold to the highest bidder. To strangers, who knew nothing of the pride in Jenny's face as she presented her first finger painting to her father, who had just as proudly framed it and hung it in his den. Nothing of the marks on the kitchen door frame telling of the growth of a little girl into a young woman, or the significance of the countless nicks and scratches and dents accumulated over the past twenty years.

Upstairs, Culley paused in the doorway of the master bedroom before entering to sit on the edge of the bed. He picked up the framed photograph on the nightstand and held it before him, staring at it as he fought back the tears welling in his eyes. It was the last photograph taken of Janet and Jenny, just before his trial began. They smiled out at him, giving him a thumbs-up, and holding up one of Bubba's paws to simulate the same gesture of encouragement and support. He carefully pealed off the inventory sticker and went to the closet, where he pulled a leather carryall from the shelf. He put the photograph in the carryall, then began stuffing it with clothes from the built-in drawers he had installed himself on weekends, with Bubba lying nearby, watching his every move and waiting patiently for their evening run.

Culley stripped off the prison-issue civilian clothes they had given him that morning and put on an old pair of jeans, a turtleneck, a pair of Nike cross trainers, and his favorite leather jacket. He then removed one of the drawers and reached behind the frame to pull out his old backup gun in an ankle holster: a Walther .380-caliber semiautomatic pistol that had traveled the world with him. From the same hiding place he removed four passports, all perfect forgeries provided by the Agency, from four separate countries, each bearing his photograph under a different name. He checked them for expiration dates and found them all to be good for at least another three years. He tossed the weapon and the passports into the bag, zipped it closed, and went back downstairs to the kitchen.

He stood staring at the door leading to the attached garage, finally bringing himself to open it. He entered slowly, stopping on the bottom step. The old riding mower was still parked in the far corner where he had left it. His Harley-Davidson Low Rider motorcycle, covered with a tarp, leaned on its kickstand in the middle of the floor. He smiled at the memory of Janet laughing and kissing him passionately the day he'd brought it home; she'd attributed the purchase to the onset of his midlife crisis, and thanked him, tongue-in-cheek, for choosing a grown-up toy rather than a love affair to recapture his youth. He saw a tag dangling from the part of the handlebar that protruded from under the tarp and went over to read it. It was a reserve tag, setting the bike apart from the auction for its new owner. The name on the tag was George Kincaid. His lawyer.

Despite his efforts to prevent it from happening, visions of Janet, sitting in her car, the engine running, waiting to die, completely overwhelmed him. He sat heavily on the steps, and noticed his battered old guitar case propped against the wall, an inventory sticker on its side. He reached over, opened the case, and took the instrument out. The simple act of strumming a few chords caused the tears, held back for so long, to flow freely.

"I'm sorry, honey," he whispered softly, his words choked with emotion. "I'm so sorry."

And then he saw Janet's face before him, smiling at him in her loving and compassionate way on the day he'd left home to go to prison.

"I miss you, honey. God knows I miss you."

He played a few introductory cords, then began to sing "Danny Boy," in a strong, clear Irish tenor. It was the song Janet had always asked for first.

But come ye back, when summer's in the meadow was as far as he got before breaking down and sobbing. He didn't know how long he sat there crying before the sorrow and the pain were replaced by an explosive rage. He got to his feet and smashed the guitar to pieces on the cement floor. He stood there trembling, on the verge of losing control completely, before he knew what he had to do.

He unlocked the garage door and threw it open, almost tearing it off its track. He then removed the cover from the motorcycle and wheeled it outside, finding, to his surprise, that the battery still had enough of a charge to start the engine. A two-day-old service sticker on the left front fork explained the mystery. His ever thoughtful and attentive attorney had had the bike serviced in preparation to be driven away tomorrow.

Culley took the money, and the information packet with the NROC photos of Malik, from the Agency car and put them in the carryall, strapping it across the motorcycle's jump seat with bungee cords. He pulled on the shoulder holster with the nine-millimeter semiauto pistol Gregus had left for him, then returned to the garage.

The two five-gallon gas cans in the corner by the old riding mower were full, and Culley carried them into the house. He sloshed the gas throughout the first floor, drenching the draperies and upholstered furniture and pegged wood floors. He threw the cans in the center of the living room, then stood in the kitchen doorway and ignited a pack of matches, tossing it into a trickle of gasoline. A sudden *whoosh* of flames ignited and spread quickly as he walked calmly from the kitchen and back outside through the garage.

The Harley roared to life, its exhaust rumbling and crackling as he spun it around and sped down the driveway. He paused at the end, looking back to see the first floor of the house consumed by flames. He watched as the fire spread to the second level, then pulled away, accelerating rapidly and taking the winding country road at breathtaking speed.

11

"WHERE'S THE SURVEILLANCE team now?" the CIA's deputy director for operations asked, making no attempt on the phone to disguise the anger in his voice.

"On their way back from Nags Head, North Carolina," Gregus said. "They should be here in another hour or so."

"Idiots. Sucked into the oldest trick in the book. The procedure is that anytime the target vehicle stops and then begins to move again, you close in until you can identify it as the right vehicle, then you drop back."

"They're young," Gregus offered.

"I was never that young," the DDO said, quickly changing the unproductive subject. "There's no doubt in your mind that Culley torched his house?"

"None at all. I sent two of my men to Clifton to see if he went there after he shook the surveillance team. The place was a roaring inferno surrounded by fire trucks when they arrived. The car we left at the prison for him was parked in the driveway."

"That's wonderful. Just wonderful. It's really going to make the director's day when the local cops trace the car back to us."

"That's taken care of. One of the people I sent thinks well on his feet. He spotted the keys in the ignition and told a fireman he was moving the car out of harm's way. With all the excitement and confusion no one even bothered to question who he was. He just drove it out of there."

"Well, that's not the only problem we have. Once they figure out the most likely suspect, which should take them all of two minutes, they're going to discover the amazing coincidence that Culley got out of prison the same day his house went up in smoke. At approximately the same time it would have taken him to drive there from Lewisburg."

"That won't bring it home to us," Gregus said. "I can absolutely guarantee that the Honorable Judge Hendricks will attribute his vacating Culley's sentence to a judicial review and a change of heart. There's no way in hell he'll take the chance of laying it on our doorstep."

"The cops will still go after Culley," the DDO said. "Can you guarantee what he's going to tell them when they find him?"

"I've already taken some diversionary measures," Gregus said. "A little smoke screen. The local sheriff's department got two calls from passing motorists who reported seeing a group of kids running from the property just as the fire started."

"They're going to want to talk to those 'passing motorists.'"

"And they will," Gregus said. "The callers are two contract people I've used on occasion. They live in the vicinity and could have been passing by at the time for any number of reasons."

"Nice touch," the DDO said, his admiration genuine. "Damage control always was your specialty."

The DDO then lapsed into a long silence. "I should have known better," he finally said, more to himself than Gregus. "Take away everything a man cares about, leave him with nothing, and he has nothing to lose. Which makes him very dangerous and unpredictable."

"The operation is still salvageable," Gregus said.

"Pack it in, Lou. We've got a rogue on our hands. It's time to cut our losses."

"No, sir. I disagree. Culley took the file on Malik, and the photos, from the car. If I'm right, he's on his way to Charlottesville. I still believe he'll carry out the contract. I've never known him to lie before, or not see an operation through once he has committed to it."

"You've never known him to burn down his goddamn house before either."

"All things considered, I don't know that I wouldn't have done the same."

"I'm not out on this limb alone, you know," the DDO said. "So you'd better hope you're right about him."

"I'd bet my career on it."

"You already have."

"Yes, sir," Gregus said. "The logical first step for Culley is to check out Malik's house and place of business for anything that might give him a clue to where he's hiding out."

"Logic doesn't seem to be Culley's strong suit these days."

"I've sent someone down to Charlottesville to see if he shows up there. If he does, and it looks like he's back on track, I'll pull the surveillance immediately and let Culley run with it."

"And if he doesn't show?"

"I'll put someone on his daughter in New York. He'll definitely go to see her, sooner or later. We'll grab him when he does."

"All right, Lou. One more toss of the dice. But if he screws up again, in any way, I want him brought in. Immediately. Understood?"

"Yes, sir," Gregus said, and heard the line go dead.

Gregus went into the first-floor bedroom at the back of the safe house, where the communications and computer room was set up. The curtains were drawn, shutting out the natural light, and a large electronics console, taking up most of one wall, shone brightly with green and red and amber lights. Four computer workstations filled the adjacent wall, their color monitors displaying various menus and data. He found one of his assistants, a computer whiz recruited from MIT and known as Hack, busy at work at one of the stations. Given enough time, and the Agency's state-of-the-art equipment, Hack could break into any system in the world, regardless of its security measures, usually without leaving a trace of his ever having done so.

"Anything new?"

"Nothing that's made the earth move for me," Hack said, without looking up from the terminal. "I got into all of Malik's credit-card files: American

Express, Visa, MasterCard, and Discover. There's nothing outside normal parameters."

"What were you looking for?"

"Purchases made on a regular basis outside of Charlottesville but still in the same general area. Something that might indicate where he was spending a lot of time. Maybe the little hideaway you're looking for."

"What about parking or speeding tickets?"

"Nothing. He's either a safe driver or a real lucky one."

Hack riffled through a stack of printouts cluttering the top of his workstation and pulled one out.

"I also ran a check on his gas credit card. Got a little something. Two purchases on the second of September. One in Delaware and another in New York City. Brooklyn, to be exact. Two more on the fourth of September. The first again in Brooklyn, the second in Warrenton, Virginia. The dates coincide with the Secret Service sniffing around about the currency-paper hijacking. I'd say our boy went to Brooklyn to see his Russian mafia buddies, then came home two days later.

"Oh, yeah," Hack added, and dug through the computer printouts again, quickly finding what he was looking for.

"I got some background on Julie Houser for you, that *Washington Post* reporter?"

Gregus's temper flared. "I explicitly told you to stay the hell out of the *Post*'s system!"

"I didn't get it from the *Post*, boss," Hack said. "I got her plate number from the surveillance team we put on her to spook her. She's got Virginia tags. Virginia uses social security numbers for their driver's license ID numbers. I had a little electronic conversation with their computer and found that Houser handed in a New York license when she got her Virginia license. Long story short. I tapped into Albany, then the New York City employment records, and checked her out using her social security number. She's an ex-cop. New York City homicide detective. Ten years on the job before she quit. Want me to find out why?"

Gregus paused for a moment, intrigued. "Yeah. Get whatever you can."

"Hey, boss," Hack said with a broad grin. "That'll be everything since the day she was born, maybe before."

"Try to restrain yourself," Gregus said. "The pertinent stuff will do just fine."

"I'll get right on it."

"What about Malik's telephone records?"

"I was just about to reach out and touch Centel's system when you came through the door."

"Do that first," Gregus said. "If you come up with anything, I'll be in the study."

Gregus entered the small walnut-paneled study off the kitchen and slipped on a headset as he sat at the desk. He pushed the play button on the reel-to-reel recorder, and again heard Malik's arrogant and self-assured voice. He sounded as American as the debriefer interviewing him, perhaps even more so with his relaxed banter and liberal use of colloquialisms.

The reels of tape stacked on the desk in front of Gregus amounted to over six hundred hours of conversation recorded during Malik's eight-month debriefing. Gregus had no idea what insights the tapes might give into Malik's present behavior or plans, but it was all he had for the moment. He rummaged through the desk drawers, looking for his oral-dependency support system: the box of toothpicks he was seldom without since he quit smoking.

A pack of cigarettes lay temptingly on top of a stack of logbooks in the bottom drawer. Gregus stared at them for a long time before reaching for them. It had been ten months since he quit. So much for grace under pressure, he thought, and tore off the wrapper. He flicked the desk lighter to life and drew a deep, luxurious breath, sighing contentedly as Malik's voice filled the headset.

12

HE FIRST GRAY light of dawn appeared on the eastern horizon as the Bell Jet Ranger helicopter lifted off the pad at the FBI academy in Quantico, Virginia. Seated alone in the back, trying to grab a quick nap on the short flight back to Charlottesville, was FBI Special Agent Jack Matthews. The eight-hour day had become a thing of the past with the discovery of the first body, and with only seven hours' sleep in the past two days, Matthews was both physically and mentally exhausted. He had spent most of the previous day at the FBI's Behavioral Science Unit in a grueling fourteen-hour skull session with the BSU's top experts in abnormal criminal psychology, sociology, police sciences, criminology, and homicide.

In most murder cases serology, DNA testing, microscopic matching of fibers, fingerprinting, and all the other wonders of forensic science from the FBI's evidence analysis laboratories were invaluable in the solving of a crime, once a suspect was in custody. But they were virtually useless when it came to determining what type of person had committed the crime.

The BSU team, all agent-analysts specializing in psychological profiling of serial killers, looked at the same evidence, but in a different way. They were more interested in the killer's psychic loops and whorls. His method and style, and the small, seemingly irrelevant acts, bearing no relationship to the actual murder, that disclosed an individual personality—a psychological personality print. Lab reports, color photos of the dump site and the body, and any other available evidence, were all examined, but not viewed as evidence of the crime itself, rather as a symptom of the deviant nature of the person who had committed the crime, providing subtle clues that revealed the "signature" of the killer and took them inside his mind.

In the case of the Mix & Match killer—a label they personally considered repulsive, but which was repeated so often by the media that they found themselves using it for convenience' sake—specific questions needed to be answered. Why the explicit mutilations? Why cut out only the heart? Had he kept it as a souvenir? Was he cannibalistic? (They believed not.) Were the mutilations ritualistic or part of an elaborate psychosexual fantasy? Why that particular dump site and open display of the body? Why take great pains to leave no personal clues that could identify him, yet leave a note and a paint chip that might eventually aid in tracking him down?

Tests revealed that the small clump of red clay found on the stage of the amphitheater could have come from anywhere within a two-hundred-square-mile area of Charlottesville, and the hair samples were from the head on the body found at the dump site. The two pieces of physical evidence directly linked to the killer, the note and the paint chip, so far held nothing but a faint promise. The paper on which the note was written was a generic type that would be nearly impossible to trace, and the same held true for the felt-tip pen used to write the note. The FBI labs had identified the metallic green paint chip as being from a Chrysler product; the color was used, under different names, on various 1993 models of cars and vans produced by Chrysler, Dodge, Plymouth, Eagle, and Jeep. Determining the number of vehicles painted in that color and sold in the Charlottesville area would help somewhat, but Matthews suspected there would be hundreds, with no guarantee that the vehicle, if it was the killer's, had been purchased there.

Everything had been gathered and analyzed that could be shaped into a profile of the killer's personality. By ten o'clock that evening, after fourteen non-stop hours in the conference room, with meals of pizza, soft drinks, and coffee, a firm psychological profile began to take shape. The Mix & Match killer was a highly organized killer. A disorganized killer made sudden attacks, killing his victim quickly, in a rage, usually making no attempt to hide the body or remove it from the crime scene. He fled the scene immediately, often unintentionally leaving behind physical evidence and numerous clues to his identity. His crimes were spontaneous, with little or no planning. If the disorganized killer mutilated his victim, it was usually done in a crude and savage way.

The Mix & Match killer's mutilations were precise and purposeful. His abductions were carefully calculated, well planned, structured, and methodical. He left no physical evidence without intention; an attempt to control, even direct, the course of the investigation, the BSU team theorized, or perhaps to show contempt for his pursuers, or to raise the level of tension and excitement for his own twisted needs.

All agreed that the murders had been committed by one person. He would be a white male between the ages of twenty-five and forty-five, probably closer to the upper limit because the full-blown psychosis he exhibited would have taken years to develop. He was probably a paranoid schizophrenic, and had definitely killed before. His current accelerated pace indicated that he may have been dormant for a number of years. The high level of violence and mutilation further indicated that he would strike again, soon. He would live in the Charlottesville area, judging from his familiarity with the university grounds and the pattern of activity there. He harbored a deep hatred of women. Was probably a single-parent child, with a mother who was abusive. He had never had a strong father-figure in his life and no older siblings. He was highly intelligent, persuasive, articulate, physically strong, and probably physically attractive. He would be neat and orderly in his habits and appearance. His victims would not have been killed quickly, and handcuffs, or other implements of restraint and torture, would be found wherever he kept them before killing them.

He may have posed as a law-enforcement officer or authority figure during the abductions, to gain immediate and unchallenged control of his victims. That would explain no one's having heard any screams or seen any signs of a struggle. He would have lived in a fantasy world as a child. His fantasies were more than likely used as an escape and to experience repressed emotions, and were rehearsals for the crimes he would commit as an adult. Sexual fantasy was clearly evident in the mutilations, though preliminary indications were that no sex act had been committed. He was probably unsuccessful in close personal relationships with women. He was obsessed with his fantasies and would be driven to kill again and again in ever more bizarre ways.

He was a predatory animal, very controlled and controlling, always looking for his next victim and always prepared to seize an immediate opportunity. His need for control would dominate his personality, and he would achieve his ultimate pleasure in exerting the ultimate control: the decision over life and death. He would follow reports of his crimes closely and whenever possible join onlookers at the dump sites for his victims' bodies.

Matthews was aware that the profile was only guesswork, most useful in eliminating suspects and narrowing the field. But it was well-educated guesswork based on years of experience and on interviews with serial killers already in prison. With the completed profile in hand he began searching the Violent Criminal Apprehension Program and Behavioral Science Unit data bases. The world's largest data bases on violent criminals, they were run on artificial-intelligence computers, and contained facts about killers' crimes, methods, and personalities.

Matthews entered the analysts' information, looking for any known or active serial killers who might match the profile. He checked under Primary Intent, searching for matches under the motive of the crime: sexual, criminal, or emotional. He then queried Scene Dynamics, where a killer's style, symptoms of behavior, and personality were listed. And finally Escalation, entering known details of the sequence of acts committed during the crime. He got two "hits," two remote possibilities with a few things in common. They were quickly eliminated upon checking their FBI files: both men had been spree killers, not serial killers, and both had been in prison for at least eight years.

Matthews knew that the chances of finding the Mix & Match killer quickly were at best remote. History showed that the odds favored a serial killer not being caught. The FBI had never caught one, and most of their concerted efforts had been high-visibility failures. When the killers were caught it was either through the hard street-level work of local cops or through sheer luck, the former usually leading to the latter. The statistics, unknown to the general public, were frightening. Between 1960 and 1980 serial-killer cases had averaged eleven a year. In the past decade the rate had escalated to two a month.

Sixty women murdered in Kansas City since 1972. Fifty-one women murdered by the Green River killer in Seattle since 1983. Forty-two in San Diego since 1988. Thirty-one in Miami since 1986. To date fifty-two known serial killers were active in the country, and neither the FBI nor any of the local jurisdictions involved had the slightest idea who any of them were.

Matthews was not surprised that none of the active serial killers fit the Mix & Match killer's "signature." What he had witnessed at the amphitheater on the university grounds left little doubt in his mind that he was dealing with a unique monster, working at a fast, bloodthirsty pace, who would claim more victims before they could stop him. But based on the BSU team's analysis and profile, Matthews believed that the killer had told him something he had not intended.

The killer was obviously highly intelligent, but like many intelligent people, he was given to underestimating his adversaries. He had left no physical evidence that could directly link him to the crimes if he came under suspicion, even going to the extreme of cutting out the bite marks on the inner thighs of his victims to prevent any identification by forensic odontologists. Yet he had purposefully left other clues that the BSU team believed were an attempt to direct the course of the investigation. This alone gave Matthews his first real clue to the killer's background: he knew how the FBI operated and was familiar with investigative procedures. Information that was not known to the average person. It wasn't much, but it was a place to start.

▽

As THE HELICOPTER settled onto the pad in front of the general aviation hangar at the Albemarle County airport, Matthews saw the special agent in charge of the Charlottesville FBI office standing beside his car, sipping coffee from a foam cup, awaiting his arrival.

Matthews glanced at his watch as he crossed the apron to the parking lot. It was six-fifteen. His scheduled briefing of the local task force was not for another two hours. Plenty of time for some breakfast, his stomach reminded him. The Charlottesville SAIC handed him a copy of the medical examiner's autopsy protocols as he slid into the front passenger seat of the waiting vehicle. They had no sooner backed out of the parking space when the car phone chirped. The conversation was brief and one-sided, and the SAIC's jaw was clenched when he hung up.

"He's dumped the other bodies," he told Matthews.

"All three of them?"

"All three of them. Scott Stadium. Right in the middle of the damn football field on the fifty-yard line."

13

THE POLICE OFFICERS gathered around the macabre scene were grim and silent. Jack Matthews at first involuntarily averted his eyes, then composed himself and looked on in revulsion. In his entire life he had never seen anything as grisly or horrid, and he hoped to God that he never would again.

The naked, mutilated bodies of the three young women lay sprawled in the center of the football field. Their arms were outstretched and their legs spread wide, directed inward, arranged so the feet of all three bodies touched to form a crude triangular shape in the center; some grotesque symbolism of which Matthews could not begin to imagine the significance.

Neal Brady, the Charlottesville chief of police, stood nearby, his arms folded tightly across his chest as he talked with one of his detectives. He acknowledged Matthews with a bleak look and a shake of his head as he approached.

"This is a horror show, Jack."

Matthews nodded in agreement. "Is the stadium sealed off?"

"Yeah. But look at those ghouls," Brady said, motioning to the north end of the field and the chaotic scene just outside the fence.

Through the one open section of the stadium where there were no grandstands, Matthews had a clear view of Alderman Road. He counted fourteen mobile news vans parked on the shoulder, satellite antennas for live feed transmissions bristling from their roofs. A grassy slope, leading down to the fence enclosing the stadium, provided an unobstructed view of the playing field. The area was rapidly filling with reporters and television news crews jockeying for positions and aiming their huge telephoto lenses at the scene a few hundred yards away. Brady had strategically placed eight of his tallest uniformed officers in a tight semicircle close to the bodies, between the reporters and the dump site, preventing them from getting any shots of the victims.

"They descended on the town yesterday morning like a plague of locusts," Brady said. "Television crews from all the Richmond and Washington stations, the major networks, CNN, reporters from newspapers, newsmagazines, producers from tabloid talk shows. There must be hundreds of them. They're driving everyone on the task force nuts, shoving microphones and cameras and tape recorders in their faces every time they turn around."

"When were the bodies found?" Matthews asked.

"A few minutes before we reached your local man at the airport. About thirty minutes ago."

"Who found them?"

"University cop making his rounds. He noticed that the chain on Gate One had been cut. There's a big game here tonight with Clemson. A few years ago some Georgia Tech students broke in and tried to burn the school's initials into the field. Morons set fire to the Astroturf. The cop on patrol thought some of the Clemson kids might be up to a similar harebrained stunt, so he checked it out and found the bodies. He immediately called it in and secured the area."

"Anyone see anything?"

"So far no one."

"I want the university president informed that there won't be any football game here tonight," Matthews said. "This stadium is sealed off for at least twenty-four hours."

"Considering the circumstances I don't think we'll get any argument on that."

"Where's the ME?" Matthews asked, noticing his absence among the forensic technicians, who were taking photographs of the scene and looking for evidence in the immediate vicinity of the bodies, but giving them a wide berth—no one was allowed to touch or move the bodies until the medical examiner conducted his preliminary examination.

"He was in Richmond for the night," Brady said. "He's on his way back. I arranged a police escort. Should be here anytime."

"How did the canvassing go yesterday?"

"Hell, between my people, the state, and county, we had over eighty officers on the grounds. I don't know how many hundreds of students we interviewed and reinterviewed since the first body showed up. Everyone who knew or had classes with the missing kids, any faculty or employees they came in contact with, anyone who might have argued with them or had a grudge against them, any jilted boyfriend, anyone who might have asked all four of them for a date and got turned down. By now we've talked to everyone who even walked across the grounds on the nights they disappeared and the morning the first body turned up. Nothing. Nobody saw or heard anything."

"And yet he managed to drag four women out of here, presumably against their will, and then bring their bodies back," Matthews said. "If I didn't know better, I'd swear we were dealing with a phantom."

"You missed a real fiasco last night," Brady said. "I had three of my female officers working undercover, trolling the grounds after dark as decoys. One of them got a strike and radioed for her backup. The guy started to run and a sheriff's deputy panicked and fired two shots at him before he was even close enough to ID him. Fortunately his aim was as good as his judgment."

"Who was he shooting at?"

"Some poor bastard with a history of mental illness, out to catch the serial killer on his own. Dumb shit was dressed in cammies with greasepaint on his face."

"How's the university population holding up?"

"It's a mass exodus. Like registration week in reverse," Brady said. "Half of the coeds are packing up and leaving town as fast as they can. Those without cars are renting them, or their terrified parents have come to take them home. All of the off-campus hangouts were virtually deserted last night. I don't think there's one woman left at school with brown hair or shorter than five eight."

"I'm afraid it's going to get a lot worse before it gets better."

"Tell me about it," Brady said. "What's left of the student body and half the damn town has armed itself to the teeth. Every gun shop within a hundred miles has had a run on rifles, pistols, shotguns, stun guns, tear gas, Mace, pepper sprays. The sporting goods stores are even sold out of baseball bats. You name it, they're carrying it around with them. They've turned their dormitories and off-campus quarters into armed camps.

"And this mess hasn't even gotten out yet," Brady added, gesturing toward the bodies. "After tonight's news broadcasts I'm going to have an all-out panic on my hands."

"We'll take it a step at a time," Matthews said. It was the only reassuring comment he could make with any conviction.

Matthews felt someone brush past him and turned to see Dave Maurer, the medical examiner, anxious and out of breath.

"Sorry, fellows," Maurer said. "I got here as soon as I could." He took his first look at the bodies and paused to collect himself before moving closer.

Matthews turned his attention to the ME as he snapped on a pair of surgical gloves and knelt beside one of the victims. Maurer carefully raised her head to examine the back of her skull, then moved to each of the bodies in turn, again placing special emphasis on the same area.

Matthews pulled on a pair of gloves and knelt beside him as he continued his preliminary examination. "What were you looking for? Rear head wounds?"

"I take it you haven't read my autopsy report

on the first body?" Maurer said as he continued his work.

"Just got it. I haven't had time."

"Fifth page. Fourth paragraph."

Matthews took the folded report from the inside pocket of his trench coat, where he had stuffed it during the high-speed drive from the airport. He turned to the section Maurer had indicated and read it through once, then again, frowning even deeper the second time.

"Did he do the same thing to these three?"

"No. Just the first one."

"I've never come across it before."

"That doesn't surprise me. I don't get the variety of homicide cases that a big city ME does, but I've never even heard of it being done."

"Why would he do it? To what purpose?"

"Good question," Maurer said as he gently probed a gap between the sutures in the chest of one of the victims. "I can tell you this, it had nothing to do with any frenzied sexual mutilations. It was cold and calculated. The physical pain involved would be negligible, but if he was doing what I think he was doing, the results would be the worst form of psychological torture imaginable."

"You mean she was *alive* when he did that?"

"It wouldn't make any sense to do it if she wasn't."

"Who else got a copy of your report?"

"Just your office. The next person to see it will be the United States attorney when you've got a suspect in custody who's going to trial."

Matthews had been angered by the leaking of the information about the paint chip and did not want a repeat of the incident. He had learned the hard way not to trust small-town cops to keep information to themselves; they were too familiar with the local media.

"I'd appreciate it if you make sure it stays that way," he told Maurer. "I can use this along with the note to eliminate false confessions. And on a personal level I don't want the family of that girl ever finding out about it. They've been through enough already without adding another horror to their nightmares."

"I'll do what I can, but I've got ten people working in my office."

Matthews began moving his eyes slowly over each body. He saw the now familiar cut-out sections of flesh on the inner thighs of three of the legs. He stared at the face of the victim farthest from him and felt a knot form in his stomach. It was the daughter of the FBI assistant director.

"The pattern of mutilations and the sutures looks identical to the first body."

"With some minor variations."

"Are the hearts missing?"

"Again, I won't be certain until I do the autopsies," Maurer said, "but it looks like they are."

Matthews noticed the same gray-blue sheen glistening on the surface of the victims' skin that he had seen on the first body. He placed a hand on the arm closest to him. It was damp, and cold to the touch.

"Frozen like the first one?"

"And still defrosting."

"Do me a favor," Matthews said. "Give me a quick summary of your autopsy report on the first body. I'll read it at length later."

"It was definitely made up of parts from four

people. Little doubt that these three provided them. I found no traces of semen or any extraneous fluids. Blood smears were of the victim's blood, and three others that will probably match up with these."

"Cause of death?"

"In layman's terms—she bled to death while being tortured."

"She was alive during the mutilations?"

"For some of them," Maurer said, "and judging from the time frames of the abductions, neither she nor any of the others was killed immediately. They were kept alive for at least a few days."

Maurer looked away, changing a subject he chose not to dwell on. "I may have found the answer to how the killer abducted them without a struggle."

Matthews waited for him to continue.

"The toxicologic studies on the tissue sections from the composite parts of the first body showed traces of a morphine-based drug. Which means it was used on all four of them. The lab hasn't been able to positively identify it yet. But in all probability it was extremely fast acting, and if administered in the right dosage it was definitely capable of placing someone in a very manageable and compliant state without rendering her unconscious, probably leaving them enough motor skills to walk, but not enough to resist."

"How was it administered?"

"I found small puncture wounds, from a single hypodermic needle, on the upper sections of both arms on the first body; and those arms came from two separate people. The same punctures are evident on two of the arms here. My guess is a spring-loaded

Syrette was used to inject a premeasured dose of the drug."

"Why spring loaded?"

"The punctures on the arms on the first body were exactly the same depth. Which means precisely the same amount of pressure was used to inject the drug both times. It's unlikely someone jabbing a needle into a person's arm could manage that. But use a spring-loaded Syrette and it will penetrate the same distance every time. If the same holds true for the punctures on the arms here, I'd say it's conclusive."

"Spring-loaded Syrettes aren't generally available, are they?"

"I doubt that you'll find a hospital or medical supply company that stocks them."

Maurer turned his attention back to the bodies, and Matthews watched as he examined the vaginal cavity of one of the girls and withdrew the first note. Two more followed from the other victims.

Matthews unfolded and read each one in turn as Maurer handed them to him with the forceps. Brady looked over his shoulder.

The first note read: *You Smiled at Me*. The second: *Your Friends All Said*. The third: *You Took My Breath Aw*. The last word on the third note was smeared and impossible to read. Matthews guessed *Away*, but he would have to wait for the lab to restore it if possible.

"Any help?" Maurer asked.

Matthews shook his head. "I have no idea what they mean."

"There's something awfully familiar about those phrases," Brady said as Matthews slipped each note into a separate evidence bag. "The one found in the first body was, what? *The Day We Met*?"

Matthews confirmed that it was.

"I've heard them before. I just can't remember where," Brady said, then repeated the words to himself. "It'll come to me."

Matthews stood and again looked toward the north end of the stadium. A much larger crowd was gathering on the grassy slope outside the fence, mixing with the reporters and television crews.

"Is anyone taking pictures of the crowd?"

Brady looked to the detective standing beside him.

The chagrined cop shook his head. "Sorry, Chief. I'm just not thinking straight with all of this."

"Damn it, Charlie!" Brady said. "Get out there."

As the detective hurried off with his partner, cameras in hand, Matthews continued to stare at the growing crowd of spectators along the northern perimeter of the stadium. Students were drifting over from the student housing complex on the opposite side of Alderman Road, and cars were stopping, bringing traffic to a standstill.

Was the killer up there among them? Matthews wondered. Was he staring back at him at this very moment, smug and self-confident in his anonymity? He thought of the section of the autopsy report Maurer had told him to read. What kind of depraved monster was he dealing with?

Matthews looked down at the bodies sprawled on the ground before him. He took a deep breath and let it out slowly, then again scanned the crowd outside the stadium.

I'll get you, you twisted son of a bitch. No matter

*how well you think you've planned it all, you've made
a mistake somewhere, and sooner or later I'll find it.*

▽

JOHN MALIK LOWERED his binoculars and
backed slowly out of the mob of reporters and gawk-
ers until he reached the edge of Alderman Road. He
smiled to himself as he crossed to the opposite side
and walked to where he had left his car, near the
student housing complex a short distance away. He
paused as he approached the Jeep Cherokee, inspect-
ing the quickie paint job done the previous morning
in Richmond. The maroon color was pleasing
enough, but the mix had been too heavy with metallic
sparkle, and in the bright morning sun it had an
overall candy-apple effect. He shrugged it off. It
really didn't matter. He planned to ditch the car when
he was finished here.

Just two more little bitches; he'd hate to waste all
of the time he had spent scouting their routines.
Maybe three. The angel-faced one who had played
the violin at the recital he attended at Old Cabell Hall
a few days ago had piqued his interest.

They might all be gone by now, he reminded
himself. Run home to Mommy and Daddy. But they
would start trickling back soon enough, when no
more were abducted and the panic subsided. A week,
ten days tops. He had his videotapes until then. He
could wait. Use the time to reconnoiter abduction
and dump sites, establish his routes to and from
them. Prepare for the little bitches' return. Decide on
how best to use them to heighten his pleasure.

After them he would move on. First to New York

to take care of his business there; then, who knew? With the enormous amount of money he would have, his options would be unlimited, for the rest of his life, he reminded himself with relish. But he would definitely stay with college towns. The campus pickings were so easy. The choice of victims prime. So trusting and naive. God bless America.

He spotted the two plainclothes cops taking pictures of the crowd as he pulled onto Alderman Road and turned left, toward the heart of the university section. He almost tooted the horn at them, but restrained himself at the last moment. *Don't get too cocky. Never beard them in their den.* He turned on the radio, selected a country music station, and sang along as he drove.

A quick stop at a hardware store for a larger drill bit, to improve on his latest innovation, perhaps a leisurely lunch at the Corner for some people-watching, and then back to the cabin. The first in-depth news reports should be airing just about the time he got there. CNN was his favorite. Bobbie Battista would really squirm when she reported this morning's extravaganza. She had such pretty, expressive blue eyes.

14

JULIE HOUSER HAD not found quite the atmosphere of near panic she had expected to find when she arrived in Charlottesville. But that soon changed when the news of the bodies found that morning spread throughout the student population. In the past few hours the fear had become palpable and the deluge of reporters and television crews roaming the grounds only added to the feeling of a town under siege.

Houser had already seen at least six print and television reporters from the D.C. area she knew by name. Two others, one from *The New York Times* and another from *Newsweek*, she recognized from her years as a New York City cop. She had also kept a watchful eye for any more obvious surveillance that she assumed had been meant to scare her off. Seeing none, she further assumed that the FBI now considered it an exercise in futility, with the massive media attention the killings had attracted.

She had spent the early part of the previous day interviewing students and faculty, looking for a fresh

angle with little success. Those cops on the Mix &
Match killer's task force, who would stop long
enough for her to introduce herself, gave nothing
more than a terse "no comment." Frustrated, but not
about to give up, she called in a marker. A telephone
call to a friend with the Washington, D.C., police
force, a lieutenant who owed her a few favors, produced the name of a close friend of his, a state police
homicide investigator assigned to the task force.
Within the hour Houser knew about the note found
on the first body, and its content.

The Xerox copy of the autopsy report was delivered to her that same evening, in a dark corner booth
of a local pub. It had cost her only a pitcher of beer
and an hour of conversation with an eager-to-help,
but very nervous, secretary from the medical examiner's office, whom she had zeroed in on when she
heard her New York City accent. The secretary was
originally from Manhattan—her family had moved
to Charlottesville five years ago when her father
retired—and she longed for the excitement and energy of the Big Apple.

The common bond gave Houser the opening she
needed, but just in case, she laid on the accent and
speech patterns a little thick as the two expatriate
Manhattanites reminisced and became instant, if temporary, buddies. She assured the young woman that
her lifelong dream of becoming a New York City cop
was well within the realm of possibility. She should
apply to take the entrance exam for the academy at
her earliest opportunity. Of course she had a chance
at being a homicide detective. With her experience in
the ME's office? Absolutely.

A follow-up call to the state police homicide

investigator the following morning, a few hours after
the bodies were found at the stadium, confirmed
what Houser suspected. There had indeed been more
notes, and again he provided her with the contents,
promising to personally pound her into the ground
like a tent peg if his complicity was ever revealed.

Houser then returned to her motel room, wrote
a story on what she had witnessed and learned, then
plugged the telephone jack into her computer and
used the built-in modem to send it on to the *Post*.
Still a cop at heart, she included the information
about the four notes, but did not include their contents, nor would she ever print one word of the
terrible details she had found on the fifth page of the
autopsy report. Enough of the gruesome acts the
killer had committed were now public knowledge,
and she was not going to add to the sensationalism or
put the families of the victims through any more pain;
it was not something they ever needed to know. As a
New York City cop she had become inured to most
of the savagery human beings can inflict on one
another, but what had been done to that girl, and the
fact that she had been alive while it happened, had
made Houser cringe as she read it.

Shortly after two o'clock Houser followed a leafy,
sun-dappled path across the university grounds
toward the Corner. A collection of shops, sidewalk
cafés, bookstores, restaurants, and night spots, the
Corner was a busy and lively gathering place for
students and faculty, especially during the lunch
hour. And it was lunch that was foremost on Houser's
mind, as she had skipped breakfast to cover the scene
at the stadium.

As she stepped into the crosswalk at University

Avenue, something familiar caught her eye. She paused and stared at the man astride the rumbling Harley-Davidson motorcycle waiting for her to cross the street. He wasn't wearing a helmet and his face was clearly visible. She looked back over her shoulder as she walked, her eyes fixed on him. He had what her mother had always referred to as Irish good looks. The "Black" Irish. Ruddy complexion, with dark curly hair and dark blue eyes. He was tall and strikingly handsome, the kind of man who turned women's heads, she thought, and perhaps that was why he drew her attention. No. It was more than that. She had seen him before. But where?

She stopped on the opposite side of the street and watched as the motorcycle swung left off University Avenue onto Elliewood, a narrow side street of shops and cafés that dead-ended a few hundred yards away. The Harley passed within a few feet of where she stood on the sidewalk, and it was then that she remembered where she had seen him. And who he was.

Michael Culley. CIA case officer convicted of contempt of Congress and lying to Congress during the BCCI scandal. Sentenced to four years in federal prison about this time last year. As a court reporter she had covered his trial. She also remembered her reaction to his conviction. Sold down the river by his buddies at Langley. And there was something else. She searched her memory for a moment and then recalled reading the article in the *Post* about his wife's suicide.

Houser's reporter instincts took over as she watched him drive up the narrow street. His four-year prison sentence had started about a year ago.

What was he doing out? Parole? No. The feds had abolished parole. He would have had to serve at least three years of his sentence. Worth looking into? The scheduled briefing by the FBI agent in charge of the task force wasn't until three o'clock. Maybe she should talk to Culley. Couldn't hurt.

She saw the motorcycle slow and swing into the parking garage halfway up Elliewood. She walked quickly, closing the distance and catching up with Culley as he left the garage and began to walk toward the far end of the street.

"Mike Culley?" she called out from a few steps behind him.

Culley stopped and turned, and she was briefly taken aback by the hard, challenging look in his dark blue eyes.

"Who are you?"

"Julie Houser," she said, and extended her hand.

Culley hesitated, then shook the proffered hand. He was still feeling the effects of the Coors twelve-pack and most of a fifth of Jack Daniel's he had downed the previous night while holed up in the motel room feeling sorry for himself.

"What do you want?"

"I covered your trial last year."

"A reporter?"

"Yes. With the *Post*."

"I'm old news, lady."

Houser was not accustomed to indifference to her obvious physical attributes, but Culley's eyes, hard and penetrating, were fixed steadily on hers when not scanning the street. Not for a second had he stolen a quick appraising glance to mentally undress her. Nevertheless, she tried her best smile.

"I'm glad to see you're out of prison."

"Is that right?"

"Yes. I never thought you deserved it."

"Yeah, well, it's an imperfect world."

"How did you get out so soon?" She knew the question was leading and out of sync as soon as she asked it, and she saw his eyes narrow and his antenna go up.

"Hey! I told you, I'm old news."

With that he turned and walked away. The last question had angered him, but Houser had detected a hint of something else when his eyes moved suspiciously over every inch of the street as they talked.

Her Porsche was parked in the same garage, only a few spaces away from the motorcycle, and she went to it, pretending to unlock the door. She gave him a ten-count before she left the garage on foot and began to follow him at a distance from the opposite side of the street.

At the end of the block he stopped at a small shop that had once been a tiny gingerbread Victorian home. A sign advertised used textbooks, and an assortment of T-shirts and other university souvenirs adorned the display windows. She stood partially hidden behind a large oak tree in front of a sidewalk café and watched him rattle the front door of the shop twice, then disappear around the back of the building.

Houser stepped aside, into a quiet corner of the café where she could still see the front of the shop. She took the small portable cellular telephone out of her shoulder bag and pressed the number programmed to autodial the city editor's office at the *Post*. She kept her eyes on the shop as she heard the number ring.

"I got your story," Peter Davidson said. "Good stuff. Keep it coming."

"I need a favor."

"If I can."

"This may be completely off the wall, but I've got a real strong gut feeling."

"Spit it out."

"Remember Mike Culley, the CIA case officer sent to prison last year?"

"Vaguely. BCCI. Lied to Congress."

"That's him. Well, I just saw him here in Charlottesville."

"So?"

"So he was sentenced to four years in prison about a year ago. What's he doing out?"

"Ever hear of parole?"

"That's the first thing I thought of. Then I remembered there's no parole for federal prisoners since the feds changed their sentencing guidelines a few years back. They get one day a week good time if they don't screw up in prison. That would give Culley less than a year off his sentence."

"His lawyer could have appealed and gotten him a new trial. That would put him out on bond."

"Possible," Houser said. "But humor me. Have someone covering Justice check it out."

"What are you onto?"

"Probably nothing. Like I said, just a hunch."

"Give me an hour," Davidson said, and hung up.

Houser took a small table with a view of the shop and ordered a Perrier with lime. She was famished, but had no intentions of paying for a meal she might not get a chance to eat. She sat nursing the drink for the better part of an hour before she saw Culley appear around the side of the shop from the rear and begin walking toward her. She angled her chair, placing her back to him, then craned her neck to watch him enter the garage across the street, pay the attendant, and climb on his motorcycle.

She waited until Culley had pulled out of the garage, then ran across the street, stuffed more than enough money to cover the amount she owed into the attendant's hand, and dashed to her car.

She pulled the Porsche out of the garage to find Culley sitting at the end of Elliewood. He was waiting for a break in traffic to turn right onto University Avenue. She held back until he'd made the turn, then stopped at the same corner, waited until two cars had passed by so she wouldn't be the first car behind him, and pulled out to follow.

Culley went only two blocks before turning right at the light onto Rugby Road. A few more blocks, past a row of fraternity houses, and he turned into a quiet, tree-lined street of single-family homes. He pulled into the driveway of a small brick colonial near the end of the first block, and Houser slipped the Porsche into the curb on the opposite side of the street behind another car.

She saw Culley go through the same routine he had followed at the shop. He tried the front door of the house before disappearing behind a tall hedge as he went toward the back. Houser waited a few moments, then took the portable phone from her shoulder bag.

"What did you get?"

"Curious," Davidson said. "No appeals in the works. But someone somewhere pulled some strings."

"What kind of strings?"

"The kind that get things done, quickly and quietly. That got me interested, so I called a friend at the Bureau of Prisons. Culley got a visitor, CIA type, at the Lewisburg penitentiary two days ago. The next morning he was out."

"That fast?"

"That fast. Sentence vacated. I called the sentencing judge. Hang-'em-high Hendricks. He said he'd had a change of heart, end of story. Except Hendricks is a stone-cold prick; he doesn't have a heart."

"Thanks, boss."

"Stay on the serial-killer story for now, Julie. No sidetracks."

"Maybe the two are connected."

"That's a stretch."

"You're probably right. But you know how I am about coincidences."

"Keep in touch."

At the precise moment Houser slipped the telephone back in her bag, the passenger-side door of the Porsche flew open and she found herself staring down the barrel of a semiautomatic pistol only inches from her head.

Another incident flashed through her mind. A little over two years ago, in an apartment on East Eighty-sixth Street in New York City; another gun stuck in her face. She had frozen then too. She quickly shook the painful memory but was still so fixated on the gun barrel that she did not see the face of the man who slid into the seat beside her. When she finally recovered her senses, she saw that the hammer of the gun was cocked, a finger firmly on the trigger, and the dark blue eyes in the handsome Irish face were ice-cold and deadly serious.

15

"GET THAT GODDAMN gun out of my face!" Houser said as she recovered from the initial shock.

"Just shut up and sit tight, lady." Culley lowered the gun but kept it pointed at her chest. "Let's see who you really are."

"I told you who I am."

Culley grabbed her shoulder bag and emptied it onto the floor in front of his seat. He used his free hand to rummage through the contents, picking out a fat, overstuffed combination wallet-checkbook and a thin leather ID case. He flipped open the ID case containing her press credentials, then slipped the driver's license out of the wallet and compared the information and the two photographs.

"Satisfied?" Houser said. She remained perfectly still, her eyes on the gun.

"Satisfied that you aren't lying about who you are."

Culley carefully released the hammer on the semiauto and flicked on the safety before tucking it back in the shoulder holster beneath his leather jacket.

"I'm only going to say this once. Stay the hell away from me."

"That's not very friendly," Houser said, her composure fully restored with the gun safely tucked away.

"I'm not a friendly kind of guy," Culley said, and reached for the door handle.

"What do you think I'll find when I check on who owns the shop and the house you were so interested in?"

"More trouble than you bargained for."

"I'll tell you what I think. I think—"

"I don't care what you think."

"A former heavy hitter in CIA special operations is suddenly and mysteriously released from prison two days ago by a judge who hated his guts, and the first place he shows up is in a town where there's an all-out manhunt on for a serial killer. Coincidence?"

"As you said, *former* CIA. I'm not with them anymore."

"Once in, never out."

"That's the mafia. And I don't know anything about a serial killer."

"Where the hell have you been for the past month—scratch that. You're telling me you don't know anything about what's going on in this town?"

"I don't watch television, and I haven't read a newspaper in a week," Culley said, and again reached for the door.

"Why are you in Charlottesville?"

"It doesn't concern you. So walk away from it while you still can."

"Maybe I'll let my editor decide if it concerns me. The CIA's presence in Charlottesville in the middle of a hunt for a serial killer? Might be an interesting sidebar."

"You got a real set of balls on you, lady."

"Not likely," Houser said, and pulled a comical face that relieved some of the tension. "Have lunch with me. My treat."

"Lunch? Why in the name of God would I want to have lunch with you?"

"Convince me we're not here for the same reason and I'll leave you alone. No story. No more hassles. Promise."

Culley hesitated, considering the fallout if Houser was just foolish enough to print something that would draw attention to his release from prison, compromise his temporary affiliation with the Agency, and jeopardize the operation he had promised to carry out.

He remembered the tone of the *Post*'s stories during his trial, and if she was the one who wrote them, she had been more than fair in her reporting. What the hell. He had not eaten since the previous morning, and he had dined in worse company in the past year. Much worse. Her table manners had to be an improvement over Crazy Jack's.

"All right. Lunch. Then you're out of my life. Right?"

"Right. There's a sidewalk café across from the garage you just left. Meet you there."

Culley got out of the car, looked back once,

shook his head, then continued down the street to where he had parked his motorcycle.

▽

CULLEY WAS EVEN HUNGRIER than he'd thought. He wolfed down most of the basket of bread set before them and was halfway through the refill when his plate of pasta arrived.

Houser studied his face when he wasn't looking. He seemed to relax after she'd thanked him for the compliment about the fairness of her articles on his trial, and she actually saw a trace of a smile when she again told him she thought he had gotten a raw deal, and how his kiss-my-ass attitude with the judge had been highly entertaining theater, but questionable tactics given his situation.

"You really haven't heard about the murders here?"

"I remember reading something a week or so ago; about some college kids being missing."

"Well, in the past few days they all turned up dead. Mutilated and tortured."

"That's why all the press is in town? I thought it was because of a football game."

Houser watched Culley's eyes as he spoke. She began to believe she had made a mistake in attributing his presence to anything more than some arcane Agency business. It occurred to her that, with his background, he might have some insight into something that had been troubling her since she read it. She took the copy of the autopsy report from a zippered outside pouch on her shoulder bag and handed it to him.

"Would you read the fourth paragraph on the fifth page of this and tell me what you think? And please, it's confidential. Agreed?"

Culley nodded, took the neatly creased document, and opened it to the page Houser had indicated. He laid it on the table beside him and read as he ate. Halfway through the paragraph he raised a forkful of pasta to his mouth, then slowly put it back on his plate and looked up at Houser.

"What is this?"

"The autopsy report on the first body they found."

She noticed that Culley's eyes had gone cold again. The muscles along his jawline twitched.

"What's wrong?"

He handed the report back to her and ignored the question.

"Come on. You know something. Give."

"What else do you have?"

"What do you know, Culley?"

"My rules. You want my help, tell me what else you have."

"The killer left a note with each of the bodies. I found out what they said, but they don't make any sense."

"What do they say?"

Houser removed her notepad from her bag and turned to the page on which she had scribbled the information.

"*The Day We Met. You Smiled at Me. Your Friends All Said.* And, *You Took My Breath A-w. . . .*" she said, pronouncing the last two letters separately. "Part of the last word in the fourth note is illegible."

Culley sat quietly for a few moments; then, to

Houser's surprise, he began to sing in a voice just above a whisper.

> *The day we met you smiled at me;*
> *you took my breath away.*
> *Your friends all said your heart was*
> *cold and you would never stay.*
> *I'd give most anything it takes to*
> *hold you just once more—*

"You have a very sick sense of humor," Houser said, cutting him off in mid-verse and glaring at him with an expression of anger and disappointment. "That's not in the least bit funny. How can you make up some little ditty about something so twisted?"

"I take it you're not a country music fan."

"Billy Bob's house burned down, his wife left him, his pickup got repossessed, his dog up and died; he went down to the railroad station, had a cup of coffee, smoked a cigarette, and jumped a freight. That about covers every country song ever written."

"You've missed a lot."

"Leave me some illusions," Houser said, her voice still tinged with anger. "How could you make light of something like that?"

"No humor was intended. You had the words out of order. They're from an old country music classic. And if the killer's going to complete that verse with four- and five-word notes, the cops are going to find a lot more bodies before he's finished."

"Sorry," Houser said, and she genuinely was. "What did you see in the autopsy report that made you tense up?"

"I've heard of it being done before."

"Where?"

"In the former Soviet Union, during the nineteen thirties, at the height of Stalin's purges," Culley said. "A man by the name of Lavrenti Pavlovich Beria thought it up; he was head of the NKVD at the time, the forerunner of the KGB."

"The autopsy report says that the actual process involves very little pain. Is that true?"

"You sure you want to hear this?"

Houser hesitated, then said, "Yes."

"When you drill a hole in the back of the skull, the only pain the person feels is the piercing of the skin. It's no worse than cutting your finger. The skull and the brain itself feel no pain."

"Then why do it?"

"It wasn't done to inflict pain," Culley said. "The idea was to have someone you were interrogating, who had information you wanted, watch while you did it to another person."

"To what purpose?"

"To instill sheer terror in the person watching. Beria's torturers would take a small knife and begin cutting out sections of the brain. The effects were gradual: the person felt nothing, but first his speech might begin to slur, then maybe his eyesight would begin to go, or his hearing, he might lose control of his bodily functions, begin to drool or salivate, a paralysis would eventually spread throughout his body. If the torturer knew what he was doing, he could keep the victim alive for days, as long as he kept the bleeding down to a minimum."

"The autopsy report said the killer used a soldering iron to cauterize the area around the sections of the brain he cut out. That was done to stop the bleeding?"

Culley nodded that it was. "It was a pretty effective form of psychological torture. But to my knowledge it hasn't been used in more than forty years. The KGB later developed drugs that had the same effect, and worse."

Culley saw the wheels turning in Houser's mind as she sat there staring at him. She had not missed the correlation of the KGB, the CIA, and his presence in Charlottesville where a serial killer was using an old NKVD method of torture.

Culley had the same suspicions as his thoughts went back to his conversation with Lou Gregus in the prison visiting room. He had asked Gregus why he thought Malik would still be in Charlottesville if he knew the Secret Service and the Agency were looking for him. Just a strong hunch, had been Gregus's reply, and then he had quickly changed the subject. And there was something else. For the six years he had acted as Malik's control in Moscow, the arrogant bastard had constantly bugged him to leave the latest country music tapes in the dead drops they used to exchange information and instructions.

"You son of a bitch, Lou!" Culley said aloud, without meaning to.

"What?" Houser said. "Who's Lou?"

"Nothing." He looked into her eyes and saw the next question coming.

"Off the record, Culley. Are you looking for the serial killer?"

"Off the record. The man I'm looking for is suspected of being involved in a counterfeiting operation," Culley said, though he now had serious reason to doubt that Gregus had given him the whole story on why he had been recruited to bring Malik in.

"Why would the CIA be involved in a counterfeiting case? That's the domain of the Secret Service. Stop insulting my intelligence."

Culley said nothing.

"The killer's ex-CIA, isn't he, Culley? Of course. It makes sense. That's why they got you out of prison. To find him. Is he an old friend? Someone you used to work with who went off the deep end? You know who the killer is, don't you?"

"I don't *know* anything. But the man I'm looking for is definitely not CIA or former CIA."

"Former KGB?"

Culley didn't answer.

"Who owns the shop and the house you broke into?"

"I can't tell you that."

"You know I can find out. It's a matter of public record. What were you looking for?"

"Anything that might tell me where he went."

"He's missing? For how long?"

"A few weeks," Culley said, sorry he'd ever started the conversation, but determined to get a handle on it. "And don't add more weight to that than it can support."

"What color car does he drive?"

Culley thought for a moment. "Dark green. Why?"

"The killer left a dark green paint chip on the first body. The FBI labs identified it as coming from a Chrysler product: a Plymouth, Dodge, Chrysler, Eagle, or Jeep. What model car does the man you're looking for drive?"

"This conversation's over."

"What make of car? When I get his name I can get the information from the Department of Motor Vehicles."

"Jeep Cherokee," Culley said.

"Damn it, Culley! If you know who he is, you've got to tell the FBI. This monster has killed four women in the past month . . . four that they know of."

"Look, let's say you're right; I know who the killer is, okay? It won't do a damn bit of good to tell the FBI, because if it's who I think it is, from what you've told me so far, he's playing games with them, and believe me, he knows how to play games they never heard of."

"Well, if you don't tell them, I will."

"No, you won't."

"Are you threatening me?"

"I'm warning you. For your own good," Culley said. "There's a lot you don't know."

"It was the CIA, not the FBI, who was following me, wasn't it?" Houser said. "And they broke into my apartment and read my computer files, didn't they?"

"I don't know anything about that."

"I'm not going to let go of this."

"You have no idea what you're setting in motion."

"I think I do."

"Let me disabuse you of a serious misconception you reporters have come to consider gospel," Culley said. "Forget everything you ever read about how bungling and inept the CIA is. Believe me when I tell you they are not. All you ever hear about are their occasional failures. You never hear about the successes, and you never will. And success is the rule, not the exception. When they want something done, it gets done. One way or another. No holds barred if it's deemed in the national interest, or in many cases in their own interest, which they consider one and the same."

"If you're trying to scare me off, forget it. I don't scare easily."

"I'm trying to enlighten you. And to prevent you from making a serious mistake. You can't go around accusing someone of being a murderer on purely circumstantial evidence, not when there are things at stake you know nothing about."

"Come on, Culley. You know as well as I do that grand juries have indicted people on less than what we're talking about here."

"Sure. The press coverage creates political pressure. Some opportunistic assistant district attorney sees a chance to advance his career, so he presents circumstantial evidence as facts and leads the grand jury around by their noses."

"At the very least there's enough to have him picked up and questioned."

"Maybe. But if it turns out you're wrong, and he's not the killer? By the time you and your friends in the media get finished with him the accusations will stick like a guilty verdict for the rest of his life. And in the process you'll succeed in exposing some highly classified operations."

"Are you going to sit there with a straight face and tell me that you don't think the person you're looking for just might be the serial killer?"

"I'm telling you I don't know."

"So you're going to do nothing?"

"I'm going to look into it. I might know someone who can help sort it out."

"Who?"

"Give me one day before you go running your mouth about a lot of suppositions and assumptions that might add up to nothing more than coincidence. If I learn anything—"

"If *we* learn anything," Houser said emphatically. "That's the deal. I'm sticking with you. Take it or leave it. Leave it, and I go to the FBI and then my editor with what I've already got."

"You've got nothing. Granted, you'll have no trouble getting the name of the man who owns the shop and the house, but you still won't be any closer to learning his identity."

"What's that supposed to mean?"

"It means you don't have what you think you have."

"I've got enough. And I'll get more," Houser said with conviction. "CIA INVESTIGATION LINKED TO HUNT FOR SERIAL KILLER. How's that for a catchy headline?"

Culley struggled with a conflict of emotions as he sat shoving his food around his plate with his fork. He owed the Agency nothing. If they had lied to him from the start about why they wanted Malik, then he owed them less than nothing. Certainly not his loyalty. But he had never gone back on his word in his life, and although there were strong indications that Malik was involved in the murders up to his eyeballs, he did not have any conclusive proof of that. Not enough to throw Gregus and the deputy director for operations to the wolves.

They had paid him, and he had given his word. Accepted the contract. The time-honored Agency practice of "need to know" had resulted in his being kept in the dark about the true purpose of any number of operations he was involved in. He accepted that as one of the rules of the game. But this had nothing to do with the national interest. It was nothing more than a cover-your-ass operation. And while covering up a counterfeiting case involving a defector-gone-bad was one thing, a murderer was something far different, especially if his own inability to find Malik and bring him in resulted in any more deaths.

Culley locked eyes with Houser, considering her ultimatum. She wasn't going to back off, and there was no way to convince her that she was wrong, especially when every indication was that she was right. She was smart and intuitive and would put it all together quickly. Hell, she had most of it figured out already. And there were good, sound operational reasons to keep her close at hand, and under control, until he could talk with the one person who might have the answers he needed. And if it turned out it was Malik, he would call Gregus and dump the whole mess, *Washington Post* reporter and all, in his lap and walk away from it. *Jesus Christ, Lou! A serial killer!*

"All right. Here's the way it's going to go," he said. "If you're in, you're in until the end. No stories until we know beyond a reasonable doubt that the killer is the man I'm looking for."

"And if that turns out to be the case, I'm not going to hold anything back. And I'll get no interference from you, right?"

"From me? No. But if Malik is the killer you've got to know up front that the Agency will do whatever it has to do to cover it up. And trust me on this; they're some very serious people."

"You said Malik. Who's Malik?"

"John Malik, that's his name. Or the name he was given when he was resettled in this country a few years ago."

"Resettled?" Houser said. "Then I was right. He is former KGB."

"A defector. I was his control for six years in Moscow while we ran him as an agent-in-place."

Houser smiled inwardly. She knew a great story when she heard one. This had Pulitzer Prize written all over it. Not to mention a book contract. And she would have the inside track.

"You've got a deal," she said, and held out her hand. Culley shook it. "Now, who is it we're going to talk to?"

"I'll tell you on the way there," Culley said, and signaled the waiter for the check.

"My treat, remember?"

Culley waited as she paid the bill. Then they crossed the street to the parking garage.

"We'll go in your car," Culley said. He unstrapped the leather carryall from the motorcycle and tossed it in the back of the Porsche.

"Where are we going?"

"Hampden-Sydney College. It's about an hour and a half south of here."

Houser looked over at the motorcycle. "You left your key in the ignition."

"I know."

"That's an open invitation for someone to steal it."

Culley shrugged. "That's what I did."

"You're kidding, right?"

"Let's go."

16

THE OUTDOOR TERRACE of the Biltmore Grill, located across the street from the sidewalk café where Mike Culley and Julie Houser had eaten lunch, is enclosed by a wooden latticework trellis covered with vines. Anyone sitting at one of the tables at the far end of the terrace overlooking the sidewalk on Elliewood Avenue is concealed from the immediate view of passersby. Yet from the cool and shady spot they can peer through breaks in the creeping vines and observe the activity in the surrounding area. It was while sitting in just that location that John Malik had seen Culley pull his motorcycle into the parking garage, then cross the street to join a woman he himself had been watching with some interest.

For a brief moment Malik believed he was mistaken. It couldn't be Culley. He had followed the accounts of his trial in the paper and was aware of the length of the sentence he had received. It did not make sense that he was out of prison so soon. But then he realized that it made perfect sense. And he knew immediately why Culley was in Charlottesville:

the CIA had sent his old handler after him. Who better? It was a smart move on the deputy director for operations' part. But was Culley being sent to find a resettled defector discovered missing by his NROC case officer, a counterfeiter, or a serial killer?

Malik believed it was the last, the result of a logical progression: the Agency had learned of the hijacking and suspected his involvement; his NROC case officer was then sent to talk to him and found him missing. Aware of the concurrent disappearances of the little bitches, they had done their homework, discovered lingering questions about his checkered past, and put the pieces together.

When most of the currency paper from the truck his Russian mafia friends had hijacked was recovered by the Secret Service, Malik knew there was a chance his involvement might be uncovered. He had anticipated that, as well as the inevitability of where it would logically lead them. But he had not anticipated Culley's being sent in response, although that confirmed another judgment he had made at the outset: the CIA would tell the Secret Service and the FBI nothing. They would keep it in-house, try to bring him in themselves, and if unsuccessful, destroy any and all of his files, enabling them to deny him in the event he came under investigation by any outside agencies.

But where would any such investigation lead? There no longer was a John Malik. He had disappeared without a trace. The printer in Brighton Beach had seen to that. An old KGB forger, he had created an entirely new identity for him, complete with all the necessary backup documents. The Secret Service, or the FBI, if they were smart enough to unravel his clues, would eventually be led to John Malik. A man who, further investigation would reveal, had not existed until three years ago. They would suspect CIA involvement, but by then the purging of the Agency records and files would be complete, if they weren't already, and any queries would be met with bald-faced stares of incomprehension and innocence. It was his little game. His tweaking of the Agency's beard. And it could still play out the way he had planned.

He had been more than careful in renting the remote cabin in the woods, leaving no paper trail, and anyone would be hard-pressed to discover where he had gone. Yet, despite all the careful planning and the precautions he had taken, they had almost stumbled across him by accident. Had he arrived at the restaurant a few minutes later, Culley would surely have seen him, and there would have been a confrontation. He did not fear Culley, but he did have a healthy respect for his abilities. He would have to be more cautious.

He had kept to himself since he was resettled in Charlottesville, and few people knew him well enough to strike up a conversation. And he had stayed away from his house and shop since setting his plan in motion. But now, with confirmation that the Agency was looking for him in earnest, he could no longer take any unnecessary risks. He would not panic and leave Charlottesville immediately, there would be no sport in that. But no more daytime trips into town without disguising his appearance, and then only to scout his routes to and from the abduction and dump sites to be used for what he still had planned.

Culley's presence, however, was something he had not factored into the original equation. He was a formidable adversary, who knew him well, and, as he recalled from their relationship in Moscow, played by his own rules. A change of tactics was in order. His timetable would now have to be moved up. He would go to New York and complete his business there. The one pallet of currency paper, enough to print thirty million dollars, part of his share that he had managed to move from the warehouse before the Secret Service raid, was safely tucked away in Brighton Beach, awaiting the engraved plates in his possession that were needed to print the money. With that completed he could still return to the cabin to harvest the last of the little bitches in Charlottesville before disappearing to resurface wherever he chose. Knowing that Culley was out there somewhere would make the game that much more interesting and challenging. He would show his old handler who had really held the reins all along.

But first he would find out what Culley and his lady friend were up to. Their activities might reveal how much or how little they knew. He had watched them leave the café together, and was now four cars behind the old Porsche as it left I-64 and drove south on Route 20 toward Scottsville. He had not yet reached a conclusion on how the woman fit into the picture. Perhaps part of an Agency surveillance team assigned to work with Culley. He did recall that Culley was a loner; he did not like working with partners. But this one was quite alluring. Perhaps Culley was attracted to her. He knew that *he* was. Her shoulder-length chestnut-brown hair, dark brown eyes, and stunning figure had drawn his attention the moment he saw her crossing the street to the sidewalk café. She might be an interesting addition.

All in good time, he thought as he slowed to let another car pass and kept his distance from the Porsche up ahead.

▽

"ARE YOU STILL following them?" Gregus asked the man calling from the surveillance vehicle in Charlottesville.

"No. I established that he was searching Malik's shop and house, and when I saw him having lunch with the reporter I broke it off as you instructed."

"Good. Head back here," Gregus said, and hung up.

He left the small study off the safe-house kitchen and went to the computer room, where he found Hack busy at work.

"What else did you come up with on Julie Houser?"

"During her tenth year on the Job she was awarded the department's medal of honor. She retired with a disability pension three months later."

"What did she do to get the medal?"

"Couldn't get that," Hack said. "Not in the computers. Must be in a hard-copy file."

"What disability does she have?"

"Same story. Not in the computer. My guess would be she was wounded in whatever action was involved in her getting the medal. They don't give those things away for nothing.

"By the way," Hack added, "the ruse worked perfectly. The local cops in the Clifton area have chalked up the fire at Culley's house to a group of teenage vandals. So far they aren't looking any farther."

"Good," Gregus said. "Let me know if it changes."

Gregus was intrigued by Culley's involvement with the reporter, and he had no difficulty imagining the scenario that had led to it: somehow their paths had crossed, her reasons for being in Charlottesville discussed, and Culley would now know, or strongly suspect, the counterfeiting story was not the only reason he was after Malik.

Houser was a potential problem, but one Gregus felt could be handled when the time came. At least Culley was back on track, and that was what mattered. Whatever his reason for teaming up with Houser, Gregus knew him well enough to feel certain that he would not violate operational security. He was probably more than a little pissed at the moment, Gregus thought, but he was a big boy and knew how the game was played. When he called in, he would stroke him and smooth things over.

17

HOUSER WAS DETERMINED to wring every last thrill from the near perfect merger of a road and a sports car meant for each other. For the fifth time in as many minutes Culley gripped the handhold on the door as she expertly downshifted and powered the Porsche through another tight turn.

"You always drive like this?"

"Every chance I get. Now, who are we going to see?"

"His name's Boris Novikov. Or at least it was until three years ago. It's now George Spirko."

"Another KGB defector? How many has the Agency brought into the country?"

"I don't know. Maybe three or four hundred over forty years."

"And they all go into the government's witness protection program?"

"Something like that. But the Agency has its own operation."

Culley gave her a brief, sanitized synopsis, without mentioning the National Resettlement Operations

Center by name, or explaining how the defectors were debriefed, given new identities, relocated, and monitored until they were fully adjusted to their new lives.

"What's this Novikov, or Spirko, doing at a yuppie school like Hampden-Sydney?"

"Teaching theology."

"You're kidding."

"That's another misconception everyone has. The stereotypical KGB officer. You think of them as stupid thugs with bad teeth in poorly tailored blue suits, green shirts, white socks, and brown shoes. The truth is most of them have at least a master's degree or a Ph.D., and more than a few are better trained, more experienced, and better dressed than our own people."

"But theology? That's not exactly a subject you'd expect a former KGB officer to be well versed in."

"It's even more ironic when you consider that Spirko spent his early years in the KGB directorate that suppressed religion inside their own country."

"Why the affinity for college towns?"

"Some of them teach, usually Russian studies, or continue their own educations. Some go to work for the Agency as intelligence analysts. Others don't do a damn thing but live off the tax-free income the American taxpayer provides for the rest of their lives."

"And some murder people," Houser said pointedly.

After a long silence Culley turned in his seat to face Houser, who was again driving as though a trophy and a garland of flowers were to be awarded at the end of the trip.

"I don't want to give you the wrong impression of these guys," he said. "You'd be hard-pressed to find one with any character, integrity, or honor. The majority of them didn't become double agents and defect for any strong moral or religious convictions, or for any belief in democratic principles, although that's what they like to claim. The motive was usually money, or revenge for being passed over for promotion, or just to get a taste of the good life. For the most part they're liars, cheats, and sneaks who betrayed their country. The fact that they helped us doesn't make them less of a traitor. Spirko is one of the few exceptions. He couldn't stomach the treatment of the clergy and those who held on to their religious faith. He got religion himself while in the process of sending them off to labor camps to be starved and worked to death."

"How convenient," Houser said. "If their new identities are so highly classified, how is it you know who they are and where they live?"

"I don't," Culley said. "I know about Spirko because I got his wife and daughter out."

"Out of what?"

"Russia," Culley said. "The KGB was closing in on him. He had to leave in a hurry. He left his wife and six-year-old daughter behind."

"That was nice of him."

"It was either that or die," Culley said. "One of our agents warned us the KGB were onto him. We literally got him out by the skin of his teeth. They were waiting at his apartment to arrest him when we grabbed him off the street on his way home and put him under wraps. Six months after he defected, the Agency kept their promise to get his wife and daughter out. They sent me in; I used the same escape route I'd used for Malik the year before."

"What do you think he can tell you about Malik?"

"Maybe nothing I don't already know. But he knew him in Moscow. They worked together for ten or twelve years. If Malik did kill those kids, he didn't just sprout fully formed as a serial killer a month ago. He must have had some history that led up to it."

∇

THE LAST OF the evening light was fading fast as Houser slowed the Porsche to somewhere close to the speed limit and drove past the ivy-covered brick columns at the entrance to Hampden-Sydney. Set among the rolling hills of southern Virginia, the college, founded in 1776, had a picture-perfect campus of federal-style brick buildings and sprawling lawns and paths shaded by towering oaks and maples, some that were mere saplings during the American Revolution. With fewer than nine hundred students and a student-faculty ratio of one to twelve, it was a highly accredited and acclaimed institution, well-known for its abundance of students from some of the most wealthy and powerful families in the country.

"This place is loaded with atmosphere," Houser said, admiring the grounds as they drove along College Road. "I can see it all now, long leafy walks, plaid skirts, cashmere sweaters worn over the shoulders, the boys in Brooks Brothers shirts, chinos, loafers, and no socks. My kind of college."

"I don't think so," Culley said.

"And why not?"

"It's a men's college. One of only three left in the country."

"As I said. My kind of college." She wiggled her eyebrows and flashed a broad grin. "Where do we find Spirko?"

"I don't know, we'll have to ask."

Houser spotted four young men walking along the sidewalk and swung into the curb in front of Graham Hall. She had the students' immediate and undivided attention the moment she stepped out of the car. Yes, they knew where Professor Spirko could be found. He was giving a recital in a few days and was practicing his cello on the third floor of Winston Hall, next to the president's residence on Via Sacra.

Three of the students fell all over themselves in offering their assistance to personally escort Houser there. Then they noticed Culley sitting in the Porsche, at which time they simply pointed in the direction of the hall, visible a short distance away on the far side of a broad sweep of lawn.

Gabriel Fauré's "Après un rêve" drifted down to the first-floor Commons, filling the high-ceilinged room with its melancholy strains as Culley and Houser entered the building. They had no trouble following the sound to where Spirko sat in the center of a large room, his eyes closed, lost in the music as he played.

Houser's first impression of Spirko was one of contradiction. He was a mostly bald, middle-aged man with strong Slavic features. Short and powerfully built, he had a bull neck and beefy hands, and at a glance one would suspect he would be more comfortable with a tuba wrapped around his neck than a cello between his knees. But his delicate touch and the sweet music it created belied that outward impression.

He was unaware of their presence, and they stood silently in the doorway until he had finished, then applauded politely and approached. Spirko's brow furrowed for a moment, but as they drew closer a warm smile came with the moment of recognition.

"Michael, it is so good to see you."

"Hello, Boris."

"Please, Michael. It is George now. You don't want to confuse my students should any of them overhear you. I give them enough to worry about as it is." He smiled at Houser and nodded. "And who is your lovely friend?"

"Julie Houser," Houser said, and stepped forward to shake hands.

Spirko took the outstretched hand. "A pleasure, Ms. Houser."

"You still play very well," Culley said.

"And you still lie very well," Spirko said with a smile. "And so, to what do I owe this unexpected but welcome visit?"

"I need to talk with you about some old business," Culley said.

"First you must come and say hello to Anna and Katrina. They will be very pleased to see you. You and Ms. Houser will be our guests for dinner this evening."

"I'm afraid I can't. This isn't a social call."

Houser noticed Spirko's eyes: the eyes of someone who knew and kept secrets, secrets others had probably given their lives trying to learn. A wariness replaced the slight twinkle that had first greeted them.

"Ms. Houser is from Langley too?"

"No. But it's all right to talk."

"I was sorry to read about your troubles, Michael," Spirko said. "I assume that nasty business is all straightened out now?"

"You assume correctly."

Spirko nodded. "You were the chosen sacrificial lamb, my old friend. But, as they say, it goes with the territory."

"Something like that." His expression told Spirko the subject was closed to further discussion.

"So, what is it that brings you here?"

"I need some information about an old friend of yours, Nikolai Lubanov," Culley said, using Malik's true name, the only one Spirko would know him by.

Houser again noticed a sharp change in Spirko's eyes. The wary gaze hardened into a cold stare that made her reassess her earlier evaluation: the eyes now spoke not of a cello or a tuba in his hands, but a meat-ax.

"*Friend* is hardly the appropriate term," Spirko said at length. "Is Nikolai giving you trouble?"

"I'm not sure. What can you tell me about him, other than what I already know about his KGB history?"

"What specifically do you want to know?"

"Did he have a dark side we knew nothing about?" Culley did not want to lead him, and kept it at that.

"A dark side?" Spirko smiled grimly. "I take it you are not aware of the information I gave my debriefers when I defected."

"I wasn't told anything about it."

"Nikolai was under suspicion of murder when he defected," Spirko said. "Not one murder, but many.

There were questions about young women who had been brutally killed in a number of Soviet cities, and in others where he had been stationed over the years."

"And you told your debriefers this three years ago?"

"Of course. They told me they would pass the information along and 'take the appropriate action,' I believe is how they put it."

"Was there compelling evidence against him at the time?"

"Very strong circumstantial evidence," Spirko said. "And one eyewitness who saw Nikolai in the company of one of the victims the night of her death. KGB internal security conducted a rather vigorous investigation into the allegations on their own, but then it was suddenly dropped."

"Why was that?"

"The eyewitness was killed by a car that witnesses claim climbed the curb and chased him down the sidewalk before crushing him against a wall."

"And that was the end of it?"

"They didn't see the driver of the car, and with the only eyewitness dead there was little they could do. The Moscow police continued their investigation, but it went nowhere. Nikolai had friends in high places. Friends who let it be known that any further harassment of a fellow KGB officer would not be looked upon kindly." Spirko searched Culley's eyes for a brief moment, then said, "I take this to mean that nothing was done about my warning."

"Apparently not."

"I find that very difficult to believe."

"Believe it," Houser said, breaking her long silence.

"And where is Nikolai now?"

"Charlottesville, Virginia," Houser said, catching the angry look that Culley directed at her.

"Stay out of this," Culley said sharply.

"Stay out of it? That's what your buddies did three years ago and now there are four people dead."

"The murders at the University of Virginia," Spirko said. "Of course. They are similar."

"I have to ask you not to mention my visit to anyone, or to say anything about Nikolai's possible involvement in the murders in Charlottesville."

"Possible involvement?" Houser said. "What do you need, Culley, a wall to fall on you?"

Culley shot her another angry look. Spirko studied her face for a moment.

"What is it you do, Ms. Houser?"

"I'm a reporter for *The Washington Post*."

The look Spirko gave Culley was one of shock and incredulity that left no doubt in Culley's mind that the former KGB officer considered Houser's presence a serious breach of security.

"I had no choice," Culley said by way of explanation to Spirko's unspoken question.

"The FBI is not aware of Nikolai's background or of his presence in Charlottesville?"

"Not yet," Culley said.

"And you are not going to tell them?"

"It's not my decision to make."

"You are placing me in a rather untenable position," Spirko said.

"I'm sorry. There are good reasons that I'm not at liberty to discuss."

"Of course. There always are."

"I need to know something else."

Spirko's gaze shifted to Houser, then back to Culley.

"It's all right," Culley said. "I take full responsibility for her."

The remark rankled Houser, but she said nothing.

"Was Nikolai ever involved in KGB counterfeiting operations?"

Spirko thought for a moment and then said, "Periodically, we provided East German State Security with engraved plates to produce counterfeit West German deutsche marks, English pounds, and American dollars. Nikolai oversaw that operation."

"Why did you use the East Germans?"

"They had a well-organized and ingenious distribution method. They never got greedy, so there was never enough circulated through the international monetary system to arouse suspicions. Only a few million dollars a year was printed in each of the currencies. The money was used to fund some of their espionage operations. The KGB got half of it."

"And the counterfeit money was good enough to pass for the real thing?"

"Unless examined in a laboratory by people who knew precisely what they were looking for, it was perfect," Spirko said. "The engraved plates were made by a master engraver, an old man who had done the same thing for the Nazis. We manufactured the currency paper and provided the plates. The East Germans printed the money and distributed it."

"What happened to the engraved plates when East Germany fell?"

"That's an interesting question," Spirko said.

"Does it have an interesting answer?"

"When it became obvious that the East German government was about to disintegrate, Nikolai and two of his men were sent to State Security headquarters in East Berlin to retrieve the plates and destroy any records or files that would reveal our involvement in the counterfeiting operation. It is my understanding that he accomplished his mission, with the exception of retrieving the set of engraved plates for the American dollars. Fifty- and one-hundred-dollar bills were the denominations, I believe. Nikolai claimed they were stolen by someone within the State Security apparatus. Someone who had fled to the West only days before he got there."

"And the plates would still be useful today."

"Of course. The engraver created new plates whenever any of the governments made changes that outdated those we were using. The ones they were using at the time the DDR fell were only a year or two old. With the right paper they could still produce the same-quality currency."

"I'm sorry I had to lay this at your feet," Culley said. "But you were the only person I knew who might be able to help."

"The Agency is pursuing Nikolai on their own, to avoid embarrassing complications?"

"That's the plan."

Spirko smiled knowingly. "And they have sent you to find him, but did not tell you the real reason why?"

Culley nodded and Spirko rose to embrace him, kissing him on both cheeks. "I owe you a great deal, Michael. Anna and Katrina will be disappointed they did not get to see you."

"Perhaps another time."

Spirko turned to Houser. "I would appreciate you not making public my past or my present situation, Ms. Houser."

"There would be no reason to mention it."

"Thank you."

A full moon was shining brightly when Spirko walked Culley and Houser outside to where the Porsche was parked at the curb. He again embraced Culley.

"Good luck, my friend. And be careful. You know Nikolai as well as anyone, but do not let your familiarity lead to overconfidence. He is a very capable and dangerous man."

"I remember," Culley said. "And I won't mention our conversation to anyone."

"Nor will I."

Houser remained silent until they were seated in the car. She started the engine and then turned angrily to Culley.

"No one is responsible for me but me, Culley. Understood?"

"I understand you occasionally don't engage your brain before you put your mouth in gear. Never volunteer information when you question someone. You tell them only what they need to know to give you the information you want. If I'm right, Spirko will find some anonymous way to get the information about Malik to the FBI."

"What difference does it make? That's exactly what I'm going to do, or are you forgetting our deal?"

Culley did not reply. He stared out the window at the moonlit campus as Houser pulled away from the curb and ran quickly through the gears.

18

GEORGE SPIRKO WALKED along the moonlit pathway, savoring the crisp fall air and the scent of autumn carried on the night breeze. He replayed his conversation with Culley over in his mind, and made his decision. He could not possibly ignore the information about the murders in Charlottesville. After dinner he would go to a pay phone off campus and make an anonymous call to the FBI. Had he known that Nikolai Lubanov had been resettled in Charlottesville, he would have immediately passed the information on to the authorities. He hated to go back on his word to his old friend, but lives could be at stake if the CIA were not immediately successful in their hunt for Lubanov. If indeed they were even trying to find him. Had they not ignored his warnings before?

Spirko left the path and took his usual shortcut across the grounds. He walked through a thick grove of old maples in the direction of his on-campus residence, already tasting the pork roast and dumplings he knew Anna was preparing. The dappled

moonlight filtering down through the dying leaves
did little to light the way in the deeply shadowed
area, and he slowed his pace after stumbling once.

He paused to light a cigarette, and in his peripheral vision he thought he saw something move among
the trees off to his left. He stared in the direction he
had seen the movement, but it was still and silent,
with the exception of the branches swaying in the
breeze. A lone leaf fluttered to the ground, account-
ing, he believed, for what had drawn his attention.

He continued on his way, then paused again.
There *was* something out there. And it was not a
falling leaf. Just ahead of him but still to his left, for
an instant, a long shadow had passed across an open
space between two trees, not twenty yards away.
Perhaps a student on his way to the residence halls
across the lawn at the opposite end of the grove.
Again he stood quietly and watched, but saw nothing
more. He smiled to himself; too many years of dark
alleys and secret meetings, he mused. His past coming
back to haunt him.

He resumed walking and focused his thoughts on
the upcoming recital that he and another faculty
member, a pianist, were giving to welcome the new
college president. In his mind he went over the selec-
tions he would play, thinking that perhaps he might
rearrange their order to better set the mood for the
special evening. Leave the more difficult pieces until
last, he reminded himself.

He was humming one of the more intricate passages when again his attention was drawn to the deep
shadows beneath the trees. There. Yes. Ten yards
ahead, just off to his left. Someone had stepped

out from among the trees and was walking slowly toward him.

The figure appeared in silhouette, backlit by the lights from the complex of buildings ahead in the distance. His arms hung loosely at his sides as he moved with a calm, easy gait. He held something in his right hand, and as he drew closer, Spirko recognized its ominous shape and stopped walking. His senses came alive and he was back fifteen years to a time when he would have been prepared to react immediately. But not here, not now. Was it just another faculty member or a student? Was he imagining the gun in the man's hand? He must be. That was all behind him. But then he knew it wasn't, and never could be.

The silhouetted figure stopped a few yards from Spirko and raised the sound-suppressed semiautomatic pistol, pointing it at his head.

"Boris Nikolaevich," Malik said, in a soft, almost friendly voice, "you've been a very bad boy."

Spirko looked quickly to his left and right; his instincts told him to run. But his reflexes were not what they used to be, and he knew he could never reach the cover of the closest trees in time.

"You've been telling stories about me, haven't you? Shame on you."

"You're insane, Nikolai. You'll be caught. They know it's you."

"Of course they do. I planned it that way, you fool."

Spirko again glanced about for anything that might divert Malik's attention, someone he could call out to and cause a distraction if only for a moment, just long enough for him to break away. But there was no one in sight.

Malik smiled and shook his head. "There is no salvation tonight, comrade."

And with that he fired three rapid shots into Spirko's head. The shots made no more noise than three quick finger snaps. Spirko was dead before his body crumpled to the ground.

Malik moved quickly, dragging the lifeless body into the deep shadows at the base of a maple tree, its branches low to the ground. He scanned the surrounding area, making certain they were still alone, then removed a switchblade knife from his jacket pocket and flicked it open.

"I would like to spend more time with you, dear Boris, to be more creative. I truly would. But unfortunately tonight I am forced by circumstances to improvise."

"See no evil," he whispered, and deftly removed both of Spirko's eyes with swift, practiced gouging cuts.

"Hear no evil." Just as quickly both ears were cleanly sliced off.

"And most important of all. You must speak no evil." And he pried open Spirko's mouth and grasped his tongue.

19

CULLEY SLOUCHED AGAINST the wall beside the pay phone in a darkened corner of a roadside tavern ten miles north of the Hampden-Sydney campus. He took a drink from a long-neck bottle of Bud as he listened to Lou Gregus on the other end of the line. He had told him nothing of his meeting with Spirko.

"You fuckin' lied to me, Lou."

"All you needed to know was that we wanted him brought in," Gregus said. "What difference does it make why?"

"Did it ever occur to you that a man responds differently when he's looking at a death sentence for multiple murders as opposed to a few years for a counterfeiting rap?"

"I felt you could handle it, regardless."

"Your confidence in me is inspiring. But you're full of shit."

"Just find him, Mike. Before the feds do."

"I'm not going to take him out for you. If we get

into a shoot-out and he goes down, that's one thing. But I'm not going to assassinate him."

"Just find him and call us in. We'll take care of the rest."

"I'll find him, but only because I don't want it on my conscience if he murders any more kids."

It was the reaction Gregus had been counting on. "That's all I ask."

"And that's all you'll get."

"Good. We'll work it from this end and keep you informed. Anything you need, just call."

"There's one little hitch; something you're going to have to deal with sooner or later."

"I know about her," Gregus said. "Julie Houser. Reporter from *The Washington Post*."

"You know about her?" Culley's temper flared. "You put another surveillance team on me?"

"Only until I was sure you were going after Malik. When you showed up in Charlottesville I pulled them."

"Well, keep them the hell away from me. If Malik spots them he'll be in the wind and you can kiss his ass good-bye."

"Done," Gregus said.

"And I want your personal guarantee, and the DDO's, that there won't be any rough stuff where Houser is concerned."

"No problem. We have any number of ways of handling her when the time comes."

"I'm serious about this, Lou. She gets hurt in any way, I'll see to it that you and the DDO end up eating dinner in the Lewisburg penitentiary with Crazy Jack and Spaceship Smith."

"Who?"

"Never mind. Take me at my word, it's an experience you can do without."

"There'll be no rough stuff," Gregus said. "How much does she know?"

Culley told him of the serendipitous meeting and how quickly Houser had pieced together what was going on.

"She's nobody's fool," Culley said. "The only option was to keep her close."

"Then continue to keep her with you. Let her think she's got the story of her life at the end of the line. In the meantime we can set things in motion here."

"Forget that. I'm not dragging some reporter around with me. I don't need to be worrying about her getting blown away if I get into it with Malik."

"She might be more of an asset than you think."

"Pain in the ass is more like it."

"She didn't tell you about her background?"

"What background? She's a newsie."

"She's an ex-cop, Mike."

"A cop?"

"Ten years. New York City. Highly decorated."

Culley peeked around the corner to the bar where Houser sat nursing a beer and chatting with the oversolicitous bartender. "A cop. I'll be damned."

"Apparently a gutsy one. Worked undercover narcotics for almost two years, and took a round for her partner as a homicide detective. She retired on a disability pension two years ago. Don't have the details on that yet. But she's more than qualified to watch your flank."

"A cop," Culley said again. "You got any ideas where Malik might be hiding out?"

"Not yet. But we're working on it."

"I'm on my way back to Charlottesville. I'm going to toss his house and shop again. See if I missed anything."

"Good idea. Where are you staying?"

"Holiday Inn. On Twenty-nine North."

"I'll call you the minute we come up with anything. You do the same. By the way, I covered your ass on the fire. That wasn't the smartest move you ever made, but I can't say that I blame you."

"Mind your own business, Lou."

Culley hung up and stood staring at Houser before returning to the bar to join her. He had always prided himself on sizing people up. He had assumed her underlying toughness to be that of a cynical reporter; he should have known there was more to her.

"So, what's the verdict?" she asked as he sat on the stool beside her.

Culley ignored the question, taking some time to figure out how he was going to handle her. He got the bartender's attention away from the front of Houser's silk blouse, where the two open buttons at the neck promised an enticing view if the bartender could only lean forward far enough. Culley pointed to his beer, remained silent until a second one arrived, then gave the bartender a look that sent him to the far end of the bar, out of earshot.

Houser met and held his eyes. "You're going after him yourself. Aren't you?"

"You think that's a bad idea?"

"I think in this situation the FBI is better equipped to find him than you are."

"Not a chance," Culley said. "Let me tell you a few things about the Feebs. Their forensic labs are hands down the best in the world. And their computer boys can follow a paper trail as well as anyone. But their street-level work sucks. Their arrest and conviction rate looks good on paper, but when you're willing to spend ten million to investigate and prosecute some poor sap who forged a five-hundred-dollar check, or to sting some idiot politicians, that's not effective law enforcement. They're borderline morons when it comes to solving any crime they didn't set up themselves as an entrapment operation. And their Ten Most Wanted list is a joke; they never put anyone on it until they know where he is and how long he's going to be there."

Houser smiled. She had her own personal frame of reference for the merits of the FBI from her days as a cop. She knew Culley was right. Every joint operation they had worked with them had turned into a disaster.

"And what can the CIA do that the FBI can't?"

"Grow up, Houser. Forget proper procedure. Forget Miranda. Forget the rules of evidence. If it's important enough you can even forget the Constitution. We can do anything we want, and usually do."

"Yeah, that's what got you in prison."

Houser regretted the biting comment as soon as she heard herself say it. "Sorry. That was a low blow."

"No, you're right. I went to prison. But the game still went on. We're all expendable."

"Look, I know where this is headed. And I'm

not holding off on my story. We had a deal. You said if your buddies were lying to you, and it turned out that Malik was the Mix and Match killer, you were backing away from it and I was under no obligation to sit on the information."

"And just what do you think you have so far?"

"Enough to write one hell of a good story."

"You've got nothing without Agency confirmation. And there's no way in hell you'll get that. And in case you're considering selling out Spirko, you're forgetting who controls his life. He'll deny everything we discussed. And if you do manage to get past that, the Agency can bring considerable pressure to bear on your paper."

"My editor won't knuckle under to the CIA. I can guarantee you that."

"Your editor won't have anything to say about it. It'll be done on a much higher level. The old-boy network will come into play. The director calls in a few favors, claims you're off the wall with your information, that the true story has to stay buried for reasons of national security. So you're discredited, your story's dead, and you end up looking like some conspiracy-theory nut case."

"We're talking about stopping a serial killer, Culley. Not my career. If I tell the FBI what I know right now, they've got a much better chance of finding Malik."

"I promise you they don't," Culley said. "Let me run it down for you. You give the FBI Malik's name and tell them he's a KGB defector. The Agency denies him from top to bottom. But in the process you've succeeded in getting the FBI watching their every move. So they've got no choice but to cease and desist with their operation. That leaves the FBI on their own, trying to find someone who is no longer using the name you gave them, a name Malik intended for them to find out from the start anyway. Get the picture? You're back to square one.

"And I've got something going for me that the FBI doesn't," Culley added. "Malik expects them to come after him, he's anticipating their moves and playing with them. He doesn't know I'm in the game."

After a long silence Houser suddenly glared at Culley. "And I don't sell people out," she said, still smarting over the insinuation about Spirko.

"I owed you that one; for the smart-assed prison remark."

"I apologized for that."

"And I apologize for mine."

Houser lapsed into silence again, staring into her glass. Culley followed her lead. Waiting.

"Okay, Culley. Out with it. What are you proposing?"

"Sit on your story. Hang in with me, just for a couple of days, until we see if we get anywhere. If the FBI finds Malik first, you've still got your story. One that nobody else has."

"And if you find him, then I'm still in the same situation. You'll cover it up like it never happened."

"It's not that easy. You dig deep enough and you can establish that Malik existed. Then, alive or dead, someone's going to have to explain who he is. The likely scenario is that if I find Malik before the feds, the Agency gets to announce his capture, or death, whichever way it goes down. Bottom line, he wasn't one of their own gone bad. They play it as the ever-diligent heroes who cleaned up an unfortunate mess. They come out looking as much like a victim as everyone else."

Culley was not particularly proud of himself for trying to convince Houser of something that he knew to be a highly improbable outcome. But even though any personal loyalty he had left for the CIA was hanging by a thread, he owed even less to a reporter.

"I find it unconscionable that the CIA would simply ignore the warning Spirko gave them about Malik. How can they possible justify doing that?"

"The CIA is a bureaucracy like every other government agency," Culley said. "With one exception: It's so compartmentalized that the right hand seldom knows what the left hand is doing. Spirko's warning could have been filed away and nobody paid any attention to it. Or it could have been purposely ignored. Malik was a high-level defector. One of the most valuable we ever got. He's the kind people build careers on, and his champions would take a dim view of anyone who rains on their parade."

Culley checked the time. It was six-thirty. They could be in Charlottesville within the half hour. He settled up with the bartender as Houser tossed down the last of her beer and slid off the stool. The bartender took a final wistful look at the long, shapely legs in the snug-fitting jeans as Houser walked out the door.

Outside, Houser paused in the neon glow cast across the parking lot. She stared long and hard at Culley. What he had said made sense. And a reporter was lucky to stumble across an exclusive story like this once in a lifetime. Accolades and awards loomed large in the distance. And then there was the opportunity to relive what she missed most about being a cop: the action.

"Okay. I'm in. Only as long as you're making some progress. And I assure you, regardless of any pressure, I'm going to get the story out when this is over. If not in the *Post*, then somewhere else."

Culley extended his hand and they shook. "Deal," he said.

Culley slipped into the passenger seat of the Porsche and reached into the rear compartment, where the backs of the jump seats were positioned forward to form a shelf. He unzipped his leather carryall and brought out the Walther .380-caliber semiautomatic pistol in the ankle holster. Houser watched as he checked the gun to make certain a round was in the chamber and the safety was on.

"I've been told you're more than just a pretty face," Culley said, and handed her the weapon.

"So your buddies at Langley have been doing their homework," Houser said, and gave the gun back. "I don't need it."

"If we run into Malik, believe me, you'll need it."

Houser pulled her shoulder bag from the rear shelf and held it in her lap. To all but someone who knew of its dual purpose, it looked like any other oversized shoulder bag. Houser pulled apart a concealed Velcro fastener that revealed a hidden compartment in the center of the bag, accessible from the outside at either end. She slipped her hand inside and withdrew a squared-off semiautomatic pistol.

"Glock .40-caliber," she said. "Beats the hell out of that puny peashooter you wanted to give me."

Culley laughed for the first time since Houser

had met him. He had a wonderful laugh, she thought, and a devilish twinkle that she had not seen before.

"A reporter carrying?"

"You should see some of the neighborhoods I go into at all hours of the night."

"You have a permit for that?"

"I don't break the law, Culley."

"Why didn't you tell me you used to be a cop?"

"You didn't ask."

"Dumb answer."

"Dumb question," Houser said, and started the engine. She pulled out of the parking lot leaving a goose-tail of gravel in her wake.

"Oh, shit," Culley said. "Here we go again."

20

THE STRETCH OF Route 20 that snaked its way north to Charlottesville was pitch-black beneath the canopy of trees crowding both sides of the road. The moon had disappeared behind a bank of low-lying clouds, and a ground fog further reduced visibility. The center line, in need of paint, was barely visible in the narrow funnel of brightness cast by the Porsche's headlights, forcing Houser to slow to the legal speed limit. She felt deprived by conditions that kept her from again enjoying the challenge of the road. Culley experienced no such deprivation, considering anything that would slow her down an answered prayer.

The road was deserted; they had not seen another car since turning off Route 15, and as they came out of a long S-turn the lights that suddenly appeared in the rearview mirror caught Houser by surprise. She flipped the mirror to deflect the glare and concentrated on the road ahead.

As she entered a short straightaway, she noticed the car behind was closing at a high rate of speed.

The straightaway ended one hundred yards ahead, and recognizing an accident waiting to happen, Houser slowed to let the fool pass before it was too late. But the car only pulled closer and stayed there. The headlights were higher off the ground than a normal car's, and Houser guessed it was a pickup truck or a sport utility vehicle of some kind. The windows of the Porsche were open to the cool night air, and she put her arm out and signaled for the vehicle to pass. But it stayed on her tail, inching closer.

"Redneck jackass," she muttered.

Culley turned in his seat to squint into the glaring light. "Let him pass."

"I tried that. It's probably some drunk getting his kicks."

"Then lose him."

Houser dropped the Porsche into third gear and punched the accelerator. The finely tuned engine responded instantly with a burst of speed. The quickness of the little sports car left her tormentor behind, but a minute later he was back riding her bumper.

"Moron!" Houser said.

▽

MALIK CHUCKLED WITH delight. The big V-8 engine in the Grand Cherokee could not match the sudden acceleration of the Porsche, but it did have the power to recover and stay with it. Malik, following the same route back to Charlottesville he had taken to Hampden-Sydney, had passed the roadside tavern fifteen minutes earlier and seen the distinctive Porsche in the parking lot.

A small voice at the back of his head had said, *Don't play with him; he's dangerous.* It was the voice that had governed his actions for the past four years, suppressing his murderous impulses with soothing logic and reason. But Malik had stopped listening to it a month ago. And tonight, still tingling from the thrill of killing Spirko, he was in the mood for a game. He had turned off the highway onto a gravel side road a half mile from the tavern, and waited until he saw the Porsche pass by, then pulled out to follow.

Don't be a fool! the voice said. "Fuck you! Fuck you! Shut up!" Malik had screamed. And the voice was stilled.

▽

HOUSER TOOK THE Porsche to the maximum speed the fog and the twisting, poorly banked road would allow. She was doing over seventy miles per hour, but Malik stayed with her. He was now dangerously close, only inches from her rear bumper. If she had to stop suddenly for anything in the road, it would be impossible to avoid a rear-end collision.

She decided to try an old trick she remembered her father using when he encountered a tailgater.

"Hang on," she said to Culley.

Culley, not needing to be told twice, gripped the handhold on the door and braced his other arm against the dashboard, preparing himself for God knew what.

Houser swung the Porsche off the side of the road, just enough so the wheels on the right side hit the small strip of gravel on the shoulder. The rear tire sent a spray of small stones into the front of the Jeep and up onto windshield.

Malik backed off immediately. "Little bitch!" he shouted, and closed in again as soon as the Porsche pulled back onto the roadway.

Houser gained ground through a long, winding turn, but the Jeep came out of it fast and closed in again.

"Pull over and stop," Culley said. "That idiot's going to get us all killed."

Houser strained to see through the ground fog, searching the side of the road for an open spot. She saw a break in the trees ahead, halfway into a sharp S-curve. She lightly tapped the pedal to flash her brake lights as a warning that she was about to slow down.

Malik, heedless of any oncoming traffic, swung into the left lane and came abreast of the Porsche just as it reached the curve.

"Looks like he's tired of his game," Houser said, and got as far to the right as she could without going off the road.

Malik pulled slightly ahead and cut the wheel hard to the right. Houser's quick reflexes were all that prevented a collision, but Malik, aware of the Porsche's limitations, had timed the move perfectly. He had cut her off at the sharpest point of the curve.

The nimble sports car's weakness was its rear engine. Any hard braking at speed in a tight turn always held the threat of losing control. And the Porsche did just that. The rear end swayed and the tires lost their grip. Houser did what any good driver familiar with the car's idiosyncrasies would have done, she rode it out as opposed to trying to muscle the car back under control. The Porsche spun wildly, turning two complete circles before rocking up on two wheels, on the verge of flipping over, then bounced back down on all fours.

Culley's forehead slammed into the dash with a thud as the side of Houser's head hit the driver's-side window. The car sat half off the road facing oncoming traffic, the front end pointing toward Malik's Jeep, which had stopped just ahead of where the Porsche came to rest.

Culley, momentarily stunned, shook off a wave of dizziness and leaned across to Houser, who was uninjured with the exception of a small knot rising on the side of her head.

"You okay?"

"Yeah," Houser said, and looked up to see Malik standing behind his Jeep, fifty feet away. The lower portion of his body was partially obscured by the ground fog, but his face was clearly visible in the lights of the Porsche. He had a gun in his hand, pointed at the windshield.

"Culley!"

Culley turned and recognized Malik immediately. He was waving at him, wiggling his fingers and grinning.

Culley pulled the gun out of his shoulder holster as he threw open the passenger-side door and rolled out onto the ground. He sprang to his feet, crouched behind the fender, and trained the gun on the spot where he had last seen Malik. He was gone.

"Get down below the dash," Culley called out to Houser, and at the same moment saw her open her door and get out to take cover behind it, her weapon in a two-handed grip, braced between the inside door edge and the body of the car.

Culley inched closer to the front of the Porsche, staying low. The barrel of his gun followed every movement of his eyes as they swept the area around them.

The Jeep was parked in the middle of the road, still running. A sudden roar from the engine drew Culley's attention. He took aim to fire through the rear window. A split second later he saw the lights of another car coming through the curve toward them. Afraid that any ricochets might hit the innocent passerby, he released pressure on the trigger just as Malik sped away, disappearing from sight in a matter of seconds around the far end of the curve.

The driver of the oncoming car swerved to avoid hitting the Porsche, stopped to look back, saw two people with guns in their hands, and took off, tires howling.

"Get in," Culley shouted. "Put your suicidal driving skills to good use. He can't outrun you."

"Forget it," Houser said, and gestured with her head to the front of the Porsche. "The left front tire's blown."

Houser stood up and leaned over the roof of the car. She held the gun as though it were a natural extension of her hand. Culley noticed that she was calm and collected, not the least bit shaken by what had just happened.

"Malik?" she said, knowing what the answer would be.

Culley nodded.

"Wrong color Jeep, but he could have had it

painted," she said. "So much for your theory about him not knowing you're in the game."

She saw Culley's expression change from one of anger and frustration to one of shock as his eyes widened and his body went stiff.

"What is it?"

"Spirko. Malik must have followed us there."

"Oh, my God!"

Houser pulled the Porsche completely off the road and Culley used her cellular phone. He rhythmically thumped the dash with his fist as he waited for the operator to give him Spirko's home number. He tapped out the number and pressed send, then waited as the phone rang six times before it was answered by a man with a gruff voice, who said simply, "Sheriff Mahanes."

Houser heard only Culley's side of the conversation, but it was enough to tell her that Spirko was dead.

"The guy who answered the phone was the local sheriff," Culley said when he hung up. "He wouldn't tell me anything, but I could hear crying in the background. That sick bastard killed Spirko. And I led him there."

"They're going to think we did it," Houser said.

"They don't know who we are. I didn't give him my name, and it's unlikely the kids we asked for directions noticed your plate number."

"But we were probably the last people seen with him before he died."

"No. There were three students crossing the street to talk with him when we pulled out. They saw us drive away while he was still alive."

"I'd still want to talk with us if I was the investigating officer."

"We can't do that."

Houser noticed that her hands were shaking and knew what was happening. The surge of adrenaline that had coursed through her veins was ebbing. She had been through it countless times before and knew the worst of it would pass in a matter of minutes.

"He could have killed us if he wanted to," she said. "Why didn't he?"

"Because he's arrogant and crazy enough to believe he can win any game he plays."

"What did he do for the KGB?" Houser said. "Something tells me it wasn't a desk job."

"He did it all," Culley said. And began to fill her in on Malik's background as they got the spare tire from the trunk at the front of the Porsche.

21

CULLEY AND HOUSER stood in the darkness at the back door of Malik's house, pulling on the thin cotton gloves they had stopped to purchase at a drugstore. Culley was about to kick in the door when Houser stepped in front of him and used a credit card to slip the lock.

"Typical," she said, with a playful smile. "Put a hammer in your hand and everything looks like a nail."

"Saves time. And it feels good."

"Try a little finesse once in a while, saves wear and tear on the body."

They entered the darkened kitchen and Culley turned on the flashlight he had taken from the glove compartment of the Porsche. Houser used the small penlight kept in her shoulder bag. The house was screened by thick evergreens on all sides, but they shielded the lights with their hands as they moved from room to room and drew all of the curtains.

"I assume you know how to toss a house," Houser said.

"I'll manage."

"I'll do the first floor," she said.

Culley took the stairs two at a time as Houser began her search with systematic expertise. The interior of the house was immaculate. Nothing was out of place. Magazines were stacked neatly on the coffee tables in the living room and the den. The stacks were positioned in the same places on both tables, arranged so the titles were visible at a glance and placed exactly one inch from the ends of the table and centered; separate stacks for different categories, with old newsmagazines arranged by date, the most recent at the top.

The compulsive tidiness and order were evident throughout. Culley found clothes left in the upstairs closets zipped inside garment bags and hung at two-inch intervals. Shoes were stored in plastic freezer bags and lined neatly along the floor of the closet. The contents of the medicine cabinet above the master bathroom sink reminded him of a military formation awaiting inspection. Towels hung equidistant on the racks, folded precisely, the outside of the folds all facing in the same direction. The bureau drawers held the same order: socks, arranged by color and weight, summer weight in one drawer, winter in another, underwear folded and ironed, and shirts, heavily starched and folded and stored in plastic bags.

By the time Culley had finished, the upstairs looked as if someone had tossed a hand grenade into each room. Clothes were strewn across the floors. Framed prints taken down from the walls had the backing cut open. Books thrown from the shelves in the master bedroom littered the room. Sheets and blankets were stripped from the beds and the mattresses were overturned and thrown against the walls.

An hour of tearing the place apart yielded nothing more than an old movie stub left in the bottom of an otherwise empty wastebasket. Besides the anal-retentive order of the place, the only insights into the man who lived there were a collection of textbooks on anatomy and surgical procedures, and an extensive collection of pornographic videos kept on the top shelf of the linen closet behind the spare sheets and pillowcases.

Houser's efforts were no more successful. Her equally thorough search, however, had left the downstairs looking as though it had never been touched. They both descended the stairs to the partial basement to find the room barren of anything but a hot water heater, a gas furnace, and a fuse box. A thick layer of dust covered every flat surface and, along with the tangles of cobwebs, suggested that no one had been down there in years.

As they were about to leave through the kitchen door, Culley noticed a telephone answering unit on the counter beside the phone. The red message light was on and the display indicated three calls were still on the unit. He pressed the playback button and listened to the messages. The first was from a dry cleaner reminding Malik that his clothes were ready to be picked up. The second was from the power company telling him to come to the credit office to make arrangements to pay his delinquent bill, now one month overdue.

The third message was from a woman with a French accent and a very distinctive voice, low and husky. Culley paid particular attention to it, playing the message back three times.

> *This is Odette. I shall be returning to George-*
> *town tomorrow and will be waiting to hear*
> *from you at your convenience.*

"Odette, with a French accent from Washington," Houser said. "Should only take about two years to track her down."

Culley said nothing, certain that the Georgetown the woman had mentioned was not the exclusive section of Washington, D.C. He pressed the erase button and the messages were gone.

"Why did you do that?" Houser said.

"Force of habit."

"She could be his next victim."

"From what you've told me, he doesn't make dates with them; he drags them off the streets."

"That was thoughtless, Culley. That message could have been useful."

"My mistake. Come on, we've still got work to do."

▽

AN HOUR IN Malik's shop on Elliewood Avenue again gave them nothing, and shortly after ten o'clock they left the premises and drove to the Holiday Inn.

"Have your support people check with the post office tomorrow," Houser said as they got out of the car. "There was no mail in the boxes at the house or the shop. Maybe he's got a PO box."

"He's too smart to have overlooked anything that

obvious. I guarantee you he stopped delivery on his mail and left a phony forwarding address, if any."

"So what's next?"

"Right now I need some sleep," Culley said. "We'll figure the rest out tomorrow morning. See you around seven."

"You're not going to fold your tent and silently steal away in the night on me, are you?"

"I couldn't if I wanted to. I got about two hours' sleep last night."

Culley's room was on the opposite side of the building, and Houser stood by the car and watched as he walked across the parking lot. He was trouble, and she knew it, but at that moment she was feeling the effects of the immediate bond formed when two people share and survive a harrowing experience. And there was more. When their eyes met, he seemed to be looking deep inside her. And she liked it. She hadn't felt that way for a while.

He had a stillness about him, she thought. A coiled readiness, and at times his intense, watchful, and oh-so-goddamn-blue eyes were devoid of emotion, reflecting the calm awareness of the supremely confident. But he had been betrayed by people he trusted; like a kid beaten up by his best friend. On the outside he looked as tough as twisted steel, but just below the surface he was hurt and wary and in need of help and reassurance. Her nurturing instincts had been stirred for the first time in longer than she cared to remember. She had had no one of consequence in her life for the past year, just the occasional dinner date with men she considered friends. She had known other men like Culley; dangerously handsome. And he was the last thing she needed, but that had never stopped her before.

Houser spent the better part of an hour propped up in bed with her laptop computer, writing a summary of the day's events. It was just after eleven o'clock when she called her editor at home.

"Great timing, Julie. I just stepped out of the shower," Peter Davidson said, "but I'll forgive you. You scooped everyone on the notes. The *Times* didn't even have it; I like when that happens. Makes my week."

"I'm going to be out of touch for a while," Houser said.

"Is there an explanation that goes with that?"

"You're going to have to trust me on this one, boss."

Davidson knew better than to press; he had been through this with her before. "Okay, but I expect one hell of a story when you get back."

"That's precisely what you're going to get."

"If you're digging into the affairs of the SANV," Davidson said, recalling their earlier conversation, "be careful. Those boys play for keeps."

"SANV?" Houser said.

"Secret Army of Northern Virginia. Otherwise known as the CIA."

Houser laughed and said good night. She switched off the light on the nightstand and lay staring at the ceiling in the dark. She again saw Culley roll out of the Porsche and come up in a crouch, his gun sweeping the area around him. A practiced move that had become almost instinctive. Not the slightest hesitation or sign of fear.

"Just what you need, Julie. A man at home with violence."

She turned on her side, nestled into the pillows, and watched the day's events in her mind's eye until she fell asleep.

22

MALIK WAS IN his glory. The sound of country music echoed from the rafters in the jam-packed room as he twirled and stomped and swayed along with the phalanx of line dancers that stretched the entire length of a sixty-foot barroom dance floor sprinkled with sawdust and littered with peanut husks.

It was close to midnight, on a typical Saturday night, and the crowd had not yet reached its zenith. The place reeked of stale beer and cigarette smoke, and the decibel level of the music, the bellowing drunks, and the raucous squeals of women either delighted or offended by the attention they were receiving, made conversation impossible unless screaming directly into someone's ear. The mediocre band was on a raised stage behind a wire mesh screen that protected them from the hail of beer bottles or the occasional chair thrown in their direction whenever they played a song that did not meet with the approval of the more rowdy and out-of-control customers. A dozen hulking, no-neck bouncers, positioned strategically about the room, broke up the inevitable fistfights, unceremoniously throwing the offenders through a rear double door, without first opening it.

Hannigan's Country Roadhouse and Emporium was two miles off the New Jersey Turnpike near Mansfield. Malik had discovered it a few months earlier on one of his trips to New York City. He had made it a point to stop on each successive trip, both on his way there and on his return. He made good time on I-95 that evening, averaging ninety miles an hour with Hannigan's in mind, and had arrived at ten-thirty, less than four hours after he ran Culley and Houser off the road. He ate a quick meal in the stick-to-your-ribs, bring-your-own-Mylanta restaurant at one end of the building, and purchased a new cowboy hat and boots in the adjoining store that sold an assortment of overpriced, gaudy western clothing.

The new hat, complete with phony silver adornment and a few scraggly feathers, was perched on the back of his head. He was breathing heavily and perspiring in his tweed sport coat when the line dance ended and the song blended into a slow ballad sung in a twangy nasal voice by the bandleader, who was all hat and hair and no talent. Malik's dancing partner was a sexy, twenty-year-old, fox-faced hard body; Tammi with an *i*, she had told him. She wore skintight jeans, pink boots, and a revealing tank top beneath an open leather vest. Far from being danced out, she began swaying to the ballad and rubbing up against him, giving him her most seductive look.

"I love this song," she said, moving her hand slowly along the inside of his thigh.

Malik took her in his arms and smiled to himself

as she pressed her body firmly into his, grinding her pelvis as they moved in a small circle in the middle of the crowded floor.

When the slow dance ended, Malik looked at his watch. He had called Yuri in Brooklyn and told him to wait for him no matter how late, so there was no hurry to leave. But he had had enough dancing for one night, and was eager to get to the unexpected bonus he knew was waiting for him.

"That's a gold Rolex, huh?" Tammi said, staring at his watch.

"Yes, it is."

"You're pretty sexy for an older guy, ya know?"

"That's very kind of you."

Tammi hung on his arm as he walked off the dance floor. She was growing more brazen by the minute, as Malik had anticipated she would. With the music stopped, conversation was now possible, if shouted.

"You ain't leavin', are ya?"

"I'm afraid so. But it's been a most enjoyable evening, my dear."

"I just fuckin' *love* the way you talk." Her hand went to his belt buckle, then down inside his trousers as she winked salaciously and took him in her hand. "Maybe we could go somewhere? Just the two of us. Somewhere nice and quiet."

"And what did you have in mind?" Malik said, removing her hand from his trousers.

"Fun and games?"

Malik laughed and Tammi clung to him as he shouldered his way through the milling crowd and outside to the dimly lit parking lot packed with cars and pickup trucks. The Jeep was parked in a far, dark corner, and Malik looked around to make certain they were alone. The front lot was full, and new arrivals drove around to the rear, well out of sight. A few drunks staggered in and out of the front entrance, but the Jeep was hidden behind four rows of cars. The look of amusement on Malik's face had nothing to do with the antics of his sluttish companion; he had seen the tall, skinny kid leave just ahead of them and now spotted him leaning against the side of the building in the shadows.

Malik eagerly anticipated what he knew was coming next. He had noticed the pair of them sizing him up earlier in the clothing store. They had been so obvious and amateurish that he had almost laughed. To amuse himself he had flashed a wallet fat with fifties and full of credit cards, and made certain they saw his watch. Tammi's approach at the bar, made with all the subtlety of a strung-out hooker with a bad habit, came as soon as he ordered his first drink. And now he had to restrain himself from laughing again when he saw the skinny kid flick his cigarette in tough-guy fashion and swagger across the parking lot trying to look both nonchalant and threatening.

The kid approached from the rear of the Jeep and pulled a switchblade knife from his boot. He released the blade and waved it in a tight circle in front of Malik's face.

Tammi giggled with excitement. "Cut him, Dwayne. Cut him."

"Hand over the fuckin' Rolex, the wallet, and the car keys, asshole, and just maybe I won't cut ya up too bad."

They were the last words Dwayne ever spoke.

Malik grinned, feigned reaching for his wallet,

and pulled the sound-suppressed pistol from inside his waistband at the small of his back. He shot the kid twice in the head before he knew what was happening, then calmly stepped over the body and threw Tammi against the side of the Jeep, jamming the tip of the sound-suppressor under her chin.

"Now, be very quiet and get in the car."

Tammi stared in horror at her boyfriend lying at her feet, his head leaking a pool of blood. She was too frightened to move or scream. Malik opened the car door and shoved her inside, over the center console to the passenger seat. She immediately tried the door, but Malik jumped in and grabbed her arm, twisting it roughly.

"Please, mister. He made me do it."

"I'm sure he did."

"You're not takin' me to the cops, are ya?"

"I don't think that will be necessary."

"I ain't never done nothin' like this before, I swear."

"Of course you haven't. You're a paragon of virtue. I knew it the moment I laid eyes on you."

"Yeah. I didn't want no part of it. He beats me, ya know."

"Well, we've solved that problem, haven't we?"

"What are you going to do to me, mister? Don't hurt me, please."

"You mentioned something earlier about fun and games," Malik said, and closed the car door as he started the engine.

"Yeah, sure, sure. Hey, I'm real good too," Tammi said, ever the opportunist and trying desperately to please. "The guys say I'm a natural. I can give you a California French, get you off between my tits. And I give great head. I can deep-throat you, swallow the load, you name it."

"How charming."

"You won't be disappointed. I promise you that."

"Well, then, Tammi-with-an-*i*, it's fun and games you wanted, and it's fun and games you will get."

Malik took her by the back of the neck and shoved her face in his lap as he drove out of the parking lot. He groaned softly as she undid his trousers and took him in her mouth.

"Now, do your best work," he said as he pulled onto the highway. "You'll be judged accordingly."

A few miles from Hannigan's Malik found what he was looking for: a gravel road that led into a large construction site deserted for the weekend. He pulled in behind a bulldozer, hidden from view of anyone passing by on the road, and he cut the engine and lights.

Tammi looked up from her work, disappointed. "Hey, your dick's goin' soft on me. And I ain't finished yet."

Malik grabbed her by the hair and slammed her head against the far door. "Neither am I, my little bitch."

▽

ONE HOUR LATER a New Jersey state trooper left the murder scene at Hannigan's parking lot. The shooting was being covered by the local cops and sheriff's department and there was nothing for him to do. He continued with his normal routine and swung into the construction site a few miles down the road, checking to make certain no one was stealing a truckload of building materials as had happened the previous week.

The trooper made a slow sweep through the site and was about to leave when he noticed someone sitting behind the controls of the bulldozer. He drove closer, holding the hand-held spotlight out the window. The person looked naked and asleep. Some drunk, he thought, and stopped the cruiser and got out.

He climbed up on the bulldozer and played his flashlight over the interior. The sight of the horribly mutilated body caused him to gasp and fall backward to the ground, where he rose to his knees, retched, and vomited before collecting himself and running back to the radio in his car.

23

THE REPORT FROM Hampden-Sydney reached the Charlottesville task force office less than an hour after George Spirko's murder. Just as quickly FBI Special Agent Jack Matthews had dismissed it as being unrelated. The victim was male, the mutilations had no sexual overtones, and the Mix & Match killer had not used a gun in the previous four killings. Shortly after eleven o'clock Matthews was about to call it a day, when one of Chief Brady's officers caught a break in running down the dark green metallic vehicles manufactured by Chrysler and purchased in the Charlottesville area.

The list numbered three hundred and sixty-eight, but they got lucky with number one hundred and twelve. The officer had received no response at the home of John Malik, the owner of a Jeep Grand Cherokee. The next-door neighbor, an elderly man, returning from a late-evening walk, told the officer that he had not seen Malik in about a month. Just disappeared. And he didn't miss him either; playing that damn country music at all hours of the night, loud enough to wake the dead. They might want to check his shop down on Elliewood, but then he thought that had been closed for about the same length of time; he had ordered a book on Elizabethan dramatists from him six months ago and still hadn't gotten it.

The officer began questioning other neighbors, rousing some of them from their beds, but none had anything of consequence to add, only that Malik kept to himself and wasn't very friendly, often ignoring their greetings on the rare occasions when they saw him.

Disappeared a month ago, Jack Matthews repeated to himself when the officer reported in. The time frame fit. The color of the vehicle was a match. And the country music. Shortly after leaving the dump site in the stadium Chief Brady had remembered where he'd heard the familiar words written on the notes; he had been unconsciously humming the old country song when he suddenly realized what he was doing.

Matthews was aware that at this point he had only the thinnest kind of circumstantial evidence—small, inconclusive pieces that might never fit together upon further investigation. He had a long way to go. Still, it made the hair stand up on the nape of his neck. It felt right.

They now had a photograph and social security number from Malik's driver's license, issued three years ago. It showed him with a full beard and mustache, which Matthews suspected, if Malik was the killer, he would have done away with when he went into hiding and began abducting the coeds, significantly altering his appearance. And, Matthews had noticed with interest on the VDOT report, no out-of-state license had been surrendered when Malik applied for his Virginia license. A man of forty-three who had not previously had a driver's license was something Matthews found difficult to believe—and the first thought that occurred to him was that the name was an alias.

A clerk from the commissioner of revenue's office was pulled away from the *Tonight* show and driven to city hall to get the information from Malik's business-license application and his real-estate and personal-property tax records, adding more pieces to the puzzle. Malik had moved to Charlottesville three years ago and immediately purchased the home and shop, paying in cash. His gross receipts from his shop for the past three years had averaged eighteen thousand dollars, which told Matthews it was highly unlikely Malik's primary source of income was coming from his business. The large amount of cash, over four hundred thousand dollars, used to purchase the house and the shop could have come from prior criminal enterprises, Matthews thought, but there could also be any number of legitimate explanations. The Bureau's liaison with the IRS could start digging into that in the morning.

At two A.M. the lights still burned in the room taken over by the task force at the Charlottesville police station. Chief Brady sat slumped in a chair, his eyes red with fatigue and his face tight with stress as he listened to one side of the call Matthews had just received from the VICAP unit at Quantico, who had been burning the midnight oil as well since the first body surfaced.

Matthews hung up the phone and got up from

the conference table, walking around the room to stretch his cramped leg muscles. He picked up his coffee cup, then put it back down without drinking; it was his seventh cup in the past three hours and it was beginning to taste like battery acid. His eyes went to the large corkboard at the front of the room, moving over the grisly photos of the young girls' bodies taken at the dump sites, and reading for the hundredth time the contents of the notes chalked on the blackboard, looking for some message hidden within the lyrics that might be eluding them.

"NCIC has no outstanding warrants for a John Malik," Matthews finally said to Chief Brady, relaying what he had just learned from Quantico's search of the National Criminal Information Center data base. "And there's nothing in our own criminal history files."

"No one who used the name as an alias?"

"Nothing. No intersects with the name Malik. A complete blank."

"We could get a search warrant for the house and shop," Brady said. "We're bound to find his fingerprints. If John Malik is an alias, odds are he's hiding a criminal record and somebody's got his prints somewhere."

"We need probable cause for a search warrant," Matthews said. "And we're not even close to having that."

"How about bank statements, credit history, telephone records?"

"That we can do. I'll get subpoenas for them from the United States attorney first thing in the morning," Matthews said. "I've got a strong feeling about this guy, Chief. So much so that I want you to pull all your officers off the vehicle search to concentrate on Malik exclusively. Have them talk to anyone who even passed him on the street in the past three years."

"I'll get copies of the driver's license photo made up and distributed to everyone on the task force," Brady said. "With and without the beard and glasses."

"Have it shown around at all the medical-supply places, hardware stores . . . you know the drill."

"You want a statewide APB on the Jeep?" Brady asked.

"Yes," Matthews said. "But with instructions not to stop the vehicle. If they locate it they are to inform this office and maintain contact until we can get surveillance in place. But under no circumstances are they to confront him."

"We could have him pulled over on a ruse," Brady offered. "Claim a taillight is out, any number of things. Give him a ticket, make sure he touches something we can get his prints off."

"Absolutely not. I want this done by the book. If he's the killer, there's no way in hell I want him walking on a technicality."

One of Brady's men entered the room holding a fax that had just come in from the New Jersey state police. The man's eyes were wide with apprehension as he handed it to Matthews.

"Goddammit!" Matthews said after reading the message.

"What is it?" Brady said.

Matthews crossed to the blackboard. "What are the next words in this song?"

Brady thought for a moment, repeating aloud the

words in the notes found on the four bodies. " 'The day we met, you smiled at me, you took my breath away. Your friends all said . . . your heart was cold.' *Your Heart Was Cold*," he said. "Is there another body?"

"In New Jersey. Mansfield."

"New Jersey?" Brady said. "Christ! It's only what? Eighteen, twenty hours since he dumped the bodies in the stadium."

"It can't be a copycat. Only one reporter found out about the notes, and if she knew the contents, she didn't print them. And the chances of this being a coincidence aren't even worth considering."

"A note with *Your Heart Was Cold* on it was found in the same place on her body as the others?"

Matthews nodded. "Sexual mutilations similar to our victims, but not as elaborate, as though they were done in a hurry."

"A college student?"

"They only found the body about a half hour ago; haven't identified her yet."

"Mansfield, New Jersey. That's what? Three or four hundred miles from here?"

"About three hundred and fifty."

"That shoots a hole in your theory about him stalking local victims and making careful preparations before he grabs them."

"Nothing's carved in stone with these monsters. What we have are general guidelines from our profiles and psychological studies based on case histories and the interviews we've done with the ones we've got locked up," Matthews said. "And changing locations isn't that unusual. Most serial killers operate across a wide area. Ted Bundy started out in Seattle and ended up in Florida. It's not unusual for them to put as many as twenty-five or thirty thousand miles a year on their cars searching for victims. But this one doesn't gel. There's usually a break in the killings when they change locations. Until they're completely familiar with the new area."

"Maybe she was a student from here, someone he had stalked before who was going home, and he followed her."

"Possible," Matthews said. "But more than likely she was a target of opportunity he just came across in the course of doing something else. The first four were highly organized, this one appears to have the signature of a disorganized killer acting on impulse. Which indicates he's capable of operating on different levels."

"You think he's gone from here for good?"

"No. I don't. Everything about him says that if he was going to settle in New Jersey he wouldn't have killed this soon," Matthews said. "He went to a lot of trouble to find a hideout near Charlottesville where he can torture and mutilate his victims. And judging from the clues he's left, he isn't afraid of being caught. My gut says he's in New Jersey for some completely unrelated reason. But what?"

Matthews shook his head in frustration. He picked up his coffee cup and grimaced as he swallowed. "Make the APB on the vehicle nationwide, with instructions to advise the closest FBI office if they locate it. I'll get out an advisory to our field-office network."

24

MIKE CULLEY FLAILED wildly as he fought his way through the fire to reach his wife. He was almost there, within inches of her outstretched arms, and then she was gone, consumed by the conflagration that was destroying his home and his family. He could hear his daughter's screams from somewhere among the flames and the thick black smoke, but he could not see her. He crashed through another door and saw Malik standing in the center of the living room, surrounded by the fire, yet untouched, laughing and taunting him. The telephone rang from somewhere in the room as he saw his wife again, a single tear rolling down one side of her face. She beckoned to him and then was immediately engulfed by the flames. He ran into the heart of the fire, shouting her name, and he heard the telephone again.

Culley awoke with a start from the fitful dream to realize that the telephone on the nightstand was ringing; he had incorporated it into his dream. He sat on the edge of the bed, glistening with sweat and breathing heavily, the sheet twisted around his legs. He let the phone ring three more times, until his breathing returned to normal and his heart stopped racing. The bright green numbers on the clock radio read four-twenty-four A.M.

"Yeah," Culley said as he snatched the phone from the cradle, his voice heavy with sleep.

"Mike, it's Lou," Gregus said.

Culley shook the gossamer veil of sleep from his mind and cleared his throat. "What is it?"

"Malik's on the move."

"On the move where?"

"He was in New Jersey around eleven-thirty last night."

"You sure? He ran us off the road about seven down here."

"Positive. He apparently hasn't had time to get new credit cards under whatever identity he's assumed, and he used one of his old ones. We've been tapping into the computer records of his charges every hour or so and we found one called in from a place called Hannigan's in Mansfield."

"Don't you ever sleep?"

"I do, but my computer genius likes to work in the small hours of the morning. Says it's easier to gain access to the systems then."

"Look, there's something I have to tell you," Culley began hesitantly.

"I know about Spirko," Gregus said, cutting him short. "His wife called his case officer at NROC, whose boss informed me immediately. It didn't require a rocket scientist to figure out what had happened."

"I'm sorry," Culley said. "I screwed up."

"Yeah, well, it happens to the best of us."

"If the FBI puts it together with the serial killings and starts looking into his background, it's not going to take them long to track him and Malik back to the Agency."

"Let me worry about that. Right now I want you in New York City. Brooklyn, to be precise."

"What's in Brooklyn?"

"The Gardenia Restaurant on Brighton Beach Avenue."

"You want to elaborate on that a little?"

"It's a place to start. A Russian mafia hangout. A couple of Malik's old KGB buddies we've been keeping tabs on have been spotted there on occasion over the past month. We believe they're the ones who were involved in the hijacking of the currency paper."

"You think Malik's headed there to pick up his share of the counterfeit money?"

"I think his end of the deal was to provide the engraved plates to print the money, and he's on his way to do just that."

"I'm going to need something other than commercial transportation," Culley said.

"There's a Lear en route to the Charlottesville-Albemarle Airport as we speak. ETA is about thirty minutes."

"I'll need a car to get around the city."

"You'll find one waiting for you at the Marine Air Terminal at LaGuardia Airport when you arrive."

"What else do you have on Malik's KGB buddies?"

"Not much. But you know one of them. Viktor Silkin."

Silkin's image flashed before Culley. "Yeah. I

remember him. He was a major in special operations. Left side of his face is paralyzed from a gunshot wound. Got a permanent scowl. We had him targeted for recruitment but backed off because Malik said he wouldn't be receptive."

"That's him. We lost track of him after he ran for cover when Yeltsin came to power; he had the misfortune of choosing the wrong side of the coup. He was deep into the Russian mafia operations in Moscow, and it seems he's picked up where he left off over here."

"You have anyone on Silkin now?"

"No, I pulled them two days ago, when you came aboard."

"Keep it that way. I don't want to be tripping over any operations out of the New York office."

"You've got a clear field," Gregus said. "Did you learn anything at Malik's house and shop?"

"Only that he's a neat freak."

"If you need anything in New York, just shout."

Culley hung up and continued to sit on the edge of the bed, staring at the darkness outside the window. Part of the dream came back to him, and he shook it off, then showered and dressed before calling Houser's room to wake her.

He found her waiting for him in the parking lot, sitting behind the wheel of the Porsche. He tossed his bag on the rear shelf and slipped in beside her.

"Why are we going to New York?"

Culley told her, and saw a wry smile appear.

"Now we're operating on my turf," she said.

"Don't get too smug. Remember, Malik worked in New York City as an illegal for ten years. He knows it as well as you do, if not better."

"Not a chance," Houser said. "Do you think after he gets the money he'll leave Charlottesville? Start killing somewhere else?"

"Probably. The only reason he'd leave the FBI clues is because he's not going to be there when they finally ID him. And in order to break away from the Agency and stay lost, he's going to need money. Serious money. The kind that can buy silence, protection, numbered accounts, a new face, whatever he needs."

"How much money are we talking about?"

"Thirty million."

Houser let out a low whistle. "So if there are two others involved, that's at least ten million for him, if it's an even split. What do you think he'll get for it when he sells it to whoever is going to distribute it for him? Twenty, thirty cents on the dollar?"

"You're forgetting that it's going to be as good as the real thing. He won't have to sell it to someone else. He'll use some of his connections from his KGB days and launder it through the international monetary system. No one will ever know."

"Dollar for dollar?" Houser said as she started the car and pulled out of the parking lot onto Route 29 North and headed toward the airport.

"Dollar for dollar," Culley replied.

"Hey, what about your motorcycle? It's still back at that parking garage."

"It's not mine."

"You really did steal it?"

"Sort of. But from a bigger thief, so it's okay."

25

THE WAREHOUSE WAS two blocks off Surf Avenue in the Coney Island section of Brooklyn, a short distance from the famed amusement park and beach. The exterior was badly in need of paint, and all that was left of the original owner's sign were faded, weather-beaten, indecipherable letters that had once proudly proclaimed the printing company of Kasanoff and Son. The only window facing the street was in the small Judas door at one side of the sliding bay doors, the glass covered with tar paper.

From the outside the warehouse looked abandoned and long out of use. Inside, taking up the front section of the huge open floor space, was a high-speed, sheet-fed typographic printing press, an intaglio press, a letterpress, a guillotine cutter, and a banding machine, all meticulously restored to working condition within the past month. Against one wall were three large commercial dryers, and a long worktable stood at the front of the bay near the doors. Sitting on a stool, leaning over the table, his head resting on folded arms, fast asleep, was Yuri Belikov.

It was just after five-thirty A.M. on Sunday morning when Malik pulled into the alley beside the warehouse and parked his Jeep, now bearing New Jersey license plates stolen from a car in the parking lot at Hannigan's. He had stopped at a service station on the way into the city and used the rest room to strip off his bloodstained jacket and slacks, and to wash and change before disposing of the clothing in a nearby Dumpster. He looked out of place in the rundown neighborhood in his blue blazer, gray slacks, crisp white shirt, and neatly knotted silk tie as he got out of the Jeep and walked out of the alley to the front of the building.

The side street on which the warehouse fronted was dark and eerily quiet. Malik tried the Judas door to find it locked. He had noticed Belikov's minivan parked farther down the alley where he had left the Jeep, and he knocked lightly and listened, hearing no response from inside. The sound of footsteps followed the second series of slightly more forceful knocks.

Belikov, still groggy with sleep, opened the door and stepped aside to let Malik in, then took a quick look outside at the deserted street and locked the door behind him.

"I was expecting you sooner," Belikov said. He was a small, wiry man with the face of a ferret and the quick, darting eyes and furtive movements to match. His gaze seldom settled in one place for more than a second or two. A career criminal, he had spent ten years of his life in a Siberian prison camp and had learned to accept impending doom as a way of life. Trusting him on any level would have been a serious mistake, unless fear was involved. And Belikov had a deep and abiding fear of the man standing before him.

"I was unavoidably detained," Malik said, suppressing a small smile; he was still feeling some of the excitement from his time with Tammi. His eyes moved over the array of printing equipment at the front of the bay and came to rest on a pallet of paper sitting on the floor beside the workbench. The pallet was less than four feet high and two feet deep and wide.

"That's it?" Malik said. "That amount of paper will produce thirty million dollars?"

"Thirty-two million to be exact. Deceiving, isn't it?" Belikov said. "There are ten thousand sheets to a pallet. Thirty-two notes to a sheet. Four across and eight down. We will be printing one-hundred-dollar notes. Three thousand two hundred dollars per sheet, times ten thousand sheets, equals thirty-two million dollars."

Malik's eyes went to the commercial dryers against the wall. "What are they for?"

"Roughing up the money," Yuri said. "There are clothespins, rags, and plastic blocks inside that go through the fluff cycle with the money. When it is finished it no longer has the just-printed look."

"How soon can you have it ready?"

Belikov shrugged. "Perhaps ten hours, if I begin immediately."

Malik looked at his watch. "Three o'clock this afternoon?"

"If all goes well."

"See that it does."

Malik opened the briefcase he was carrying and removed the engraved plates, each enclosed in an individual hardcover case with thick padding inside. He handed them to Belikov, who immediately took them to the worktable, where he pulled a high-intensity light into position and fixed a jeweler's eyepiece in place.

Belikov studied each of the plates in turn, carefully going over every detail of the hand-engraved designs. He scrutinized the treasury seal and the federal reserve seal. Both were clear, distinct, and sharp, with no uneven or broken sawtooth points. The portrait of Benjamin Franklin for the front of the bill appeared remarkably lifelike and stood out from the fine screenlike background, as did the rendering of Independence Hall for the back of the bill. The fine lines and scrollwork at the borders were equally well done.

"Magnificent!" he said. "The best I have ever seen."

"Then the finished product will be virtually undetectable from the real thing?" Malik said.

"All we are lacking is the exact green and black ink used by the Bureau of Engraving and Printing."

Malik frowned. "What you have is a different color?"

"No. The color will be identical. But it will not have the magnetic properties the government adds to the official ink."

"How easy is it to determine that?"

"It is impossible to determine outside of a laboratory," Belikov said. "No one will even think to question the money we will produce. Not with the authentic currency paper and engraved plates of the quality we have here.

"Almost all counterfeit money produced today is of such inferior quality as to be laughable," Belikov went on. Counterfeiting money and credit cards had been his criminal area of expertise for the past twenty-five years, and he spoke with conviction and authority. "The fools who attempt to make it use poor-quality paper that is often distinguishable by touch, and they do not use engraved plates. They simply use photocopiers, or the more ambitious use an offset method to make a plate from a photograph or a genuine bill. Most, however, use copying machines of the type found in offices. The paper and the images on the notes are usually so poor that a convenience-store clerk could tell at a glance. I would guess that the Secret Service hasn't had an engraved-plate counterfeiting case in twenty-five years. And they have never had one involving authentic paper. Consequently, our money will be undetectable and above suspicion."

"As long as it passes the inspection of a banker," Malik said. "That's all that is necessary. Once it gets into the international monetary system there will be no retrieving it or tracing it."

"I can assure you, that will not be a problem."

"I want it packaged and banded in ten-thousand-dollar bundles," Malik said. "And I will be back here at three o'clock to pick it up."

"To pick up your share," Belikov said warily.

"Of course. My share. Ten million, six hundred and sixty-six thousand dollars. Correct?"

"Correct," Belikov said, relaxing a bit.

"I will bring Viktor with me," Malik said, referring to Viktor Silkin, the remaining partner. "We can divide the money at that time."

"And the others who took part in the hijacking will be paid by whom?" Belikov asked.

"Viktor and I will take care of them from our share," Malik said, knowing that the three men, brought in from Moscow specifically for the job, had already been dealt with: Silken killed them after the Secret Service raided the first warehouse where the contents of the Crane Paper Company truck had been taken immediately after the hijacking. Their bodies were weighted and dumped in Jamaica Bay. Silken and Malik still bristled at the loss of all but one pallet of the official currency paper, a loss attributable to the stupidity of the three men. Had Silkin not taken a pallet to Belikov for inspection only minutes before the raid by the Secret Service, they would have lost all of it.

"I want to change cars with you," Malik said. "I will take the minivan and leave the Jeep for you."

"Of course," Belikov said agreeably, and exchanged keys with him. "After tomorrow I will be driving something much more suitable."

"Three o'clock," Malik said, leaving Belikov to his work as he went out through the Judas door.

26

M ALIK STOOD IN the darkened street outside the warehouse and breathed deeply of the early-morning air that carried with it the scent of the ocean. It was close to six o'clock, and his scheduled meeting for breakfast at the Gardenia Restaurant with Silkin was not for another three hours. He did not feel the least bit tired, he never did after a killing, and he drove the short distance to Brighton Beach and left the minivan on Brighton Fifth Street. From there he walked to the boardwalk and sat on a bench looking out at the ocean as the morning light grew on the horizon.

He felt comfortable whenever he visited Brighton Beach, familiar with the area from his days as a KGB illegal in New York City; it always felt like a homecoming of sorts. A once abandoned and decaying enclave, in the seventies it had been rejuvenated into a thriving community by an influx of Russian émigrés that now numbered over forty thousand. Entire blocks that had once been boarded up were crowded with Russian delicatessens, groceries, restaurants, shops, and lively nightclubs. Quiet wealth, accumulated from both legitimate and criminal enterprises, was there just beneath the surface, and old, run-down art deco apartment buildings with ocean views that once were difficult to sell at forty thousand dollars now brought more than half a million.

Malik had come here often during the ten years he spent in the city, especially when he was homesick for things Russian. On warm summer evenings he would sit on the boardwalk and drink kvass—a brew made from fermented black bread—and listen to the minstrels play their balalaikas and sing of the motherland. But love of all things Russian was not the only reason he came. The cloistered community was a natural place for illegals to disappear into the population, and infiltrated among the legal immigrants were dozens of KGB officers with whom Malik had coordinated his espionage operations.

It was during that same time that the seeds for the present criminal structure in the area had been sown. In the early seventies, much as Castro would do several years later, the KGB emptied their jails, sending thousands of hard-core criminals to the United States, mostly into the working-class community of Brighton Beach, along with the legitimate political refugees who were allowed to leave the Soviet Union in the largest wave of Russian immigration since World War II.

Malik had long-standing ties to the leaders of the Russian criminal element, formed during his years in the city and in Moscow. In Russia they could not run their black-market operations without KGB complicity, and in New York they had served as spotters for the KGB, targeting potential recruits among former patriots now disillusioned with their lives in America, and desperate people in need of money, or indebted to the criminals.

At first what later would become known as the Russian mafia, or the Organizatsiya, was no more than loose-knit gangs of criminals who terrorized and extorted money from the émigré community. But it was not long before they branched out into far more lucrative enterprises that included insurance and medicare fraud and, upon gaining control of the gasoline distribution network throughout the city, defrauding the government of hundreds of millions of dollars in tax revenues. By the nineties they were a tightly run organization with central controls, spreading from their base in Brighton Beach to the remnants of communist Eastern Europe, Africa, and Southeast Asia, and, with the advent of the Yeltsin government, back into the former Soviet Union where ex-KGB agents now ran their black-market and drug-smuggling operations for them.

Malik smiled to himself, thinking about how the counterfeiting scheme had come about. A chance meeting with Silkin on a visit to Brighton Beach six months ago had resulted in their reminiscing about old times. Silkin had brought up the old KGB counterfeiting operations, confiding that he now had a reliable contact working inside the company that manufactured the official currency paper for the United States government. He planned to hijack one of the shipments and produce counterfeit money, using a photocopying process. He had asked Malik if he wished to be part of it; his expertise at laundering money would be invaluable. Malik still recalled the look on Silkin's face when he told him about the engraved plates he had stolen in East Berlin. And the deal was made.

Needing only to wait until the money was printed, Malik now sat watching the gentle surf, relaxing to its soothing rhythm, until he saw a lone early-morning jogger running along the beach toward him. She was sprinting, with the fluid, graceful stride of an athlete. A lovely young woman, a brunette, of medium height, with wide-set, expressive eyes, her shoulder-length hair tied back in a ponytail.

The runner finished her sprint and slowed to a walk along the edge of the water as she drew near. Malik's eyes clung to her, examining every part of her body as she walked past, not twenty yards away. The ridge of muscles along the front of her long, curving thighs rippled with the tension of a bent sapling, echoing the demands made of them during the all-out sprint. A dew of perspiration covered her body, and her chest rose in rhythmic swells of controlled, even breaths. Her thin nylon tank top and running shorts clung to her skin, the top taut across her firm, round breasts, deep rib cage, and tightly knitted abdominal muscles that tapered to a narrow, tiny waist.

A magnificent figure, Malik thought, near perfect in its symmetry and proportion, sculpted from within by finely tuned, superbly conditioned layers of muscle. He put his hand inside his jacket pocket and felt the switchblade there. He envisioned the razor-sharp knife edge cutting cleanly, effortlessly, through the runner's abdomen, the horror on her face as he did it. He thought of following her, perhaps to find out where she lived and visit with her later, when his work was completed. But the part of his thought process that occasionally exercised some control over his actions made him dismiss the idea as too impulsive. He would need to stalk her, learn her movements and schedule, and this was not the time or the place.

He continued to watch as she moved farther up the beach, and then his thoughts went to the future, and how he would launder the money. Should he do it before or after finishing his work in Charlottesville? The small voice he had learned to despise told him to take the money and start over. Change his life, his looks, and stop the killing and live out the rest of his life in quiet luxury. But in his mind's eye he saw the young women he had already selected at the university as his next victims, and the urge to go on with his plans was overwhelming. The violin player intrigued him most. There was something about her, an innocence he looked forward to violating.

The once subconscious urges had become a palpable thing when he began to kill again one month ago. They had changed greatly since the early years, when it had begun as a game, with no conscious thoughts of killing until he found himself trolling for victims and stalking those who aroused him. He had often gone for months without having the urges. There had even been lapses of a year or more. But after the three-year gap following his defection, debriefing, and resettlement, the urges became far more frequent, arising almost weekly. And they were much stronger and more pronounced, growing in intensity with each killing. He could now recognize them at the onset; feel them coming on. A twilight world beckoning to him. Colors were heightened. Time slowed. His skin became more sensitive. Bizarre, sexually charged homicidal fantasies would begin to dominate his every thought. The fantasies soon became realities, demanding action. An irresistible compulsion to fulfill them took over, sending him into another cycle of murderous rage followed by progressively shorter periods of relief and gratification.

The cycle never completely ended with the death of a victim and the period of inactivity. He had his videotapes and his souvenirs: panties, bras, and other personal items kept from each of his victims, even a tiny locket from his first, some thirty years ago, in the village where he was born. They allowed him to relive and savor the excitement of the killings over and over in private and at will. His vivid memories and the souvenirs from his earlier victims had helped sustain him through his three-year period of inactivity, yet they never equaled the actual killing, eventually serving only to whet his appetite and compel him to kill again.

He sat quietly looking out at the ocean, finding himself mentally reenacting the torture and mutilation of Tammi-with-an-*i*. He had waited patiently, undressing her and fondling her, until she regained consciousness from having had her head slammed against the car door. His mind retained the smallest details of the brief time spent with her. He could still hear the pleading and crying and screaming as he dragged her from the car and went to work on her. Her final scream of torment echoed loudly in his head, and it was at that moment that the jogger came back into his vision, and his thoughts returned to her. She had continued a few hundred yards up the beach and then turned to walk back in his direction. And he began to feel a stirring deep within.

Her name was Carole Jordan, and following her

usual morning routine after finishing her run, she turned and walked up the beach to the boardwalk and the outdoor water fountain not ten yards from where Malik sat.

The immediate area was deserted at this time of year; the shops and concession stands along the boardwalk closed and boarded up with the closing of the amusement park after the Labor Day weekend. The beach was empty, and Malik saw no one else along the boardwalk in either direction. He did see, almost directly behind the bench where he sat, a narrow passageway between two concession stands. Partway down the passage was a side door leading into the rear of one of the boarded-up stands.

Perfect, he thought. *No!* the small voice inside his head shouted. *Not here! Not now!* Malik gritted his teeth and shook his head violently in silent rage, and the voice was quieted.

His attention went back to the jogger, who stood with her hands on her hips, pausing between drinks. And the stirring within him quickly rose to a crescendo. He sat quietly, seemingly staring out to sea, but in his peripheral vision he was watching her every move; his senses alert, clear and sharp, focused, like those of a cheetah in tall grass stalking an antelope.

Carole Jordan had no permit for the snub-nosed .38 revolver she carried in her waist-pack when she ran alone or went out at night in a questionable neighborhood. Like a growing number of New Yorkers who live daily with the constant threat of explosive, senseless violence, she subscribed to the axiom Better to be judged by twelve than carried by six.

But at the moment she was not feeling the least bit threatened as she bent over the water fountain and

took another long drink. Nor did she see any reason
to look with apprehension upon the man sitting on
the bench a short distance from where she stood. She
gave him only a cursory glance as she approached,
discounting him as any sort of threat—he was too well
groomed and nicely dressed, and rather handsome in
a rugged sort of way.

As she passed in front of the bench, Malik moved
with a quickness that belied his size and age. He was
on her before she realized what was happening. He
wrapped one arm around her, pinning her arms to
her sides. He used his free hand to cup her mouth,
stifling her cry of alarm. He lifted her up off the
ground, holding her off to one side, like a parcel
under his arm, negating her attempts to kick at him.

He ran, carrying her into the passageway to the
side door, where he reared back and kicked solidly at
the flimsy plywood. Once, then twice. The door
splintered around the lock and swung open with a
loud bang. Malik rushed inside, out of sight, knocking the door closed with his shoulder. It had taken
no more than six seconds from the time he grabbed
her. No one had seen or heard a thing.

The inside of the concession stand was dimly lit
by shafts of light that slanted through the tiny spaces
in the boards covering the side windows and the front
of the stand, which opened to the boardwalk. Carole
Jordan struggled helplessly in the powerful arms that
gripped her and held her feet off the floor. She could
feel his warm breath on her neck and thought she felt
him licking the side of her face. She fought back the
paralyzing terror that was fast overtaking her.

Her arms were pinned at the elbows, but her
hands were free. She felt for the quick-pull tab on the

waist-pack and found it. She tore it open and gripped the butt of the revolver, curling her finger around the trigger as she withdrew it.

At that moment, one of her thrashing feet caught Malik in the shins, and he threw her roughly against the wall, face first. She was momentarily stunned by the impact, but found the strength and composure to spin around to face her attacker. And Malik found himself staring down the barrel of the snub-nosed revolver.

"Get away from me!" she screamed, and began inching her way along the wall to the door. "Get away!"

Malik took a step closer, a sick, humorless smile on his face.

"Take one more step toward me and, so help me God, I'll shoot you!" she screamed again, her eyes wide with terror.

Malik judged the one step he had taken to be enough.

She stood facing him, her back to the door, feeling behind her for the handle. The tip of the gun barrel wavered in Malik's face, less than two feet from his head. But she had already made the fatal mistake of all those who found themselves in life-and-death situations and did not live by the gun: She did not fire the instant she had the advantage.

It was then that Malik made his carefully calculated move. He looked quickly to his right, as though seeing something in a darkened corner. Carole Jordan's eyes instinctively followed, distracting her for the split second it took for Malik's arm to come up and take the gun away from her with a lightning-fast sweep of his hand.

She summoned what remained of her inner strength and lunged at him. Malik grabbed her throat in a powerful grip with his left hand and held her at arm's length. Her fingernails clawed the air only inches from his face. He threw the gun into a far corner and lowered his right shoulder as he drove a powerful punch into her midsection, eliciting a forceful rush of air and a terrible guttural sound. He released his grip on her throat and she slumped to her knees at his feet, gasping for breath.

"Never, never talk about what you are going to do," Malik said calmly. "There is only one reason to point a weapon at someone. And that is to shoot them. Immediately. Before they have time to react."

Carole Jordan began to shake, gulping in huge breaths of air. She was quickly losing all control over her actions. She braced herself against the wall, slowly pulled herself to her feet, to a less vulnerable position, and began to cry and plead.

"Please! I have some money with me," she said desperately, and took the two twenty-dollar bills she kept as emergency money in the waist-pack. Her hands shook uncontrollably as she reached toward him.

"It's all I have. Take it. Just let me go. I promise I won't tell anyone. I promise. Just please let me go. Please!"

Malik stood silently for a long moment, the expression on his face one of calm deliberation.

"Take off your clothes," he finally said, his voice flat and unemotional, just above a whisper.

"No! Please!"

A sharp backhanded blow cracked across the side

of her face, sending her reeling into the wall. A small trickle of blood ran from the corner of her mouth.

"Each command will be given only once," Malik said in the same low monotone. "If it is not obeyed immediately and without question, swift punishment will follow."

Carole Jordan looked into the eyes of her tormentor and saw only darkness and evil. He seemed in a daze, his facial muscles gone slack and his mouth turned cruelly downward at the corners. She had never known such fear, and she trembled terribly as she undressed, fumbling with the clasp on the waistpack before she freed it and let it drop to the floor.

"The running shoes and socks too," Malik said. "Quickly."

She immediately complied, pulling the shoes off without undoing the laces. She pulled the tank top and her running bra over her head, and slipped her shorts and panties down over her hips, letting them drop to the floor where she kicked them free of her feet. She stood naked before him, one arm across her breasts, her other hand placed over her crotch.

"Put your hands at your sides."

Carole Jordan did as she was told, feeling totally helpless for the first time in her young life. Her eyes filled with tears, and she felt weak and light-headed. She wavered slightly as her legs turned to jelly. She lost all control as her eyes rolled back in her head and she fainted, collapsing on the floor.

Malik dropped to one knee beside her, running his hands in a gentle caress over the length of her body. He then roughly pinched her nipples and got no response. Convinced that she truly was unconscious, he began to undress himself. He folded his clothes neatly, laying them on the serving counter at the front of the stand after dusting it with a dish towel, which he subsequently stuffed in his victim's mouth. He found two aprons and a ball of twine on the shelf beneath the counter and used them to tie her spread-eagled and immobile, anchoring the ends of the constraints on the legs of a pizza oven and the support struts of the counter.

He stood naked, staring down at her, feeling unprepared and unsure of how to proceed. As with Tammi, there had been no preliminaries of stalking, lurking, and organizing that allowed his fantasies to develop into a set plan of action as they had with those he took to his cabin. He would have to improvise again, be as creative as possible without the use of his carefully selected tools. Something would come to him. It always did. The possibilities were endless.

He stepped over her and stood straddling her naked body. He began to fondle himself and masturbate, tilting his head back and closing his eyes, envisioning the ritual he was about to perform. His groans of pleasure soon turned to irritable grunts when he could not sustain his erection. He heard her moan softly and saw her eyes open, staring up at him, and he flew into a rage. He kicked her savagely, then knelt and pummeled her with his fists, stopping short of knocking her unconscious. He did not want that. Not yet.

Carole Jordan lay helpless before him, numbed in the places he had hit her, but still sentient and clearly aware of what was happening to her. She watched Malik get up and go to the counter. Her eyes widened in horror and she let out a long, muffled scream when he turned to face her. The switchblade knife he held in his hand flicked open as he grinned and knelt beside her.

"Are you ready, my little bitch?"

Carole Jordan's muted screams went unheard outside the small enclosed space. In a last desperate but futile attempt she tried to twist away, her body writhing to avoid the knife he drew slowly through the outer layer of skin on her abdomen.

"Not ready?" Malik said in a childlike, singsong voice. "Well, ready or not, here I come."

▽

SHABAZ JOHNSON MOVED erratically along the boardwalk, on the lookout for the cops, or anyone who might rob him of his recently acquired treasures. He was emaciated, his blotchy skin covered with scabies, his rheumy eyes streaked with red, the whites tinted a pale yellow. His clothes were tattered and filthy, and his jerky, barely controlled gait, somewhere between a strut and a lunge, would have been comical if it were not for the obvious fact that the man had a serious problem. In Shabaz's case the problem was crack. But he had just scored. Big time. Five rocks. And he was looking for a place to hide and fire up his pipe. Someplace he wouldn't have to worry about anyone bothering him. He needed to get straight. Real bad.

He stayed to the inside of the boardwalk, moving slowly along the fronts of the shops until he came abreast of a passageway between two concession stands and spotted his salvation. The door at the side of one of the stands was ajar, and he headed directly for it, slipping inside and kneeling in a darkened corner as he prepared to escape his misery, however temporarily.

He fumbled inside his pocket for one of the small glass bottles containing his crack, and stopped to sniff the air. A strong coppery scent made his nostrils twitch. He knew that smell. What was it? He felt something wet and sticky at his knees, and reached down and touched the partly congealed pool of liquid he had inadvertently knelt in. He brought his hand up to his nose and sniffed again. And then he knew.

Shabaz Johnson jumped to his feet and stepped out of the pool of blood. He backed farther away, toward the front of the concession stand, and the smell grew stronger. He felt something behind him snag his foot, and he turned to squint into the dimly lit space behind the counter. What he saw sent him scrambling and stumbling out the door into the passageway, along which he ran, tripping and falling, out to the boardwalk, nearly knocking over an old couple who were about to begin their morning stroll along the beach.

The old couple shuffled away, shocked by the sight of Shabaz and his incoherent shouts and wild gestures toward the passageway. They walked quickly with small, frightened steps back down the access ramp to the street. A police car turned the corner just ahead of them and they waved frantically.

27

IT WAS SEVEN-FIFTEEN when Julie Houser turned right off Brooklyn's Ocean Parkway onto Surf Avenue. She slowed at the first intersection and craned her neck to read the street sign.

"We passed Brighton Beach Avenue about a block back on the left," Culley said.

"I know. I want to make a stop first."

Culley had noticed something different about her since they arrived in the city. A subtle but tangible change, an edge to her that he hadn't seen before. Her body language was part of it, but mostly it was in her eyes, constantly moving, watching everything around her. Sizing people up in the cars they passed, or those standing on corners or gathered in the playgrounds and small parks around the housing projects they drove by. And then he realized what it was. She was watching the city as a cop would. Everyone was suspect until her data bank of street experience identified them as harmless or threat, perp or victim.

Houser's eyes continued to scan the street as they

passed the Brightwater Towers high-rises on the right, and behind them Trump Village.

"It's around here somewhere," she said. "On West Eighth, I think. Behind the aquarium."

"What is?" Culley said.

Houser slowed again and read the upcoming sign. "Here we are."

She swung onto West Eighth Street and drove halfway down the block, looking for a place to park in front of the Sixtieth Precinct station house.

Culley saw the cluster of blue-and-whites angled into the curb and the sign above the station-house entrance. "This is a police station."

"Yes. The Six-oh."

"What the hell are we doing at a police station?"

"I've got an old friend here, Tony Grimaldi," Houser said. "I want to check in with him. Say hello."

Culley took her by the arm as she cut off the engine and went to open the car door. "No cops. The deal was, we work this alone."

"We can show him Malik's photo; ask him to keep an eye out."

"No way."

"Okay. I'll just ask him about the guy you're looking for. Silkin. He might know him, where he hangs out."

"I know Silkin," Culley said. "And I don't need any help. We've got a place to start looking."

"All right. But I'm not running around this precinct without telling Tony I'm here," Houser said. "I'll just say I'm working on a story, which in my case isn't a lie."

Culley reluctantly got out of the car and followed her up the steps into the station house.

"Hey, Lou," Houser called to the desk officer, using the generic term of respect for lieutenants. "Tony Grimaldi?"

"Who's askin'?"

"His old partner."

"Detective squad. Up the stairs. Take a left," the lieutenant called back, studying Houser's face. "I know you?"

"No. But don't you wish you did?"

The lieutenant laughed and went back to his paperwork. Houser started up the stairs, Culley following, intrigued by another side of her he had not seen. Her accent was solidly New York now. The easy, familiar banter with the desk officer was natural and unaffected. She was a street cop again, back in what had clearly been her element, at home, comfortable and energized, confident. He wondered why she had ever left.

They entered the detective squad room and Houser's eyes moved over the desks lining the wall to the right. Three detectives sat hunched over battered old typewriters, hunting and pecking away, while two more talked on the telephone. The one closest to them looked up.

"Yeah. Can I help you?"

"Tony Grimaldi?"

The detective jerked a thumb to a doorway leading off the main squad room and went back to his typing. The small room served as a sitting area; a few rickety tables and chairs were scattered about, littered with coffee cups and newspapers, a television set was perched on a wall bracket; and a refrigerator, a coffeemaker, and a vending machine filled with snacks lined one wall.

Houser stood in the doorway smiling down at Tony Grimaldi, who sat at one of the tables, coffee cup at his side, a doughnut in his hand, brushing crumbs from a case file he was reading. He had his suit coat off, his shirtsleeves rolled up, his snub-nosed detective's special secured in a shoulder holster beneath his left arm. Stocky and muscular, he had a smooth olive complexion and wore his dark wavy hair short on the sides and top, but over-the-collar-long at the back. A tiny diamond-chip earring flashed from his right ear. He looked every inch the hotshot New York City detective.

"Still stuffing your face every chance you get? You Gindaloon hump," Houser said with a broad smile.

Grimaldi looked up, his darkly handsome face beaming with recognition.

"Julie," he called out, and jumped up to embrace her, then held her at arm's length. "Look at you, you Mick-Kraut hag. I don't believe it." He hugged her again.

"Believe it," Houser said, and kissed him on the cheek.

Houser was wearing a somewhat baggy gray tweed coat over faded jeans and a black silk blouse that had seen better days. Well-worn Nikes completed the ensemble. Grimaldi reared back and gave her an exaggerated stage look.

"Nice outfit. I didn't know they settled the Mary Poppins estate."

The instant rapport between the old friends was genuine and heartfelt, the mutual respect and affection immediately evident. Culley found himself smiling. It was clear they had history. The kind of lasting bond forged in tough, dangerous places where each had depended on the other and neither had been found wanting. A part of him envied their relationship; something he missed and knew was lost to him forever. He could never trust anyone that way again.

"Hey, Sullivan," Grimaldi called to the detective sitting at a desk in the squad room directly across from the doorway. "Look who's here."

Sullivan looked up, the map of Ireland on his face. "Who?" he said, giving Houser the once-over.

"Julie Houser. We worked narcotics together. I told you about her."

"Oh, yeah?" Sullivan said.

"Yeah. She quit the Job about two years ago. She's a hooker now."

"Christ, Grimaldi," Houser said with a chuckle. "I'm a reporter, not a hooker," she said to Sullivan.

"There's a difference?" Sullivan wasn't kidding.

Houser laughed. "Play nice."

"It's been what?" Grimaldi said. "Three . . . four years?"

"About three."

"You married yet?"

"No, not yet."

"That's what this is about. You're waiting for me. You miss me, right?"

"Terribly. Dream about you every night."

"Figures. It's the Grimaldi curse. I can't help it. Wherever I go, people stare at me in dumb admiration."

"Still suffering from delusions of grandeur, I see. So, fill me in. How are you doing?"

"About as well as a white, male heterosexual can do on the Job."

"Ah, poor politically incorrect baby. I take it that means you flunked the sergeant's exam again."

"For the fifth time. Between you and me? I think it's rigged against Italians."

"What? Too many big words?"

Grimaldi laughed and hugged her again. "I miss you, Houser. We had some good times."

"That we did."

"So, what are you doing here? Just happened to be in the neighborhood kind of thing?"

"A story."

"Last I heard you were with *The Washington Post*, right? You cover New York?"

"We cover the world, Grimaldi," Houser said, and gestured to a copy of the *Daily News* on the table beside him. "Not like these supermarket tabloids you call newspapers."

"Good paper. Lots of pictures. So what's the story you're workin' on? Anything I should know about?"

"Just a follow-up on the currency-paper hijacking about six weeks ago."

Culley, standing off to the side, shot her a warning glance. Grimaldi took it in. It was the first he realized that Culley and Houser were together.

"Yeah. I was in on that. We helped the Secret Service make the raid on the warehouse where it was stashed. They got it all back except one pallet. About thirty million bucks' worth, if the perps ever put it to use. Never found any of them. But that's the feds' problem. You got something new on it?"

"No. Just sniffing around."

Grimaldi pointed his chin in Culley's direction. "He's with you?"

"Oh, sorry. Mike Culley. Tony Grimaldi," Houser said. The two men shook hands, Grimaldi's cop eyes sizing him up.

"You on the Job?" Grimaldi made him for a player.

"No," Culley said. "Just tagging along."

"Yeah?" Grimaldi said, not buying it.

"You need some background on the case?" he asked Houser.

"Maybe later. I just wanted to touch base. Let you know I was in the area."

"We've got to have dinner, a few drinks, something before you leave. Tell some lies. Talk about the old days. It's been too long."

"If I can."

A burly detective, a lieutenant, nattily dressed in a three-piece suit, appeared in the doorway. "Grimaldi. You're up. We got a body on the boardwalk off Brighton Second. Officer on the scene says it's a bad one." With that the lieutenant was gone.

"Duty calls," Grimaldi said, and pulled on his suit coat, then paused and said to Houser, "Hey, why don't you come along? My partner's in court today. You worked homicide. It's only a couple of blocks. Look in, it'll be like old times." He turned to Culley. "You too."

"You don't mind?" Houser said.

"Hell, no. I could use a woman's perspective."

"Fuck you."

"Promises, promises."

Grimaldi headed for the stairs and Houser turned to Culley. "I won't stay long, then we'll get to work. Besides it's only seven-thirty. Nothing's open around here yet anyway. And it's right in Brighton Beach."

Culley thought of going after Malik on his own and meeting her later, but quickly recognized the danger of leaving Houser alone with her cop friends. He looked at his watch and gave an acquiescent shrug. "We hit the streets no later than eight-thirty."

"Right," Houser said, and started after Grimaldi.

▽

THE CRIME SCENE Unit and the medical examiner were already at the scene, and Grimaldi slipped his shield case in the outside chest pocket of his suit coat as he ducked under the yellow tape, holding it up for Houser and Culley. He ignored the shouted questions of the horde of television and newspaper reporters already gathered on the perimeter and being held at bay by a line of uniformed officers.

"They're with me," he said to one of the uniforms who was about to challenge Culley and Houser. "Who found the body?"

"Some crack-head," the cop said, pointing to Shabaz, who was standing nearby, nearly jumping out of his skin for need of a fix as he gave his statement to another uniform.

"Where's the victim?"

The cop pointed to the passageway between the two concession stands. Grimaldi led the way to the open door on the right. Culley and Houser followed him inside. The front of the stand had been unhooked and propped open, flooding the interior with bright morning light for the Crime Scene Unit, who were meticulously going about their work.

The medical examiner knelt beside Carole Jordan's horribly mutilated body, and Grimaldi joined him, pulling on a pair of surgical gloves he took from his pocket.

Culley and Houser stood against the wall, out of the way, but still able to see and hear all that went on.

Culley grimaced and looked away when he first saw the body. He noticed that Houser's eyes had hardened, but her composure was unshaken and her expression had not changed. She had seen worse. Her eyes now held his, and he knew what she was thinking.

"What do we have?" Grimaldi asked the medical examiner, his passive expression mirroring Houser's.

"A slice and dice," the ME said without looking up from his work. "You heard about the one in New Jersey last night?"

"Yeah. We got a fax on it early this morning. The FBI tied it to the Mix and Match killer. Looks like things got too hot for him in Virginia."

"Well, by the looks of this, he just hit the Big Apple."

"He killed again? In New Jersey?" Houser said, moving closer to the body. "Last night?"

"Mansfield," Grimaldi said. "Young girl in her twenties, like the others."

"Did they find a note?" Houser asked.

"Yeah." Grimaldi realized what he had just confirmed, and what his old friend now did for a living. "Forget I said that, Julie. The feds aren't releasing anything about the notes to the press."

"And lookee here," the medical examiner said as he used forceps to remove a folded piece of paper from Carole Jordan's vaginal cavity. Grimaldi took the note and began to carefully unfold it.

Houser noticed that the note was written on a sales receipt. A thick pad of them lay on the counter above the body. A ballpoint pen lay next to the pad.

"Bag the pad of sales receipts and the pen," she said to a detective with the Crime Scene Unit.

The detective gave her a who-the-hell-are-you look.

"She's okay," Grimaldi said.

"Sorry," Houser said by way of apology. "I used to be on the Job."

Grimaldi was about to read the contents of the note aloud when Houser preempted him.

"*And You Would Never Stay,*" she said, and looked hard at Culley. "And the one they found in New Jersey would have said *Your Heart Was Cold.*"

Grimaldi's eyes met hers. He had seen the interplay between her and Culley, and cast a questioning look at his old undercover partner. "Am I missing something here?"

"A source gave me the contents of the first four notes, but I didn't print them. They're the words to a country song. The killer's been using short word groups from the lyrics. *And You Would Never Stay* comes next."

"You've been covering the serial-killer story?"

Houser nodded. Grimaldi stood up and gestured with his head for her to follow him outside. Culley joined them as Grimaldi led them away from the cops and the reporters, stopping farther up the boardwalk.

"Hey, Julie, you're my friend and I love you,"

Grimaldi said. "But something tells me you're not being straight with me. You're covering the serial killings and you just happen to show up at the same time and place where he whacks his next victim? The hijacking story's bullshit, isn't it?"

"It's part of it."

"What's the rest?"

"We can't tell you that," Culley interjected, afraid things were getting out of hand, and expecting Houser, with good reason, to blurt it all out at any moment.

Grimaldi's voice dropped an octave and took on a rough edge, his index finger hard in Culley's face.

"Hey! You I don't know. But I did notice that bulge from the cannon you're carryin' under your leather jacket. You wouldn't happen to have a permit for that, would you?"

"Not with me," Culley bluffed. "I can give you a number to call that will put your mind at ease, but I don't think you want to open up that can of worms."

"Maybe. Maybe not. You a fed? What? Secret Service? FBI?"

"No. How 'bout if I don't tell you that part?"

"I think you just did."

Grimaldi turned back to Houser. "You want to tell me what's going down here?"

"I can't. Not right now."

"Hey, Julie. It's me. Tony."

"I know." She looked to Culley, who looked away and slowly shook his head. "Let us talk alone for a few minutes. Okay, Tony?"

"Yeah, sure. But don't jerk me around on this. If you know anything about the wackadoo who cut that girl up, I want to hear it. I'll be inside," he said, and walked away.

"We've got to tell him," Houser said to Culley. "Give him Malik's picture."

"No. I don't like what's happened any more than you do, but I'll get Malik. I promise you."

"Before he kills again? When I made the deal to keep quiet about this, it was on the condition that he didn't kill anyone else while you were trying to find him. He killed one a week in the past month, now it's one a day. This is a hell of a lot more than I bargained for."

Culley was on shaky ground, and he knew it, but he was not ready to give it up. "It's more than I bargained for too. But I've got to see it through. We're close, I can feel it."

"My God, Culley! You can't possibly let this continue. Tony knows this precinct; he's got informants here, he knows the players in the Russian mafia, and he stands a much better chance of finding Malik than we do, or than the FBI for that matter."

"Look, in all probability Malik's here to get his share of the counterfeit money. And if Gregus is right about him supplying the engraved plates, that means the printer just got them late last night or early this morning. It's going to take him the better part of a day, maybe more, to print the money. That means Malik's going to be here for at least that long."

"And if he kills someone else in the meantime?"

"Right now, Malik doesn't know we're here, but if the cops come out in force, running around showing his picture to everyone, he'll sure as hell hear about it. All we'll accomplish by bringing your friend in is to drive Malik into hiding until he can pick up the money. Then he's gone and we've lost him for good."

"And if he gets the money before you find him, then he's gone for good anyway."

"Give me until the end of the day," Culley said. "If I haven't found him by then, I'll tell Gregus I'm out, and I'll work with Grimaldi."

"You just said the money would be ready by the end of the day, so Malik will be gone by then. What kind of deal is that?"

Houser stood staring out across the beach. As much as she wanted the exclusive story, she could no longer justify withholding information that might lead to Malik's capture. She turned back to Culley, believing she had found a compromise she could live with.

"Here's the way it's going to be. Take it or leave it. Leave it, and I tell Tony everything I know right now. You give Malik's picture to him on the condition that if he finds him you're in on the bust. If you find him first, you've got no problem. If Tony does . . . well, I'm sure your friends at Langley will find some way to cover their asses." She looked deep into his eyes, imploring. "You've got to tell him, Culley, work with him. Anything less would be unconscionable."

Culley knew she was right. The sight of the mutilated girl in the concession stand had made it all too real for him. It was no longer just a sterile Agency damage-control operation removed from the horror at its core. He also knew that the odds were Malik would never allow himself to be taken alive, an end that would satisfy everyone's needs.

"We don't tell your friend about the Agency's

interest in this, or anything about Malik's background," Culley finally said. "Agreed?"

"Agreed. But you're underestimating him. You think he hasn't already figured out who you represent?"

"Thinking it is one thing; knowing it and having it confirmed are entirely different."

"Then, fine. Don't tell him about the CIA connection. Make up any story you want to explain your interest. All he needs to know is who he's looking for."

"Get him out here," Culley said. "And I'll do the talking."

Houser hurried back to the crime scene, to return moments later with Grimaldi.

"You got something for me?" he asked Culley.

"Let's set the rules. I give you what I can and you work it yourself. No FBI."

"No problem. I want to find this guy, not turn the investigation into a three-ring circus and a series of high-profile press conferences."

"And if you find him I want to be there when you take him down."

"You got my word."

Culley took the photo of Malik, taken during his debriefing, from an envelope in the zippered pocket inside his jacket and handed it to Grimaldi. "This is the guy you're looking for."

"This is him? The Mix and Match killer?"

"That's him."

"You're sure?"

"Positive."

"And . . ."

"And what?"

"Name. Some background information. What's he doing here? How come you know where to look for him? And like that."

"I don't know what name he's using now."

"What's his real name?"

"You don't need to know that."

"Why don't you let me decide what I need to know?"

"That's not how this is going to work."

"Is that right?"

"Look, Grimaldi, I'm willing to cooperate with you as much as I can, but don't play tough guy with me and don't push too hard. If I push back, by the time I'm finished you'll be on a scooter working traffic. Now, I'm way out of line giving you as much as I have already, so why don't we knock off the my-dick's-bigger-than-yours contest and call a truce."

Grimaldi backed off. "Okay, but I need to know why he's here if I'm gonna know where to start looking for him."

"He was involved with the hijacking of the currency paper. We have reason to believe he's got the engraved plates they're going to use to print the money. If we're right, that's the only reason he's here, and as soon as he gets the money he'll be gone. So we don't have much time. Find the place the money's being printed and we find him."

"How many more of your people are operating in my precinct?"

"None."

"You know any of this guy's contacts here?"

"One, and Houser and I will follow that up."

Grimaldi studied the photo of Malik. "This recent?"

"Three years ago."

"He ever wear glasses, beard, mustache?"

"He wasn't last night."

"You saw him last night?"

"Around seven o'clock. He ran us off the road in Virginia."

"You want to give me a little more on that?"

"No," Culley said.

"How come I knew you were gonna say that? All right, but you keep a low profile. You find him, you call me in. You've got no jurisdiction here, and I don't want any Gunfight at the OK Corral in the middle of Brighton Beach."

Grimaldi turned to Houser. "Be careful, Julie. These Russians make the wiseguys, the Colombian cartels, and the Jamaican posses we went up against look like a bunch of choirboys. They got former Soviet Olympic weightlifters as enforcers and they're heavy into drugs now, heroin, out of the old Soviet republics. They're smart and they're tough and they'll kill you in a heartbeat. I got eighteen unsolved homicides already this year. Most of them happened in broad daylight and nobody saw a thing. We try to investigate and all the doors are closed. Nobody wants to be branded a *stukatch*, what they call a snitch. To top it off we got no Russian-speaking cops; I took a course and picked up a little, for all the good it did me. The only phrase I really needed to learn was, *Ya nechevo ne znayu*, which means 'I don't know anything,' because that's all I ever get out of them.

"I had one of them in for questioning the other day? His left leg looked like a pretzel. Some of his friends didn't like the company he was keeping. I tried to sweat him on a guy we think did one of the murders? He laughs, points to the leg, and says, 'You gonna do worse to me?' Most of them have been in Soviet prisons, so ours are like country clubs for them. They've survived the KGB and the gulag, and they're not afraid of us or anybody else, and they're more violence-prone than any drugged-out crazy you and me ever ran into. Most of our guys are afraid of them; they won't hesitate to go after a cop's family."

"I get the picture," Houser said.

"Yeah, well, don't even think about takin' them on yourself," Grimaldi said, and handed her one of his cards. "My beeper number's on the back. I want to hear from you the minute you get so much as a nibble."

Grimaldi looked at Culley. "Anything more you can tell me about this guy?"

"Yes. He's everything you just said, and more. A lot more than your usual psycho. He won't go down easy, so forget about any warnings. Shoot first, and shoot to kill, because I guarantee you he won't let you arrest him."

"I take it you know this guy."

"Only too well."

"Answer me this. Is he CIA or ex-CIA?"

"No. He's not."

"Not for nothin', but you're CIA, right?"

Culley didn't reply.

"Okay, like you said, we'll skip that part."

"Good. Because that's all you're going to get."

"No gunplay," Grimaldi said. "Call the beeper number the second you got anything. Understood?"

"Understood," Culley said, knowing that the

chances of it ever happening that way were remote at best. "And you'll do the same."

"Like I said."

Houser scribbled down the number for her portable telephone and handed it to Grimaldi. "The phone's in my bag. I'll be with Culley."

Grimaldi took the number. "Remember, Julie. Don't play around with these people." With that he left and went back to the crime scene.

"You were a good cop, weren't you?" Culley said to Houser as they left the boardwalk and returned to the car.

"Yes, I was."

"Why did you quit?"

"That's a long story."

"Tell me about it."

"Maybe some other time." Her tone left no doubt the subject was closed.

"Mick-Kraut?" Culley said.

"What?"

"Grimaldi called you a Mick-Kraut hag."

Houser smiled. "I'm half Irish, half German."

"Bad combination. Get drunk, sing 'Galway Bay,' and invade Poland."

28

THE WINDOW TABLE in the coffee shop on Brighton Beach Avenue had an unobstructed view of the entrance to the Gardenia Restaurant on the opposite side of the street. The restaurant had opened for breakfast thirty minutes earlier and Culley and Houser sat watching and waiting until enough people entered. They did not want to draw attention to themselves by walking into a nearly empty dining room.

An express train roared overhead on the elevated subway tracks that ran down the center of the broad avenue, showering the deeply shadowed area below with sparks as Culley and Houser left the coffee shop and crossed to the restaurant. The steel gates were rolled back on the shops lining both sides of the street, and the sidewalks were already crowded with beefy, heavy-boned men and squat, thickset women. All had strong Slavic features, and most were garishly dressed in polyester and patent leather, carrying net shopping bags filled to the brim with fresh fruits and vegetables and various items from well-stocked shops they had never experienced in their homeland.

The feeling of being in a closed ethnic world, inhospitable to outsiders, was reinforced by the coarse, guttural sound of the Russian language that was clearly the dominant if not the only language spoken in the community. Culley would have sworn he was back in the old Soviet Union, in Moscow, or Kiev, or the seaside town of Odessa in particular for its physical resemblance, were it not for the abundance of goods and groceries in the shops and stands and the steady stream of cars flowing past.

The owner-manager, who greeted Culley and Houser upon entering the Gardenia Restaurant, had the bright eyes and round, rosy-cheeked face of a cherub, the image of friendliness and conviviality. The Cyrillic letters tattooed on the backs of his fingers—the mark of a made man in the Organizat-siya—told a different story.

The restaurant was one long, narrow room, three quarters full, smelling of the motherland and crackling with animated conversations in the mother tongue. Culley spotted an empty table tucked into a corner near the door and pointed to it. The cherub in disguise nodded and led them to the table, gesturing to a waiter with the countenance of a hangman, who hurried over, gave them menus, and splashed water into their glasses before walking away without a word.

Culley had a clear view down the length of the room. His eyes moved slowly over the small groups of diners, some casting suspicious glances at him and Houser, immediately pegging them as outsiders.

Culley's eyes came to rest on a table at the far end near the swinging doors into the kitchen.

Three men, all dressed in expensive designer suits, looking like escaped convicts who had just looted an Armani men's store, sat hunched over their food, tossing down glasses of vodka as though they were water. A shoulder holster peeked out from beneath the suit coat of a man with the hooded eyes of a psychopath, who sat facing Culley and Houser. They were all big, bull-necked, barrel-chested men, with the look of hired muscle, and Culley logged them in.

"What does Silkin look like?" Houser asked, studying the room, taking in the watercolors and cheap oil paintings depicting overly romantic scenes of the Russian landscape and the Volga River.

"He's about six two, kind of rawboned and slender. Blond hair, blue eyes. One side of his face is paralyzed, so he looks just like the stupid son of a bitch that he is."

"He and Malik are friends?"

"They worked in the same section of the KGB for a while. They had a little side venture. Silkin took care of collecting the tribute paid by the Russian mafia while Malik made sure a blind eye was turned to their activities."

"Was Silkin part of the hijacking?"

"Probably."

Culley's distant tone of voice and his lack of eye contact were not lost on Houser. She sat quietly for a few minutes and then said, "Are you angry with me for insisting that you bring Grimaldi in?"

"No. I'm angry that I was stupid and desperate enough to get involved in this in the first place."

"I don't know that the decision to get involved

was wrong. You're probably a lot closer to getting Malik than the FBI is at this point, or would be if you had simply told them what you know. I think you were right in that respect."

"I'm beginning to have my doubts."

"Well, believe me, confiding in Grimaldi was a smart move. He's the best street cop I've ever known."

They fell silent when the waiter returned to take their orders. Culley convinced Houser to try the Russian version of pierogi—a pastry shell filled with spicy pork—one of the few Russian dishes he had learned to enjoy during his years at the CIA's Moscow station. The waiter spoke no English, and Culley simply pointed to what they wanted on the menu, choosing not to speak the language he knew well and spoke without a trace of an accent.

Shortly after their food arrived, Culley saw one of the men at the rear table get up and go into the kitchen in response to another man who had signaled to him from the swinging doors. The two who remained at the table seemed more alert. They kept turning their heads in the direction their companion had gone, as though expecting to be summoned at any moment.

Culley ignored his food, his eyes riveted on the back of the room and the narrow hallway that led past the kitchen to the rear exit. The man who had been summoned returned to the table, joined by another man who immediately drew Culley's attention.

Houser, never one to pass up a meal, was enjoying the unusual but tasty dish. She saw the change in Culley's demeanor and turned to follow his gaze. She studied the recent arrival's face as he approached the table and sat down, then recognized him from Culley's description.

"That's Silkin?"

"Yeah. Don't stare at him. Look at me as though we're having a normal conversation."

"What are you going to do?"

"Nothing. But there's something you can do for me," Culley said. "If I'm right, he'll lead us to Malik. I want you to leave and go around to the back of the building. I noticed there's an alley between the restaurant and the shop next door. Position yourself where you can see the back door and the head of the alley where it fronts on Brighton Beach Avenue. If he comes out the back, follow him. I'll leave by the front and join up with you."

"And if he goes out the front?"

"When I come out I'll signal you in the alley. You know how to work a leapfrog surveillance?"

"We follow from opposite sides of the street and trade off taking the lead so he doesn't always see the same person behind him."

"Right."

"Doesn't he know you by sight?"

"No. I watched the surveillance films we had of him and read the biographical and psychological workup we did when we were thinking of recruiting him in Moscow. But we never met."

Houser started to leave and Culley put a hand on her arm to keep her in her seat. "Wait until I give you the word, then stand up, lean over and kiss me on the cheek, and give me a short wave on your way out the door."

Culley continued to watch Silkin and the other

men at the table unobserved, waiting until they were engrossed in conversation.

"Now," he said to Houser, who got up and followed his instructions calmly and coolly, without a hint of apprehension.

The man with the hooded eyes took note of Houser leaving, but went back to his conversation. Culley picked at his food, watching Silkin out of the corner of his eye. The double doors to the kitchen swung open and a man came out, immediately turning his back to finish his conversation with whoever was on the other side of the doors.

Culley stared hard at the back of the man's head, the slope of his shoulders, the way he stood with one hip cocked. He felt his skin pebble and the hair rise on the back of his neck. The man turned slightly, providing a full profile, and Culley knew without a doubt that it was Malik.

Culley tensed, averting his eyes and lowering his head. His first thoughts were of Houser. If Malik went out the back door and saw her, or she confronted him, she was dead. No matter how good a cop she was, no matter how many tough situations she had been in, she was no match for Malik one-on-one.

His mind raced, working out a plan of action if Malik started for the back door. But by then it would be too late. And if he went after him now, he would bolt for the door and be outside before he could ever reach him.

The dilemma resolved itself as Malik headed toward the table where Silkin sat. He scanned the restaurant, his cold, suspicious gaze moving slowly over the crowd. His eyes passed over Culley, then immediately snapped back and widened.

Malik's initial expression was one of shock that soon turned to a mocking smile. His hand went to the inside of his jacket when he saw Culley draw his gun and get up, walking slowly, purposefully across the dining room. At the sight of Culley's gun shouts and screams filled the room as people dived for cover and scrambled out of his path.

Malik had his hand around the grip of the gun tucked inside his waistband at the front of his slacks. He hesitated, deciding for his own reason not to draw the weapon. Culley closed fast, his gun held at his side as people scattered in every direction. A few of the diners in front of him stood paralyzed with fear in the center of the room, momentarily obscuring his view of Malik.

Malik said something to Silkin, then smiled again and waved to Culley before turning and running for the rear door. Silkin got to his feet, joined by the three other men at the table. They formed a blockade at the entrance to the narrow hallway.

Culley kept coming. Ten feet from the human blockade he slowed and stopped, pointing his gun at Silkin's head. The other three men had their hands on the grips of their weapons secured in the shoulder holsters inside their jackets.

Culley increased the pressure on the trigger. "Bring your hands out empty, boys, or your friend is a dead man."

The three men did not understand a word of English, but clearly understood the sense of the threat.

"No guns!" Silkin shouted in Russian.

They quickly complied, bringing their hands into plain view.

Culley moved in close, his gun leveled directly between Silkin's eyes. He swung the barrel across Silkin's temple, clubbing him to the floor, unconscious. In an almost continuous, fluid motion Culley spun to his left and drove the knife edge of his hand into the throat of the man with the hooded eyes, dropping him to his knees gasping for breath. The third man charged and Culley kicked him in the groin, then brought a knee up into his face as he doubled over. He fell into a fetal position on the floor, his hands cupped over his shattered nose. The fourth man hadn't budged: he stood four-square blocking the hallway, staring down the barrel of Culley's gun with no sign of fear and no intention of giving ground.

Culley heard two muffled shots coming from outside, behind the restaurant, and fearing the worst, he feinted a left hook at the final man, then swept his knee with a powerful kick, sending him screaming to the floor in pain.

Culley leapt over him and ran into the hallway. In his peripheral vision he saw a face appear in the small window in the kitchen door. The man behind it shoved it open. Culley drove a shoulder into the door, slamming it into the man's face and sending him reeling back into the kitchen.

Culley ran to the end of the hallway and crashed through the rear door out into the passageway behind the restaurant. He crouched into a stable firing stance, the barrel of his gun following his eyes as they moved quickly over the area. Malik was nowhere in sight. Culley sprinted the short distance to the alley between the buildings and hugged the wall, taking a quick look around the corner and then drawing back.

He spotted Malik at the far end of the alley, exiting onto Brighton Beach Avenue at an all-out run. Culley stepped around the corner of the building looking for Houser and didn't see her.

"Houser!" he called out, and then saw her getting to her feet from behind a pile of crates and garbage bags.

He ran over to her, his eyes still watching Malik as he darted out into traffic on the busy avenue.

"You all right?"

She stood with her gun in her hand, unshaken. "I'm okay. I challenged him, he fired, and I dived for the ground."

Culley immediately gave chase, running to the end of the alley, Houser close behind him.

Culley reached the sidewalk on Brighton Beach Avenue and saw Malik halfway to the other side. He was running beneath the el, looking for a gap in the traffic to get to the opposite sidewalk.

Culley ran out into the street, heedless of the oncoming traffic. Brakes screeched and tires howled as drivers swerved to avoid hitting him. He rolled over the hood of a car that had stopped directly in his path, landing on his feet as he came off the other side.

Malik spotted a gap in the traffic and sprinted through. He glanced over his shoulder to see Culley in pursuit, then dropped to one knee, bracing his gun to take aim. Culley saw him and darted behind one of the el's steel support beams. Malik fired twice. Both shots missed by only inches, ricocheting off the support beam, causing more cars to veer and swerve away from the gunfire.

A top-heavy delivery truck overturned from a swift evasive move, and a car plowed into the back of it as it lay on its side, its cargo of crated produce skittering across the street to be hit by another car that swung up onto the sidewalk and crashed into a shop window.

Culley braced his gun against the support beam and looked for an open shot. Pedestrians were running in every direction, and he could not fire with effect without endangering their lives. He watched as Malik jumped to his feet and disappeared down Brighton Fourth Street, heading away from the avenue.

Houser reached Culley's side just as he ran from behind the support beam and across the last lane of traffic, now halted in both directions along the avenue in the midst of a cacophony of blaring horns and shouted obscenities. He was running flat out as he reached the entrance to Brighton Fourth. Houser ran after him, keeping pace as best she could.

The area into which Malik had disappeared was the second community in Brighton Beach. Separate and apart from the Russian section, it had once been the summer colony of the well-to-do in Brooklyn. The once charming brick and stucco bungalows and small clapboard homes were now hollow, decaying shells, many stripped of pipes and fixtures and anything else of value that could be sold for scrap to provide money for drugs. What remained were crack houses and shooting galleries; a dangerous third-world enclave of hookers and junkies and dealers ruled by vicious Jamaican and Haitian gangs.

Culley slowed to a jog as he entered Brighton Fourth. He kept the gun in close, chest-high in a two-handed grip as his eyes scanned both sides of the narrow street. It was eerily quiet, not a morning place. He saw no one ahead of him except a lone, emaciated junkie leaning over the fender of a stripped car and vomiting.

The junkie, believing Culley was a cop, assumed the position over the hood of the abandoned car.

"I'm clean, man. I'm clean," he cried from his torment.

Culley ran past him, picking up his pace. When he reached the next intersection, he stopped to look up and down the cross street. He heard shouts coming from halfway down the block to his right, and saw two black women run from the yard in front of a pink stucco bungalow with boarded-up windows on the opposite side of the street. The women stopped on the sidewalk to look back and then continued running down the street.

Houser reached his side, breathing heavily. "Anything?"

"Down there."

Culley pointed with the barrel of his gun in the direction of the pink bungalow. They began moving toward it. Houser kept her weapon inside the compartment of her shoulder bag, her hand on the grip and her finger on the trigger. They moved along together, staying in a crouch, using the cars lining the street for cover.

They came abreast of the bungalow and darted across the street, taking cover behind a Toyota 4-Runner parked at the curb. Gunfire suddenly erupted at the back of the bungalow, echoing loudly throughout the area. A second volley immediately followed, and Culley recognized it as coming from fully auto-

matic weapons. He saw Malik bolt from behind the
bungalow, turning back to fire at three black men,
their shoulder-length hair worn in dreadlocks. All
three carried Uzi submachine guns, firing them inac-
curately from the hip. Malik fired again and one of
the black men staggered and fell.

"Who the hell are they?" Culley said.

"Probably dealers," Houser said. "They must
think Malik's trying to rip them off."

Malik came into view, dashing across the rear
lawn from tree to tree, toward an alley at the back of
the property. Culley ran from behind the Toyota and
took the waist-high fence in stride into the front yard.
He fired at Malik as he ran. Two of his four shots
impacted in a tree, close to Malik's head. Houser,
against her better judgment considering the overwhelming firepower of the dealers, was right behind
Culley, her gun now out of her shoulder bag.

The dealers, believing they were under attack
from the rear, stopped chasing Malik in response to
Culley's shots. They turned and fired sustained bursts
from the submachine guns. The barrage of rounds
tore up the ground at Culley's feet. He saw Malik
vault the rear fence just as he dived for cover into a
tall thicket of untrimmed hedges that ran the length
of the bungalow.

Houser dived in right behind him, rolling into a
prone position, her gun pointed toward the backyard.
The two remaining dealers lost sight of them, unable
to see the hedges from where they stood on the rear
lawn. They came around the corner of the bungalow,
their submachine guns sweeping the area ahead of
them.

"We're in deep shit, Culley," Houser whispered. "Those guys have Uzis."

"Tell me about it."

The dealers were at the far end of the bungalow, moving cautiously forward. Culley's left foot protruded from beneath the hedge, and the taller of the two men spotted it and signaled to his companion. They both stared at the spot where Culley and Houser lay hidden, training the muzzles of the Uzis directly at them as they closed in.

"Take the guy on the right," Culley whispered. "Just fire until your gun's empty. It's the only chance we have."

At that moment the *whoop, whoop, whoop* of a siren filled the air, and the two dealers froze in position, looking out toward the street. Grimaldi, the red light flashing from the dash of his unmarked car, jumped the curb, drove through the fence onto the lawn, and skidded to a stop. He threw the door open and in an instant was crouched behind it, his gun pointed at the dealers.

"Police!" Grimaldi shouted. "Drop 'em! Now!"

The two dealers hesitated but a second, then turned and ran around the back of the house. Grimaldi, assuming that Culley and Houser had walked into the middle of a drug deal while chasing the Mix & Match killer, looked quickly around the backyard, then stood up and shouted to them as they got to their feet.

"Where is he?"

"He ran down the alley behind the house," Culley said.

"Get in the car!" Grimaldi said, and got back behind the wheel.

Culley jumped in the back as Houser got in beside Grimaldi. They had no sooner closed the doors than Grimaldi floored the accelerator and tore across the lawn. He caught a quick glimpse of the two drug dealers disappearing from sight around the adjacent house.

"Which way?"

"To the right," Culley said.

Grimaldi smashed through the rear fence without hesitation and swung wildly into the alley.

"What's he wearing?"

"Blue blazer, gray slacks, white shirt," Culley said, watching the small passageways and walks between the houses as Grimaldi sped down the alley, driving with one hand on the wheel, the other holding his portable radio. He broadcast Malik's description and location last seen to the other units in the area, and passed on a description of the two drug dealers, pointing out that they were carrying Uzis.

Grimaldi braked hard and stopped where the alley intersected with Brighton Fifth, looking down the length of the street in both directions. Seeing nothing, he shot across the intersection and continued down the alley and did the same at Brighton Sixth. Still no sign of Malik. He turned right, and raced back toward Brighton Beach Avenue.

"If he's got any sense, he's going to get out of this neighborhood as fast as he can," Grimaldi said. "He'll try to blend in with the crowd along the avenue, or duck into one of the shops or restaurants."

"You okay, Julie?" he asked as he picked up speed, his eyes constantly moving over the street.

"I am now."

"What the fuck is wrong with you, Culley? You were supposed to call me when you found him."

"No time. He showed up in the restaurant and spotted me."

"That's the way it went down, Tony," Houser said. "There was only time to react."

"Yeah? Well, nice work," Grimaldi went on, venting his anger. "You left Brighton Beach Avenue looking like a redneck demolition derby and turned the streets into a free-fire zone."

Culley said nothing, looking out the window as a blue-and-white roared by in the opposite direction, its light bar on and siren wailing, responding to another unit that had spotted the Uzi-toting drug dealers and called for backup.

Grimaldi stopped again as he reached Brighton Beach Avenue, checking the sidewalks along with Culley and Houser.

"Nothing," Grimaldi said. "He went to ground somewhere."

Culley got out of the car and stood looking up and down the street. Malik was nowhere in sight.

"Get in the godamn car!" Grimaldi yelled.

Culley stood watching the street, then shook his head in disgust and got back in.

"I want you out of here," Grimaldi said.

"Not yet."

"You're out of here now! Don't make me play hardball, Culley. Fuck you and the CIA. I'm not gonna let you run around here like the fuckin' Lone Ranger. This bullshit is over."

"Not as long as Malik's still out there."

"You said yourself, the way to find him was to find where the money was being printed. I was working on that when you started a fuckin' war. Now let me do my job."

Culley slumped in the backseat, feeling defeated and helpless. If he bucked Grimaldi he had little doubt that he would end up in a holding cell at the station house, or worse. And Malik now knew he was there, and might also assume the cops had his description. He believed Grimaldi was right; Malik would go to ground and stay there until the money was ready. There was nothing more to do for the moment.

"Have you got any reliable snitches?" Houser said to Grimaldi, breaking the strained silence in the car.

"One or two who might know something about who would be printing the money," Grimaldi said. "I was trying to find them when this shit went down."

"All right," Houser said. "You work the precinct. I've got a good friend with the Intelligence Division; we went through the academy together. She's with the Organized Crime Unit. They've got a squad that keeps track of the Russian mafia, right?"

"Right."

"Culley and I can go down there and see if she can give us anything on who might have been in on the hijacking."

"Fine by me," Grimaldi said.

"You'll call me if you come up with anything?"

"I said I would."

"Okay. Give us a ride back to the car. I left it over near the boardwalk at the crime scene."

"You go," Culley said to Houser. "I've got something I have to do."

"What?" Grimaldi said.

"It's got nothing to do with this."

"How can I reach you if we come up with anything?" Houser said.

"You can't." Culley looked at his watch. "I'll be in Manhattan. Tell me where to meet you in about two hours."

"The Intelligence Division is in lower Manhattan. I'll give you a ride to wherever you're going."

"No, thanks. I'll take a cab."

"Where in Manhattan are you going?"

"Upper East Side."

Houser thought for a moment. "There's a neighborhood pub on the northeast corner of Fifty-second and First called Billy's. I'll pick you up there in two hours."

Culley got out of the car. Houser leaned out the open window. "You're not going to dump me and take off on your own, are you?"

"Billy's. Fifty-second and First. Two hours," Culley said, and signaled to a taxi that had pulled into the curb farther up the avenue to discharge a passenger.

Houser watched after Culley as he jogged over to the taxi. Grimaldi studied her face.

"Hey, Julie. That guy mean anything to you?"

"I don't know. Maybe."

"Take it from an old friend. Something's not right about him. He's trouble."

"Story of my life."

▽

MALIK SAT BEHIND the wheel of the minivan on a side street directly across Brighton Beach Avenue, fifty yards from where Grimaldi had swung into the curb. He had jumped into the vehicle only seconds before Grimaldi screeched to a halt, and was about to pull out when he saw Culley get out of the car and search the sidewalks. They had not seen him, and he decided to wait and let the scene unfold. He saw the unmarked police car pull away with the cop and the girl in it, and watched as Culley got into the taxi.

"Fuck your mother," he said through gritted teeth, in one of his rare lapses into colloquial Russian. His head was throbbing, and he could feel the rage rising within with a will of its own.

"Fuck you, Michael Timothy Culley. Fuck you," he swore, pressing his palms against the sides of his head to relieve the mounting pressure.

"Enough is enough!" And he started the minivan as the taxi pulled out into the traffic on Brighton Beach Avenue, weaving slowly through the still congested area.

29

FBI Special Agent Jack Matthews got the
break he needed when, shortly after six o'clock in
the morning, the Newark, New Jersey, field office
reported that one of the bartenders at Hannigan's
Roadhouse in Mansfield had positively identified the
photograph of Malik as the man he had seen leaving
with the Mix & Match killer's victim, now identified
as Tammi Maldinado—the agents had learned of her
affiliation with Dwayne Becker, found dead in Hannigan's parking lot, providing the link to the roadhouse. It was all that was needed for a search warrant
for Malik's home and place of business.

Matthews had gotten the local assistant United
States attorney out of bed to approve and authorize
the affidavit he had quickly prepared, and then personally hand-delivered to the federal magistrate's
home for the approval and issuance of the search
warrant, interrupting the magistrate's breakfast in
the process. By seven-thirty a team of FBI forensic
specialists, flown down from Washington headquarters in one of the Bureau's jets, was at work in Malik's

house and shop. Within an hour the fingerprints lifted from both places were flown back to the FBI labs in Washington, where they were quickly classified and run through their computerized identification system. Thirty minutes later the disappointing report came back. There was no match in the FBI criminal files.

No sooner had Matthews finished talking to headquarters than what was left of his optimism was dissipated by another phone call, apprising him of the mutilation murder of Carole Jordan in the Brighton Beach section of Brooklyn. The agents from the FBI's New York field office, called to the scene by the Sixtieth Precinct, reported that a note was found bearing the next word group in the song. There was no doubt it was Malik's work.

In the interim one of Chief Brady's men, interviewing a clerk at a local hardware store, got a positive identification from Malik's photo as the man who had purchased a power drill, and a bit the same size as the one used to drill through the skull of one of the murdered coeds.

By nine-thirty Malik's bank, telephone, and credit-card records were accessed, the charge at Hannigan's the previous night confirming what they already knew. They found the bank accounts had been closed around the time the abductions of the coeds began. Social security records were checked, and the Bureau's liaison with the IRS got an immediate response; Malik's tax returns went back only three years. By then the pattern was painfully clear. John Malik was a man who had not existed anywhere until three years ago.

Matthews sat in the room set aside for the joint

task force at the Charlottesville police station, going over the reports and computer printouts, looking for anything he might have missed. For the past three years Malik had claimed sixty thousand dollars of tax-free income, but no W2P form was included with the returns to indicate the source of the income. There was something there. But what? Check on the source of the money. Tax-free income could mean a disability pension from somewhere. The military? A police department? Malik showed an uncanny ability to predict the course the investigation would take; an ex-cop would know that.

Matthews was also bothered by something the head of the forensic team had told him: Malik's house and shop had been tossed recently. Probably by two people. One who worked the downstairs of the house and knew what they were doing, taking great pains to put things back the way they were found, and another who obviously didn't know any better, or didn't care if anyone knew what they had done.

Matthews's first thoughts were that a couple of Chief Brady's men had taken matters into their own hands and pulled a black-bag job on the house and the shop. Brady, more than a little angry about the accusation, assured him that none of his men, or anyone else on the task force, had set foot in either place.

Matthews felt guilty about going off half-cocked. The pressure was getting to him. Brady was a good cop, and his men were well trained. He made a mental note to apologize again when he next saw him. It was at that moment that Chief Brady entered the room and sat down at the conference table across from him.

"Listen," Matthews said. "About what I said earlier . . ."

"Forget it," Brady said, and meant it. "The twenty-hour days are taking their toll."

"Do you have anyone working the telephone records?"

"I've got three people on it."

Matthews sat rubbing his eyes with the palms of his hands. He could not remember ever having been this physically tired or mentally exhausted.

"How could this guy not exist anywhere in the system until three years ago?" he said to himself as much as to Brady. "Everyone has a history we can trace one way or another, back to the day they were born, in most cases, no matter how hard they try to bury it. What the hell aren't we seeing here? How could he have wiped the slate that clean?"

"My officers working the street tell me that so far everyone who knew Malik or came in contact with him on a regular basis, and there weren't many, knew nothing about him. The guy who ran the shop next to his said he said hello to him in passing on occasion, but that was it. Said he thought he had a nondescript accent, maybe Midwest, but he wasn't sure. The man apparently kept himself to himself."

Matthews shook his head in dismay. "The lab said all of the prints in the house belonged to one person. They found a few others in the shop, probably customers."

"A real loner," Brady said.

"He fits the profile to a T. But I still don't understand how he could have erased every trace of himself from the system."

Brady got up to pour a cup of coffee, and stood

staring at the dump-site photographs. He suddenly turned to face Matthews, a look of revelation on his face.

"He couldn't. Not unless the system did it for him."

Matthews's head snapped up, his eyes wide. "Damn! You're right. How could I have missed it? The Witness Protection Program."

Matthews pulled the telephone on the conference table over to him and quickly punched out the private number that skirted the secretary of the assistant director who was coordinating the investigation for him at FBI headquarters. He put the phone on the speaker so Brady could hear both sides of the conversation.

"Johnson," the assistant director said curtly, answering the phone on the first ring.

"Tom, this is Jack Matthews. How quickly can you run a check with the Marshal Service to see if someone is in the Witness Protection Program?"

"Are we talking about the suspect, John Malik?"

"Yes."

"Minutes," Johnson said. "Stay on the line; I'm putting you on hold."

Matthews face brightened, his spirit buoyed. "We've got him, Chief. We've got him."

He and Brady sat listening to the silence, waiting for Johnson to come back on the line. Seven minutes later they heard a click, and leaned toward the speaker expectantly.

"Sorry, Jack. No John Malik in the program."

"Shit!" Matthews said, crestfallen. "I was positive that was it."

"Good thinking, but no go. I'm here if you need me," Johnson added, and hung up.

"Looks like we're back to square one," Matthews said.

One of Brady's sergeants entered the room and handed Matthews a six-page fax. "Just came in from Washington for your immediate attention."

Matthews took the material and quickly scanned it. "And then again, maybe we're not," he said, and began carefully reading over the reports.

"What do you have?" Brady asked as the sergeant left.

"Supplemental lab reports, with an annotation from our Counterintelligence Division."

"Counterintelligence? How'd they get into this?"

Matthews finished reading a paragraph and looked up. "Do you remember what the medical examiner said about the hole drilled in the back of the girl's head? Why he said it was done?"

"To terrorize a victim who was forced to watch while he did it to someone else."

"It seems the practice was developed by the Russians back in the thirties. They supposedly stopped it years ago, but some of their state security buddies in Eastern Europe were using it right up until the Communists were driven out. Particularly, the Czech STB and the East German Stasi."

"Was the practice commonly known?"

"Not according to this report. It rang a bell with an old CI hand at headquarters and he called the Counterintelligence Division to ask around."

"So how does our boy Malik know about it?"

"Good question. And there's more. The morphine-based drug the university hospital labs couldn't identify?"

"They said it had the ability to incapacitate, but would leave the person mobile with reduced capacity to resist," Brady said.

"Right. Our lab people identified its origin."

"Let me guess. Russia and the former Eastern Bloc countries again?"

"Exactly. According to this the KGB and the Stasi were known to use it to subdue people they snatched off the streets and dragged in for interrogation.

"And the spring-loaded Syrette the ME thought was used to inject the drug into the victims?" Matthews went on. "There are autoinjectors available in this country, but they come with premeasured doses of drugs, for people allergic to bee stings and things like that. But no one sells them empty so you can load your own drug. Again, according to this report, the KGB and the East Germans were known to use them in their abductions."

Brady's face had a distant look, his brow furrowed. Then, "The murder at Hampden-Sydney College yesterday evening."

"What about it?"

"What was his name . . . ? Spirko. He was a professor. He taught Russian and theology."

"Russian drug. Russian torture technique. Russian professor," Matthews said. "And the murder in Brooklyn this morning was at Brighton Beach; a Russian émigré community. We've got a common thread running through this mess, and I think I know who's spinning the web."

"The Russians?" Brady said.

"No. The CIA," Matthews said. "They have a program similar to the Marshal Service's Witness Protection Program, for the defectors they bring into this country. I don't know what they call it, but I can find out."

"That puts the black-bag jobs at Malik's house and shop in a different light, doesn't it?" Brady said.

"Yes, it does. My apologies again."

"But if they already know who he is, what would they have been looking for?"

Matthews smiled, believing he had it all now. "The same thing we are—if Malik is a former intelligence officer they resettled in this country, and they found out he's a serial killer. Think about it. They want him worse than we do."

"And a former intelligence officer would also have in-depth knowledge of investigation procedures," Brady said.

"Absolutely," Matthews said. "And the clues he's been leaving? No wonder he doesn't care if we find out who he is. He knows we can only track him as far as the CIA. And he also knows there is no way in hell they're going to give him up."

"You're not serious?" Brady said. "They'd protect a serial killer to cover their asses?"

"You're damn right they would. Until they could clean up their own mess."

Matthews steepled his hands beneath his chin and sat staring at the table. "Tell you what, Chief. We're going to keep this to ourselves. I don't want the boys at Langley to get even the slightest hint of where we're going with this. Not until I'm good and ready to confront them."

"No problem. How do you want to handle it?"

"First I'll have our Counterintelligence Division check to see if the name Malik crops up in any of their Russian or Eastern Bloc files. They keep track of all foreign intelligence officers who operated in this country. Any cover names they used. How long they were here, and in most cases where they were reassigned when they left the country. If Malik is former KGB, STB, or Stasi, and worked here before he defected, they should have a file on him."

"What about following up on the professor . . . Spirko? Nail down the connection, if there is one."

"We'll take the helicopter down to Hampden-Sydney and talk with his family, if he had any, and to the people who knew him. I want to be loaded for bear when I confront the CIA; they aren't known for giving out information unless they're between a rock and a hard place; and that's exactly where I intend to put them."

30

MARYMOUNT MANHATTAN COLLEGE, on New York's Upper East Side, had been Jenny's first and only choice of where she wanted to attend school. Culley and his wife, Janet, had questioned the wisdom of her living in an urban environment, especially one as dangerous as New York City could be for the young and uninitiated. But Jenny had made her case persuasively. She wanted to major in theater with an applied minor in art, and Marymount Manhattan offered unparalleled opportunities with the whole of New York City as a campus, and world-renowned libraries, museums, galleries, and theaters all within walking distance. In the end they had given their approval; she was an intelligent, strong-willed, and highly independent young girl with a great deal of common sense and good judgment. Neither of them could allow their overprotectiveness to deny her what she wanted most.

Overcome by the need to see his daughter again, to see for himself that she was all right, Culley had taken the taxi from Brighton Beach to Ninety-second and Third, to a luxury high-rise apartment building that served as one of the college's student residences. He was pleased to see that the building had two doormen in the lobby, and a twenty-four-hour security service. He stood outside, working up the courage to face his daughter, not knowing what he would say, or how she would feel about him after all that had happened. It had only been fourteen months, but it seemed so long ago, and he feared an enormous chasm had opened between them, one that might never be bridged.

Finally overcoming his doubts and fears, driven by the strength of the love he'd had for her since the day she was born, he called her apartment from the lobby, only to learn from her roommate that she had just left for work; one of her part-time jobs at a café. The roommate gave Culley the name and location, and when she asked who was calling, he hung up without replying. He gave one of the doormen a thick envelope to put in Jenny's mailbox, then left, taking another taxi to the Upper West Side, where he got out at Seventy-second and Columbus Avenue, two blocks south of the café.

Each step brought with it more inner conflict and apprehension as Culley walked slowly up the avenue, past row upon row of trendy boutiques and shops and gourmet groceries, and more sushi bars than he remembered having seen in Tokyo. The once run-down section of the city had, in the past decade, been transformed into a thriving, affluent neighborhood of thirtysomething people, commonly referred to as the yuppie capital of the world.

Culley stopped as he reached the corner at Seventy-fourth Street, and stood on the opposite side of the street from the café, watching the waiters and waitresses setting the sidewalk tables beneath a blue-and-white-striped awning, preparing for the Sunday brunch crowd that would soon arrive.

The doubts and fears arose again, and Culley considered leaving without actually talking with Jenny. To have her reject him would be more than he could bear. He could still be her father, help her from a distance whenever he was able. But he believed he had no right to interfere with the life she had rebuilt for herself over the past year, without anyone's help, overcoming the devastating things that had torn her world apart. Things that he had caused, which had forced her to become a self-sufficient adult, with all the burdens and responsibilities that went with it, at a time that should have been her carefree student days.

He would stay just until he saw her from a distance; that would be enough, he told himself. Then he would leave, and call her later. They could have a long talk over the telephone. It would be easier that way. He would not have to see the hurt and disappointment in her eyes.

And then he saw her, coming out from the indoor dining area, carrying a tray of silverware and dishes. He watched as she moved about under the awning, setting up the tables. He felt his chest tighten and a lump rise in his throat. His little girl, his baby, the image of her mother, with Janet's fine, aristocratic features, but with his coloring; his dark hair and deep blue eyes. She seemed to have matured so much, and was even more beautiful than he remembered. He wanted terribly to hold her, to comfort her, and tell her that everything would be all right, and how sorry he was for what had happened, and that he would always be there for her no matter what.

He stood transfixed by her image, feeling as though he had regained part of all he had lost, if only for the moment. He was no more than fifty feet away, and he watched as she laughed and joked with one of her co-workers. He stood there for the longest time, his mind filled with fond and precious memories of her and Janet and the life they once had together. He felt his eyes brim with tears and he fought to hold them back. Overcome with emotion, and so afraid of what her reaction to him might be, he could not bring himself to face her, and began to walk back down the avenue.

▽

IT WAS THEN THAT Jenny Culley finished setting up the last of the tables and turned to go back inside the café. She looked out over the street and paused, a sad smile moving slowly across her face. It was the jacket on the man across the street that brought the poignant memory as she recalled the scent of her father's leather jacket, identical to the one she now saw. She looked away, then stood stock-still; she felt her heart quicken as her eyes went back to the man walking down the far side of the avenue. She hesitated in a moment of confusion and disbelief, then the empty tray she was carrying clattered noisily to the ground.

"Daddy!" she cried, and ran toward him, out into the street, where she drew to a sudden stop waiting for a break in the traffic so she could cross to the other side.

The man continued walking away. She had only seen his face for an instant. Was she wrong? Could it simply be the mental image the memory of the leather jacket had invoked and made so real that she was imagining it was her father. And then he turned in response to a taxi pulling into the curb behind him, and she knew there was no mistake.

"Daddy!" she cried again, her voice cracking with emotion as she reached the far sidewalk, ten feet from where Culley was walking south along the avenue.

▽

CULLEY HEARD THE second cry over the sound of the traffic and street noise, and turned to see his daughter rushing toward him. She flew into his outstretched arms, and in that instant the doubts and fears, the pain and torment of the past year, were swept away in her embrace.

"Daddy," Jenny said breathlessly, holding on to him tightly. "I can't believe it's you. What are you doing here? The last time I talked to your caseworker he said that nothing had changed, that you weren't going to be released for at least two more years."

"Something changed," Culley said. "You talked to my caseworker?"

"Every month. I wanted to know how you were."

"He never told me."

"I asked him not to."

They stood in the middle of the sidewalk, people walking around them. Culley held her at arm's length. "You look terrific, honey. How have you been?"

"I'm okay, Daddy. Even better now that you're here."

"I love you, Jenny." He could no longer hold back the tears, and turned his face away to keep her from seeing them.

Jenny cried, too, hugging him again, holding on with all her strength. "It's okay, Daddy. I love you too."

They began to walk along the avenue, and Jenny slipped her arm through his, holding on tight, afraid to let go.

"What about your job?"

"The brunch crowd won't arrive for at least another hour; I could get the rest of the day off," she said hopefully.

"I'm here on business," Culley said. "I only have an hour or so."

"Business? Like before?"

"Sort of."

She didn't press. "I only work until four. Then I'm free for the rest of the day."

"I'm sorry, honey. I don't know how long I'll be tied up."

"How long will you be in the city? I want to spend more than an hour with you. Can't you rearrange things?"

"I can't now. But soon. We'll work it out. I promise. It'll take some time, though."

They walked along in silence, Jenny resting her head on his shoulder as she clung to his arm. Culley couldn't find the words he had so carefully rehearsed over and over again in his prison cell at night; all of the things he wanted to tell her were lost in the moment. They turned left on Seventy-third Street and walked over to Central Park, glorious with its mantle of brilliant fall foliage. They sat on a bench overlooking the lake and the graceful arch of the bow bridge.

"How are things at school?" Culley asked, still not able to say the things he wanted so badly to say.

"I got a merit scholarship," Jenny said proudly, still holding on to his arm. "And I'm okay financially, too, so don't worry about that. I work this job on weekends and three evenings a week, tips are great, then Thursday nights at Bloomingdale's, and I have a part-time job with the Theater Department's set construction crew at school. I'm making it, Daddy. I'm tough, like you. And stubborn." She squeezed his arm and smiled up at him. "Remember what you told me about never giving up?"

"I remember."

"Stubbornness is the basis of endurance; endurance is the basis of survival. Well, you're looking at a survivor."

Culley sat silently staring out across the calm waters of the lake, watching a man and woman with their two young children in a rowboat pass beneath the bridge. He turned to Jenny and found the strength to say what he had been avoiding.

"I'm so sorry about what happened to Mom. I know there's no way I can ever make that up to you. And I'll understand if you can't forgive me for it."

"There's nothing to forgive, Daddy. It wasn't your fault. Mom had problems with depression for years. You were away so much, you never saw the worst of it."

"It's okay, honey. I've accepted the blame and the responsibility for what happened, and I'm learning to live with it, a day at a time."

"There's no blame to accept. Mom tried to commit suicide once before."

Culley looked at her in disbelief.

"It's true, Daddy. Right after we came back from Moscow, when you began traveling so much."

"I never knew."

"She made me promise never to tell you. I came home from school one day and found her in the bedroom. She had taken an entire bottle of sleeping pills. Fortunately I got there just in time. I called nine-one-one and they got her to the hospital and pumped her stomach."

Culley stared at his daughter, still stunned by what she had said. "I remember she used to get in bad moods, but she always seemed to snap out of them sooner or later."

"It was a lot more than that. She was never that strong, Daddy. She put on a brave front when you were around; she was very good at hiding the things that were bothering her."

Culley lapsed into another long silence. Then he said, "I still think about her. All the time."

"So do I. I still love her, and I miss her terribly and I always will. And I'm thankful for the time I had with her. But that doesn't blind me to the reasons she took her life, and I don't blame you or anyone else for that."

Culley's eyes again filled with tears. "I'm so damned ashamed, honey."

"Ashamed of what, Daddy? You have nothing to be ashamed of. What you did had nothing to do with right and wrong. It was politics at its worst. But you stood up to them, and you lived up to your oath and protected your friends, which is more than they did for you."

Culley sat quietly, regaining his composure.

"I never knew you worked for the CIA until you were called to testify before Congress," Jenny went on. "Did you know that? All the time Mom and I lived with you in Moscow, I thought you did what you told everyone you did, worked for the State Department as a political affairs officer."

"That's what you were supposed to think."

"When the hearings started, and I found out what you really did, I was even more proud of you. You were my hero, Daddy. And you still are."

Culley put his arm around his daughter's shoulder and pulled her close, kissing her gently on the forehead.

"You've got to be careful of heroes. They're usually reckless and excessive in everything they do in life. And in the end they pay dearly for it."

"And they're usually loyal, trustworthy, and inherently decent people."

Culley smiled and turned to face her. "You're all grown up, aren't you, honey?"

"Pretty much. But there's still a lot of the little girl inside me who needs her father, and that's never going to change."

"You sure you want me back in your life? I'm an ex-con now, and future prospects aren't all that bright."

"Of course I want you in my life. Forever."

"I left an envelope for you at your apartment house. It's in your mailbox," Culley said. "There's fifteen thousand dollars in it. Put it in your bank account for school, or whatever else you might need it for."

"That's not necessary, Daddy. I can manage. Honest."

"I know you can. But I want you to have it. I'll send more whenever I can."

"When will I see you again?"

"I don't know. This thing I'm working on may take a while."

"Are you working for the CIA again?"

"I can't answer that."

Jenny nodded knowingly. "Please don't ever cut me out of your life again, Daddy. Promise me that."

"I promise. I won't."

"That was a very selfish and inconsiderate thing you did, not letting me write to you or come to visit you."

"I know. I just couldn't bear to be reminded of what I'd lost, and how I let you and Mom down."

"You didn't lose me, Daddy, and you never will. And you didn't let us down. You gave Mom a lot of happiness. Whether you know it or not, you were her knight in shining armor—most of the joy she got from life came from you. She treasured her time with you. When you were away, she used to sit for hours and listen to the tapes she made of you playing the guitar and singing to her. It helped her over the rough spots."

"I'd like to believe that."

"It's true, Daddy. You know I've never lied to you."

Culley looked at his watch and got up from the bench. "I've got to go. I'll walk you back to work."

They left the park, and walked back to Columbus Avenue, Jenny still clinging to her father's arm. They stopped at the corner near the café and Culley put his hands on his daughter's shoulders and looked into her eyes.

"I want you to know that, no matter what happens from here on out, I love you."

"That has an ominous sound to it. What aren't you telling me?"

"There's a lot I can't tell you right now. But if you don't hear from me for a while, it's not because I don't love you, or that I don't care. It's just that things are going to be a little unpredictable until I get my life turned around. And if anything should happen to me, know that I've always loved you, with all my heart."

"You're scaring me, Daddy." And her eyes filled with tears.

"There's nothing to be afraid of. Sometimes things happen, things we can't control. But I'll do my best to get through this, and as soon as I do, I'll be in touch."

He embraced her again, then kissed her on the forehead and smiled as he turned to leave. "You look just like Mom, you know."

"I know."

"Lucky you."

Jenny stared after her father until he turned the corner and was gone from sight, then sat heavily at one of the tables and buried her face in her hands and cried with joy.

31

BILLY'S WAS THE quintessential neighborhood pub, cozy and intimate, with rich cherry paneling, gleaming brass fixtures, dim lighting, and small tables with red-checked tablecloths. Culley derived a small, familiar solace from the atmosphere as he came in off First Avenue and slid onto a stool at one end of the ornately carved bar to the right of the dining area. He ordered a Jack Daniel's, double, and sat glaring at himself in the mirror behind the neatly arranged rows of bottles.

He was still awash with the powerful emotions of his brief visit with Jenny, and the revelation of Janet's hidden struggle with depression. How could he not have known? But he knew the answer to that. If he had only been there for her, he could have made certain she got the professional help she needed. There were drugs that could have solved the problem, made her feel that life was worth living. And she would still be here, and they would still be a family.

Culley tossed down his drink, caught the bartender's eye, and pointed for a refill, which he dispatched just as quickly in an attempt to numb his senses and ease the odd mixture of pain and joy: the joy of seeing Jenny, and how she had matured into a young woman of strength and courage, and the pain of learning that in placing his career above his family, he had destroyed them in the process. His thoughts returned to Jenny, tough, determined Jenny, but not that tough, deep down still hurting over the loss of her mother; he had heard the tremor in her voice when she spoke of how she missed her and always would.

"Fuck the Agency," he muttered, louder than intended. "Fuck me for believing in them. Fuck Gregus. Fuck Malik. Fuck it all."

"Sounds like you had a real bad day at the office," the bartender said, in an attempt to lighten his only customer's load.

"Fuck you too," Culley said. "Keep 'em coming. Doubles."

The bartender shrugged an apology for the intrusion, then filled Culley's glass. "I'll leave the bottle. Help yourself."

"Sorry about what I just said."

"No problem. I've been there."

"No. You haven't. And if you're lucky you never will be."

The bartender retreated. Went back to polishing glasses. He didn't need any belligerent drunk making an already shitty day even worse.

Culley fought back the circular madness of guilt and what might have been, trying to focus on what remained. Jenny. She was all he had left, and he vowed never to do anything to hurt her again. He would somehow make it right. He would find a way out. He still had a few friends from the old days; people who had left the Agency to start their own businesses. Maybe one of them could find something for him. Anything. He didn't need much; he never had. Just enough to live on, and to provide Jenny with things she might need.

He was on his fourth double Jack Daniel's and feeling the effects when Julie Houser came through the door. One look at his posture as he sat slumped at the bar, his eyes beginning to glaze, told her all she needed to know. She climbed onto the stool beside him and gave him an admonishing look.

"Smart, Culley. Real smart." She shoved the bottle toward the bartender and ordered a Perrier with lime. "Intelligence Division didn't have anything we could use. Grimaldi knows more about the Russian mafia than they do."

"Doesn't matter. I'm out," Culley said.

"You're what?"

"I'm out. Write your story, help your friend Grimaldi, do whatever you like, but I'm out."

"You're not serious."

"Oh yes I am."

Houser lowered her voice. "Look, I don't know where you've been, or who you've been talking to, but if this is some ploy to cut me out, you can forget about it. This isn't just about a story anymore. There's a serial killer out there and he's got to be stopped. You can't just quit; you have a better chance of catching him than anyone. I believed that when we started this and I believe it even more now."

"If Grimaldi finds out where the money's being printed in time, he's got him. If he doesn't, I've got no more of an inside track on where Malik's going next than anyone else does. He's someone else's problem now, not mine."

"You *are* serious."

"I said I was. How many times do you have to hear it?"

Houser's temper flared. "What is this? Poor-me time? Drown your sorrows in booze and wallow in self-pity? You're pathetic. You don't have the right to indulge yourself while Malik is still out there. You have responsibilities. You and your friends are the ones who set that monster loose."

"I had nothing to do with it."

Culley was suddenly overcome by a powerful surge of emotions, haunted by an image of Janet on the day he left for prison; the last time he had seen her. Her brave smile, her loving embrace, her words of encouragement. He finished the drink before him and reached for the bottle.

Houser shoved it farther away. "You drink any more of that stuff, you'll be driving the porcelain bus and calling seals."

"Shut up, Houser. Just shut the fuck up."

"All right, but first tell me where you've been. If you're going to cut me out, at least have the decency to tell me why."

Culley hesitated, then, feeling the need to open up to someone, said, "I went to see my daughter."

"Your daughter?"

"She's in college here in the city."

Houser saw it all before her eyes, and realized the pain and the anguish that seeing his daughter must have brought back to him with a vengeance. She reached over and took his hand, feeling an empathy and compassion she had not felt in years.

"Come on, Culley. I've got a friend with an apartment around the corner. She lets me use it when I'm in town. We'll get some coffee into you and talk this out."

"There's nothing to talk about."

"You're feeling like a loser, aren't you? Like you let your daughter down. Ruined her life. Right?"

"She's making it, though. Holding down three part-time jobs, got a scholarship. Goddammit!" he blurted out. "It wasn't supposed to be that way for her. But, yeah, you're right. I let her down. I systematically destroyed the two people she needed most."

"Culley, my father once told me that our triumph in life isn't in never getting knocked down; it's in getting back up every time it happens. It seems your daughter's learned that at a very young age."

"Too young."

"You can't just quit on life," Houser said. "You can't let the bastards win."

"They already have."

"Bullshit."

"Platitudes and a pep talk aren't what I need right now, okay?"

"No. What you need is a good swift kick in the ass."

"Is that right? Well, if you're such a proponent of hanging in there, never quitting, why is it you quit the police force? By your own admission you were a good cop."

"Fair question," Houser said. "After I got shot I couldn't do the Job anymore."

"Physically couldn't do it? I haven't seen any

indication of that. As a matter of fact, I saw quite the opposite just a few hours ago."

"I had a shot at Malik when he came out the back door of the restaurant, and I didn't take it."

"I wouldn't beat myself up over that. You were better off hitting the ground in his case."

"It's the same thing that made me quit the force," Houser said. "Two months after I got shot, my partner and I were conducting a homicide investigation. We were chasing down our primary suspect and he ran into the basement of an apartment building. About thirty blocks from here, on East Eighty-sixth. He hid in the laundry room and got the drop on my partner. I came through the door with a uniform behind me. I could have dropped the guy easy, but I froze. I couldn't take the shot. Fortunately for my partner the uniform did, at the same time the guy fired. The perp's shot only nicked my partner's shoulder, but if the uniform hadn't been there, he'd have been dead, because of me."

"You were highly decorated, right? For what?"

"I took a bullet for my partner three months earlier."

"Then it's a wash."

"It doesn't work that way, and you know it. My partner could have died because I hesitated. Apparently getting shot had more of an effect on me than I realized, as well as the fact that I had to kill the guy who fired it."

"Everyone freezes at one time or another. The shit gets to you after a while. You get over it. I know."

"Well, I didn't think I would. And I didn't want to ever put anyone in that situation again. So, after a few sessions with a Department shrink, I took her advice and got out on a disability pension. I get three quarters of my salary, thirty-five thousand a year, tax free for the rest of my life. I call it my fuck-you money. Gives me a lot of freedom. I left the city to start over, but if things don't work out at the *Post*, I don't have to worry about giving up my livelihood. I can move on, try something else, or just bag it and go to some Caribbean island and kick back. I live a pretty simple life, and thirty-five thousand tax free goes a long way. End of story. Now, how about we get you straight, check in with Grimaldi, and get back to work."

Culley smiled. "Fuck-you money, huh? You've got a way with words, Houser."

"Come on. Some coffee and a cold shower will bring you back to the land of the living."

"You're beating a dead horse. I don't have it in me anymore. I'm forty-two years old, with a prison record and the best years of my life behind me."

"Get a grip, Culley. You still have a lot to do, a lot to give; you've just got to put the bad stuff behind you and get on with your life. And you've got to learn to distinguish between reputation and character. Reputation is just other people's opinion based on gossip and interpretation. None of us have any control over that. But character, that's something we can make a conscious effort to improve on throughout our lives. And you've got plenty of character and integrity. You've proven that, even though it meant going to jail for your so-called friends. And, hey, I believe in you; and I don't believe in anybody."

Culley turned to face her. "You're good people, Houser. You know that?"

"And you're drunk."

"Not by a long shot."

Culley slipped off the stool onto slightly unsteady legs. "Well, maybe just a little."

Houser put one arm around his waist and his arm over her shoulder as they left Billy's and stepped outside. The cool, crisp October air immediately began to revive Culley. He was mostly recovered, with the exception of a slight buzz, by the time they reached the Sutton House condominiums a short block away. Houser had parked the car on Fifty-second Street, near the entrance, and got Culley's carryall from the trunk before they took the elevator to the fifth floor.

▽

HOUSER STEPPED INTO the bathroom to grab a hairbrush. She intended nothing more when she paused to watch Culley through the steamed-up glass doors of the large walk-in shower, his hand circling a bar of soap over his body. It happened on impulse, with no planning or forethought, and, if she had taken the time to think about it, it was the last thing she'd have wanted to happen. At least that was what she told herself as she took off her clothes and stepped into the shower, sliding the door closed behind her. Culley had his face to the stream of water, rinsing soap from his hair, when he was startled by her arms slipping around his waist from behind. He turned to face her, their bodies pressed together.

They stood there, silently, water streaming over them. Culley's hands were at his sides, he felt awkward, uncertain, then he put his arms around her, clasping his hands in the small of her back and drawing her closer.

Houser looked up and saw the profound sadness in the deep blue eyes that so captivated her whenever she allowed herself to look into them.

"It's okay, Culley. At least I think it is."

He said nothing, gazing down at her, her skin glistening with water. It had been more than a year since he touched anyone in that way. Janet was the only woman with whom he had been intimate since the day they were married. His personal code had been: Look but don't touch. And although he had occasionally been tempted to violate it, he had kept the faith. He had never strayed, never cheated on her. Never had to, she was all that he needed or wanted. But she was gone now, and although he would have been at a loss to explain it beyond a natural human response, he wanted the woman now resting her head on his chest. He wanted her as much as he had ever wanted anyone, or maybe it was just that he needed her, needed someone to make him feel as though something mattered beyond his own devastated life. Needed the warmth and the comfort, the reassurance that he was still desirable, still worthy of someone who cared enough to give herself to him.

He cupped her face in his hands and looked into her eyes, his thumbs massaging the soft hollows beneath her ears. A brief hesitation, a moment of self-consciousness, and then he kissed her, tentatively at first, then passionately as she responded to him. Her lips were soft, giving, her tongue searching, reaching for some past tender, evocative moment in his life and finding it. She put her arms around his neck as she pressed herself tighter against him, murmuring a small sound of contentment from deep within. Culley's hands moved slowly downward to cup her breasts. His fingers found her nipples, and she shivered. One of her arms left his neck, her fingers descending, lightly tracing the outline of his upper body until her hand slipped between his legs and began stroking him gently, rhythmically.

She stopped kissing him and slowly lowered herself to her knees, caressing him with her tongue, kissing his chest, his stomach, and finally, taking him in her mouth. First with just her lips, tightening on him, then letting go, and then taking all she could of him to the back of her throat. Culley's head went back, his eyes closed. He quivered and let out a long, low groan over which he had no control. Houser stayed there for what seemed a blissful eternity, Culley's hands on the back of her head, following each ecstatic movement, pressing into her. She whimpered a small sound of desire and delight as she paused briefly, licking the length of him. And then her mouth went wild, taking him inside again, then almost out, again and again with mounting pressure and long, sucking strokes.

Something Culley thought lost was found, a long-suppressed passion, carrying him far away from his doubts and fears and pain. Finally, she released him, her lips glistening, her eyes looking up at him as she got to her feet and kissed him again. His hand went to her thighs, and his finger slipped inside her, feeling the soft, silky heat.

He took her by the shoulders and turned her around, slowly, gently. She bent at the waist, spreading her legs and bracing herself with her palms against the tile wall of the shower. He entered her from behind with one steady, even stroke, holding himself inside her briefly. He felt her tighten around him, and then he began to move in and out, all the way, each time. They moved together in a perfect primal rhythm, prisoners of the moment, then both let go with wild abandon until the last deep thrust, when she pressed backward to keep him inside her as he shuddered and felt as though a terrible burden had been swept away.

They made love again, later, less urgently, in the bed, where they now lay side by side. Culley's eyes moved slowly over her body. He gently touched the puckered scar beneath her rib cage, then bent down and kissed it.

"The bullet entered just below the last rib," Houser said, her hand moving through his hair. "I was lucky. It hit at an angle and went out the side. Cracked the rib, tore up some muscle and tissue, but that was it."

Culley sat up and pointed to a bullet-wound scar on his shoulder. "Prague. Nineteen eighty-two." Then to another just above his hip. "Budapest. Nineteen eighty-four."

Houser laughed. "Does this seem at all perverse to you? Laying here comparing bullet wounds?"

"Think it might be something to build on?"

Houser laughed again and looked over at the clock radio. It was almost two o'clock. They had left Billy's an hour ago.

"If we don't hear from Grimaldi within the next thirty minutes, I'll call his beeper number."

Culley said nothing.

"You're not going to walk away from this, are you?"

"No. I gave them my word, and I'll stick with it," Culley said. "You were right. I was feeling sorry for myself."

"Don't you think you should check in with the Agency? They might have something for you."

"I'll call Gregus after we hear what Grimaldi has to say."

With that he kissed her tenderly, his right hand caressing the inside of her thigh.

"Again?" Houser said.

"You started it."

"You like me. You really like me," Houser mugged, doing a bad imitation of Sally Fields's Oscar acceptance speech.

"Don't read too much into it. I've been in prison for over a year. Anything would look good to me."

32

THE FBI BELL Jet Ranger helicopter settled onto a broad expanse of lawn near a cluster of faculty and student housing at Blake Village on the Hampden-Sydney campus. Jack Matthews had called ahead, but unable to reach J. D. Guthrie, the campus police chief, he had left a message that he and Chief Brady would arrive within the hour. Guthrie was there to meet them as they climbed out of the helicopter.

"I'm afraid you made the trip for nothin'," Guthrie shouted above the noise of the dying rotor blades. He had a slow, southern good-ole-boy drawl that masked the sharp mind behind it. "They're gone."

"Who's gone?"

"Professor Spirko's wife and daughter. Left this mornin'."

"You mean left for good?"

"Sure looks that way, but you tell me. The house is right over here."

Guthrie led Matthews and Chief Brady across the lawn to one of the small brick colonials that served as faculty housing. He opened the front door wide and, with a sweeping gesture of his arm, stepped aside as they entered.

Their footsteps echoed loudly as they moved from room to room over the bare hardwood floors edged with tacking strips. The house was completely empty. Not a trace of human habitation remained.

Chief Brady pointed to the window casements in the living room. "Even the drapery rods are gone."

Matthews knelt on one knee and ran his hand over a corner of the floor. "Jesus Christ! They not only tore up the damn carpeting, they vacuumed the place clean."

"I'll bet if we dusted for prints, we'd come up empty," Brady said.

"I didn't see it," Guthrie said. "But Professor Janklow's wife next door said a big semi, followed by a van carryin' eight men, pulled up about six this mornin' and emptied the house out. They were packed up and gone by eight-fifteen."

"And his wife and daughter?"

"One of those big limousines with blacked-out windows arrived and took them away just before the movin' van took off."

"Mrs. Spirko didn't talk to any of her friends before she left?"

"Didn't say boo. Just got in the limo without a word to anybody."

"Do any of the neighbors have any idea where they went?"

"Nope. I thought maybe they arranged a quick funeral, so I called the local coroner; he told me the autopsy was completed around eleven, and at twelve-fifteen a hearse showed up for the body. The undertaker had all the right signatures, and the coroner released it."

"Where did they bury him?"

"They didn't. Not that I know of."

Matthews looked at Chief Brady, who simply shook his head.

"I'll need a copy of the autopsy report," Matthews said. "And the crime-scene photos and whatever else you have."

"Thought you might," Guthrie said. "They're waitin' at my office. You want to talk to Professor Janklow's wife?"

"Not at the moment," Matthews said. "What can you tell me about Spirko?"

"Not much," Guthrie said. "Except he was a mysterious sort of fellow."

"Mysterious how?"

"I went over his file in the administration office after the murder. He came to Hampden-Sydney about two years ago from McGill University in Montreal, Canada. Supposedly he taught Russian there before he came here."

"Supposedly?"

"Funny thing," Guthrie said. "I called up there, to see if I could get some background. Any problems he might have had; any enemies? You know, talk to some people who knew him? Seems nobody did. The university's records show he was on the faculty there all right, but I checked with the language department and the Russian studies department and none of the other professors remember him, never even heard of him; all of them had been there for at least fifteen years."

"Did you check with the university's finance department?"

"Sure did. Never issued a check to a George Spirko," Guthrie said. "Either the man taught for free, or he never taught there at all. If I was a betting man, I'd put all my money on him having been there in name only."

"Sounds like a safe bet," Matthews said. "Does the coroner have the name of the funeral parlor that sent the hearse for the body?"

"Sure does. Holt Brothers out of Richmond. But that's not going to take you anywhere."

"Why not?"

"I already checked," Guthrie said. "No Holt Brothers funeral home in Richmond. Get's curiouser and curiouser, doesn't it, fellows?"

"Was Spirko Russian by birth?"

"Don't know for sure."

"He was on the faculty here for two years and no one knows anything about him?" Matthews said.

"Played his cards pretty close to the vest. Spent a lot of his spare time with his cello. Professor Janklow's wife got to know Mrs. Spirko some, but she said she always clammed up whenever the subject got around to their past. Same with the daughter."

"Was there anything in his file here at the college about other family, relatives?"

"Just a name and number to call in case of his death. A David Henderson."

"Do you have the number?"

"Already checked it out. A company called Global Demographics, Incorporated, in Reston, Virginia. No David Henderson there and never has been.

Might be the number was copied wrong in his file. I haven't had time to check that out yet."

"Don't bother. It's probably a proprietary company."

"You mean sort of like a cover for something else? A cutout number?"

"Yes. Exactly like that."

"How about that?" Guthrie said. "I take it we're talking about a certain government agency here?"

"Probably."

"You figure Professor Spirko's death is tied in with this Mix and Match killer you're looking for?"

"As you said, Chief; if I was a betting man . . ."

"Well, I'd sure appreciate it if you boys would keep me informed. I don't like having an unsolved homicide case. First one we've ever had on campus."

"I'll do that, Chief, and thanks for your help. I'll stop by your office before I leave."

Matthews gestured with his head for Brady to follow him outside and back to the helicopter, where he retrieved his briefcase and took out his portable cellular telephone. He stepped away from the helicopter, unfolded the telephone, and tapped out the number for the CIA's National Resettlement Operations Center he had gotten earlier from the Bureau's liaison with the Agency.

∇

JOHN QUINLAN, THE NROC chief, followed the explicit instructions the deputy director for operations had given him earlier—any calls about Malik or Spirko were to be patched through on a dedicated line, set up in anticipation of the FBI inquiry, to Lou Gregus at the safe-house operations center.

"Jim Monaghan," Gregus said, using one of the cover names all CIA case officers are given upon completing their training.

"This is FBI Special Agent Jack Matthews. I believe we have a mutual problem."

"And what problem is that, Agent Matthews?"

"John Malik."

"Malik? The name doesn't ring any bells."

"Think harder."

"Give me a second and I'll see if we've got anyone by that name in the system."

Gregus pointed to Hack, who was listening in on the speaker at his request. Hack tapped out a few lines of gibberish on his computer keyboard. Gregus waited a moment, then said, "No John Malik. What's this about?"

"It's about one of your resettled defectors being a serial killer."

Gregus paused for what he thought was the appropriate time, and put just the right inflection of surprise in his voice.

"I find that hard to believe. Very hard to believe, as a matter of fact. I'm not at liberty to go into details about our program, but I can assure you that we maintain very tight controls on our people."

"Does the name George Spirko do anything for you?"

"Never heard of the man, but let me see if he pops up."

A few more lines of gibberish by Hack, and Gregus said, "Same story."

"Have you heard about the Mix and Match killer?" Matthews said, his voice heavy with sarcasm.

"I've seen the news reports."

"I'm not on a fishing expedition, Monaghan. I know what I know," Matthews said. "The fine hand of the CIA is all over this, and I need a little inter-agency cooperation here."

"All over what?"

"A damage-control operation to protect a serial killer."

"That's a pretty wild accusation, Agent Matthews. I would hope you have something to back it up."

"I'm working on it, as you damn well know by now."

"I don't know any such thing. Why don't you enlighten me?"

"Knock off the bullshit. Your man Malik killed two more women in the last fourteen hours, and you're doing everything you can to keep us from finding out who the hell he really is—my guess is until you can find him yourself and bury him so deep, nobody will ever find him."

"Agent Matthews," Gregus said, "I'll tell you once more, I don't know what you're talking about and I resent the accusations."

"But do you deny them?"

"Don't get cute with me."

Matthews tried a change of tack. "Look, it only makes sense that we work together on this. Worry about the political fallout later, okay? Right now we've got to get a crazed killer off the streets."

"I can assure you if I had any information that would help your investigation in any way, I would give it to you without hesitation. But I'm afraid I don't have any idea what you're talking about."

Matthews lost it. "Listen to me, and listen good, you turf-conscious, ass-covering, lying, arrogant, bureaucratic son of a bitch. When I tie Malik to you, and I will, sooner or later, you'll wish to God you bailed out when you had the chance, because I'll dump this whole fucking mess at your feet. Cooperate with me now, and I'll do what I can to help with your damage-control operation. But keep stonewalling me and you and everyone else involved can kiss their careers and their pensions good-bye."

"This conversation is over, Agent Matthews. Good day, and good luck with your investigation."

Matthews was fuming, and took a moment to calm himself, folding the telephone and putting it back in his briefcase.

"Any possibility we're barking up the wrong tree?" Brady asked, having only heard one side of the conversation.

"No way in hell. They're lying through their teeth. They might have convinced me if they had said less. Under any other circumstances, with a cold call like that, all they would have told me was that what I was asking for was highly classified information, and they were not at liberty to confirm or deny that anyone was in their program. But they wanted me to think I was completely off base. "

"You think they're close to finding Malik?" Brady said.

"I don't know. But it's not just finding him they have to be concerned with; it's making him disappear and erasing any trace that he ever existed in the first place."

"Can they do that?"

"Without leaving a ripple."

▽

At the CIA safe house in Alexandria, Gregus turned to Hack. "As you just heard, the Feebs are getting a little too close."

"Doesn't sound like they've got anything they can sink their teeth into."

"Maybe not, but it's time to get phase two wrapped up," Gregus said. "Any likely candidates?"

"Not yet, but I'm logging on to every police-department computer from Washington to Miami. Something will crop up."

"Expand the search to include the Northeast."

"How far? Up to Boston?"

"He's killed in New Jersey and New York. It's conceivable he'd move on to Boston."

"A mid-Atlantic state would be more believable."

"Concentrate there, but keep tabs on the whole East Coast; we can't be too choosy. I want to be in a position to act as soon as possible after Culley gets to Malik."

"*If* he gets to him," Hack said. "Has he checked in yet?"

"Not yet. But then, staying in close touch was never his style."

33

ALIK HAD FOLLOWED Culley's taxi into Manhattan, almost losing it twice in the heavy, erratic traffic along Third Avenue; having to cut off any number of drivers and run three red lights to keep it in sight. He watched Culley enter the apartment building at Ninety-second and Third, only to come out ten minutes later and take another taxi to the West Side, where Malik pulled into the curb and watched him walk north along Columbus Avenue. He was growing tired of the game, wanting to end it then and there, to kill his old handler in broad daylight, in the middle of the crowded avenue.

He sat in the minivan, keeping Culley in sight, half expecting him to quickly hail another taxi headed in the opposite direction, a countersurveillance routine to shake anyone following him, although he was certain Culley was unaware of his presence. But when he saw him stop and linger on the corner at Seventy-fourth Street, he was puzzled by his behavior, and got out of the van to take up a position in a doorway on the opposite side of the street. Malik was only thirty yards away from the focus of Culley's attention, and he could clearly see there were no customers at the sidewalk café, only employees setting the tables.

What was he doing? Securing a meeting site? Waiting for his lady friend? Perhaps a "brush contact" with someone from the Agency? A busy street was perfect for that. Malik decided to act, before complications set in, and he prepared to cross the street to make his approach. He took the pistol from inside his waistband at the small of his back and slipped it into the front of his trousers. He ran through the scenario in his mind: Get right next to him, give him a smile, maybe even a wink, then blow his brains out in front of everyone, and walk casually away.

As he was about to leave the doorway, the unexpected drama unfolded before him. He heard the beautiful young girl cry "Daddy," and saw her run into Culley's arms. And Malik felt the familiar stirring deep inside. The thrill of anticipation caused his breathing to quicken, his pulse rate to increase. The wonderful, unlimited possibilities now available to him to cause his hated adversary the worst kind of psychic pain and torment brought a smile to his face. He could not believe his good fortune. The marvelous synchronicity of it. Much more than he could ever have hoped for. No longer would it be a split-second flash of pain as the bullet entered Culley's skull, allowing him only an instant to taunt him before he pulled the trigger.

He relished the discovery and all that it promised; the watching unseen, the stalking, the abduction, and finally . . . Yes, he would take her back to the cabin. Everything to make it perfect was there. If you want to hurt someone, truly hurt him, you did not kill him, rather you destroyed all that he loved and held dear, and then let him live. First his wife had been taken from him; now his daughter would be as well. He drew a sharp, audible breath of excitement, and as he made a conscious effort to calm himself, the small voice at the back of his head asserted itself once again. More forceful than ever. *Don't be a fool! Get the money and get out before it's too late! People are looking for you! They know who you are! Get the money and run for your life!*

But the voice no longer had any authority; he was beyond that now, far beyond the rationality that had kept his impulses under control until his more analytical side could work out a sensible plan that would cut the risk involved to a minimum. He knew now how to stop the voice, had mastered it, and he placed the flat of his hands on the sides of his head and pressed hard, grunting unintelligible obscenities until it was once again quieted. It was a predator's instinct that carried him forward, and years of training that had become second nature.

He had watched Culley and Jenny walk arm in arm down the avenue, and followed them to Central Park, observing from a distance, then back to the café. There was no mistaking their relationship; the depth of his love for her. Their body language was unmistakable. She was the light of his life. His precious, irreplaceable daughter.

With Culley's departure, and Jenny busy at work, Malik had moved the minivan to a legal parking zone just off Columbus Avenue on Seventy-sixth Street, then walked back to the café and took a table after determining which station she was working. He studied her figure, stunning, and let his vivid imagination run wild with fantasy. He breathed deeply of her scent when she reached around him to pour his wine; a wonderful natural scent, just a hint of perfume. Such beautifully smooth skin and wonderfully expressive eyes; her father's eyes, he realized, and again smiled with anticipation. Young, firm breasts peeked out from beneath her blouse when she bent over to put his plate before him. At one point during his meal, when she leaned across to refill his water glass, he lightly brushed her arm. His skin sparked at her touch and his forehead began to perspire. He had ordered two more glasses of the house wine than he'd intended to, just to feel her presence again.

He chatted amiably with her at every opportunity throughout his purposely prolonged brunch, and gave her an outrageous tip, waving a cheerful good-bye as he left. He took up an observation post where he could watch her, patiently waiting until she was through working. He did not want to rush any part of it, savoring every moment of the preliminaries. He watched her move, and smile flirtatiously with a handsome young man who kept trying to keep her from her work. He would make her smile exactly like that for him, later. Then punish her for her cheap, slutty ways. He stood near a small shop selling comforters and sheets, and ducked inside and bought a down comforter, taking it back to the van and then quickly returning to his post. Two hours later he shivered with excitement when he saw her leave the café and walk north along Columbus Avenue, in the direction where he had parked the minivan.

▽

J ENNY C ULLEY LEFT work an hour early, after the initial rush of customers had died down. She was happier than she could ever remember having been; maybe just a little less than the day her father returned home, after having been away for six months, in time to attend her high-school swim meet to see her win the district one-hundred-meter freestyle. She skipped across Seventy-seventh Street, then adjusted to the pace of the meandering crowd ahead of her. For the next four blocks, on the east side of the avenue, along the perimeter of the parklike grounds of the Museum of Natural History, hundreds of people milled about the small stalls of the arts-and-crafts fair, crammed onto every square inch of the sidewalk.

Jenny paused at a tentlike display booth, admiring a hand-knit sweater. Why not? she thought. Compliments of the nice man who had left her a thirty-five-dollar tip for a fifty-dollar check. God, how she needed some new clothes; it was the one area in which she had denied herself, out of necessity rather than any iron-willed discipline. But Daddy said he had left her some money. Quite a bit. Maybe the sweater, and a few things at Bloomingdale's. After all, she did get an employee's discount there. She inched her way through the crowd at the stall's counter and picked up a multicolored cable-knit sweater. Alpaca. She looked at the price tag—two hundred and fifty dollars—and immediately placed it back on the display table. Maybe something in a nice cotton. More in her price range. And she sifted through the stacks of sweaters, people pressing in around her.

She suddenly flinched, feeling a sharp, burning pain, like a beesting, in her upper arm. And then it was gone. She frowned and rubbed the spot to soothe the pain, then went back to looking at the sweaters. A few moments later she began to feel light-headed and dizzy. Her legs and arms went numb, and she felt someone take hold of her around her waist.

She turned to look into the face of the man from the café. He was smiling at her. His features began to blur as he held her against his side. He was saying something to her, the voice sounding as though it were coming from the end of a long tunnel, reverberating and indistinct.

Jenny tried to move away, but couldn't. She saw concern on the face of the woman behind the counter, heard her say something, but wasn't sure what it was. She felt as if she had lost all control over her body.

"I'm her father. She'll be all right," Jenny heard the man holding her say. "She occasionally has seizures."

"No . . . no seizures"—her voice weak, her words slurred. "No . . . father."

"She'll be fine in a few minutes," Malik said to the people close in who backed away to give them room.

"Who are . . . ? Who . . . ?" Her voice now a faint whisper to those nearby, but echoing loudly inside her head. The words refused to come out as she intended. She was completely aware of what was going on around her. Knew precisely what she wanted to do: get away from this man. But her body would not respond to her commands.

"It's all right, darling, I have your medication in the car," Malik said, leading her away from the booth and along the sidewalk through the parting crowd.

"No . . . no . . . don't . . ." Jenny said, but by

now her words were nothing more than hollow, incoherent sounds from the back of her throat. People tried not to stare as they went by.

At the corner of Seventy-sixth Street Malik scooped her up in his arms as he waited for the light and crossed to the other side, to where the van was parked just off the avenue. A few passersby glanced in their direction, then quickly looked away. He put her down, propping her upright against the van, holding her in place with one hand for the few seconds it took him to open the rear door. Then he picked her up again and laid her on the carpeted floor in the back of the van, where he checked her pulse rate, and saw that her eyes were now closed and she was breathing evenly, firmly in the grasp of the drug for at least another two hours. He covered her with the comforter, and quickly closed the door and locked it.

Malik got behind the wheel, smiling contentedly. He looked at his watch. It was three-fifteen. Yuri should be finished by now. A quick stop at the warehouse to pick up the money, and then back to Virginia. He started the engine and pulled smoothly out into the traffic on Columbus Avenue, humming to himself and tapping his fingers on the steering wheel. A thought occurred to him, and the more he considered it, the more he liked it. He spotted a public telephone booth and swung into the curb. He chuckled softly to himself as he picked up the receiver and dialed his case officer's number at the National Resettlement Operations Center.

34

Tony Grimaldi turned off Brightwater Court onto Brighton Fourth Street and pulled his unmarked police car into the curb across from a twelve-story apartment building overlooking the boardwalk and the ocean. He had learned from an informant that the man he was looking for, Sasha Lysenko, had entered the building only a few minutes ago, to visit one of his girlfriends, an exotic dancer at one of the local clubs. The informant did not know the woman's name, or which apartment she lived in, so Grimaldi slouched down behind the wheel and lit a cigarette, settling in to watch the entrance, when his beeper sounded. He glanced at the display, recognized the number as the one Julie Houser had given him, and took his portable telephone out of the glove compartment.

"Any luck?" Houser asked. She was sitting on the edge of the bed, watching Culley pull on his shirt after toweling himself dry from their second shower of the afternoon.

"Perfect timing," Grimaldi said. "I was about to

call you. I'm sitting on a guy right now who might be able to help us, so get over here." He gave her his location and hung up.

Houser relayed the information to Culley, pulled the towel loose from around herself, and quickly began to dress.

"We can be there in thirty minutes, tops," she said, tugging her jeans up over her hips.

"I'll check in with Gregus now," Culley said, and used the telephone on the nightstand.

"Where the hell have you been, Mike?" Gregus said, his voice unusually tense.

"What do you have for me, Lou?"

Gregus hesitated, took a deep breath, and said, "It's not good, Mike." Another pause, and then, "Malik has Jenny."

Culley felt as though someone had driven a sledgehammer into his chest. His legs turned to rubber and he sat heavily on the bed. "No. No. You're wrong. I just saw her."

Houser stopped brushing her hair and turned to see Culley's body go rigid, his eyes wild.

"How do you know he's got her? How?"

"The son of a bitch called his case officer at NROC and he transferred the call over to me."

Culley closed his eyes. *Please, God. Please.* And then he asked the question. "Is she dead? Did he kill her?"

"I don't think so."

And then came the awful realization. "I led him to her. I led him right to her."

"Listen, Mike. There's still a chance. I talked to one of our shrinks. He says the fact that Malik called to tell us about it means he's not going to kill her right away." Gregus did not tell Culley why the psychiatrist believed that to be the case: Malik would torture her first, probably for an extended period of time.

Houser grasped what had happened. She went over and sat on the bed next to Culley, and took his arm, wanting to do something, anything, to help, knowing there was nothing she could do at the moment.

"What else did Malik say?"

"He said to tell you to back off, or your daughter would . . ."

"Or my daughter would what?"

"He's a sick bastard, Mike."

"Then I'll back off. You've got to find some way to let him know I'll stay out of it. Just tell him I'll do anything he wants if he'll let her go. You've got a file on his Russian mafia contacts . . . maybe he's in touch with them or some of his old KGB buddies. We could have our people at the New York office get a message to him through their agents in the Russian community."

"Mike . . ."

"You've got to help me on this one, Lou. No bullshit. No games. This is my daughter. My baby."

"It won't work, Mike. Even if we could manage to get a message to him. He hates you; he always has. You remember the trouble you had handling him; you had to beat the hell out of him once. This is personal for him." He hesitated, then reluctantly said, "The shrink says that in the end he'll kill her no matter what we do."

"No! It's not going to happen that way. Not to Jenny."

"We've got one thing on our side," Gregus said.

"No. No. No. You've got to get word to him. Give him anything he wants. Tell him he can have me instead. Just let Jenny go."

The desperation in Culley's voice caused Gregus to feel some of his old friend's pain. He had a daughter of his own.

"How long ago did you see Jenny?"

Culley looked at his watch. "I left her at the place she works less than three hours ago."

Gregus thought for a moment. "He must have waited until she finished working to grab her. What time did she get off?"

"I don't know." He turned to Houser. "Call the Allegro Café on Columbus Avenue on your phone. Find out what time Jenny Culley got off work." He was beginning to think clearly now.

Houser ran to her purse and grabbed the phone, quickly tapping out the number for local information.

"We got Malik's call exactly . . . twenty-eight minutes ago," Gregus said. "We have our own version of caller identification here; it put him at a pay phone in Manhattan. The telephone company said it was located on Columbus Avenue at Seventy-first. Where does Jenny work?"

"Columbus Avenue and Seventy-fourth."

"What time did you leave Brighton Beach to go and see her?"

"About ten-thirty."

"So that's when he had to follow you. He killed a girl in New Jersey last night, so he didn't get into the city until early this morning. No way in hell could he have the money yet if the printer didn't get the engraved plates until then. He's been hanging around waiting for it."

"Jenny was at work until about forty minutes ago," Houser called from across the room.

Gregus heard her. "He phoned us only three blocks away from where she worked; must have been right after he snatched her. So he hasn't had her for much longer than thirty minutes, Mike. If he's anywhere, he's back in Brighton Beach to get the money. I'd bet my life on it. And the shrink says everything about his past behavior indicates he'll take her back to wherever he took the girls he abducted in Charlottesville. If he's right, we've got time. He's not going to leave New York without the money. And if he's going back to Virginia, that's at least a six-hour drive before he can—" Gregus brought himself up short, not wanting to say anything to make Culley think of the consequences if they failed.

Brief vignettes of the CNN newscast Culley had seen only minutes ago as he and Houser lay in bed came back to him; the solemn expression on the anchor's face as she told of the mutilations and the dark suspicions of prolonged torture. Horrible images flashed before him, and he fought the crippling panic that held him in its icy grip. He had to think rationally if he was to be of any use to Jenny.

"What about the FBI? Maybe they have something we don't." His mind working now, clicking rapidly through a range of possibilities, beginning to function on an operational level. "Maybe they're closer to finding where he took the other girls."

"We've got a source wired into their task force, Mike. They're no closer than we are. And just maybe we've got an edge."

"What kind of an edge?"

"We've been brainstorming it since Malik called. Whoever is printing the money for him must have had some way of contacting him to let him know he was ready to proceed. If Malik is already gone, and you can find the printer, he might have a telephone number, even the location of the place in Virginia. It's our best hope at the moment."

"Does anyone have any idea of the general area of where he took the other girls? How close to Charlottesville it is?"

"According to the ME who examined the first four bodies, it has to be within forty-five minutes of the university. Something about the time it took for the bodies to defrost. And it's got to be someplace secluded, but accessible."

"Forty-five minutes? In any direction? That could be anywhere within a hundred square miles."

"Like I said, Mike. Our best bet is to find where the money is being printed. It stands to reason the printer, or maybe Silkin, would have some way of contacting Malik, so let's work it from that angle for now."

Culley was about to tell Gregus that Grimaldi was sitting on an informant, but he did not want him to know he had told the cop about Malik.

Houser quickly scribbled the number for her portable phone on a pad on the nightstand. Culley read it off to Gregus.

"I'm leaving for Brighton Beach right now. The phone will be with us all the time. Call the second you come up with anything."

"Will do. We're working on Malik's phone records. So far nothing, but we'll stay on it."

"And keep tabs on the FBI's progress."

"We're doing that too. Hang in there, Mike. It's far from over. You have my solemn promise we'll do everything we can to get Jenny back."

▽

IN A SKILLFUL, aggressive, and highly illegal display of city driving, Houser made the trip from midtown Manhattan to Brooklyn in under twenty minutes. She slipped into the curb around the corner from where she'd spotted Grimaldi, and she and Culley walked back to where the unmarked car was parked and got in.

"He's still in there," Grimaldi said, indicating an apartment building farther up the block on the opposite side of the street. Houser sat beside him in the passenger seat, and Grimaldi turned to look at Culley in the back.

"What have you been doing? You look like shit."

"He's got my daughter," Culley said, the words catching in his throat.

The look on Grimaldi's face said all the things he knew Culley did not need to hear. "Who? The guy we're looking for? The Mix and Match killer?"

"I led him to her," he said, and looked away.

"Jesus, Culley. I'm sorry. Look, I didn't bring the squad in on this, because I think you were right. Word gets out that we're looking for this guy, he'll be long gone. I've been working it myself, hoping to catch a break, but we can flood this whole area with cops. Hell, it's a kidnapping, we can call in the feds."

"No! You do that and Jenny's dead. We can't let him know we're still hunting him. This is personal;

he wants to get back at me. If he thinks he's trapped with no way out, he'll kill her then and there."

"What makes you think he hasn't already?" No sooner were the words out of his mouth than Grimaldi winced an apology. "Sorry. Cop question." .

"He'll want to draw it out," Culley said, saying nothing more for fear that even mentioning what he knew Malik was capable of would drive him over the edge.

"Who are you sitting on?" Houser asked.

"A local sleazoid by the name of Sasha Lysenko. I've jacked him up on occasion; some of what I got out of him was righteous, some pure bullshit. He's a paranoid little puke of a bottom feeder; a small-time thief who sucks up to the heavyweights. But he's on the fringes of the Organizatsiya, and he keeps his ears open for anything he can use to buy a walk from us whenever we bust him."

"We've got to find the guy who's printing the money," Culley said.

"If my boy Sasha doesn't know, he might know someone who does. Right now he's all I've got."

At that moment Grimaldi's eyes narrowed and he leaned forward in the seat. He was watching a small, wiry man with close-set eyes and a heavily pockmarked face come out of the apartment building. His hair was combed to perfection, and he wore an expensive, well-tailored double-breasted gabardine suit.

"That's him," Grimaldi said. "Ten-cent face and a two-thousand-dollar suit. Like putting a tuxedo on a trash can."

Culley reached for the rear door handle.

"Sit tight," Grimaldi said. "See if he comes

toward us. I don't want him to bolt from any distance; the little fucker can run like a rabbit."

Sasha Lysenko stopped just outside the building, his head on a swivel, watching the street. He moved cautiously away from the entrance and onto the sidewalk, turning to walk in the direction where Grimaldi was parked. He had gone less than fifty feet when he looked across the street and spotted the car with three people in it, immediately recognizing Grimaldi as one of them. He took off as though he came out of starting blocks.

"Shit!" Grimaldi shouted, then grinned when he saw where Sasha was headed. "Wrong choice, asshole. Gotcha!"

Sasha reached the ramp leading up to the boardwalk as Grimaldi brought the engine to life and roared away from the curb, tires squealing and smoking. He was facing in the wrong direction, and expertly spun the car around in the middle of the street and gave chase.

Sasha turned a corner and was gone, running flat out as Grimaldi sped up the ramp, with less than a few inches to spare between the wall of a building and the guardrail on either side of the car. He swung onto the broad expanse of the boardwalk, nearly going into a spin before straightening the car out. Sasha was thirty yards ahead, a speedy broken-field runner, dodging and weaving through the people strolling along in front of him. Grimaldi hit the siren and floored the accelerator. People ran to either side, clearing a path for him down the middle of the wooden roadway.

Grimaldi closed quickly, pulled slightly ahead, then swerved sharply to the left and slammed on the brakes to cut Sasha off. He was out of the car in a second with Culley and Houser right behind him. Sasha bounced off the fender of the car and tried to run back in the direction he had come, but Houser kicked one of his legs out from underneath him and sent him to the ground. Grimaldi grabbed him by the scruff of his neck, pulled him to his feet, and threw him against the wall of a boarded-up restaurant.

"Sasha, my man. What the fuck is this? You're not happy to see me? I'm crushed."

"Fuck you, Grimaldi."

Grimaldi grabbed Sasha's lower lip in his fist and twisted. Sasha squealed in pain. "That's 'Fuck you, *Detective* Grimaldi.'"

Culley moved forward, about to intervene, when Houser held out an arm to stop him. "No. Let Tony handle it. He knows what he's doing."

"What do you want with me, Grimal—Detective Grimaldi?" Sasha said, rubbing his lower lip when Grimaldi released him.

"That's much better. Now, shut your stupid mouth and listen very carefully to what I have to say. Hang on my every word. Your worthless life depends on it. Understand?"

Sasha nodded vigorously, meticulously smoothing his hair back in place and straightening his suit coat.

"Now, I can't slap you around and heel-stomp your head the way I'd like to, but you see that guy behind me?" Grimaldi jerked his thumb toward Culley.

Grimaldi was right in Sasha's face, and he had to peek around him to see Culley standing there glaring at him.

"Yeah. I see him."

"Well, he's not a cop, so he's not bound by any of the rules and regulations that I unfortunately have to adhere to. And if I turn my back? And I can't see what he's doin' to you? It never happened. Right? And I'll tell you up front, Sasha, I've seen what he can do; last guy he worked over is gonna spend the rest of his life in a wheelchair, wearin' a diaper and a drool bib. Get the picture?"

Sasha nodded again. "What does he want? I did nothing. I don't know him."

"Just pay attention, and don't even fuckin' think about lying to me." Grimaldi took the photo of Malik from his pocket and held it in front of Sasha's face. "You seen this guy around?"

Sasha stared hard at the picture. "No." His expression gave the lie to his answer.

Grimaldi frowned and shook his head. "Wrong answer. Now, one more time. Have you seen this guy?"

"Maybe. I don't know."

Grimaldi turned to Culley. "I think he's lying. What do you think?"

Culley moved forward, standing over Sasha, staring at him hard. Sasha cringed, waiting for the blows. Culley guessed correctly that punching him silly would be counterproductive. He had the look of a man who was accustomed to being knocked around.

Culley began to speak to him in rapid, flawless Russian. Sasha's eyes widened and fixed on Houser. He responded immediately to Culley's questions in Russian, hurrying to get the words out, his frightened eyes on Houser as he spoke.

"In English," Culley said.

"I don't know his name," Sasha said. "I saw him around a few weeks ago, maybe a month. I'm not sure when. He was with Viktor Silkin and Yuri Belikov."

Grimaldi knew Silkin by reputation. The other name meant nothing to him. "Who's Yuri Belikov?"

Sasha looked away, reluctant to answer until he again glanced at Houser. "I heard—I only heard—they were involved in the hijacking of the currency paper."

"What did Belikov have to do with it?" Culley pressed.

Sasha hesitated again. Culley looked to Houser and smiled, making certain Sasha saw him.

"Maybe—maybe he was to print the money for them."

"Where was he going to print the money?"

Sasha threw his hands up. "I don't know details. I only heard, you know, rumors." His eyes again went to Houser.

Houser had no idea what Culley had said to Sasha in Russian, but she quickly caught on that whatever it was, it involved her and it had frightened him, and that Culley was using that fear as a wedge. She played along, taking a few steps toward the man pinned against the wall.

Sasha's eyes widened at Houser's movement. "Somewhere around here. Maybe over by Coney Island."

Houser took another step forward, glowering at Sasha. Culley saw what she was doing and nodded to her. "He's all yours."

"Okay. Okay. A warehouse on West Twenty-ninth. Between Neptune and Mermaid. That is all I know."

"That's five minutes from here," Grimaldi said to Culley. "It's out of my precinct, but fuck it, let's go." He turned to Sasha. "Get in the car. I'm not taking any chances of you calling them before we get there."

"If they see me with you, they will kill me."

"They kill you, we kill you, what's the difference? Get the fuck in the car. I'll cut you loose when we find the place and make sure you're not lying."

Culley grabbed Sasha by the hair, literally throwing him into the backseat and jumping in beside him.

Grimaldi sped back down the boardwalk and swung onto the ramp, this time taking out the galvanized pipe guardrail as he raced toward Brighton Beach Avenue.

Sasha sat tight in the corner against the rear door, watching Houser's every move. He flinched when she turned in the seat to look at Culley.

"What did you say to him?" she asked.

"Just some gentle persuasion," Culley said, his mind on Jenny, hoping, praying that she was still alive and had not been harmed.

Grimaldi smiled as he swung onto the avenue on two wheels. "He said you were an insane lesbian, and that the guy he was looking for had raped and killed your lover. And if Sasha didn't tell him what he wanted to know, he was going to let you cut his dick off. And I think he said you had done it to three men before and enjoyed it."

Grimaldi glanced in the rearview mirror at Culley. "Accurate translation?"

"Close enough," Culley said, and grabbed the handhold on the door as Grimaldi swung wildly around another corner toward Surf Avenue.

35

Viktor Silkin immediately pulled the bay door closed after Malik had backed the minivan inside the warehouse. He returned to stand beside Yuri Belikov, paying no attention to Malik as he got out of the van and went to the rear to open the door and check to see that Jenny Culley was still incapacitated by the drug.

Jenny stirred and let out a faint whimper as Malik lifted the comforter. Her head lolled to the side, her eyes fluttered open, then closed, and she was still again. Malik covered her up, then went around to the side of the van and folded the rear seat forward to extend the cargo area. With that he walked over to where Silkin and Belikov stood watching the binding machine eject the money in neat ten-thousand-dollar packets.

Malik took a one-hundred-dollar bill from his pocket, then removed another from one of the packets. He studied them both, feeling the texture of the paper. He smiled and handed both bills to Silkin, who made the same comparison.

"There is no difference," Silkin said, pleased.

"Of course not," Belikov said. "Nothing that can be distinguished outside of a laboratory."

The three men continued to watch until the last of the packets came out of the binding machine. Belikov had been stacking the money in three equal piles on the long worktable, and rubbed his hands together gleefully as he added the final packet. He pointed to six four-foot-long ballistic nylon equipment bags lying beside the table.

"Two for each of us," he said. "They are very expandable. Each will hold a little over five million dollars if packed tightly."

The three men began stuffing the money into the bags, making a careful count as they did so.

"The plates," Malik said to Belikov.

"Of course." He went and got them from the small office off the left side of the bay and gave them to Malik, who opened the padded containers to make certain the engraved plates were inside, then placed them in with the money.

"Remember, Yuri," Silkin said. "Do not purchase anything with large amounts of cash. Especially not automobiles. The dealer might report it to the authorities. The same is true for banks—make no large cash deposits, unless you can make an arrangement with a bank that will launder the money for you for a fee."

"I understand," Belikov said as he hurriedly filled the bags at his feet.

Malik knew that Silkin's words had fallen on deaf ears. The first thing the fool would do would be to buy an expensive car and flash his money around the nightclubs. If the Organizatsiya did not demand a share of the money for protection, or simply kill him and take it all, the Secret Service, still looking for any trace of the currency paper they had not recovered, or counterfeit money produced from it, would have him in custody within a week. And despite Silkin's sage advice Malik doubted that he would be much more circumspect in how he handled his share.

Malik zipped the second of his two bags closed, and carried them over to the minivan. He placed them in front of where Jenny Culley lay under the comforter, then closed the door and went back to the worktable, where Silkin and Belikov were finishing their tasks. He stood ten feet from them, their backs to him, and he took out his pistol and screwed the sound-suppressor onto the tip of the barrel. He stood quietly, watching until they had stuffed the last bag full.

It was Silkin who first noticed him standing there with the gun in his hand. His expression was one of shock that turned quickly to anger and then to stark fear when he saw the look in Malik's eyes. It was the last thing he had expected. He had known Malik for more than twenty years and had trusted him through all of their nefarious dealings during their years with the KGB.

"I'm sorry, Viktor. But it wouldn't be a week before you were in custody and telling them all about me. I'm afraid I can't have that."

Two silent shots struck Silkin in the head. He crumpled to the ground at Belikov's feet, startling him and causing him to spin around to face Malik. He reacted much quicker than Silkin, diving under the long wooden worktable, his hands reaching, grasping something beneath the tabletop. Two bullets tore into his chest just as he pulled the compact H & K submachine gun loose from the bracket he had attached under the table. He died before he had the chance to bring the deadly weapon into play.

Malik walked calmly over to where both men lay, and fired one shot directly into the heart of each of them. He pried the submachine gun loose from Belikov's death grip and tossed it in the front of the van, then took his time loading the other four bags. He placed one on each side of Jenny, one behind her against the rear door, and then put the last one in the expanded cargo area just behind the front seat.

He went to the Judas door at the front of the bay and pulled back a corner of the tar paper covering the window. First one side, then the other, looking up and down the street. His eyes fixed on the corner to his right, where the street intersected with Mermaid Avenue. He saw a man get out of a car with three other people in it, and run around the corner. He could not make out the faces of those in the car, but he did recognize the vehicle as the one he had seen Culley get out of that morning.

Malik stood watching for a few moments, then cursed under his breath and rushed back to the van.

∇

GRIMALDI HAD CREPT slowly around the corner off Mermaid Avenue onto West Twenty-ninth, where he pulled into the curb at the beginning of a street that reminded Culley of Beirut with its burned-out, mostly windowless buildings. Some showed signs of habitation, but most were hollow shells. Culley's eyes moved slowly down the block, stopping at the wide bay doors of a warehouse forty yards away on the far side of the street. They had driven around the block twice, scouting the immediate vicinity, and had noticed a rear entrance in the alley behind the warehouse.

"Cut him loose," Grimaldi said to Culley, who opened the door. Sasha ran back to the corner and disappeared from sight.

"Culley, you take the front. Julie and I will cover the back."

Grimaldi turned to Houser. "You carrying?"

"Yes." She patted her shoulder bag.

"What?"

"Forty-caliber Glock. Fifteen-round magazine. One in the chamber."

"I'm going to get my head handed to me on a platter if this goes down wrong," Grimaldi said. "If it wasn't for your daughter, Culley, it wouldn't be happening this way."

Grimaldi took his department portable radio and stuffed it in his pocket, then reached into the glove compartment and took out two miniature hand-held radios. He gave one to Culley and clipped the other to his belt.

"The volume is set low, so hold it to your ear." He looked at Houser. "You sure you're okay with this?"

"Yes." There wasn't a hint of nervousness, only a cold, willful determination Grimaldi had seen before.

"Okay. Let's do it. I'll let you know when we're in position, Culley. We all go in together."

"Make sure you know where Jenny is before you start shooting," Culley said.

"We've done this before," Grimaldi said.

They got out of the car, and Houser and Grimaldi went around the corner to the entrance to the alley. Culley kept close to the buildings on the same side of the street as the warehouse. An elderly black woman, sitting on the stoop outside of a dilapidated row house, got to her feet and hurried inside without a word. Out of the corner of his eye Culley saw a curtain being drawn across a thick sheet of plastic that served as a window in a house across the street, and then another farther down. A door slammed shut behind him. Culley turned and drew his gun in response to it and saw four black teenagers staring at him. One, thinking he was a cop, shouted, "Five Oh," and they all ran around the corner. The neighborhood was no stranger to trouble.

Culley reached the warehouse Judas door and crouched low, under the small window. He raised his head just far enough to peer through a thin sliver of glass the tar paper did not cover, but he could not see anything inside other than a small section of the far wall.

He stood and pressed his ear to the glass and heard nothing, then slowly, painstakingly, turned the doorknob, stopping when he met resistance. The door was unsubstantial, the wood framing old and weathered. It would give with one good kick.

He flattened himself against the outside wall to the left of the door and raised the small portable radio to his ear, waiting for Grimaldi to report in. He glanced at his watch. What was taking them so long? His thoughts went to Jenny; her smiling up at him as they walked through Central Park. And then he heard Grimaldi's voice, a low whisper, filled with the tension of the moment.

"There's a blind alleyway on the right side of the building we didn't see. Two cars are parked in it. A Mercedes, and a Jeep that Julie says belongs to the guy you're looking for. We checked them both. Empty. So your daughter could be inside the warehouse."

"The front door is locked," Culley said. "I'm going to have to kick it in. Shouldn't be a problem."

"Same here," Grimaldi said. "You in position?"

"In position."

"On three," Grimaldi said. "One. Two. *Three!*"

Culley reared back and kicked in the door. It gave instantly, crashing back into the inside wall and shattering the glass in the window. He heard the door slam open at the rear of the bay as he darted inside and dropped into a crouch, the barrel of his gun following his eyes as they swept the huge bay. Split-second images flashed by. The wooden worktable on his right. Two men dead on the floor beside it. The printing machinery. A blue minivan. And then he froze.

The engine of the van came to life, echoing off the high ceiling. Malik sat in the driver's seat, smiling at him. One hand on the steering wheel, the other holding the compact H & K submachine gun to Jenny's head as she sat in the front passenger seat, held upright by the shoulder harness.

Jenny's head moved slightly, and Culley saw that she was alive. He felt a few seconds of relief and said a brief prayer of thanks. Gregus had been right. Malik had not killed her. And from what Culley could see, she had not been harmed at all. Drugged, he thought, as he recalled what the newscaster had said about how the other girls had been abducted. He heard

Houser's and Grimaldi's footsteps as they rushed to the front of the bay.

"Don't shoot! Don't shoot!" he cried out as they came into view around one of the printing presses. "He's got Jenny."

Houser and Grimaldi moved slowly forward, their guns fixed on the rear of the van.

"Don't come any closer," Culley shouted. "They're in the front of the van. He's holding a gun to her head."

They stopped in their tracks. Grimaldi held up a finger to Culley and pointed to the rear tires; he was going to shoot them out. He moved a few steps forward, took careful aim, and slowly squeezed the trigger.

Malik was watching him through the sideview mirror. "If he shoots out the tires, I'll shoot your daughter, Michael. Not a very fair trade, is it?"

Grimaldi immediately lowered the gun and backed off.

Culley saw that Jenny was at best semiconscious, her head resting on her shoulder. He felt utterly helpless, so close and yet unable to do anything. He still had his gun trained on Malik, looking for a shot that could take him out in an instant. But he could clearly see Malik's finger on the trigger of the submachine gun. A brain-stem shot, impossible from Culley's angle of fire, was the only chance of killing Malik and preventing a reflex action that might still allow him to fire the gun pressed against Jenny's head.

"Open the bay doors," Malik called to Culley.

"Me for my daughter," Culley said. "It's me you want. Let her go. She's done nothing to you."

Culley let his gun dangle from one finger, then

bent down to place it on the floor and kick it away. He held his arms out wide, his empty hands palms forward.

"Kill me. Do anything you want to me, just let my daughter go." He moved another step closer to the van.

"I don't want to kill *you*, Michael. Open the doors. Do it now. Or I'll shoot her in the leg right here." He lowered the gun and held it at Jenny's kneecap.

"No!" Culley shouted. "I'll open the doors. I'll open them."

Culley went to the front of the bay and slid open the portion of the door in front of the van. He turned to face Malik, standing directly in front of the vehicle.

"I'll send you a video postcard, Michael," Malik called out, the gun back at Jenny's head. "For old times' sake. You can play it on her birthday. Ta-ta."

He saw Malik smile as he put the van in gear and stomped on the accelerator. The van roared ahead, missing Culley by inches as he jumped out of the way.

"Jenny! Jenny!" he shouted, his last image of her the moment her eyes opened, blurred and confused.

Malik swung wide as he came out of the warehouse, climbing the curb on the far side of the street before gaining control. Culley grabbed his gun and ran into the street to see the van turn the corner onto Neptune Avenue and drive out of sight.

Houser and Grimaldi reached his side. Culley's face was a tortured mask. He heard Grimaldi speaking into his department portable radio and he grabbed it from him.

"No!" Culley said, realizing that Grimaldi was about to call in the license number and description of the van. His voice cracked as he spoke. "If they stop him he'll kill her, before he kills himself. He'll never let them take him alive."

Grimaldi snatched the radio back. "Sorry, Culley. I'm already stretched too thin. I've got a double homicide in there, plus the woman he killed this morning. It's time to bring in the cavalry."

Culley knew it was a losing cause. Grimaldi no longer had any choice but to follow procedure from here on out. His first thoughts were of taking one of the cars and giving chase, but Malik could have gone in any direction on a warren of side streets and alleys. If the CIA psychiatrist was right about his going back to Virginia, locating the hideout where he had taken the other girls was the best hope he had of getting to him before he could kill Jenny. He stood, helpless and frightened for his daughter, staring down the empty street.

Grimaldi keyed the radio and called Central, putting out a citywide APB, giving the location last seen, the information on the vehicle, and a description of Malik, making it clear that he had a hostage. He next called in to the station house and gave the location of the warehouse and reported the two homicides.

"If they stop him, you've just signed my daughter's death warrant," Culley said to Grimaldi. Then, with the initial panic and adrenaline rush subsiding, Culley realized what Malik was almost certain to do as quickly as possible. Ditch the van and get another car. He kept the thought to himself and went back inside the warehouse.

Out of Grimaldi's sight Culley knelt beside Belikov's body and quickly removed the wallet from the dead man's pocket and slipped it inside his jacket. He took a ring of keys from another pocket and just as quickly put them in with the wallet.

Grimaldi and Houser came back into the warehouse to see Culley entering the small office off the bay. He began to open the drawers in an old rolltop desk, sorting through the papers.

"What are you looking for?" Grimaldi said.

"Anything that might tell me where he's gone," Culley said, casting a warning glance at Houser to silence her as she was about to speak.

Grimaldi stepped in front of him. "You're disturbing a crime scene. We'll take it from here."

Culley, in his desperation, had almost told Grimaldi that he was looking for a telephone number with an 804 area code, or directions to a location near Charlottesville, Virginia, but had stopped short of that. If the cops found the information and passed it on to the FBI and they got to wherever Malik was taking Jenny first, it was all over. They would bring in a hostage rescue team and Jenny would be killed. His instincts told him that what he was looking for probably was not in the warehouse, and he stepped away from the desk.

"You're out of it now, Culley," Grimaldi said. "This place will be crawling with detectives in about ten minutes, plus the Crime Scene Unit, and Emergency Services. We'll tear the place apart. We find anything, I'll let you know. You and Julie have got to get out of here, unless you want to spend the rest of the day answering questions at the station house."

"I appreciate what you've done," Culley said. "And I'm sorry about what I said before, about signing Jenny's death warrant. If that turns out to be the case, my decisions were ultimately responsible for it, not yours."

"These things don't always end badly," Grimaldi said. "Just keep the faith."

Three blue-and-whites, followed immediately by two detectives in an unmarked car, screeched to a halt outside the open door of the warehouse.

"I'll have one of the uniforms give you and Julie a ride back to your car. And like I said, I'll call you if we come up with anything."

The two men shook hands, and Grimaldi gave Houser a hug. "Never was a dull moment with you around, Julie. I'll be in touch."

"What are you up to?" Houser said as she and Culley walked out to the street.

"I've got Belikov's address and keys. If he's got anything written down on where to contact Malik, it's probably where he lives. Where's Fourteen Brightwater Court?"

"About a block down from where we left the car," Houser said. "We could be wasting a lot of time if he called Malik from the warehouse."

"Did you see a telephone in the office?"

"No."

"Neither did I, and I looked for one."

Houser took Culley's hand and squeezed it. "Tony's right, you know. It doesn't always end badly. Jenny's still alive, so the psychiatrist could be right about the rest. We still have time."

"I've got to keep believing that, or I'll lose it completely."

"Take them where they want to go," Grimaldi called out to one of the uniformed policemen.

The cop pointed to his radio patrol car, and

Culley and Houser got in. "What happened in there?" the cop asked as he slid behind the wheel.

"I don't know," Culley said. "We were just riding around with Detective Grimaldi."

▽

MALIK PULLED INTO the parking lot behind a small electronics store off Bay Ridge Parkway in Brooklyn. The store was closed for business, but as he sat at a traffic light at the intersection, he had watched a man in a Ford Explorer drive into the lot and back up to the rear door of the shop. At five o'clock on a Sunday afternoon the half block of discount stores in the minimall were all closed, leaving the area deserted. Malik slowed to a stop alongside the Explorer and put down the window, just as the man opened the rear door to his shop and walked back to open the tailgate of the vehicle to unload a stack of boxes.

"Can you help me? I'm afraid I'm lost," Malik called out.

The man turned to stare down the barrel of a sound-suppressed pistol. Malik shot him twice in the head, then jumped out of the van and quickly threw the man's body through the rear door of the shop and slammed it shut. He looked about the deserted parking lot, then began emptying out the back of the Explorer and transferring the large nylon bags full of money.

He carried Jenny to the rear of the Explorer, and placed her in the space he had left between the bags. She offered some resistance, an indication that the drug was beginning to wear off, but he could not risk giving her another dose; one of his early victims, years ago, had gone into a coma from an overdose and had spoiled all of his fun. He took the roll of tape he had found in the glove compartment of the van and bound Jenny's ankles together, then her hands behind her back, placing a final strip over her mouth before covering her with the comforter.

He checked the time as he pulled into the street. It was approximately four hundred miles to Charlottesville. Seven hours, if he kept to the speed limit on the interstates, which he fully intended to do. He should arrive at the cottage no later than twelve-thirty. He heard a few muffled sounds from Jenny as she struggled briefly against her restraints, then lay quietly again.

36

ULLEY AND HOUSER had been inside the fourth-floor apartment at 14 Brighton Court for three and a half hours. They had systematically and meticulously gone through all five of the rooms and found nothing to indicate that Belikov, if he had a way of contacting Malik, had ever written it down and kept it.

Culley was going through the contents of a small desk in a corner of the bedroom for the second time, each minute an eternity, the barely controlled rage and dread inside tearing him apart. Houser suddenly appeared in the doorway, startling him.

"Did you find something?" he asked.

"What the hell are we doing, Culley?"

"What are you talking about?"

"We're a couple of morons, that's what I'm talking about," Houser said. "We've been so intent on finding anything Belikov had written down that we overlooked the most logical avenue of approach."

"What?"

"Didn't you tell me that your friend Gregus had someone who could access any computer system?"

"Yes. He does."

"If Belikov called a number in Virginia from this apartment, it's on his billing records at NYNEX."

"Jesus!" Culley picked up the phone on the desk and called the CIA safe house in Alexandria. He quickly filled Gregus in on what had happened at the warehouse and where he and Houser were at the moment.

"Can you get into the NYNEX billing computer?"

Hack was listening in on the speaker and nodded emphatically. "Yes," Gregus said. "What have you got?"

He gave Gregus Belikov's telephone number. "See if he made any calls to the eight-oh-four or seven-oh-three area codes from this number."

"I'll take care of it," Gregus said. "In the meantime, you go to the airport. No sense sitting around there until we see if we get a hit. Your best bet is still to get back to Charlottesville as soon as possible."

"Have you come up with anything since we last talked?"

"No. But we have two of the best shrinks in the Agency going over everything we have on Malik, and they are absolutely positive he's going back there. The consensus is that his fantasies are in complete control of him now, not the logic and discipline of a trained intelligence officer. So get to the airport, the Lear is still there on standby. We'll call you the minute we have anything."

▽

THE SUNDAY SOUTHBOUND traffic on I-95 had been heavy, but flowing smoothly at an average rate of seventy miles per hour. Malik made better time than expected, and had left the interstate for the Beltway around Washington, then headed west on Route 66 to 29 South. His thoughts preoccupied with his plans for Jenny Culley, he had not noticed the gas gauge on the Explorer reading empty as he bypassed Warrenton, Virginia, just over one hour north of his destination. He was running on little more than fumes by the time he saw the fuel warning light and the needle sitting all the way to the left of the gauge. Four miles out of Warrenton he spotted a gas station at the side of the road and immediately pulled into what was a small mom-and-pop convenience store with two self-service pumps. He looked into the rear of the Explorer to see that Jenny was laying motionless under the comforter, then got out to fill the gas tank.

▽

JENNY HAD BEEN wide awake for the last fifteen minutes of the drive, her mind finally free of the drug haze that had kept her from thinking clearly and fully realizing what had happened to her. But with that realization came terror and panic, which, before she got them firmly under control, nearly caused her to fight her restraints; to kick and try to scream, anything that might bring someone to her aid. But she had enough presence of mind to know the foolishness of that, given her present circumstances, and managed to lie quietly as she tried to think of some course of action that would enable her to escape. It was then that she felt the car slow and stop, and heard Malik get out and put the gas nozzle into the tank at the rear of the vehicle only a few feet from where she lay under the comforter.

She acted immediately, but kept her movements slow to avoid rocking the back of the vehicle. Her dance classes kept her limber and agile, and she had no trouble bringing her knees up to her chin and working her hands under her hips and behind her legs and over her feet, to the front of her body. She winced as she pulled the duct tape from her mouth, then clamped her teeth on the end of the tape binding her hands and began to peel it off. She pulled the comforter aside and sat up far enough to peer through the heavily tinted rear windows. She could see Malik pumping gas, but he could not see her.

She had her hands free by the time he was finished at the pump, and she watched as he walked toward the convenience store to pay for the gas. She quickly pulled the tape from her ankles, and at the same moment that Malik stepped inside the store and out of sight, she crawled over the large nylon bags stacked in front of her and opened the rear passenger door facing away from the store and got out, closing it quietly behind her.

She was disappointed to see that she was in an isolated area, with no other cars in sight. The station was set off the road in a small clearing, surrounded by woods on both sides and at the rear. Her heart pounded in her chest as she looked for a vehicle to flag down, but the traffic was light, and she saw only a brief flash of headlights as a tractor trailer roared by in the opposite direction. She next thought of finding someplace to hide that would not require her to run out in the open. It was dark outside, but the lights over the gas pumps and in front of the convenience store illuminated the area well enough that if she tried to make it to the woods on either side of the store it was possible Malik would see her. Behind her a grassy median strip with a few trees separated the northbound and southbound lanes of the road. Jenny first checked to make certain Malik was still inside the store, then she ran across the southbound lanes to the strip and hid behind one of the trees, waiting, hoping that a car would come by.

Malik came out of the store drinking a can of Pepsi. He paused to raise his hands high above his head in an exaggerated stretch, then continued toward the car. He was about to open the driver's side door when he heard a horn blare from the northbound lanes. He looked up to catch a fleeting glimpse of Jenny caught in the headlights of an oncoming car. She stood at the edge of the median strip and waved her hands, but the driver continued on without even slowing. She looked over her shoulder and saw Malik watching her, then darted across the two northbound lanes and disappeared down an embankment.

Malik immediately gave chase, running across the road and down the steep embankment into dense woods, where he stopped to listen. A full moon cast a pale light through the trees, but the woods were deep in shadow, and he could see no more than ten feet in front of him. He heard someone directly ahead, and took off in the direction of the sound, pausing every ten yards to again listen.

Jenny thrashed wildly through the thick underbrush, following the path of least resistance. She could see nothing but the dark outlines of trees and tangles of brush ahead of her, but she kept running as fast as she could, stumbling and falling twice, jumping quickly to her feet and continuing on. The ground began to rise toward a hill, and the going became more difficult. The terrain grew steeper, and she was now scrambling on all fours up a thickly wooded hillside, grabbing on to small saplings to keep from sliding back down. She was near the top when a thin branch she was using to pull herself up snapped off, sending her sliding back to the foot of the hill on her stomach. She got up to begin the climb again, when she heard someone behind her and turned to stare into the face of the man she immediately recognized as her abductor. He was pointing a gun at her and she saw a trace of a smile in the dim light of the forest.

"We've got to stop meeting like this, Miss Culley," Malik said, between quick breaths.

"Who are you? What do you want with me?" The panic was quickly returning, and she began to scream.

Malik grabbed her and clamped a hand over her mouth, then whispered into her ear. "It will all become quite clear to you shortly." He held her until she stopped struggling, and when he felt her body relax, he removed his hand from her mouth. "If you scream again, I will have no choice but to knock you unconscious."

Jenny stood rigid with fear, gasping for breath. "Please, just let me go. I don't know who you are. I won't tell anyone about what happened. Just let me go."

"I'm afraid I can't do that. I made your father a promise, and I'm looking forward to keeping it."

"You know my father?"

"We worked together for a number of years."

"You're with the CIA?"

"You might say that," Malik said. "Now I want you to walk back to the car with me, and, please, no more attempts to run away. Do you understand?"

The fact that the man knew her father calmed her for a moment. Perhaps this all had to do with an intelligence operation, and she would be returned unharmed. But despite the man's calm, soft-spoken way, his eyes were frightening to look at, and Jenny believed there was much more to it than that. She looked desperately about. There was no escape, not with him standing right before her. She fought back the tears welling in her eyes and began walking through the woods in the direction Malik indicated. She struggled to keep herself from completely breaking down, her eyes watching for any opportunity to get away.

As they came out of the trees and reached the top of the embankment on the shoulder of the north-bound lanes, Jenny saw the headlights of a car coming around the curve toward them. Malik had her by the arm, but she pulled free and ran into the middle of the road, screaming and waving her hands frantically at the approaching vehicle. Malik ran after her, swept her off her feet, and carried her onto the median strip as the car screeched and swerved to a halt at the side of the road.

The Virginia state trooper jumped out of his patrol car and directed his flashlight at the fleeing figures crossing the southbound lanes toward the gas station.

"Stop! Police!" he shouted, and ran after them.

Malik drew his gun from his waistband, the

sound suppressor still attached, and held it at his side as he stopped near the back of the Explorer.

"Just a family argument, Officer," he called out to the state trooper, who had now reached the edge of the gas station clearing. "No problem."

"No! Help! Please help!" Jenny screamed. "I've been kidnapped!"

Malik swung Jenny around in front of him as a shield and brought his weapon up to take aim at the trooper, who was thirty feet away and moving closer, now reaching for his own weapon.

The trooper did not see the gun in Malik's hand until it was too late; his own gun had not yet cleared his holster. Malik fired twice, both bullets tearing into the trooper's chest. He was dead before he hit the ground. Jenny screamed and fought to free herself from Malik's grasp.

Malik looked toward the store. It was quiet. The elderly couple inside were completely unaware of what had taken place. Holding Jenny firmly in his arms, Malik brought the butt of the gun down hard on the back of her head and felt her go limp in his arms. He opened the tailgate of the Explorer and threw her inside. He scanned the area one last time and, seeing nothing to indicate that he had been observed, drove away from the gas station. Two miles south he pulled off the road behind a feed store that was closed for business and used the tape to bind and gag Jenny once again before continuing on.

∇

HOUSER MADE THE trip to LaGuardia's Marine Air Terminal in just over an hour, fighting the heavy

Sunday-evening traffic all the way. They were on
board the Lear and airborne fifteen minutes later.
Thirty-five thousand feet above the New Jersey coast-
line the call came from Gregus.

"We've got it."

"The location of Malik's hideout?"

"The approximate location."

"How approximate?"

"We talked to a local telephone company repairman. The phone is in a rural area of Fluvanna
County. The line runs off a terminal located on State
Route 609, about thirty minutes or so from the
airport. There are five other lines running off it. None
of them is listed to a John Malik, but then he wouldn't
be using the name we gave him if he planned on
disappearing. The one we're interested in has his
telephone listed under the name of George Anderson.
So we have to narrow down which of the houses he's
in. They're all out in the boonies, off dirt roads with
no route numbers, and scattered over a two-mile area
that's heavily wooded."

"What about outgoing calls?"

"We thought of that," Gregus said. "Hack accessed Centel's billing computer. Anderson's phone
records only go back a little over a month. Right
about the time the first girl was abducted. No calls
were made from his phone to the New York City
area. Mostly local calls, a few long distance, but we
don't have time to track them all down, and I doubt
we'd come up with anything if we did. Besides, that
wouldn't tell us which of the houses is his."

"You're positive Anderson is Malik?"

"Three calls were placed to his number from the
number you were at in Brooklyn. The dates of the

calls are even more revealing. The first was made the day of the hijacking, the second three days later, and the third four days ago. Best guess: Belikov called Malik to tell him about the success of the hijacking, then to tell him the Secret Service got back all but one pallet, and finally that he was ready to print the money. It all fits, Mike."

"Just a second," Gregus said, and looked at the map display Hack had called up on the computer. He used the mouse arrow to draw a small square around the section of Route 609 where the telephone-company terminal was located, then clicked once and the screen was filled with a large-scale detail of the area of interest.

"It looks like there are eight unmarked and un-paved roads in the immediate area," Gregus said. "According to our contact at the phone company only five of them lead to houses, the others to fallow fields."

"What about calling the other four telephone numbers?" Culley said. "Ask them where they're located and if they know where Anderson lives."

"We tried that, under the guise of a telephone company repairman. No one answered at two of them, and the other two said they never heard of Anderson and got suspicious and hung up when we began asking question about the precise locations of their homes. So we've got to come up with some other way to figure out which one is Malik's place before you get here."

"How are you going to do that?" Culley said. "You can't take the chance of sending people in there to check each one out."

"I've got a helicopter on standby at the Farm. I can have it over the area within thirty minutes."

"No!" Culley said. "If he hears the chopper he'll know we've found him. And if you try to put people in there to assault the place he'll kill Jenny the minute he sees it coming."

"I'm not ordering an assault," Gregus said. "The chopper is a Hughes Defender, a small scout helicopter. It's equipped with Forward Looking Infrared and a Thermal Imager. And it's got a four-bladed tail rotor that keeps the revolutions subsonic and cuts the noise drastically compared to a conventional helicopter. It can cover the area we're talking about from two miles out at six or seven thousand feet. With no navigation lights on, Malik will never know it's there. It can quickly eliminate the roads that don't lead to houses. So that narrows it down to five. And if we're lucky we might be able to have Malik's place located by the time you get there. Then you can go in alone."

"Hold on," Culley said, and got out of his seat and went forward to kneel in the aisle at the entrance to the cockpit. "What's our ETA?" he asked the pilot.

The pilot glanced at one of the instruments. "Twenty-seven minutes."

Culley relayed the time to Gregus. "Houser's car is at the airport. We'll be en route to the area within thirty minutes. If the chopper hasn't pinpointed the place by the time we get there, we'll just have to try all five of the roads leading to houses until we find the right one."

"We've still got time, Mike," Gregus said, hearing the stress in Culley's voice. "The shrinks are just as sure that Malik will not kill Jenny immediately. And if he drove out of the warehouse in Brooklyn only five hours ago, it's unlikely he could have gotten back there that fast. If we find the place within a half hour after you land, you could be there before he arrives, or not long after."

"I'll need precise instructions from the airport to the road where the telephone company terminal is located."

"We're already working on that," Gregus said. "I had some equipment put on board the aircraft for you: night-vision goggles, and two-way radios with headsets and throat mikes. Call me on the radio as soon as you reach the car at the airport and I'll give you the directions to the terminal; we'll all be on the same frequency with the chopper, so he can advise you of any progress. We'll also have a Blackhawk chopper in a holding pattern out of hearing range. I've got a plane waiting to take me to the Farm now. I'll be on board the Blackhawk with a cleanup team. Once you have Malik secured and Jenny is safe, call us in."

"Just make sure you keep the Blackhawk well out of range," Culley said. "On a still night you can hear those things coming from five miles out."

"I'm aware of that," Gregus said. "There's also a sniper rifle on board the aircraft for you. In case you get the opportunity to take Malik out at a distance. It's a seven-millimeter Magnum with match grade ammunition and a night scope. It shoots point-of-aim, point-of-impact out to two hundred yards.

"This is as far as the reporter goes, Mike," Gregus added.

Culley looked at Houser sitting across the aisle from him. "No. I might need her help."

Gregus hesitated; then, after a long silence:

"Okay. It's your call. Hang in there. We're going to get Jenny back safe and sound. I can feel it."

"I pray to God you're right," Culley said, and hung up.

He turned to Houser. "Are you sure you want in on this part?"

"I was afraid you weren't going to ask."

He searched her eyes, and said, "Will you be able to pull the trigger if it comes to that? It's my daughter's life we're dealing with this time."

"Yes," Houser said with conviction.

As the Learjet streamed southward through the night sky, Culley filled Houser in on all he had learned from Gregus and how he planned to use the scout helicopter. He said nothing of the Blackhawk and the cleanup team.

"What's the Farm?" Houser asked.

"The CIA's training base at Camp Peary. It's near Williamsburg, Virginia, only about a thirty-minute flight from where we're going."

They both fell silent, deep in their own thoughts, Culley calculating the time since he'd seen Malik drive out of the warehouse. He estimated it at just over five hours. With approximately twenty-five minutes until they were on the ground, and another half hour to where the telephone-company terminal was located, it was conceivable he could get there in time.

37

FBI SPECIAL AGENT Jack Matthews sat watching a CNN news report on the television in the joint-task-force conference room with Charlottesville police chief Neal Brady. The anchor reported that it was believed the Mix & Match killer was still in the New York City area after eluding police at a warehouse in Brooklyn, where he was suspected of having killed two men and fled with a hostage—a young girl—although that had not been confirmed because the first officer on the scene, a Brooklyn detective, had not actually seen the hostage in the vehicle in which the suspect had fled.

The television screen was filled with a photograph of Malik as the anchor went on to say that the man's name was not known, but that he was the principal suspect in the hunt for the Mix & Match killer.

Matthews stared at the screen. The photograph was not the same as the one he'd had blown up and enhanced from Malik's driver's license and the Bureau had sent out to their network of field offices.

"Where the hell did they get that?" He immediately picked up the phone and dialed the number of the FBI's New York City field office.

"No one in this office gave the press Malik's name or the photograph from his driver's license," the special agent in charge of the New York office said. "We've complied with the director's order to keep his identity under wraps for the time being. I've never seen the picture the press has."

"Where did they get it?"

"From a New York City detective by the name of Grimaldi. He claims he got it from an informant in Brighton Beach. But I think he's lying."

"Why would he lie?"

"My guess is he's covering for someone."

Matthews suspected the fine hand of the CIA at work again, but dismissed the thought immediately; the last thing they would want was Malik's picture in the hands of the media. "How did the detective get on to the warehouse?"

"Claims he was following up a lead on the murder of the woman in Brighton Beach this morning; his informant also told him that it might be the same guy involved in a counterfeiting operation."

"Counterfeiting?"

"Yes. And that part rings true. Two of my people checked out the warehouse. There were definite signs that someone had printed a considerable amount of money there. And they found an empty pallet with CRANE PAPER COMPANY stenciled on it, which ties it to the hijacking of the currency paper the Secret Service have been looking for."

"Whom did Malik take as a hostage?"

"The detective claims he isn't certain and he doesn't want to speculate. He said his informant could have been wrong about that. Again, I think he's lying. But the problem is, he's one of the cops who helped the Secret Service recover the bulk of the paper three days after the hijacking, so it'd make sense he would be following up on the case. There's just enough of a ring of truth to his story to cover his ass for whatever he's up to. We weren't able to shake anything else out of him."

Matthews ended the conversation and turned to Chief Brady, who had been listening in on the speaker. "Maybe the hostage is someone he grabbed for his next victim," Brady said. "If that's the case, he could be on his way back here with her."

The telephone rang and Brady answered it. "It's for you. An Agent Burruss from your Richmond office."

Matthews put the phone on speaker again. He had forgotten about the task he had assigned Burruss—to check out one of the telephone numbers found on Malik's billing records. The call had been placed from Malik's shop to someone in Richmond. It was the last one on the list; the others had proved to be dry holes.

"I checked out the number you gave me," Burruss reported. "It's listed to a Robert E. Lawrence. He's eighty-four years old, wealthy, or at least he was at one time. Socially prominent, old Richmond family, lived here all his life. I talked to him on the phone, but his memory is a little foggy. He said he only remembers talking to two people in Charlottesville in the past few months. One was an old friend who called to remind him of an upcoming University of Virginia class reunion, which he didn't attend, and the other was a professor at the university who rented a weekend retreat he owns. He said he was not acquainted with anyone by the name of John Malik. He suggested the call may have been to his house-keeper; she's a divorcée with a number of boyfriends who occasionally call her at his home. But that didn't check out. He asked her and she didn't know anyone named Malik."

Matthews felt a sudden chill. "What was the name of the man he rented the weekend retreat to?"

Burruss checked his notes. "George Anderson."

"What's the location of the place he rented?"

Burruss hesitated. "Sorry, I didn't ask when he told me it was rented to a professor. I assumed he knew the man."

"Get over to his house and talk to him in person. Find out where the rented property is located, and show him the picture of Malik, see if he can ID him as Anderson."

"I'm on my way."

"How long will it take you to get there?"

"Maybe forty-five minutes."

"Call me immediately after you talk to him, regardless of what he says."

Matthews hung up and said to Brady, "Can we get someone to do a quick check to see if there's a George Anderson on the faculty at the university?"

"I'll get the chief of the university police to scare someone up."

The telephone rang again, and Matthews grabbed it. Burruss was back on the line.

"I called Lawrence's house to let him know I was coming. His housekeeper told me he's out for the evening, having dinner with friends. She doesn't know where, or what time he'll be home."

"What time did he leave?"

"Around seven o'clock."

Matthews looked at his watch. It was a few minutes before ten. "Get over there and see if you can track him down. Get a list of his friends from the housekeeper and start calling them until you come up with something."

∇

JOHN MALIK DROVE slowly along the deserted rural highway, his eyes searching the darkened woods at the side of the road. He spotted the fallen tree that served as his guidepost, and slowed almost to a stop as he turned off Route 609 onto a narrow dirt track all but hidden from view by the encroaching branches of the trees on either side. He stopped to get out and open the farm gate blocking the entrance to the property, then drove through and stopped again to close the gate, wrapping the length of chain around the post and snapping the lock back in place.

The Explorer rocked in and out of deep ruts in the roadbed as Malik drove slowly through the woods, down a steep incline that eventually leveled off where the road skirted the edge of a lake and wound its way to the clearing in front of the cabin. He parked the Explorer at the side of the cabin and went around to the back to unlock the door and turn on the lights, then returned to open the rear of the vehicle.

Jenny Culley's head still throbbed where Malik had struck her, but she was wide awake and struggling against her restraints as he tossed her over his shoulder in a fireman's carry. She kicked her bound legs and screamed muffled protests as he took her inside and placed her on top of the large butcher-block table in the center of the room that had once served as a slaughterhouse for the hunting camp.

Jenny quickly looked about the room before Malik rolled her onto her stomach and pinned her still-kicking legs with his body as he tied one of the leather restraining straps at the end of the table to one of her wrists before removing the tape binding her hands. He then grasped her other arm firmly and tied the second strap around her other wrist. He rolled her over on her back and pulled the straps snug against the rings embedded in the end of the table, raising her hands high above her head. He then repeated the process, securing her ankles with the straps at the opposite end, leaving her tied spread-eagled on top of the butcher's block with the tape still across her mouth.

He next went to the electronics console on the wall near the door leading into the interior of the cabin. He turned on the radio, tuned to his favorite station, filling the room with country music. Jenny's muffled cries stopped as Malik came back and leaned close to her, gently brushing the back of his hand along her cheek.

"Now, my little bitch, I'm going to remove the tape from your mouth," he said. "If you cry out, no one will hear you, but it will disturb the mood, and I will be forced to sew your lips shut unless you agree to behave; and I promise you, you won't like that."

Jenny's eyes grew wild with terror. She now believed she knew who the man was. She had seen the newscasts about the Mix & Match killer, and a few moments after the radio came on, and the song ended, she heard a commercial for a car dealer in

Charlottesville, and recalled the stories of the four college students who had been murdered and mutilated there. She lay on her back, staring up at the array of knives and saws and cleavers hanging from the overhead rack directly above her. She felt faint and weak, on the verge of hysteria, but she called upon her reserves of inner strength and remained quiet when Malik pulled the tape from her mouth.

"I have some preparations to make," Malik said. "So just lie back and enjoy the music while I go about my work."

Jenny's eyes followed Malik as he went to the far end of the room and began threading a video camera onto a tripod. With his back to her she twisted her hands in the leather thongs tied to her wrists and felt them give slightly. She kept working on them, stretching them a fraction of an inch at a time until Malik turned to face her again.

He carried the tripod-mounted video camera toward the butcher's block and placed it off to one side, putting his eye to the viewer and adjusting it.

"We're going to make a tape for your father," Malik said. His eyes had a glazed look to them now, and a small, sick smile was fixed permanently in place. "Sort of a fond remembrance."

Jenny felt a wave of nausea rising from within, but she closed her eyes and breathed deeply to hold it back. Her muscles contracted throughout her body and a whimper escaped from the back of her throat as she saw Malik approach with a large pair of cutting shears in his hand.

"No! Please!"

"Quiet, now. Not to worry. I'm only going to

cut away your clothes," Malik said, his voice soft and soothing.

He opened the blades of the shears and began cutting up the leg of the cotton slacks Jenny wore. She flinched at the touch of the cold steel as the dull edge of the blade lightly brushed against the bare skin of her calf and moved upward.

"Be still. This is one of my favorite things. And I do like to take my time with it. If you move I may cut you by mistake. And you wouldn't want that, would you?" His voice was eerie, singsong, almost a chant.

Jenny lay as still as she possibly could, but a tremor shook her entire body as Malik continued cutting, removing her belt before snipping through the waistband of the slacks and then starting on the other leg. With a final snip he pulled the slacks from beneath her and tossed them into a corner. With one quick motion he cut through her bikini-style panties and pulled them off, holding them to his face and breathing deeply before tossing them aside. He again went to the other end of the room, only to return with a small pair of scissors.

Jenny jumped with an involuntary spasm as she felt the cold steel touch the inside of her thighs. She raised her head to see Malik using his fingernails to gently brush her pubic hairs upward and snip them off until nothing but stubble remained. He began running his hand slowly down the inside of her legs from top to bottom as he hummed softly to the music coming from the radio.

He felt the power now; the ultimate power of life and death. He was in complete control of the beautiful little bitch lying before him. He would take his time, be more inventive, savor each moment, and in the end present Michael Timothy Culley with a creative masterpiece for his eternal viewing pleasure.

With Malik's attention elsewhere Jenny again worked her hands against the leather straps, closely watching him as she did. She felt them give a little more, but not nearly enough, then stopped abruptly when Malik quit stroking her legs and left the table, returning with the large shears. He began to cut her blouse away, and Jenny closed her eyes and cried softly. *Please, Daddy. Please come and get me,* she silently repeated over and over as Malik continued humming, cutting away at her blouse.

▽

THE HUGHES DEFENDER scout helicopter flew the perimeter of the three square miles of heavily wooded terrain below from two miles out at an altitude of six thousand feet. The Forward Looking Infrared optics mounted on the aircraft turned the night to a green-tinted day, displaying what they saw on a monitor in the cockpit. The copilot's eyes were fixed on the FLIR monitor, watching the ground and the roads leading into the area as the pilot banked into a steep turn, then leveled off as he aligned the helicopter with another target.

The copilot leaned in close as an old farmhouse at the end of an unpaved road off Route 609 appeared on the monitor. The property looked deserted. No interior lights were on in the house. He reached over and turned on the Thermal Imager, looking for heat signatures on another screen to the right of the FLIR monitor.

The Thermal Imager was operating in an optimum environment: the crisp October night was clear and calm and cold, the air temperature at ground level approximately fifty-five degrees. While the Forward Looking Infrared was capable of detecting exceptionally hot areas at its point of focus, it was incapable of detecting anything or anyone concealed from the naked eye if the temperature difference of the surroundings did not vary greatly. The Thermal Imager, highly sensitive to the smallest temperature differences, as small as two degrees, produced thermal pictures of invisible heat radiation, which all living things emit in relation to the area around them. It was capable of discerning and delineating the heat signature of objects or persons in daylight, or in complete darkness, inside a structure, or hiding under natural cover such as trees or underbrush, and could easily distinguish between an animal and a human being, as well as detect the residual heat from the engines, tires, and brakes of a recently driven vehicle, displaying them on the cockpit screen in varying shades of gray and white, depending on the intensity of the heat the object radiated.

The copilot studied the FLIR screen as the optics zoomed in on the farmhouse; a pickup truck and a small compact car were parked in front of it. He then went back to the Thermal Imager screen.

"I'm getting a low heat signature from the house," he said to the pilot, who was flying the aircraft using the night-vision goggles attached to his helmet. "The chimney's hot. They must have had a fire going, but it's out now. And neither one of the vehicles has been driven recently, probably not in four or five hours. I'd say they've been home all evening and are tucked away in bed."

The copilot zoomed the Imager optics in to the maximum. Two smaller white spots glowed on the screen. "Yep. Two people, close together, in a second-floor room at the left rear corner. Neither one of them is moving."

"That's three down and two to go," the pilot said. "The double-wide trailer in the northeast section of the quadrant, and the place with the lake in front of it."

The pilot banked hard to the left and a few minutes later maneuvered the helicopter into position to look directly at the double-wide trailer in a small clearing at the end of a long, winding road. The copilot again studied both monitors. A bright white sphere bloomed on the Thermal Imager screen, coming from the hood of a four-wheel drive vehicle he recognized as a Chevrolet Blazer. It was parked in front of the trailer.

"Got a real hot spot. That vehicle was driven no more than fifteen minutes ago. Brakes and tires are still warm too." He glanced at the FLIR screen looking for any activity around the trailer, seeing that the lights were burning brightly inside. "I'd say he just got home."

He again zoomed in with the Imager and the screen flared with two more heat signatures. "Two people in the front room off the entrance. Some movement. Could be them."

"Let's check out the last one," the pilot said. "See if we can rule it out." He again swung the aircraft around, and maneuvered it into position to observe the cabin by the lake.

Lights glowed from a room at the back of the cabin and the Ford Explorer parked outside flared just as brightly on the Thermal Imager screen as the Blazer had, giving every indication that it, too, had been recently driven.

"The cabin's got a metal roof," the copilot said. "I'm not getting as clear a reading, but it looks like there are two people in there. I'd say we've got two solid possibles."

"That's as far as we can narrow it down from here," the pilot said. "Is the Blackhawk up yet?"

The copilot checked the radar screen and saw a large blip to the southeast of their present position.

"Looks like it," the copilot said. "I'll give him a try."

The copilot keyed his radio microphone. "Blackhawk, this is Defender. Do you read?"

There was a brief pause, then Gregus's voice came up. "Defender, this is Blackhawk. We're eighty miles out and closing."

The copilot reported what they had found, and then heard Gregus's voice again.

"Culley should be in your immediate area any minute. He'll be coming in from the north off Route Six-fifteen. Which place is closer to his avenue of approach?"

"The double-wide trailer," the copilot said.

"Then guide him in there first."

The copilot was scanning the narrow two-lane ribbons of blacktop that snaked their way through the heavily wooded rural section of northern Fluvanna County, watching for any sign of an approaching vehicle, when he saw headlights appear from beneath a canopied section of the road at the juncture where Route 609 branched off Route 615.

"I think I've got him," he said, continuing to watch as the small car veered left onto Route 609 and headed toward them.

38

CULLEY USED THE cellular telephone in the Porsche to maintain contact with Hack at the twenty-four-hour operations center in the safe house in Alexandria. The computer whiz was using an automap program to direct them from the airport, providing the route numbers and the precise mileage to each turnoff, allowing them to drive at maximum speed without watching for road signs.

As Houser swung onto Route 609, Culley thanked Hack for his help and hung up the cellular phone. He immediately switched on the small two-way radios, gotten from the equipment bag in the Learjet, and clipped them to his and Houser's waistbands, then put the tiny earpiece receivers and the voice-activated throat microphones in place as Houser kept her full attention on the road. They were now in direct contact with the scout helicopter.

"Defender, this is Culley. Can you see us yet?"

The pilot was flying a pattern that, from an altitude of six thousand feet, provided a panoramic view of the area around both the double-wide trailer and the cabin at the lake.

"That's affirmative, Culley; I see you," the co-pilot answered, his eyes on the headlights of the Porsche as it sped along the winding road. "We have the location narrowed down to two sites. The first is approximately one mile from your present location. You'll see a dirt road leading off the highway on your left, just past a utility pole. The entrance drive is about three quarters of a mile long, leading to a small clearing in the woods. A double-wide trailer is at the end of the road, and a Chevrolet Blazer is parked in front of it. The last stretch of the road is out in the open, so you'll want to cut your lights before you come out of the trees."

Houser sped into a tight turn and came out of it to again hear the copilot's calm, deliberate voice in her earpiece. "Okay, another hundred meters and you'll see the utility pole. The turnoff is ten meters past that."

Houser slowed as the pole came into view, then downshifted and swung onto the dirt road leading through the woods. She dropped into second gear, moving slowly over the uneven surface. She turned off the headlights, finding that the parking lights provided all the illumination she needed to follow the narrow track.

Culley reached into his leather carryall in the rear of the Porsche and got his backup gun, strapping the ankle holster securely on the inside of his lower left leg beneath his jeans. He next removed two pairs of night-vision goggles from the satchel taken from the Lear and placed them in his lap, then checked the

semiautomatic pistol in his shoulder holster and replaced the rounds expended earlier that day.

Houser crept down a steep section of the dirt
track, and heard the copilot again.

"At the bottom of the grade you're on, the road
turns sharply to the right, then it's twenty meters
until you hit the clearing. Cut the rest of your lights
now."

Houser did as instructed, holding her head steady
as Culley fitted her with a pair of night-vision goggles, turned them on, and pulled them in place over
her eyes. He then put on his own goggles and began
scanning the green-tinted terrain ahead.

"No one is outside the trailer," the copilot reported, his eyes flicking back and forth from the
FLIR screen to the Thermal Imager screen as he
spoke. "There are two people inside. Both in the
front room immediately off the entrance. They appear to be stationary at the moment."

Culley again reached into the back of the car. He
took the sniper rifle from its case as Houser cut the
engine and came to a stop, hidden from view of the
trailer behind a stand of cedar trees lining one side of
the road at the edge of the clearing.

"Let us know if there's any movement inside the
trailer while we're getting into position," Culley said,
and reached up to click off the switch for the interior
light that came on when the doors opened.

The clearing was bright with the light of the full
moon, and both Culley and Houser removed the
cumbersome night-vision goggles, realizing that the
ambient light was all they needed at the moment.
Houser slipped her goggles inside the bellows pocket
of her shoulder bag after removing her weapon, and

Culley put his goggles in the satchel that contained the extra ammunition for the sniper rifle, slinging the satchel across his back as they got out of the car.

They kept to the edge of the road, staying low and using thick clumps of underbrush to move from cover to cover as they closed in. They stopped twenty feet from the front of the trailer behind a tall oak tree, and Culley, whispering into the throat mike, told Houser to go around and cover the rear entrance.

"Let me know when you're in position," he added.

Houser moved out in a low crouch, disappearing around the back of the trailer as Culley ran forward to stand flat against the outside wall, beside a picture window to the left of the front entrance.

He heard Houser through his earpiece, her voice a soft whisper. "There's only one rear exit. I'm behind a small outbuilding just to the left of it."

"I'm going to try to get a look inside," Culley said. "Be alert for any reaction if they spot me."

Culley heard voices inside, and background music, and realized that what he was hearing was a television program. He inched closer to the picture window, then peeked around the edge for no more than a second, and pulled his head back. The quick glimpse of the two people in the reflected light from the television was enough to tell him they had the wrong place.

"Defender. Are you certain there are only two people in the trailer?"

"Positive," the copilot replied.

"Then we're at the wrong location. A man and a woman are sitting on a sofa watching television. The man is definitely not Malik, and the woman isn't my daughter."

"Then it's got to be the cabin on the lake," the copilot said. "Get out of there fast. When you reach the top of the driveway, I'll direct you into the other place."

Houser heard the conversation over her radio, and came around from behind the trailer, joining Culley as they ran as fast as they could back to the Porsche. Houser used the loose surface of the road to her advantage, spinning the nimble sports car around in a tight circle and racing back up the road through the woods.

▽

JACK MATTHEWS AND Charlottesville police chief Neal Brady sat drinking coffee and impatiently pacing the length of the task-force conference room. It had been over an hour since they last talked with Burruss in Richmond. The high-pitched chirp of the telephone caused both men to jump and reach for it, with Matthews grabbing it from its cradle before it could ring again.

"George Anderson and John Malik are one and the same," Burruss said, his voice crackling with excitement. "Lawrence rented the property to him just over a month ago."

"Where is it?" Matthews asked.

Burruss told him. "And get this. It's a hunting camp, complete with its own slaughterhouse for dressing out the game, and large freezer units for storing it."

"Good work," Matthews said, and immediately hung up the phone.

Brady had been listening in on the speaker. "I know the general area. It's about forty-five minutes from here."

"We've got to set up a staging area as close to the place as possible."

Brady went to the large-scale Fluvanna County map on the wall and traced his finger along the roads leading into Route 609. "There's a gravel quarry within three miles of the hunting camp. It's got a large parking area for loading the trucks that haul the stuff out of there."

"Is it large enough to handle two helicopters?"

"More than that."

"Do you know the county sheriff?"

"Yes. Burt Edwards. He's a good, solid cop."

"Call him and tell him to get as many of his deputies as possible to the gravel quarry, and to stand by until we get there. Don't tell him what's going down. We'll fill him in on the operation when we arrive. I don't want anyone near that camp until we've got everyone in place and are certain Malik is there."

"I can have our SWAT team ready to go within the hour," Brady said.

"I appreciate the offer, Chief, but we have our own Hostage Rescue Teams based at Quantico. They're on a two-hour alert status, and they can get here even sooner if need be. I'd rather use them—this is what they train for all the time. You can bring your men in for backup if you like."

▽

CULLEY CURSED UNDER his breath at finding the locked gate at the head of the road leading into the property.

"Pop the trunk lid," he said over the radio to Houser, and ran back to the car to get the jack handle, returning to snap the lock off the gate, remove the chain, and swing it open.

Houser closed the trunk and pulled past the open gate, pausing as Culley jumped back in the car. She drove slowly through the woods along the deeply rutted dirt track, staying to the right, away from where the soft shoulder of the roadbed had been washed out by the runoff from a recent heavy rain. The low-slung Porsche bottomed out twice in the ruts, but Houser kept it moving slowly ahead, dropping into first gear as they started down a steep incline.

The voice of the helicopter's copilot came over the radio. He could clearly see just how far ahead the car's headlights were reaching.

"Cut your lights now," he said. "At the bottom of the grade the road curves to the left and comes out of the woods. You don't want to take the car any farther than that. The cabin is approximately two hundred meters from where you will first see the lake."

Houser slipped the Porsche into neutral and turned off the engine. The moonlight filtering down through the trees provided just enough light as she drifted to a stop before she came out of the woods into the clearing. She and Culley got out of the car and ran along the edge of the road, using the waist-high grass bordering the lake as cover.

Houser stayed on Culley's heels, stopping and

kneeling beside him as they reached a spot to the left of the front of the cabin, where an old rowboat lay overturned in the high grass ten yards out from the porch.

Culley saw the light coming from a small window at the side toward the back. The rest of the cabin was dark. He whispered into his throat microphone, "Defender, are they still in the back room?"

"That's affirmative," the copilot said. "There's no one else in the house, and no one on the grounds outside."

"Cover the front," Culley said to Houser. "I'm going around to the window." He paused and looked hard at her. "If you have a clear shot, don't hesitate. Empty the gun into him."

Houser nodded, and took cover behind the overturned boat, training her weapon on the front door. Culley unslung the sniper rifle from across his back and went around to the side of the cabin, stopping where the Explorer was parked to look inside the open driver's-side window. The keys were in the ignition, and he reached in and removed them and put them in his pocket before running back under cover of a line of oak and maple trees that flanked the cabin.

∇

JENNY'S NAKED BODY shook with uncontrollable tremors as Malik pulled the straight razor through the layer of shaving cream that covered her from the waist down. He finished shaving her legs, and quickly removed the last of the pubic hair stubble, humming along to the sad country ballad on the radio as he toweled the excess shaving cream from her lower body.

"Now, my little bitch. Time to remove your lovely tresses," he said. "I find nothing sexier than a woman with a shaved head."

Malik smiled contentedly, and left the butcher's block, going to the far end of the room to get the scissors he had used earlier.

Jenny's eyes immediately went to the straight razor on the table near her knees beside the can of shaving cream. She saw her opportunity, and desperately tried to steel herself for what she had to do. She had never purposely hurt another living thing in her life, but she knew there was no choice if she was to survive.

While Malik was occupied with shaving her legs, she had again worked on the leather straps around her wrists, stretching them to the point where she was certain she could slip her hands through. She closed her eyes, said a silent prayer, then pulled her arms downward with all of her strength.

Her left hand came out easily; the right caught at the large knuckle of her thumb. She tugged again, her eyes never leaving Malik; his back still to her. Her right hand came free, and she quickly reached down and grabbed the straight razor. She then put her hands high above her head, taking the leather straps in her fingers, and briefly twirling her hands until the straps wrapped twice around her wrists. She held the razor off the end of the table, hoping that Malik would not see it, or the dangling ends of the straps. Another tremor shook her as she saw him turn back toward the table, pausing to adjust the lens of the video camera to frame the upper portion of her body.

▽

Culley stood inside the tree line at the side of the cabin, twenty yards from the window facing directly toward him. He was deep in shadow, and no one looking out could possibly see him. He brought the sniper rifle to his shoulder, the image in the telescopic night-vision sight appearing much brighter as he looked through the window into the well-lit room.

His angle of view precluded him from seeing all but a small section of one end of the room—a wall of shelves containing books and stereo equipment. He began to move to his right, one step at a time, staying in the shadows beneath the trees, pausing to study each section of the room as it came into his field of vision through the telescopic sight.

He fixed his gaze on a tripod-mounted video camera set off to the side of a large butcher-block table, then slowly moved the scope to track in the direction the lens of the video camera was pointing. He stiffened at the sight of a bare foot as it came into focus, then let out a rush of air as though he had been kicked in the chest.

"Oh, my God!" he gasped, nearly dropping the rifle at seeing Jenny, naked, tied spread-eagled on the large wooden table.

"What's wrong?" It was Houser, she had heard him over the radio. "Culley!"

"Stay where you are," he said, quickly recovering from the shock of what he saw. "Jenny's in there. I don't see Malik."

"Is Jenny okay?"

"I don't know," he said.

Culley put his eye back to the scope and saw Jenny's head move. "She's alive," he whispered over the radio.

"Thank God," Houser said.

Culley moved the telescopic sight the length of Jenny's body. It appeared that she had not yet been physically harmed. He focused on her head and arms. Her eyes were open, staring toward Malik. Her right arm was on the side of the table facing the window, and Culley noticed something in her hand, draped over the top edge of the table. He saw that she was gripping the leather strap to make it appear as though it was still tied to her wrist. But it definitely was not. Culley focused directly on her hand, and saw the blade of the straight razor.

He kept his eye to the scope, slowly traversing what he could see of the room, looking for Malik, finally spotting him as he came into view from the extreme right corner of the window. He was peering through the lens of the video camera, adjusting the focus.

"Okay. Malik's in the room with her," Culley said into the throat microphone. "I may have a shot."

Culley moved to his left, a step at a time, his eye to the telescopic sight, looking for an angld that would allow him a clear kill-shot. He braced the rifle against the trunk of a tree and placed the cross hairs of the scope on the side of Malik's head. He took a deep breath, let half of it out, and slowly squeezed the trigger, instantly releasing the pressure when Malik's head moved out of the cross hairs.

He took aim again, only to have Malik move completely out of the sight picture. Believing that he knew what Jenny was about to do, he decided against chancing the shot at all. She might be cut badly by the cone of broken glass that would spread out across the room at a ninety-degree angle from where the bullet shattered the window. Or if the glass was Thermopane, thicker than normal, the deflection of the bullet as it penetrated the window could be enough to prevent a one-shot kill, providing Malik the opportunity to kill Jenny before he could stop him.

"Keep watching the front of the house," he said to Houser over the radio. "I'm going around to the back to see if there's a door opening directly into the room they're in."

Culley dropped the sniper rifle and the satchel to the ground, lightening his load as he ran along the tree line. Once out of the line of sight from the window, he cut across the open area to the back of the cabin. He immediately saw the door, and drew his pistol from his shoulder holster and pressed himself flat against the outside wall. He quickly examined the heavy pine door. If it was locked, it would take more than one kick to knock it open. He could hear the music inside the room, and hoping it would mask what he was doing, he slowly turned the doorknob, finding it locked.

▽

JENNY'S HANDS were shaking so badly, she almost dropped the razor, catching it just as it began to slip from her grasp. Malik left the video camera and approached the butcher-block table, clicking the blades of the scissors to the beat of an uptempo tune he particularly liked. Jenny's breathing became erratic

as she tensed, tightening her grip on the straight
razor, terrified by what she had to do.

Malik leaned over the table and ran his hand
through her hair, and raised the scissors to make the
first cut. Jenny lashed out with the razor. Once.
Twice. And then a third time.

"Get away from me! Get away!" she screamed at
the top of her lungs as the blade cut deeply into
Malik's arm in two places, then across his shoulder as
he straightened up and drew back. Jenny sat upright,
bending forward to cut at the straps binding her legs
as Malik stood staring at her in shock and disbelief.

"You filthy little bitch!" he roared in anger, then
backed away from the table as Jenny slashed at him
again, missing his stomach by a fraction of an inch.

Malik looked at the dark bloodstains spreading
down his sleeve and across the front of his shirt. He
dropped the scissors and grabbed a ten-inch carving
knife from the rack above the table.

"Filthy little bitch!" he shouted again, and was
about to lunge forward when he heard the loud
pounding at the door at the back of the room. For a
moment he was confused, frozen in position, uncertain of what to do, the knife held above his head,
ready to swing at Jenny as she cut the last strap free
from her ankles.

Instinct took over, and Malik looked about for
his gun, immediately realizing that he had left it,
along with the submachine gun he had taken from
the warehouse, outside in the Explorer. He saw the
door hinges ripping from the frame as the pounding
continued. Four rapid shots exploded into the lock
from outside. Another forceful kick and the door
flew inward, hanging loosely from the hinges.

Malik ran through the doorway into the interior of the cabin at the same moment Culley came crashing into the room.

"Daddy!" Jenny screamed, and ran toward him.

Culley put an arm around her shoulder, and pulled her into a corner, placing himself in front of her as the barrel of his gun followed his eyes around the room.

"Where did he go?"

"He ran into the other room."

"Culley? What's happening?" Houser had heard the shots and his voice over the radio. "Are you all right?"

"I'm okay. He may be coming your way."

"I'm still in position behind the boat."

"Get back here with me," Culley said. "Stay inside the tree line until you get to the rear of the cabin. Malik is somewhere in the house. I want you to take care of Jenny while I go after him."

Culley saw a long rain slicker hanging on a nail next to the door and reached to grab it, handing it to Jenny, who quickly pulled it on and wrapped it around herself.

"The woman with me is Julie Houser. I want you to go with her."

"Don't leave me, Daddy. Please don't leave."

"You'll be all right, honey. I promise. She's an ex-cop. She knows what she's doing."

"No, Daddy. Stay with me."

"I've got to go after him."

Houser appeared in the doorway, her gun sweeping the interior of the room before she rushed inside to where Culley and Jenny stood in the corner behind the door.

Both the pilot and copilot in the scout helicopter had heard the radio transmissions between Culley and Houser and understood the situation. With no further need to conceal their presence the pilot quickly closed in on the property.

The copilot stared at the Imager screen, seeing a low heat signature near the front of the house. "Culley, your target is still in the house."

"Take Jenny outside, into the woods," Culley said to Houser. "Try to work your way back to the car."

The copilot glanced at the FLIR screen, scanning the clearing in front of the house, then checking the Imager again to make certain Malik was still inside.

"Houser, you and the girl have a clear path out the back and down to the lake," the copilot said. "Make a run for it. If Malik comes out of the house and heads in your direction, I'll see him long before he can see you."

"Be careful, Daddy. He's insane," Jenny said, then ran out the door with Houser holding on to her arm.

▽

MALIK SCRAMBLED across the living-room floor on all fours until he reached the storage closet at the front entrance. He pulled open the closet door and grabbed the lightweight bulletproof vest lying beside a twelve-gauge pump shotgun that was propped in the corner. He next took a box of three-inch Magnum shells, loaded four of them into the magazine, pumped one into the chamber, and crammed as many as he could into the pockets of his slacks.

His wounds were not painful, but he paused to examine them. The diagonal cut across his shoulder was superficial, but the two cuts on his arm had gone deep and were bleeding heavily. He grabbed a scarf from the closet, wrapped it around his arm, covering both cuts, and used his teeth to aid in tying the makeshift bandage tight. He then pulled on the bulletproof vest and slipped into a light windbreaker, zipping it up to hide the body armor.

He rose to one knee and listened for footsteps. He heard nothing, glanced out the window in the front door, and checked the clearing down to the shore of the lake. Seeing no one, he got to his feet, quietly opened the door, and stepped out onto the porch. He listened again, heard what he recognized as an approaching helicopter, ran the length of the porch, and vaulted the rail, landing in a clump of bushes below.

Culley cleared the doorway leading into the kitchen and took cover behind the half-wall separating it from the living room. He did a quick look around the corner, then pulled back, seeing little in the darkened room.

Outside, Malik crouched low and ran around to where he had parked the Ford Explorer. Upon discovering that the keys were not in the ignition where he had left them, he ran around to the back of the cabin and paused, listening and watching for Culley.

Defender's copilot kept his eyes on the Thermal Imager screen as the pilot dropped down to treetop level and made a straight-in run toward the clearing and the cabin.

Thirty-five miles farther out, Gregus, seated in

the back of the Blackhawk, had also monitored all of the radio transmissions, and he now ordered the pilot to close in on the cabin.

Defender's copilot saw a small white sphere bloom on the Imager screen as the helicopter came in low over the clearing. Two more ghostly white images appeared forty yards to the left of it.

"Houser, report your position," the copilot said.

"We're in the woods to the left of the cabin."

"Stay in the high grass and continue down to the shore of the lake," the copilot said. "You have a clear path back to the car."

He looked again at the Imager screen and saw Houser and Jenny come out from beneath the trees and run toward the lake. The first image he had seen was now moving, appearing as a long white streak leading from the rear of the cabin into the woods on the opposite side. He detected a third heat signature still inside the cabin and reasoned it to be Culley, but wanted to be certain.

"Culley, are you inside the cabin?"

"Yes. Approaching the front door."

"Your target has moved into the woods to the right of the porch. You are clear to exit."

Culley ran outside, his thermal image immediately brighter on the screen.

"Your target is approximately ten meters into the woods and still moving away from you," the copilot said.

Culley ran across the clearing into the woods, reaching for the satchel containing the night-vision goggles he had earlier slung across his back, then realizing that he had left it on the ground with the rifle.

"Your target has stopped running," the copilot reported. "He is approximately forty meters at your ten o'clock." He looked to the FLIR screen, but the infrared optics revealed nothing through the dense foliage. He went back to the Imager screen as the helicopter swung around to move in over the spot where Malik had stopped. A white spot glowed from behind a deadfall. "Looks like he's waiting in ambush."

Culley moved cautiously ahead, from tree to tree, peering through the pale moonlight filtering down to the forest floor.

Malik looked up through a break in the trees to see the helicopter directly above him, hovering at seventy or eighty feet from the ground, the downdraft from the rotor blades showering him with leaves.

"Your target is now ten meters from your present position," the copilot said, watching Culley's progress through the woods.

At that moment Culley heard the roar of the shotgun and saw the muzzle flash. He dived to the ground as a storm of pellets tore through the woods to his immediate left. He heard the distinctive sound of another round being pumped into the shotgun, followed by a second blast that went well over his head but would have hit him had he not dropped to the ground.

Culley, flat on his stomach, fired three rapid-fire shots at the point where he had seen the muzzle flash, then immediately rolled to his right. The shotgun roared again, the blast tearing into the ground where he had been lying.

Malik jumped to his feet and crashed through the underbrush, stopping abruptly where the trees ended at a long, narrow clearing cut from the forest to accommodate the power lines that ran through the property. He heard the helicopter coming closer, and looked up to see it approaching from behind, skimming the treetops as it swung into position to follow him.

"Your target has moved," the copilot reported to Culley. "He is now thirty meters at your two o'clock. Stationary at the edge of a power-line clearing."

Culley got to his feet and moved quickly in the direction of the clearing. He slowed when he saw the break in the trees ahead, his eyes searching the shadows.

The moonlit clearing was no more than thirty yards wide, the woods dark and deep on the other side. Malik bolted from beneath the trees, looking over his shoulder at the helicopter as it bore down on him, then rose quickly to avoid the power lines in its path. Once on the other side of the clearing, Malik knew he would have an excellent ambush position, with a clear shot at Culley as he came across the open space in the bright moonlight. He was halfway there, glancing back over his shoulder, when he stumbled on a rock in his path, fought to regain his balance, then fell, the shotgun flying from his hands as he landed.

He immediately rose to his knees and felt the ground around him, searching for the shotgun, unable to see it in the waist-high grass. He crawled in a small circle of where he had fallen, and found the weapon just as the helicopter swung into position on the opposite side of the clearing, hovering above the trees to mark his location for Culley.

Malik rolled onto his back and fired at the helicopter; the pellets ricocheted harmlessly off the armor plating beneath the cockpit. He pumped another round into the chamber and fired again, this time hitting the instrument pods attached to the exterior of the undercarriage.

The small scout helicopter, with no weapons to return fire, pulled quickly away, rising out of range. But the damage had been done. The instrument package had been hit.

"Shit!" the copilot said. "He knocked out the Imager optics."

Culley heard him over the radio as he reached the edge of the clearing. He stopped just inside the tree line, scanning the high grass for any sign of Malik. "Where is he?" he asked the copilot.

"The muzzle flashes came from about twenty feet into the grass from the far side of the clearing," the copilot replied, his eyes now fixed on the green-tinted screen of the Forward Looking Infrared Radar. "If he's made it into the trees, we've got a problem. The FLIR can't penetrate the heavy foliage."

But Malik had not yet reached the woods. He rose to one knee, his head and shoulders just above the grass, checking the clearing before he moved on. He saw Culley step into the open and move slowly toward him, his gun in a two-handed grip, sweeping the area ahead. Malik quickly pumped another round into the chamber, but at the sound of the shotgun's pump action, Culley was on him, pinpointing his location and instantly aligning his sights on the partially silhouetted figure thirty feet away. He fired twice before Malik could get off a shot. The two rounds hit dead center in his chest, throwing him flat on his back and out of sight in the high grass as the shotgun discharged harmlessly into the air.

Culley knew his shots had been accurate, but he still advanced cautiously toward the spot where Malik had fallen.

"He's down," he said over the radio as he moved in closer. "I hit him twice in the chest. I've lost visual contact, but I don't see any movement in the grass."

"I'll see if I can spot him," the copilot said as the pilot maneuvered the helicopter back into position to observe the clearing.

The two hollow-point bullets would have killed Malik instantly had they not struck the breastplate built into the bulletproof vest. But the vest had done its job, preventing any damage to Malik other than a bruised chest and momentarily knocking the wind out of him. Within seconds after being hit, he began low-crawling through the grass, using his elbows to pull himself forward. He reached the edge of the woods just as the helicopter swung back into position directly overhead at treetop level.

The copilot studied the FLIR screen but saw no sign of Malik in the clearing. He watched as Culley reached the spot where Malik had fallen, moving slowly over the area looking for the body.

"The son of a bitch is gone," Culley said. "I hit him with both shots. I'm sure of it."

"Then he's got to be wearing body armor."

In the glow of the moonlight, Culley then noticed the trail of flattened grass leading off toward the woods on the far side. At that same instant, he again heard the sound of the pump action on the shotgun. He immediately dived to the ground, a split second before the storm of steel pellets flew over his head, pinging off the power-line tower behind him.

Malik got to his feet and ran deeper into the woods, then paused to get his bearings. There was nothing but forest and fields for miles on three sides of him, and he headed off to his right, back toward the road that led into the property.

"Culley!" It was Houser. She had taken off her radio headset when she and Jenny reached the Porsche, but upon hearing the gunfire, she slipped it back on. "Are you all right?"

"I'm fine. How's Jenny?"

"She's okay. Her father's daughter." Jenny was now fully dressed, wearing clothes Houser had given her from her luggage in the trunk. "We're waiting where we left the car. Is it over?"

"Not yet."

Gregus came up on the radio. The Blackhawk was fast approaching the cabin site. "Houser, stay off this frequency."

Houser complied, taking off the headset as she heard the noise of the much larger helicopter off in the distance.

Culley began crawling toward the section of woods where he saw the muzzle flash when Malik had fired at him. "Any sign of him, Defender?"

"No," the copilot replied. The pilot had climbed to a higher altitude to allow them a view of a much broader area, but most of what lay below was dense woods. The copilot scanned the few open grassy patches, but saw no one other than Culley in the immediate area.

Malik ran through the woods at a dog trot, pausing occasionally to listen for the helicopter. He smiled to himself as he realized that it was now searching the area north of where he had entered the woods, in the opposite direction from which he was now headed as he ran along the edge of the clearing in the deep shadows beneath the trees. He paused to listen for Culley, but heard only the night sounds of the forest and the distant noise of the helicopter's rotors. He knelt briefly at the edge of the clearing, studying the open grassy area before dashing across to double back in the direction of the lake and the road leading to the cabin.

The brief, darting shadow on the FLIR screen appeared just as the pilot swung the craft around to cover another sector. The copilot had seen it only as a quick movement in his peripheral vision, but recognized it for what it was just before it disappeared beneath the trees.

"Culley! Your target is a quarter of a mile south of you; he's doubling back toward the cabin!"

"Are you sure?" Culley stopped moving through the trees; a sudden icy chill ran down his spine.

"Positive. He just crossed the clearing." The copilot looked at the terrain features, comparing them to Malik's line of movement. "He's moving in a direct line toward the lake. My guess is he's going back for his car."

"I've got the keys. That's probably the first thing he checked when he came out of the cabin. He's going after the Porsche," Culley said. "Houser!" There was no response. "Houser!" he tried again, then remembered that Gregus had told her to stay off the frequency. She had probably taken off her headset and could not hear him.

Culley turned and ran back through the woods,

breaking out of the trees into the power-line clearing where he could run flat out in the direction Malik had last been seen.

Defender banked steeply and roared overhead, closing in on the area around the lake. The copilot watched the terrain below, using both the FLIR screen and his natural vision. As the helicopter approached the lake, he saw that the tree line ran to within six to eight feet of where the Porsche was parked. Houser and Jenny were standing near the front of it. If Malik stayed in the woods, under the thick canopy of leaves, they would be unable to spot him until he was close enough to easily kill them.

The pilot's voice came over the radio. "Culley, I'm going to close on the car and make a couple of low passes, get their attention. Maybe drive Malik away from the area."

"Can you pick them up and pull them out of there?"

"No can do. This is a two-man cockpit; no backseat."

The copilot, watching Culley running down the open area, added, "Ten more meters to where your target entered the woods," he said. "Then you'll be in a straight line to where the Porsche is parked."

Culley made no reply. He was running as fast as he could when he cut into the woods, stumbling and thrashing through the underbrush, swatting at the low-hanging branches.

The pilot of the scout helicopter brought the craft in low over the trees, dropping even lower over the surface of the lake. He headed straight for where the Porsche was parked on the road leading into the cabin. The car was partially obscured by overhanging branches where the road came out of the woods, but the front half was out in the open. He pulled up with only seconds to spare, the skids of the helicopter less than six feet from the roof of the Porsche.

Houser and Jenny, startled by the maneuver, ducked down, then turned to watch the helicopter make a quick, agile one-hundred-eighty-degree turn and head back toward the car. It passed dangerously low overhead again, this time turning to hover less than fifteen feet from the ground ten yards from the car.

Houser stared in confusion, and in the glow from the cockpit saw the copilot gesturing wildly toward the woods around the car. She immediately understood and pulled Jenny to the ground behind the Porsche as she reached inside her shoulder bag and took out her gun. The pilot, seeing that she understood the danger, rose quickly to an altitude that allowed him to survey the area around them.

"What is it?" Jenny said.

"Malik must be headed this way. Just stay down."

Houser rose to a half crouch and moved her eyes slowly along the perimeter of the woods, watching for any movement in the deep shadows. Remembering the headset, she grabbed it from the hood of the car and pulled it on.

"Culley! Is Malik coming after us?"

"Yes, he's headed in your direction," Culley said as he continued running, his breathing heavy and labored.

"Where are you?" Her eyes continued to scan the avenues of approach from the woods to the car.

Culley could now see the shimmering surface of the lake through the trees. "I'm almost there."

"You want me to drive out of here with Jenny?"

"No. If Malik's anywhere in the woods along the road, he could kill you as you drive past. Sit tight."

"Stay close," Houser said to Jenny, "and don't leave my side no matter what."

Malik waited until the helicopter rose to sixty feet above the ground and began working its way back and forth along the edge of the woods in the vicinity of the Porsche. He stepped from behind a tree, still within the shadows of the forest, but only eight feet from where Houser and Jenny were crouched behind the car, their backs to him, completely unaware of his presence.

"Good evening, ladies."

Houser and Jenny were startled by the sound of his voice and looked around to see Malik standing at the edge of the woods, pointing a shotgun at them.

"Stay calm, my little bitches. You," he said, pointing the barrel of the shotgun directly at Houser. "I want you to get in the car, turn it around, and drive up the road until it is completely under cover of the trees, then stop and wait until I get there."

He next pointed the barrel of the weapon at Jenny. "And you will walk over here and wait with me until the car is in position. If you leave without me," he said to Houser, "I'll kill her."

Houser didn't move. Her back was still to Malik. She was looking over her shoulder at him from where she was crouched behind the car. He could not see the pistol in her hand, held at her waist.

"Move!" Malik snarled. "Or I'll take my chances

out in the open and blow both your pretty faces off right now."

Houser felt the calm descend over her that had served her well for two years as an undercover narcotics officer. Seasoned, and tested under the most extreme conditions, she did not panic when confronted with a life-or-death situation.

She nudged Jenny with an elbow. "Do as he says. Get over there with him."

Jenny's legs felt weak as she stood and stared at the monster who she believed intended to kill her no matter what she did. "I'm not going near him," she said. "Let him shoot me. I don't care."

Malik raised the barrel of the shotgun, leveling it at Jenny's face. The sound of the helicopter grew louder as it swung back in their direction, sweeping the tree line around them. Malik's eyes broke contact with Jenny for a brief moment, to make certain he had not been spotted by the helicopter.

The momentary diversion was all that Houser needed. She spun around, her finger already squeezing the trigger as she quickly brought the sights into alignment with her target. She fired three times in rapid succession. Each bullet found its mark, hitting Malik in the chest.

He held on to the shotgun as he was knocked backward and fell into the deep shadows on the ground. He felt a sharp pain on the left side of his chest, and suspected that the impact of the bullets had broken one of his ribs, but they had not penetrated the vest.

He rolled onto his stomach and turned to face the Porsche. He stayed motionless, in a prone position, the shotgun tucked into his shoulder, his finger on the trigger, as he watched Houser move cautiously toward him, her gun trained on the spot where he had fallen.

She was approaching at an angle, and a low branch blocked a clear shot at her. He knew she could not yet see him, and he waited patiently until she was past the obstruction.

Malik stiffened at the sound of a twig snapping underfoot on the forest floor directly behind him. And then he heard the familiar voice. Low. Almost a whisper.

"I should have done this years ago, you piece of shit."

Malik never heard the two shots that tore into the back of his head, killing him instantly. Houser almost fired instinctively at the silhouetted figure standing behind Malik, but released pressure on the trigger as she realized the whispered words she heard through the headset were spoken by Culley.

He stepped into the moonlight at the edge of the woods and smiled at Houser. "Now it's over."

"He was already dead, Culley. I hit him in the chest with three shots."

"He was wearing body armor."

Houser's eyes widened. "You might have mentioned that earlier."

"In all the confusion, I forgot. Anyway, dead is dead."

Jenny rushed to her father's side and threw her arms around him. He embraced her and kissed her on top of the head, holding her tightly.

"You all right, honey?" She was remarkably composed, given what she had been through, though her eyes still showed the shock of it all.

"I'm fine now, Daddy. A little shaky, but nothing a good stiff drink wouldn't cure."

"We'll spend a few days together. Go someplace where you can just kick back and relax and get all of this out of your system."

"I can't right now," Jenny said. "I've got to get back to school."

"School can wait. I want to make sure you're okay. Trust me on this one. In a few hours you're going to start feeling the full effects of what happened to you."

"Please, Daddy. I'll be fine. I've got to get back to New York. Our theater group at school has a play coming up in a week, and they need me. I can't let them down. I promise you, I'll be okay."

"We'll see."

The sound of the scout helicopter suddenly grew distant as it climbed to altitude and headed southeast, its mission completed. Culley and Houser heard Gregus's voice in their ears at the same moment the Blackhawk appeared on the horizon.

"Good work, Mike," Gregus said, having heard their conversation over the radio. "Everyone okay?"

"Everyone's just fine," Culley said, and again kissed the top of Jenny's head and held her close at his side.

The sound of the Blackhawk grew louder; the high-pitched whine of its twin turbine engines and the pulsating beat of its huge rotor blades filled the night air. It swooped in over the clearing along the shore of the lake like a great prehistoric beast, the downdraft from the swirling blades flattening the grass as it roared overhead and swung nimbly around to hover briefly before settling to the ground halfway between the cabin and where the Porsche was parked.

Four men, dressed in black fatigues and carrying large rucksacks on their backs, jumped from the helicopter and immediately ran toward the cabin. Two more men, one carrying a body bag, ran into the woods behind the Porsche.

Gregus exited the helicopter to see Culley approaching. He walked over to him and placed a fraternal arm around his shoulder.

"Turn off your radio," he shouted above the whine of the idling Blackhawk turbines, waiting until Culley did so. "Again, good work, Mike. Jenny's safe. That scumbag is dead. And all's right with the world for the moment."

Culley gestured toward the cabin. The lights were on in all the rooms, the black-clad men could be seen moving hurriedly about inside. "I suppose when your boys are finished, none of this will have ever happened."

"That's part of the plan. I'll leave it to you to make sure Jenny understands that. She's not to say anything to anyone."

"I'll take care of it. But I need a favor."

"Name it."

"Jenny insists on going back to New York tonight. I want your Lear to take her there."

"No problem. Get her to the airport."

"And I want an Agency doctor to meet her when she gets off the plane in New York. Have him take her to that private clinic you have on Long Island and keep her there overnight, just to make certain she's okay."

"Consider it done," Gregus said, and turned his

attention to one of his men, who came out of the cabin carrying a suitcase taken from a closet in the master bedroom.

"Is that it?" Gregus asked.

"Yes, sir," the man said, and tossed it into the open side door of the Blackhawk, then rushed back inside the cabin.

"What's in the suitcase?" Culley said.

"A few mementos. Anyway, your job's over, Mike. You've got about five minutes to get clear of the area after we lift off. I strongly suggest you do so."

"I'm leaving now," Culley said, and saw the two men who had entered the woods behind the Porsche returning with the body bag, now heavy with Malik's weight. They placed it in the Blackhawk and climbed inside with it.

Another of Gregus's men came out of the cabin and ran over to him. "Sir, there's something inside you should see."

Gregus clasped Culley's hand. "Stay in touch, Mike. Keep me posted on how things turn out for you."

"You'll be the first to know."

Gregus followed the man into the cabin to the room at the back. The man pulled open the door of an upright freezer for him to look inside.

"That sick bastard!" Gregus said, staring in disgust at the four freezer bags on the middle shelf. Each bag contained a frozen human heart.

▽

WITH THE HURRIED ACTIVITY inside the cabin, and the noise of the idling Blackhawk engines outside,

Culley went unnoticed and unheard as he took the Ford Explorer and drove across the clearing to where Houser and Jenny were standing beside the Porsche.

Houser's attention was on the activity in and around the cabin, making mental notes, the reporter again. She had watched the two men carry Malik's body from the woods and put it in the Blackhawk.

"What are they going to do with him?" she asked Culley.

"I don't know. And I don't care. Let's get Jenny to the airport."

Houser continued to watch as Gregus and four of his men came out of the cabin and climbed on board the Blackhawk. The noise of the turbine engines increased in pitch and volume as the huge helicopter lifted slowly off the ground, nose down, and climbed swiftly away.

"We've got to get out of here," Culley said. "I'll take Jenny with me. Meet us at the airport."

The Blackhawk rose to an altitude of four thousand feet, upwind from the cabin. Gregus knelt at the open side door, a small radio transmitter in his hand. He saw the headlights of two vehicles on the road leading out of the property, and waited until they were well out of range, then pressed the button on the transmitter, sending the detonation signal to the eighty pounds of plastic explosives placed strategically about the cabin.

Culley drove as fast as the rough road would allow, with Houser following close behind. As they reached the top of the drive, a deafening explosion tore through the air, the shock wave so powerful, it rocked both cars as they turned onto the narrow two-lane highway.

Houser slowed to look off to her right. For a few seconds night was turned to day by the bright orange fireball rising high above the trees, followed by a roiling mushroom cloud of smoke and debris. She stared in disbelief, then understood it all.

"You lying son of a bitch!" she shouted, and slammed her hand against the steering wheel repeatedly as she sped along the road.

▽

THE COPILOT of the Blackhawk saw a small blip on the radar screen, indicating that an unknown aircraft was approximately eight miles northwest of their present position.

"We've got company," he said over the intercom. "Probably another chopper, judging from the altitude and the airspeed."

"Jam their radar," Gregus said. "And haul ass out of here."

The pilot turned on the jammer and took the Blackhawk to maximum cruising speed, quickly putting a considerable distance between himself and the approaching aircraft.

▽

"WHAT THE HELL was that!" the pilot of the FBI surveillance helicopter said, having seen the brilliant fireball in the distance.

"I don't know," the copilot said, "but it's right over our target area."

"Where's the aircraft we just picked up on radar?"

The copilot looked at the radar screen; it was filled with hundreds of blips. "Someone's jamming us."

The pilot keyed his microphone, calling Special Agent Jack Matthews at the staging area for the impending assault on the cabin.

Matthews had been expecting the call. Although three miles from the cabin site, he, and all those gathered at the staging area, had heard the explosion and seen the flash from the fireball as it lit the night sky.

"Let's get over there," he said to Chief Brady, who jumped into the car beside him.

Matthews tore out of the parking area at the gravel quarry, leading a procession of twelve city, state, and county police cars off in the direction of the cabin.

▽

ON BOARD THE Blackhawk as it headed back to Camp Peary, the leader of the cleanup team came forward and sat next to Gregus.

"Sir, we didn't find any trace of the counterfeit money in the cabin."

In the rush to complete his mission and get out as quickly as possible, Gregus had forgotten about the money. "You made a thorough search?"

"Every room. Every closet. Under the beds. With the time schedule you gave us, we couldn't expand the search, so he could have had it stashed somewhere else on the property."

"If it was anywhere within fifty yards of the cabin," Gregus said, "it's nothing but dust now." ·

"Yes, sir. But it could have been in the vehicle Culley took."

"We don't know for certain that Malik had it when he left the warehouse, do we?"

"No, sir. But it's highly unlikely he left without it."

Gregus smiled to himself. "If Culley's got it, he'll turn it in."

"Yes, sir," the man said, accepting that as fact no more than he suspected Gregus did.

39

Jack Matthews hit the brakes hard as he came out of the woods, throwing Chief Brady forward in his seat as he skidded to a stop at the edge of the clearing.

"Goddamn!" Brady said as he and Matthews got out of the car, taking in the devastation spread out before them.

Across the clearing where the cabin had once stood was a shallow crater, sixty feet in diameter, filled with a glowing heap of rubble where part of the structure had caved in on itself. Smoldering debris was scattered across the open area and into the woods as far as the eye could see; splintered sections of paneling and pieces of furniture, blasted to bits by the tremendous force of the explosion, floated on the surface of the lake. The remainder of the drive up to the cabin was littered with chunks of the cinder-block foundation and parts of the roof and walls, making it impossible to proceed any farther by car. A jagged section of the fireplace mantel lay at Matthews's feet, one hundred yards from the cabin.

"Looks like somebody called in an air strike."

"Probably plastic explosives," Matthews said. "A lot of it."

Matthews and Brady walked along the edge of the road, trailed by the other officers, who came down to the clearing from where their cars were parked farther up the drive in the woods. They picked their way through the debris strewn across the road, and Matthews stopped to examine a huge slab of white-enameled metal in his path, recognizing it as part of a freezer that had been ripped in half by the blast.

"The boys from Langley?" Brady said.

"Who else? A precision military-style assault. Plastic explosives. A helicopter with radar-jamming equipment."

"If they blew the place up, it had to be to destroy anything that could prove Malik was ever here. Which probably means they got him."

Matthews nodded in agreement, torn between the relief that Malik was dead, and the anger and disappointment that they would never have the chance to learn what had made him tick, and that the families of his victims would never have the satisfaction of knowing conclusively that he was indeed the Mix & Match killer and had paid for his crimes. With no resolution, no closure to help attenuate their grief, they would spend the rest of their lives wondering, tortured by not knowing what had really happened to their loved ones.

Matthews paused to pick up what looked like the faceplate from a radio, its surface scorched by the heat from the explosion. It was still hot, and he let it drop and stared ahead at what was left of the cabin. "Something tells me this isn't where it ends."

"What else do they have to accomplish? If they got Malik, they got rid of their problem. And ours."

"They aren't known for leaving any loose ends."

"What loose ends?"

"Attribution," Matthews said. "We can't go public with what we suspect, because it's all circumstantial; we can't prove any of it. And this isn't going to go away just because the killing stops. People are going to ask a lot of questions. And the CIA isn't going to take the chance of anyone coming knocking on their door looking for the answers."

"What do you think they'll do?"

Matthews shrugged. "As much as I hate to admit it, they've got some of the smartest people in the world working for them; so they're bound to come up with something."

"What about bringing in your forensic people to go through the rubble?"

"Wasted effort. You can bet that anything that could tie Malik to the murders was removed from the cabin before they blew it up. We'd end up with twenty people here for a week with nothing to show for it."

"So where do we go from here?"

"I don't know. We'll just have to see how it shakes out."

▽

HOUSER LEANED AGAINST the fender of the Porsche, watching Culley wave good-bye to Jenny as the Learjet taxied away from the hangar. She had said nothing to him when they arrived at the airport, waiting until Jenny was gone before confronting him. The Lear roared down the runway and lifted off, heading north, as she walked over to where Culley stood on the apron.

"You lied to me."

Culley turned to face her. "No, I did not. I told you from the beginning how this was going to end. It was your decision to come along for the ride. As a matter of fact, you insisted."

"Is that all I did, Culley? Come along for the ride?"

"Sorry, figure of speech. If it wasn't for you and Grimaldi, Jenny wouldn't be on that plane right now. And I'll always be grateful to you for that."

"I don't want your gratitude. Our deal was that if I didn't tell the FBI what I knew, when this was over I had an exclusive on the story."

"So write your story."

"At the moment there is no story, you bastard. Your buddies saw to that. No hard evidence. No sources to confirm anything that could prove Malik was the killer, or to tie him to the CIA. Not unless you want to volunteer as my source."

"Not a chance."

"That's what I thought you were going to say."

"Just let it go. It's over. Malik's dead. What's the difference if people don't know all the details? He won't be killing anyone else."

"What's the difference? You can't mean that!"

"Of course I mean it. Mistakes were made, but as soon as that was realized, steps were taken to correct them."

"How convenient for those who were responsible for setting a serial killer loose in the first place!"

"Look, we're not arguing about facts that need to come out for any real purpose. This is about your story. Your own selfish interests. Nothing more or less."

"There's a lot more to it than that, and you damn well know it." Houser gestured toward the Explorer. "What's in the car, Culley?"

"You know what's in there."

"And you're going to keep it, aren't you?"

"They owe me."

"That's what this was about all along, wasn't it? The money. That's the only reason you wanted to find Malik, until he grabbed Jenny. Now that she's safe, you couldn't care less about what your friends did."

"It didn't start out that way."

"But that's the way it's going to end, isn't it? To hell with me. To hell with my story. To hell with what's right. And take off with the money."

"Hey, Houser. That's my fuck-you money in that car. You've got yours; now I've got mine."

"Don't pull that crap on me. I earned mine."

"And I didn't?"

"You lied to protect your friends and you were caught. It was your choice, you have no one to blame for what happened but yourself."

"And now it's up to me to take care of myself."

"By committing another crime in the name of some self-serving convoluted idea of personal justice?"

"That's not the way I see it."

"No, you wouldn't. And what about Jenny?"

"She'll never know."

"And that makes it all right?"

"It makes it work. That money wasn't stolen from hardworking people by savings-and-loan thieves or Wall Street manipulators. It didn't exist until yesterday. No one gets hurt by what I'm doing."

Culley looked into her eyes. "You could come with me."

"You've got to be kidding."

"There won't be any repercussion over the money. I can guarantee you that."

"And that's your only concern? Repercussions?"

"I no longer have the luxury of choosing the high road. That option was taken from me the day I went to prison."

"Do what you think you must, Culley. But sooner or later we all have to sit down to a banquet of consequences. And I don't want to be around when you have to deal with that."

"Bottom line, Houser: Taking that money is the lesser of a whole bunch of evils; and I'll learn to live with it."

"I'm sorry to hear that. I truly am. I thought you were better than that. Much better."

"I guess you thought wrong."

"I'm going to stay on the story, you know. I'm one hell of a good investigative reporter, and I've got enough to start digging in all the right places."

"Just remember what I told you when this all began: You're not dealing with a Boy Scout troop. If they think you can hurt them, they'll find a way to stop you; and I won't be able to help."

"I got along just fine without your help before we met, and as I told you: I'm not afraid of them."

"Then you're a fool."

"Maybe. But an honest one, who won't have any trouble sleeping at night or facing herself in the mirror every morning."

"I wish I could afford to share your high ideals."

"You'll spend the rest of your life looking over your shoulder, Culley."

"No. That I won't. If the Agency left me with anything, it's the knowledge and training to make certain that doesn't happen."

Culley walked over to the Explorer, then paused as he opened the door. "I'll keep in touch."

"Don't bother."

Culley smiled sadly. "Thanks again for everything you did."

"Fuck you."

She stood watching as he drove off, brushing away the single tear that ran down her cheek. "You disappointed me, Culley," she whispered softly as the Explorer turned onto the highway and disappeared from sight.

40

FOUR DAYS HAD passed since Malik's death. There had been no more killings, but with little else happening that held the same morbid fascination for the public at large, assuring high ratings and increased readership, media attention still focused on the hunt for the Mix & Match killer. Television commentators and newspaper columnists questioned who the man was in the photograph the New York City police department had released to the press, demanding answers and results from the FBI and the joint task force.

The photograph was one of Malik without the full beard and mustache he had worn before going into hiding, and a few people in Charlottesville believed they recognized him as a man by the name of John Malik, but they were not certain. The FBI confirmed that Malik was indeed a principal suspect in the case, and that they had been vigorously pursuing all leads that might link him to the serial killings. The press dug deep, establishing only that Malik was a mystery man who had disappeared one month ago.

Lou Gregus had listened carefully for any hint that the FBI might be ready to come forth with what they suspected about Malik. But they had said nothing. The twenty-four-hour operations center at the safe house in Alexandria was shut down the day after Malik's death, but Gregus still waited patiently for the final part of the damage-control operation to fall into place.

The smile on Hack's face as he entered the third-floor office in CIA headquarters at Langley, Virginia, late in the evening on the fourth day told Gregus that his computer whiz had found what they were looking for.

"You can tell the DDO that we just lucked out, big time."

"Let's hear it."

Hack filled him in on the details of his discovery, including extensive background information that was made to order for the operation. "It's perfect. We couldn't have done better if we created him out of whole cloth ourselves."

"How fresh is he?"

"Tonight. Just an hour ago. About nine-fifteen. I didn't even have to break into a system to get it. I had CNN on in the office when they interrupted *Larry King Live* with it as a breaking story. I dug up the in-depth background stuff myself."

"Where is he?"

"That's the best part. Hanover County. Fifteen miles north of Richmond. Huh? Is that beautiful, or what?"

Ten minutes later Gregus sat in the deputy director for operations' office on the seventh floor, repeating what he had learned from Hack.

"How soon can you get it under way?" the DDO asked.

"Just as soon as you give the word."

"Consider it given."

"I've had a team on twenty-four-hour standby at the Farm for the past four days." Gregus looked at his watch; it was ten-thirty. "I can have them there within the hour."

"Do it."

Gregus picked up the DDO's phone and dialed the number at Camp Peary. He quickly gave the information to the team leader and then hung up.

"They're on their way."

"Excellent," the DDO said. "By the way, did you see the article in this morning's *Post* about the Secret Service recovering twenty-five million dollars in counterfeit money, and the engraved plates used to print it?"

"I missed that."

"Seems someone called their Miami field office and told them where they could find it."

"Did you say twenty-five million?"

"Twenty-five," the DDO said. "They claim that closes the case on the Crane Paper Company hijacking."

"I'd say they can't add very well."

"I think the Treasury Department's accepted the fact that they're never going to see the rest of it, and they aren't about to admit that it's still out there."

"Smart move on their part."

"How much do you think he got away with?"

"Five or seven million."

"Not bad," the DDO said. "With Culley's know-how in laundering money, I'd be willing to bet it's already into the international monetary system and he's got a nice trust fund set up for himself and his daughter in an offshore bank."

"Sounds about right."

The DDO smiled. "No skin off our nose. I kind of like his style. Always did."

"We let it lie?"

"Absolutely. No sense opening up that can of worms. Besides, it's a kind of poetic justice."

Gregus turned to leave and stopped at the door. "What would you have done?"

"In his situation? After all he's been through? Who the hell knows? Probably just what he did."

▽

THE FOLLOWING MORNING Jack Matthews entered the Hanover County Sheriff's Office and showed his FBI credentials to the deputy behind the desk.

"Oh, yeah, Sheriff Hollins has been expecting you."

"Where is he?"

"In one of the interrogation rooms with the prisoner," the deputy said. "I'll take you in."

Matthews entered the room to find Hollins and his prisoner sitting across a table from each other, a tape recorder between them. Another deputy stood off in a corner, manning a video camera. Both devices were turned off as Matthews walked in and flashed his credentials to Hollins.

"This is him?" Matthews said.

"In the flesh. Aubrey Shifflet, otherwise known as the Mix and Match killer," Hollins said proudly.

"Sorry my boys stole your thunder, but we're all in this together. Right?"

"Right," Matthews said, and sat next to Hollins, across from the prisoner, studying him for a few moments before saying anything more.

Shifflet had the hooded eyes and flat stare of a psychopath; a sick grin was fixed permanently in place on his sallow face. He appeared to be no more than five feet six inches tall and approximately one hundred and forty pounds. His wary gaze had not left Matthews since he entered the room.

"You're the giant fuzz, right?"

"Matthews, FBI."

"I killed them bitches. Every last one of 'em. Fucked 'em up real good too."

"Is that right?"

"Damn straight."

"Tell me, Aubrey, how did you do it?"

"Waddaya mean? How'd I do it? I cut 'em up. Made 'em suffer first; for a long time. How the fuck you think I did it? Don't you read the papers? Watch TV?"

"Well, I've got to tell you, Aubrey, you sure had us puzzled."

Shifflet's grin broadened. "How's that?"

"We couldn't figure out how you managed to grab those girls at the University of Virginia without anyone seeing you. What did you use? A club? Knock them out with your gun? Or did you choke them?"

Shifflet's face went blank. "I forget."

"You forget?"

"Yeah. I forget. Sometimes shit like that comes

and goes, ya know. I'm not too good on details, 'specially if it wasn't like . . . yesterday."

Matthews kept his eyes on Shifflet. "How did you get to Mansfield and Brighton Beach?"

"Where?"

"Mansfield, New Jersey, and Brighton Beach in Brooklyn?"

"Oh, yeah. Where I killed them bitches a few days ago."

"How did you get there?"

"I flew. But I paid cash. Used an assumed name. So nobody would know. Smart, huh?"

"You flew to Mansfield, New Jersey?"

Shifflet looked to Sheriff Hollins. "Yeah. Maybe. I don't know. I could've taken a bus, ya know. Like I said. I'm not good on details. Maybe I drove. Why you askin' me all these questions? Stuff you oughtta know. You stupid or somethin'?"

"What kind of car do you drive?"

"Got me a pickup."

"Nothing else?"

"Oh, yeah. I forgot. And a Rolls-Royce, but it's in the shop." Shifflet laughed at his own joke. "Do I look like a guy who'd have two cars? Fuck's the matter with you?"

Matthews turned to Hollins. "Can I speak with you outside?"

The two men left the room and stood in the hallway.

"With all due respect, Sheriff. If he's the Mix and Match killer, you're the Second Coming of Christ."

"Then I sure hope you've been going to church regularly, son."

"At best what you've got in there is a copycat

killer. And judging from your report on the murder last night, a disorganized one who doesn't fit the profile at all. He's nothing more than a pathetic creature with the IQ of a stump. He's looking for publicity and he'll admit to anything to get it."

Hollins bristled and his face flushed. "We've got the right man, Agent Matthews. As hard as it might be for the FBI to accept, we're not just a bunch of rednecks around here."

"I didn't say you were. Tell me what you've got on him."

"The whole enchilada. More than enough to send him to the chair without a hitch."

"Could you be a little more specific?"

"He killed a young girl last night. Grabbed her and pulled her into the woods behind her house. He was in the process of cutting her up with a steak knife when someone saw him and called nine-one-one."

"That's it?"

"Not by a long shot. When Mr. Aubrey Shifflet was only sixteen years old, he hacked up two girls in his high school class with an ax because they refused to go out with him. He spent the past eighteen years of his life in a hospital for the criminally insane. Diagnosed as a severe paranoid schizophrenic and a homicidal maniac."

"And they let him out?"

"Hell, no. He escaped a little over two months ago."

"And that's the extent of your reasons for believing he's the Mix and Match killer? That, and a confession that has more holes in it than a colander?"

Hollins smiled slyly. "Oh, no. I saved the best for last. Early this morning we searched the trailer he lives in. Came up with four human hearts in the freezer; wanna bet the tissue samples match up with the four victims at the University of Virginia? We also found a suitcase full of panties and bras and jewelry; and the wallets taken from those same four victims. Plus a power drill and assorted knives and cleavers."

Matthews was momentarily stunned by what he'd heard then, "Those bastards," he muttered. "Those brilliant, diabolical bastards."

"What?" Hollins said.

"Nothing, Sheriff. Nothing," Matthews said, feeling thoroughly defeated. "Just one more thing. How large was the freezer in his trailer?"

"It was one of those refrigerator-freezer deals. Freezer on the top, not very big."

"No separate chest freezer?"

"You don't know when to cry uncle, do you? I know what you're getting at, but maybe he used another place to freeze the bodies."

"Maybe."

"So there you have it," Hollins said with finality. "Granted, he's not exactly forthcoming with any details of his crimes, but then the doctor who treated him at the insane asylum said he may be telling the truth when he says he forgets most of it. He's been off his medication since he escaped, which means he's pretty whacked out. So we aren't exactly dealing with a stable personality. But we've got more than enough to convict on the Charlottesville murders, plus the girl he killed last night."

Matthews fell silent. For the past four days the Bureau had had its Counterintelligence section digging for anything that could tie Malik to the CIA, and make a solid case against him as the killer, but they had come up with nothing. Any protestations on the FBI's part that Hollins had the wrong man, backed up only by circumstantial evidence and suspicion, would fall on deaf ears, and leave them looking like sore losers with an ax to grind against local law enforcement.

All they really had was one eyewitness who had seen Malik leaving the roadhouse in New Jersey with the girl murdered later that night. Without a lot more than that the Bureau would not put its reputation on the line, or cast aspersions on the CIA, starting an interagency dogfight that could just as well end up damaging them in the process.

For a brief moment Matthews considered telling Hollins about Malik, but he saw the handwriting on the wall. They had their killer. The media had bought it, and why not? It was all laid out for them, nice and neat and, as Hollins had said, without a hitch. The killings would stop. The public would be satisfied, feeling safe to go out again at night. The pressure would be off the Bureau and the local cops. The cases could be closed. The families of the victims would find some solace in the resolution. And the girl Shifflet had been caught in the act of murdering would have been enough to have him executed or put away for the rest of his life anyway. And, after all, Malik was dead.

"Well, it looks like congratulations are in order, Sheriff. If there's anything the Bureau can do to be of help, be sure and let us know."

"I thank you for that. But I think we can handle it from here."

Matthews sat in his car for a long time before pulling out of the parking lot. He was only thirty minutes from his home in Richmond. Thirty minutes from his wife and two-year-old daughter, whom he had not seen for nearly a week. It was over. Regardless of how it had ended, it was finally over.

"THIS IS PURE CRAP and you know it," Houser said the moment she'd closed the door to her editor's office. She held a copy of the Associated Press story on the capture of the Mix & Match killer in her hand.

"We've already had this discussion, Julie," Peter Davidson said. "Get me something you can substantiate, and I'll let you run with it, but until then there's nothing more I can or will do."

"I've got enough to raise questions that might prompt someone on the Hill to start an investigation."

"You have nothing to back up your version of what really happened. What do you want me to do? Open this paper up to a lawsuit that could ruin its reputation? The CIA and the rest of the right wing would like nothing better, but I can assure you our publisher would not."

"What about tying it into the counterfeiting story? I could approach it from that angle."

"How? The Secret Service is claiming they got it

all back, and there's no mention of a John Malik in what they released on their investigation. Julie, please. Take it from an old war-horse who's lost his share of battles; they beat us on this one. Your chances of getting what you need to break it open are virtually nonexistent. And if they perceive you as a serious threat, by the time they finish, you'll be discredited as a Pulitzer-happy, conspiracy-theory nut case. For your own good, let it go."

"Is that what you would do?"

"Yes. It would eat a hole in my gut for a while, but I'd get over it. And who knows, somewhere down the line, they may screw up and you'll get another shot at them. But for the time being I want you to put it aside and get on with your work."

"I need some time off," Houser said.

"Take a week, or two. Relax, get your mind off this whole mess. Your job will be here when you get back."

"I may not come back, Peter."

"Don't make that decision in haste. You'd be sorely missed."

▽

HOUSER ENTERED HER apartment to see the light blinking on her answering machine. She flipped through the mail first, then pressed the button to retrieve her messages. The first was a call from a man she had dated casually over the past six months, inviting her to a concert at the Kennedy Center. The second was from Tony Grimaldi. "I checked with Culley's daughter; all I got was, Malik who? What kidnapping? And like that. Sorry. Hang in there, kiddo, you can't win 'em all. See you when I see you."

The third message sent her on an emotional roller-coaster ride as she listened to it.

"Maybe I didn't live up to your expectations, but then I never claimed to be anything other than what I am. I'd like to talk. See if we can work this out. If the answer is no, I'll understand. If it's yes, I'll be arriving at Dulles Airport on a flight from Grand Cayman Island at four o'clock this afternoon. I have a one-hour-and-forty-minute layover before my connecting flight to Germany leaves. Whatever you decide, know that I never meant to hurt you."

Houser played the message back three times, sitting at her desk and staring at the machine. She went and got herself a glass of wine, then listened to it a fourth time before pressing the erase button.

The mention of Grand Cayman Island jogged her memory, and she recalled the message on the telephone answering unit in Malik's house, the one Culley had erased. The woman's name had been Odette, and Houser now realized that she had not been talking about the Georgetown section of Washington, but George Town on Grand Cayman, with its multitude of international banks and their reputation for quickly and efficiently laundering money with no questions asked. The message from Odette must have been when it started for Culley, when the seed was planted. But what difference did it make now?

There was so much that was right and good about him, and what he had said at the airport was true, he had not lied to her; he had told her at the beginning that the Agency would do whatever it took to cover it up.

She poured another glass of wine, feeling lonely and depressed and more confused than she could ever remember feeling. She recalled something her father had said to her when, as a teenager, she had confronted and berated him about his leaving her mother for another woman: "If you haven't lived my life, don't criticize my choices."

Houser looked at her watch; it was four o'clock. Dulles Airport was only thirty minutes from her apartment.

∇

CULLEY LOOKED UP from his magazine to see Houser standing at the entrance to the boarding-gate lounge, staring at him. He got up and crossed to where she stood, opening his arms to embrace her.

"I came to talk, Culley. Just talk," she said, ignoring his outstretched arms.

"I'm glad you're here."

"I'm not so sure that I am. But I couldn't leave it like this."

"I missed you."

"I missed you too. But I can't be a part of what you've done."

"You're not a part of it. You had nothing to do with it. Taking the money was my decision. I honored my commitment to them; I kept the faith and they didn't. They betrayed me and destroyed my life. Right or wrong, I've taken a part of it back. Just accept it as something I did for my own reasons."

"I'm not sure that I can. But I think I'm willing to try."

An announcement came over the public address system. "Lufthansa Airlines Flight 419 for Frankfurt will now begin boarding."

Culley raised his voice over the instructions for the boarding process. "That's my flight."

Houser held his gaze, but said nothing.

"From Frankfurt I'm going on to Munich for about a week; I've got some business to take care of. Come with me."

"I can't."

"Yes, you can."

"I can't promise you any tomorrows, Culley."

"No one can promise us tomorrow. But I'll promise you that I'll never lie to you, and I'll never do anything to hurt you. Come with me."

"I can't. . . . I don't have a ticket . . . the plane's ready to leave."

"Do you have your passport?"

"It's in my purse."

Culley reached into the inside pocket of his sport coat and took out two tickets for the flight.

"You were that sure of yourself?"

"Not at all. But I was hoping," Culley said. "And I suppose you always carry your passport with you?"

"Oh, shut up, Culley. Besides, I don't have any clothes with me . . . nothing."

"They have stores in Germany."

Houser hesitated as they again announced the boarding call. Culley took her in his arms and kissed her. She responded with equal passion.

"Please. Come with me. If it doesn't work,

you've lost nothing. If it does, maybe we'll be lucky enough to find what everyone hopes for."

"I've never been to Germany."

"You'll love it. They're into beer and leather. And they've got great music. The kind that makes you want to march—into other countries."

"And no speed limits on the autobahns."

"No way, Houser. No way. I'll do the driving."